DETOURS

DETOURS

Edited by
BRIAN JAMES FREEMAN

CEMETERY DANCE PUBLICATIONS

Baltimore
➲ 2024 ➾

Cemetery Dance Publications
132-B Industry Lane, Unit #7
Forest Hill, MD 21050
http://www.cemeterydance.com

Trade Paperback Edition Printing

ISBN: 978-1-58767-698-7

Cover Artwork and Design © 2024 by Kate Freeman Design
Interior Artwork Copyright 2019 by Mark Edward Geyer (page 29),
Alex McVey (page 37, 59, 287), Donn Albright (page 63), Will Renfro
(page 69, 145, 155), Erin S. Wells (page 81), Glenn Chadbourne (page
91, 123), Jill Bauman (page 169), Keith Minnion (page 179, 323),
Chris Odgers (page 251), Stephen C. Gilberts (page 319)
Interior Design © 2024 by Desert Isle Design, LLC

Table of Contents

An Explanation

by Brian James Freeman

I'M NOT ONE for writing introductions, but I thought this book might need a bit of an explanation before you dive into the contents since this is not a traditional anthology.

For as long as I can remember, I've been addicted to finding rare and lost material written by my favorite authors. The Internet has obviously made this task significantly easier, but there's still a real thrill when I discover something I never knew existed: an uncollected short story, an essay written for an obscure venue, or even a chapter that was deleted from a book prior to publication. Those "lost chapters" are easily my favorites, but I'm a bit of a geek when it comes to the publication process — what stays in, what gets cut, etc.

Simply put, *Detours* is meant to gather some of the fun and unusual material I've found over the years, along with a couple of original pieces that have never seen the light of day before now.

Some readers are happy sticking with the "regular" books and stories by their favorite authors, and that's perfectly okay. But if you're like me, and you're always looking beyond what you can find in the bookstore, I think you're in for a treat.

As always, please contact me at author@brianjamesfreeman.com if you have any feedback to share on this book or suggestions for the next volume of *Detours*.

Brian James Freeman
March 27, 2015

Memory

by Stephen King

→ **M**EMORIES ARE CONTRARY things; if you quit chasing them and turn your back, they often return on their own. That's what Kamen says. I tell him I never chased the memory of my accident. Some things, I say, are better forgotten.

Maybe, but that doesn't matter, either. That's what Kamen says.

My name is Edgar Freemantle. I used to be a big deal in building and construction. This was in Minnesota, in my other life. I was a genuine American-boy success in that life, worked my way up like a motherfucker, and for me, every-thing worked out. When Minneapolis-St. Paul boomed, The Freemantle Company boomed. When things tightened up, I never tried to force things. But I played my hunches, and most of them played out well. By the time I was fifty, Pam and I were worth about forty million dollars. And what we had together still worked. I looked at other women from time to time but never strayed. At the end of our particular Golden Age, one of our girls was at Brown and the other was teaching in a foreign exchange program. Just before things went wrong, my wife and I were planning to go and visit her.

I had an accident at a job site. That's what happened. I was in my pickup truck. The right side of my skull was crushed. My ribs were broken. My right hip was shattered. And although I retained sixty per cent of the sight in my right eye (more, on a good day), I lost almost all of my right arm.

I was supposed to lose my life, but I didn't. Then I was supposed to become one of the Vegetable Simpsons, a Coma Homer, but that didn't happen, either. I was one confused American when I came around, but the worst of that passed. By the time it did, my wife had passed, too. She's remarried to a fellow who owns bowling alleys. My older daughter likes him. My younger daughter thinks he's a yank-off. My wife says she'll come around.

Maybe *sí*, maybe no. That's what Kamen says.

When I say I was confused, I mean that at first I didn't know who people were, or what had happened, or why I was in such awful pain. I can't remember the quality and pitch of that pain now. I know it was excruciating, but it's all pretty academic. Like a picture of a mountain in National Geographic magazine. It wasn't academic at the time. At the time it was more like climbing a mountain.

Maybe the headache was the worst. It wouldn't stop. Behind my forehead it was always midnight in the world's biggest clock-shop. Because my right eye was fucked up, I was seeing the world through a film of blood, and I still hardly knew what the world was. Few things had names. I remember

Memory

one day when Pam was in the room—I was still in the hospital, this was before the convalescent home—and she was standing by my bed. I knew who she was, but I was extremely pissed that she should be standing when there was the thing you sit in right over in the cornhole.

"Bring the friend," I said. "Sit in the friend."

"What do you mean, Edgar?" she asked.

"The friend, the buddy!" I shouted. "Bring over the fucking pal, you dump bitch!" My head was killing me and she was starting to cry. I hated her for starting to cry. She had no business crying, because she wasn't the one in the cage, looking at everything through a red blur. She wasn't the monkey in the cage. And then it came to me. "Bring over the chum and for Christ's sake sick down!" It was the closest my rattled-up, fucked-up brain could come to chair.

I was angry all the time. There were two older nurses that I called Dry Fuck One and Dry Fuck Two, as if they were characters in a dirty Dr. Seuss story. There was a candystriper I called Pilch Lozenge—I have no idea why, but that nickname also had some sort of sexual connotation. To me, at least. As I grew stronger, I tried to hit people. Twice I tried to stab Pam, and on the first of those two occasions I succeeded, although only with a plastic knife. She still needed stitches in her forearm. I had to be tied down that day.

Here is what I remember most clearly about that part of my other life: a hot afternoon toward the end of my stay in the expensive convalescent home, the air conditioning broken, tied down in my bed, a soap opera on the television, a thousand bells ringing in my head, pain burning my right side like a poker, my missing right arm itching, my missing right fingers twitching, the morphine pump beside the bed making the hollow BONG that meant you couldn't get any more for awhile, and a nurse swims out of the red, a creature coming to look at the monkey in the cage, and the nurse says: "Are you ready to visit with your wife?" And I say: "Only if she brought a gun to shoot me with."

You don't think that kind of pain will pass, but it does. They shipped me home, the red began to drain from my vision, and Kamen showed up. Kamen's a psychologist who specializes in hypnotherapy. He showed me some neat tricks for managing phantom aches and itches in my missing arm. And he brought me Reba.

"This is not approved psychological therapy for anger management," Dr. Kamen said, although I suppose he might have been lying about that to make Reba more attractive. He told me I had to give her a hateful name, so I named her after an aunt who used to pinch my fingers when I was small if I didn't eat all of my vegetables. Then, less than two days after getting her, I forgot her name. I could only think of boy names, each one making me angrier: Randall, Russell, Rudolph, even River-fucking-Phoenix.

Pam came in with my lunch and I could see her steeling herself for an outburst. But even though I'd forgotten the name of the fluffy blond rage-doll, I remembered how I was supposed to use it in this situation.

"Pam," I said, "I need five minutes to get myself under control. I can do this."

"Are you sure—"

"Yes, just get that hamhock out of here and stick it up your face-powder. I can do this."

I didn't know if I could or not, but that was what I was supposed to say—I can do this. I couldn't remember the

Memory

fucking doll's name, but I could remember I can do this. That is clear about the convalescent part of my other life, how I kept saying I can do this even when I knew I was fucked, double-fucked, I was dead-ass-fucked in the pouring rain.

"I can do this," I said, and she backed out without a word, the tray still in her hands and the cup chattering against the plate.

When she was gone, I held the doll up in front of my face, staring into its stupid blue eyes as my thumbs disappeared into its stupid yielding body. "What's your name, you bat-faced bitch?" I shouted at it. It never once occurred to me that Pam was listening on the kitchen intercom, her and the day-nurse both. But if the intercom had been broken they could have heard me through the door. I was in good voice that day.

I shook the doll back and forth. Its head flopped and its dumb hair flew. Its blue cartoon eyes seemed to be saying *Oouuu, you nasty man!*

"What's your name, bitch? What's your name, you cunt? What's your name, you cheap plastic toe-rag? Tell me your name or I'll kill you! Tell me your name or I'll kill you! Tell me your name or I'll cut out your eyes and chop off your nose and rip off your—"

My mind cross-connected then, a thing that still happens now, four years later, although far less often. For a moment I was in my pickup truck, clipboard rattling against my old steel lunchbucket in the passenger footwell (I doubt if I was the only working millionaire in America to carry a lunchbucket, but you probably could have counted us in the dozens), my PowerBook beside me on the seat. And from the radio a woman's voice cried "It was RED!" with evangelical fervor. Only three words, but three was enough. It was the song about the poor woman who turns out her pretty daughter as a prostitute. It was "Fancy," by Reba McEntire.

I hugged the doll against me. "You're Reba. Reba-Reba-Reba. I'll never forget again." I did, but I didn't get angry next time. No. I held her against me like a little love, closed my eyes, and visualized the pickup that had been demolished in the accident. I visualized my steel lunchbucket rattling against the steel clip on my clipboard, and the woman's voice came from the radio once more, exulting with that same evangelical fervor: "It was RED!"

Dr. Kamen called it a breakthrough. My wife seemed a good deal less excited, and the kiss she put on my cheek was of the dutiful variety. It was about two months later that she told me she wanted a divorce.

By then the pain had either lessened considerably or my mind had made certain crucial adjustments when it came to dealing with it. The headaches still came, but less often and rarely with the same violence. I was always more than ready for Vicodin at five and OxyContin at eight—could hardly hobble on my bright red Canadian crutch until I'd had them—but my rebuilt hip was starting to mend.

Kathi Green the Rehab Queen came to Casa Freemantle on Mondays, Wednesdays, and Fridays. I was allowed an extra Vicodin before our sessions, and still my screams filled the house by the time we finished the leg-bends that were our grand finale. Our basement rec room had been converted into a therapy suite, complete with a hot tub I could get in and out of on my own. After two months of physical therapy—this would have been almost six months after the accident—I started to go down there on my own in the evenings. Kathi said working out a couple of hours before bed would release

Memory

endorphins and I'd sleep better. I don't know about the endorphins, but I did start getting a little more sleep.

It was during one of these evening workouts that my wife of a quarter-century came downstairs and told me she wanted a divorce.

I stopped doing crunches and looked at her. I was sitting on a floor-pad. She was standing at the foot of the stairs, prudently across the room. I could have asked her if she was serious, but the light down there was very good—those racked fluorescents—and I didn't have to. I don't think it's the sort of thing women joke about six months after their husbands have almost died in accidents, anyway. I could have asked her why, but I knew. I could see the small white scar on her arm where I had stabbed her with the plastic knife from my hospital tray, and that was really the least of it. I thought of telling her, not so long ago, to get the hamhock out of here and stick it up her face-powder. I thought of asking her to think about it, but the anger came back. In those days what Dr. Kamen called the inappropriate anger often did. And what I was feeling right then did not seem all that inappropriate.

My shirt was off. My right arm ended three and a half inches below the shoulder. I twitched it at her—a twitch was the best I could do with the muscle that was left. "This is me," I said, "giving you the finger. Get out of here if that's how you feel. Get out, you quitting birch."

The first tears had started rolling down her face, but she tried to smile. "Bitch, Edgar," she said. "You mean bitch."

"The word is what I say it is," I said, and began to do crunches again. It's harder than hell to do them with an arm gone; your body wants to pull and corkscrew to that side. "I wouldn't have left you, that's the point. I wouldn't have left you. I would have gone on through the mud and the blood and the piss and the spilled beer."

"It's different," she said. She made no effort to wipe her face. "It's different and you know it. I couldn't break you in two if I got into a rage."

"I'd have a hell of a job breaking you in two with only one amp," I said, doing crunches faster.

"You stuck me with a knife." As if that were the point.

"A plastic fife is all it was, I was half out of my mind, and it'll be your last words on your fucking beth-dead, 'Eddie staffed me with a plastic fife, goodbye cruel world.'"

"You choked me," she said in a voice I could barely hear.

I stopped doing crunches and gaped at her. "I choked you? I never choked you!"

"I know you don't remember, but you did."

"Shut up," I said. "You want a divorce, you can have a divorce. Only go do the alligator somewhere else. Get out of here."

She went up the stairs and closed the door without looking back. And it wasn't until she was gone that I realized what I'd meant to say: crocodile tears. Go cry your crocodile tears somewhere else.

Oh, well. Close enough for rock and roll. That's what Kamen says. And I was the one who ended up getting out.

EXCEPT FOR the former Pamela Gustafson, I never had a partner in my other life. I did have an accountant I trusted, however, and it was Tom Riley who helped me move the few things I needed from the house in Mendota Heights to the smaller place we kept on Lake Phalen, twenty miles away.

Memory

Tom, who had been divorced twice, worried at me all the way out. "You don't give up the house in a situation like this," he said. "Not unless the judge kicks you out. It's like giving up home field advantage in a playoff game."

Kathi Green the Rehab Queen only had one divorce under her belt, but she and Tom were on the same wavelength. She thought I was crazy to move out. She sat cross-legged on the lakeporch in her leotard, holding my feet and looking at me with grim outrage.

"What, because you poked her with a plastic hospital knife when you could barely remember your own name? Mood-swings and short-term memory loss following accident trauma are common. You suffered three subdural hematomas, for God's sake!"

"Are you sure that's not hematomae?" I asked her.

"Blow me," she said. "And if you've got a good lawyer, you can make her pay for being such a wimp." Some hair had escaped from her Rehab Gestapo ponytail and she blew it back from her forehead. "She ought to pay for it. Read my lips, Edgar, none of this is your fault."

"She says I tried to choke her."

"And if so, being choked by a one-armed invalid must have been very upsetting. Come on, Eddie, make her pay. I'm sure I'm stepping way out of my place, but I don't care. She should not be doing what she's doing. Make her pay."

⟳→

NOT LONG after I relocated to the place on Lake Phalen, the girls came to see me—the young women. They brought a picnic hamper and we sat on the piney-smelling lakeporch

STEPHEN KING

and looked out at the water and nibbled at the sandwiches. It was past Labor Day by then, most of the floating toys put away for another year. There was also a bottle of wine in the hamper, but I only drank a little. On top of the pain medication, alcohol hit me hard; a single glass could turn me into a slurring drunk. The girls—the young women—finished the rest between them, and it loosened them up. Melissa, back from France for the second time since my unfortunate argument with the crane and not happy about it, asked me if all adults in their fifties had these unpleasant regressive interludes, did she have that to look forward to. Ilse, the younger, began to cry, leaned against me, and asked why it couldn't be like it was, why couldn't we—meaning her mother and me—be like we were.

Lissa's temper and Ilse's tears weren't exactly pleasant, but at least they were honest, and I recognized both reactions from all the years the girls had spent growing up in the house where I lived with them; those responses were as familiar to me as the mole on Ilse's chin or the faint vertical frown-line, which in time would deepen into a groove like her mother's, between Lissa's eyes.

Lissa wanted to know what I was going to do. I told her I didn't know, and in a way that was true. I'd come a long distance toward deciding to end my own life, but I knew that if I did it, it must absolutely look like an accident. I would not leave these two, just starting out in their lives with nothing but fresh tickets on their belts, carrying the residual guilt of their father's suicide. Nor would I leave a load of guilt behind for the woman with whom I had once shared a milkshake in bed, both of us naked and laughing and listening to the Plastic Ono Band on the stereo.

Memory

After they'd had a chance to vent—after a full and complete exchange of feelings, in Kamen-speak—things calmed down, and my memory is that we actually had a pleasant afternoon, looking at old photo albums Ilse found in a drawer and reminiscing about the past. I think we even laughed a time or two, but not all memories of my other life are to be trusted. Kamen says when it comes to the past, we all stack the deck.

Maybe *sí*, maybe no.

SPEAKING OF Kamen, he was my next visitor at Casa Phalen. Three days later, this would have been. Or maybe six. Like many other aspects of my memory during those post-accident months, my time-sense was pretty much hors de fucky. I didn't invite him; I had my rehabilitation dominatrix to thank for that.

Although surely no more than forty, Xander Kamen walked like a much older man and wheezed even when he sat, peering at the world through thick glasses and over an enormous pear of a belly. He was very tall and very Afro-American, with features carved so large they seemed unreal. Those great staring eyeballs, that ship's figurehead of a nose, and those totemic lips were awe-inspiring. Kamen looked like a minor god in a suit from Men's Wearhouse. He also looked like a prime candidate for a fatal heart attack or stroke before his fiftieth birthday.

He refused my offer of coffee or a Coke, said he couldn't stay, then put his briefcase aside on the couch as if to contradict that. He sat sunk full fathom five beside the couch's armrest (and going deeper all the time—I feared for the thing's springs), looking at me and wheezing benignly.

"What brings you out this way?" I asked him.

"Oh, Kathi tells me you're planning to off yourself," he said. It was the tone he might have used to say Kathi tells me you're having a lawn party and there are fresh Krispy Kremes on offer. "Any truth to that?"

I opened my mouth, then closed it again. Once, when I was ten and growing up in Eau Claire, I took a comic book from a drugstore spin-around, put it down the front of my jeans, then dropped my tee-shirt over it. As I was strolling out the door, feeling clever, a clerk grabbed me by the arm. She lifted my shirt with her other hand and exposed my ill-gotten treasure. "How did that get there?" she asked me. Not in the forty years since had I been so completely stuck for an answer to a simple question.

Finally—long after such a response could have any weight— I said, "That's ridiculous. I don't know where she could have gotten such an idea."

"No?"

"No. Sure you don't want a Coke?"

"Thanks, but I'll pass."

I got up and got a Coke from the kitchen fridge. I tucked the bottle firmly between my stump and my chest-wall—possible but painful, I don't know what you may have seen in the movies, but broken ribs hurt for a long time—and spun off the cap with my left hand. I'm a southpaw. Caught a break there, *muchacho*, as Kamen says.

"I'm surprised you'd take her seriously in any case," I said as I came back in. "Kathi's a hell of a physical therapist, but a headshrinker she's not." I paused before sitting down. "Neither are you, actually. In the technical sense."

Kamen cupped one hand behind an ear that looked roughly the size of a desk drawer. "Do I hear...a ratcheting noise? I believe I do!"

Memory

"What are you talking about?"

"It's the charmingly medieval sound a person's defenses make when they go up." He tried an ironic wink, but the size of the man's face made irony impossible; he could only manage burlesque. Still, I took the point. "As for Kathi Green, you're right, what does she know? All she does is work with paraplegics, quadriplegics, accident-related amps like you, and people recovering from traumatic head injuries—again, like you. For fifteen years Kathi Green's done this work, she's had the opportunity to watch a thousand maimed patients reflect on how not even a single second of time can ever be called back, so how could she possibly recognize the signs of pre-suicidal depression?"

I sat down in the lumpy easy chair across from the couch, listing to the left as I did it to favor my bad hip, and stared at him sullenly. Here was trouble. No matter how carefully I crafted my suicide, here was trouble. And Kathi Green was more.

He leaned forward...but, given his girth, a few inches was all he could manage. "You have to wait," he said.

I gaped at him. It was the last thing I had expected.

He nodded. "You're surprised. Yes. But I'm not a Christian, let alone a Catholic, and on the subject of suicide my mind is quite open. Yet I'm a believer in responsibilities, and I tell you this: if you kill yourself now...or even six months from now... your wife and daughters will know. No matter how cleverly you do it, they'll know."

"I don't—"

"And the company that insures your life—for a very large sum, I have no doubt—they'll know, too. They may not be able to prove it...but they will try very, very hard.

The rumors they start will hurt your children, no matter how well-armored against such things you may think they are."

Melissa was well-armored. Ilse, however, was a different story.

"And in the end, they may prove it." He shrugged his enormous shoulders. "How much of a death-duty that would mean I wouldn't venture to guess, but I know it might erase a great deal of your life's treasure."

I wasn't even thinking about the money. I was thinking about a team of insurance investigators sniffing around whatever I set up, trying to overturn it. And all at once I began to laugh.

Kamen sat with his huge dark hands on his doorstop knees, looking at me with his little I've-seen-everything smile. Except on his face nothing was little. He let my laughter run its course and when it had, he asked me what was so funny.

"You're telling me I'm too rich to kill myself," I said.

"I'm telling you to give it time. I have a very strong intuition in your case—the same sort of intuition that caused me to give you the doll you named...what did you name her?"

For a second I couldn't remember. Then I thought, *It was RED!*, and told him what I had named my fluffy blond anger-doll.

He nodded. "Yes. The same sort of intuition that caused me to give you Reba. My intuition is that in your case, time may soothe you. Time and memory."

I didn't tell him I remembered everything I wanted to. He knew my position on that. "How much time are we talking about, Kamen?"

He sighed as a man does before saying something he may regret. "At least a year." He studied my face. "It seems a very long time to you. The way you are now."

"Yes," I said. "Time's different for me now."

Memory

"Of course it is," he said. "Pain-time is different. Alone-time is different. Put them together and you have something very different. So pretend you're an alcoholic and do it as they do."

"A day at a time."

He nodded. "A day at a time."

"Kamen, you are so full of bullshit."

He looked at me from the depths of the old couch, not smiling. He'd never get out of there without help.

"Maybe *sí*, maybe no," he said. "In the meantime...Edgar, does anything make you happy?"

"I don't know...I used to sketch."

"When?"

I realized I hadn't done more than doodle while taking telephone calls since an art class for extra credit in high school. I considered lying about this—I was ashamed to seem like such a fixated drudge—and then told the truth. One-armed men should tell the truth whenever possible. Kamen doesn't say that; I do.

"Take it up again," Kamen said. "You need hedges."

"Hedges," I said, bemused.

"Yes, Edgar." He looked surprised and a little disappointed, as if I had failed to understand a very simple concept. "Hedges against the night."

IT MIGHT have been a week after Kamen's visit that Tom Riley came to see me. The leaves had started to turn color, and I remember the clerks putting up Halloween posters in the Wal-Mart where I bought sketchpads and various drawing implements a few days before my former accountant's visit; that's the best I can do.

What I remember most clearly about that visit is how embarrassed and ill-at-ease Tom seemed. He was on an errand he didn't want to run.

I offered him a Coke and he took me up on it. When I came back from the kitchen, he was looking at a pen-and-ink I'd done—three palm trees silhouetted against an expanse of water, a bit of tiled roof jutting into the left foreground. "This is pretty good," he said. "You do this?"

"Nah, the elves," I said. "They come in the night. Cobble my shoes and draw the occasional picture."

He laughed too hard and set the picture back down on the desk. "Don't look much like Minnesota, dere," he said, doing a Swedish accent.

"I copied it out of a book," I said. "What can I do for you, Tom? If it's about the business—"

"Actually, Pam asked me to come out." He ducked his head. "I didn't much want to, but I didn't feel I could say no."

"Tom," I said, "go on and spit it out. I'm not going to bite you."

"She's got herself a lawyer. She's going ahead with this divorce business."

"I never thought she wouldn't." It was the truth. I still didn't remember choking her, but I remembered the look in her eyes when she told me I had. I remembered telling her she was a quitting birch and feeling that if she dropped dead at that moment, right there at the foot of the cellar stairs, that would be all right with me. Fine, in fact. And setting aside how I'd felt then, once Pam started down a road, she rarely turned around.

"She wants to know if you're going to be using Bozie."

Memory

I had to smile at that. William Bozeman III was the wheel-dog of the Minneapolis law-firm the company used, and if he knew Tom and I had been calling him Bozie for the last twenty years, he would probably have a hemorrhage.

"I hadn't thought about it. What's the deal, Tom? What exactly does she want?"

He drank off half his Coke, put the glass on a bookshelf beside my half-assed sketch, and looked at his shoes. "She said she hopes it doesn't have to be mean. She said, 'I don't want to be rich, and I don't want a fight. I just want him to be fair to me and the girls, the way he always was, will you tell him that?' So I am." He shrugged, still looking down at his shoes.

I got up, went to the big window between the living room and the porch, and looked out at the lake. When I turned back, Tom Riley didn't look himself at all. At first I thought he was sick to his stomach. Then I realized he was struggling not to cry.

"Tom, what's the matter?" I asked.

He shook his head, tried to speak, and produced only a watery croak. He cleared his throat and tried again. "Boss, I can't get used to seeing you with just the one arm. I'm so sorry."

It was artless, unrehearsed, and sweet. A straight shot to the heart, in other words. I think there was a moment when we were both close to bawling, like a couple of Sensitive Guys on The Oprah Winfrey Show. All we needed was Dr. Phil, nodding avuncular approval.

"I'm sorry, too," I said, "but I'm getting along. Really. And I'm going to give you an offer to take back to her. If she likes the shape of it, we can hammer out the details. No lawyers needed. Do-it-yourself deal."

"Are you serious, Eddie?"

"I am. You do a comprehensive accounting so we have a bottom-line figure to work with. Nothing hidden. Then we divide the swag into four shares. She takes three—seventy-five per cent—for her and the girls. I take the rest. The divorce itself…hey, Minnesota's a no-fault state, she and I can go to lunch and then buy Divorce for Dummies at Borders."

He looked dazed. "Is there such a book?"

"I haven't researched it, but if there isn't, I'll eat your shirts."

"I think the saying's 'eat my shorts.'"

"Isn't that what I said?"

"Never mind. Eddie, that kind of deal is going to trash the estate."

"Ask me if I give a shit. Or a shirt, for that matter. All I'm proposing is that we dispense with the ego that usually allows the lawyers to swallow the cream. There's plenty for all of us, if we're reasonable."

He drank some of his Coke, never taking his eyes off me. "Sometimes I wonder if you're the same man I used to work for," he said.

"That man died in his pickup truck," I said.

↩→

IF YOU'VE been picturing my convalescent retreat as a lakeside cottage standing in splendid isolation at the end of a lonely dirt road in the north woods, you better think again—this is suburban St. Paul we're talking about. Our place by the lake stands at the end of Aster Lane, a paved street running from East Hoyt Avenue to the water. In the middle of October I finally took Kathi Green's advice and began walking. They were only short outings up to East Hoyt Avenue,

Memory

but I always came back with my bad hip crying for mercy and often with tears standing in my eyes. Yet I also almost always came back feeling like a conquering hero—I'd be a liar if I didn't admit it. I was returning from one of these walks when Mrs. Fevereau hit Gandalf, the pleasant Jack Russell terrier who belonged to the little girl next door.

I was three-quarters of the way home when the Fevereau woman went past me in her ridiculous mustard-colored Hummer. As always, she had her cell phone in one hand and a cigarette in the other; as always she was going too fast. I barely noticed, and I certainly didn't see Gandalf dash into the street up ahead, concentrating only on Monica Goldstein, coming down the other side of the street in full Girl Scout uniform. I was concentrating on my reconstructed hip. As always near the end of these short strolls, this so-called medical marvel felt packed with roughly ten thousand tiny points of broken glass. My clearest memory before the scream of the Hummer's tires was thinking that the Mrs. Fevereaus of the world now lived in a different universe than the one I inhabited, one where all sensations were turned down to half-strength.

Then the tires yowled, and a little girl's scream joined them: "GANDALF, NO!" For a moment I had a clear and unearthly vision of the crane that had almost killed me filling the right window of my pickup truck, the world I'd always lived in suddenly eaten up by a yellow much brighter than Mrs. Fevereau's Hummer, and black letters floating in it, swelling, getting larger.

Then Gandalf began to scream, too, and the flashback—what Dr. Kamen would no doubt have called a recovered memory—was gone. Until that afternoon in October four years ago, I hadn't known dogs could scream.

I broke into a lurching, crabwise run, pounding the sidewalk with my red crutch. I'm sure it would have appeared ludicrous to an onlooker, but no one was paying any attention to me. Monica Goldstein was kneeling in the middle of the street beside her dog, which lay in front of the Hummer's high, boxy grille. Her face was white above her forest-green uniform, from which a sash of badges and medals hung. The end of this sash was soaking in a spreading pool of Gandalf's blood. Mrs. Fevereau half-jumped and half-fell from the Hummer's ridiculously high driver's seat. Ava Goldstein came running from the front door of the Goldstein house, crying her daughter's name. Mrs. Goldstein's blouse was half-buttoned and her feet were bare.

"Don't touch him, honey, don't touch him," Mrs. Fevereau said. She was still holding her cigarette and she puffed nervously at it. "He could bite."

Monica paid no attention. She touched Gandalf's side. The dog screamed again when she did—it was a scream—and Monica covered her eyes with the heels of her hands. She began to shake her head. I didn't blame her.

Mrs. Fevereau reached out for the girl, then changed her mind. She took two steps back, leaned against the high side of her ridiculous yellow mode of transport, and looked up at the sky.

Mrs. Goldstein knelt beside her daughter. "Honey, oh honey please don't..."

Gandalf began to howl. He lay in the street, in a pool of his spreading blood, howling. And now I could also remember the sound the crane had made. Not the meep-meep-meep it was supposed to make, because its backup warning had been broken, but the juddering stutter of its diesel engine and the sound of its treads eating up the earth.

Memory

"Get her inside, Ava," I said. "Get her in the house."

Mrs. Goldstein got her arm around her daughter's shoulders and urged her up. "Come on, honey. Come inside."

"Not without Gandalf!" Monica screamed. She was eleven, and mature for her age, but in those moments she had regressed to three. "Not without my doggy!" Her sash, the last three inches now sodden with blood, thwapped the side of her skirt and a long line of blood spattered down her calf.

"Go in and call the vet," I told her. "Say Gandalf's been hit by a car. Say he has to come right away. I'll stay with him."

Monica looked at me with eyes that were more than shocked. They were crazy. I had no trouble holding her gaze, though; I'd seen it often enough in my own mirror. "Do you promise? Big swear? Mother's name?"

"Big swear, mother's name," I said. "Go on, Monica."

She went, casting one more look back and uttering one more bereft wail before starting up the steps to her house. I knelt beside Gandalf, holding onto the Hummer's fender and going down as I always did, painfully and listing severely to the left, trying to keep my right knee from bending any more than it absolutely had to. Still, I voiced my own little cry of pain, and I wondered if I'd be able to get up again without help. It might not be forthcoming from Mrs. Fevereau; she walked over to the lefthand side of the street with her legs stiff and wide apart, then bent at the waist as if bowing to royalty, and vomited in the gutter. She held the hand with the cigarette in it off to one side as she did it.

I turned my attention to Gandalf. He had been struck in the hindquarters. His spine was crushed. Blood and shit oozed sluggishly from between his broken rear legs. His eyes turned up to me and in them I saw a horrible expression of hope. His tongue crept out and licked my inner left wrist. His tongue was dry as carpet, and cold. Gandalf was going to die, but maybe not soon enough. Monica would come out again soon, and I didn't want him alive to lick her wrist when she did.

I understood what I had to do. There was no one to see me do it. Monica and her mother were inside. Mrs. Fevereau's back was still turned. If others on this little stub of a street had come to their windows (or out on their lawns), the Hummer blocked their view of me sitting beside the dog with my bad right leg awkwardly outstretched. I had a few moments, but only a few, and if I stopped to consider, my chance would be lost.

So I took Gandalf's upper body in my good arm and without a pause I'm back at the Sutton Avenue site, where The Freemantle Company is getting ready to build a forty-story bank building. I'm in my pickup truck. Pat Green's on the radio, singing "Wave on Wave." I suddenly realize the crane's too loud even though I haven't heard any backup beeper and when I look to my right the world in that window is gone. The world on that side has been replaced by yellow. Black letters float there: **LINK-BELT**. They're swelling. I spin the Ram's wheel to the left, all the way to the stop, knowing I'm already too late as the scream of crumpling metal starts, drowning out the song on the radio and shrinking the inside of the cab right to left because the crane's invading my space, stealing my space, and the pickup is tipping. I'm trying for the driver's side door but it's no good. I should have done that right away but it got too late real early. The world in front of me disappears as the windshield turns to milk shot through with a million cracks. Then the building site is back, still turning on a hinge as the windshield pops out, flies out bent in the middle like a play-ing-card, and I'm laying on the horn with the points of both

Memory

elbows, my right arm doing its last job. I can barely hear the horn over the crane's engine. **LINK-BELT** is still moving in, pushing the passenger-side door, closing the passenger-side footwell, eating up the dashboard, splintering it in jagged hunks of plastic. The shit from the glove-compartment floats around like confetti, the radio goes dead, my lunchbucket is tanging against my clipboard, and here comes **LINK-BELT**. **LINK-BELT** is right on top of me, I could stick out my tongue and lick that fucking hyphen. I start screaming because that's when the pressure starts. The pressure is my right arm first pushing against my side, then spreading, then splitting open. Blood douses my lap like a bucket of hot water and I hear something breaking. Probably my ribs. It sounds like chickenbones under a bootheel.

I held Gandalf against me and thought *Bring the friend, sit in the friend, sit in the fucking PAL, you dump bitch!*

Now I'm in sitting in the chum, sitting in the fucking pal, it's at home but all the clocks of the world are still ringing inside my cracked head and I can't remember the name of the doll Kamen gave me, all I can remember are boy names: Randall, Russell, Rudolph, even River-fucking-Phoenix. I tell her to leave me alone when she comes in with the lunch I don't want, to give me five minutes to get myself under control. I can do this, I say, because it's the phrase Kamen has given me, it's the out, it's the *meep-meep-meep* that says watch out, Pamela, I'm backing up. But instead of leaving she takes the napkin from the lunch tray to wipe the sweat off my forehead and while she's doing that I grab her by the throat because in that moment it seems to me it's her fault I can't remember my doll's name, everything is her fault, including **LINK-BELT**. I grab her with my good left hand, caught a break there, *muchacho*. For a few seconds I want to kill her, and who knows, maybe I almost do. What I do know is I'd rather remember all the accidents in the world than the look in her eyes as she struggles in my grip like a fish stuck on a gaff. Then I think, *It was RED!* and let her go.

I held Gandalf against my chest as I once held my infant daughters and thought, *I can do this. I can do this. I can do this.* I felt Gandalf's blood soak through my pants like hot water and thought, *Go on, you sad fuck, get out of Dodge.*

I held Gandalf and thought of how it felt to be crushed alive as the cab of your truck ate the air around you and the breath left your body and the blood blew out of your nose and mouth and those snapping sounds as consciousness fled, those were the bones breaking inside your own body: your ribs, your arm, your hip, your leg, your cheek, your fucking skull.

I held Monica's dog and thought, in a kind of miserable triumph: *It was RED!*

For a moment I was in a darkness shot with that red, and I held Gandalf's neck in the crook of my left arm, which was now doing the work of two and very strong. I flexed that arm as hard as I could, flexed the way I did when I was doing my curls with the ten-pound weight. Then I opened my eyes. Gandalf was silent, staring past my face and past the sky beyond.

"Edgar?" It was Hastings, the old guy who lived two houses up from the Goldsteins. There was an expression of dismay on his face. "You can let go now. That dog is dead."

"Yes," I said, relaxing my grip on Gandalf. "Would you help me get up?"

"I'm not sure I can," Hastings said. "I'd be more apt to pull us both down."

"Then go in and see the Goldsteins," I said.

Memory

"It is her dog," he said. "I wasn't sure. I was hoping..." He shook his head.

"It's hers. And I don't want her to see him like this."

"Of course not, but—"

"I'll help him," Mrs. Fevereau said. She looked a little better, and she had ditched the cigarette. She reached for my right armpit, then hesitated. "Will that hurt you?"

It would, but less than staying the way I was. As Hastings went up the Goldsteins' walk, I took hold of the Hummer's bumper. Together we managed to get me on my feet.

"I don't suppose you've got anything to cover the dog with?" I asked.

"As a matter of fact, there's a rug remnant in the back." She started around to the rear—it would be a long trek, given the Hummer's size—then turned back. "Thank God it died before the little girl got back."

"Yes," I said. "Thank God."

"Still—she'll never forget it, will she?"

"Well," I said, "you're asking the wrong person about that, Mrs. Fevereau. I'm just a retired general contractor." But when I asked Kamen, he was surprisingly optimistic. He says it's the bad memories that wear thin first. Then, he says, they tear open and let the light through. I told him he was full of shit and he just laughed.

Maybe *sí*, he says. Maybe no.

When I was Twenty-Four and Dinosaurs Ruled the Earth

by Dean Koontz

BEASTCHILD WAS WRITTEN in 1969.
 That was a pivotal year in human affairs—though not because of *Beastchild*, much as I would like to believe my little story had something to do with changing the course of history.

In that same year, Neil Armstrong was the first man to set foot on the moon. The imprint of his boot on lunar soil marked a triumph of human ingenuity, vision, and spirit—and pretty much insured that McDonald's will one day franchise hamburger restaurants on other worlds. The Concorde supersonic jet made its first trans-Atlantic flight, whereupon it became possible for international travelers to spend less time in the air than in taxi cabs to and from the airport. Scientific and medical advances were progressing at the fastest pace in history, and there were many reasons to be optimistic.

But we were fascinated by death.

In a society increasingly interested in gossip, the big rumor of the year was that Paul McCartney, of the Beatles, had died some time ago in a car wreck, that his death was being concealed, and that references to all of this were cleverly embedded in the latest record releases by the Fab Four. For a while, this story got almost as much attention as the extension of the Vietnam War into Cambodia.

In 1969, we became fixated not merely on rumors of death but on the real thing. We tuned in the evening news to listen to daily body counts. Soldiers were dying. Four students were killed in an anti-war protest at Kent State. We concluded that death was omnipresent, that the whole world was dying from one thing or another.

The Hysteria Cult, which grows more powerful as we near the millennium, began to exert real power in 1969, when it succeeded in getting the FDA to order Cyclamate, an artificial sweetener, off the market because it was a possible carcinogen. Why we should worry so intensely about the cancerous aspects of diet soft drinks when we also believed, as we were told, that the nuclear holocaust was right around the corner, I can't explain; a case could even have been made that worldwide radiation storms from atomic weapons might cure at least a *few* cases of the tumors that Cyclamate supposedly generated, and make many other cases moot. But we had grimly turned away from all optimism. (Years later, Cyclamate proved not to be carcinogenic; however, the artificial sweeteners that replaced it came under suspicion as

When I Was Twenty-Four
and Dinosaurs Ruled the Earth

mutagens, giving rise to hideous images of babies born with insect antennae on their foreheads and lobster pincers for hands all because Mommy drank Diet Pepsi. And there was one autumn when Meryl Streep threw apple-growers into poverty by convincing us that the humble fruit was even more deadly now than in the Garden of Eden because of Alar, a chemical used in agriculture—which subsequently proved no more deadly than Cyclamate.)

In 1969, we were told, as well, that industrial emissions were polluting the atmosphere to such an extent that, before the turn of the century, so much sunlight would be prevented from reaching the surface of the planet that a catastrophic ice age would swiftly ensue, making it damned hard to get out to the nearest 7-Eleven for another six-pack of beer. Anyone predicting that this fear would be transformed into its opposite within twenty years—the fear of the Greenhouse Effect, all of humanity roasted alive like so many weenies—would have been ridiculed and derided.

In those days, people had energy for only one or two crises at a time. They didn't *thrive* on hysteria yet. We are a far hardier lot now: we have the capacity to fear everything from planetary meltdown to the deleterious effects of Saturday morning cartoon shows, yet retain enough energy to establish guidelines for politically correct behavior in every human endeavor. We are convinced that *all* of life is as dangerous as being caught in the middle of a fight between razor-wielding maniacs in a pit full of vipers and crocodiles, and that only raving lunatics would dare eat bacon or go outside wearing less than a 40 sunblock and caftan. From that small beginning with Cyclamate in '69, we have come to *embrace* doom as our just, inevitable reward as a species.

The big movies of 1969 were *Easy Rider, Midnight Cowboy, Butch Cassidy and the Sundance Kid, They Shoot Horses Don't They*—and *True Grit.* How that last John Wayne vehicle got in there among all those flicks about fate-throttled anti-heroes, I don't know. There must have been a short-circuit in the Great Hollywood Movie Sausage Machine. Like other societies that previously approached the turn of the tenth of ten centuries, we began to direct one wary eye toward the millennium, and decided we wanted our entertainment to reflect our fear of both personal and larger armageddons.

Death.

Big novels of the year included Kurt Vonnegut's black and bitter comedy, *Slaughterhouse Five*, and Mario Puzo's epic portrayal of the lives of murderous Mafiosi and their families.

To be taken seriously as a writer or filmmaker, one had to be something of a pessimist. Of course, the riches showered upon the pessimists largely *because* of their pessimism must have been disconcerting to them; but even communists have found it possible to enjoy the privileges of wealth and power without feeling like hypocrites, so the pessimists adapted easily to their success.

Doom. Sweet, dark, appealing doom.

Swimming in that grim Zeitgeist, I wrote a story about the end of the world through alien invasion—but gave it what was, in retrospect, an odd twist by making it a sometimes amusing and inspiring piece about friendship, hope, and faith. *Beastchild.* It was on the final Hugo ballot in its 40,000-word novella form, which might have indicated a turning-away from pessimism by the mass audience—except it lost to another novella that was, as I recall, darker and more cynical than my story. Furthermore, the advance and sales were so low that

When I Was Twenty-Four
and Dinosaurs Ruled the Earth

they almost shook me from an optimism as firm as that of any member of the singing Osmond family and into a brooding pessimism of my own. Almost.

1969. Death. Doom. Darkness. War in Vietnam. Nixon in the White House. Rapidly increasing nuclear arsenals. Soviet agents stirring up trouble in every corner of the world. Judy Garland dead at 47, perhaps a suicide, perhaps not. James Earl Ray sent to prison for killing Dr. Martin Luther King. Sirhan Sirhan convicted of murdering Robert Kennedy. Boris Karloff, a sweet and gentle man who portrayed monsters on the silver screen, dead at 81. Dwight Eisenhower, one of the great heroes of the century, dead at 78.

However, death can teach us lessons that lead to a renewal of hope and optimism, if we're willing to learn. For instance:

1969 was the year that Teddy Kennedy drove off the bridge from Chappaquiddick Island and left Mary Jo Kopechne for dead, trapped in a submerged car with only a small bubble of air to sustain her for precious minutes. He didn't run for help, didn't even report the accident until the next morning. The incident should have taught us everything we needed to know about the ruthlessness, brazenness, self-centeredness, and amorality of the type of men who most often become politicians. And perhaps it *has* taught us, though the effect of the lesson seems to have been long in coming, nevertheless, as I write this in August of 1992, the country shows welcome signs of having burned out on politicians of every stripe and of being less willing than it once was to make heroes of their ilk.

On August 17, 1969, the Age of Aquarius was ushered in with tremendous fanfare at the legendary Woodstock festival, where it was proclaimed that the free-love-and-drugs counterculture was the future and the only hope of paradise on earth. On December 6, at Altamont Speedway, during a Rolling Stones concert at which the Hell's Angels had been contracted for security in return for free beer, young Meredith Hunter was stabbed to death near the stage. On December 24, ex-con flower child Charles Manson and members of his counterculture free-love "family" were arrested for the murders of actress Sharon Tate and four other people, which had occurred on the night of August 10—five days before the birth of Woodstock Nation. The lesson here should have been that utopian theories, when practiced, usually lead to the circumscription of nonbelievers' rights, emphasis of form over substance, the elevation of scoundrels to the status of gurus, and murder. Perhaps a little of this lesson has sunk in too; since the fall of Communism, a utopian scheme in the name of which at least a hundred million people have been murdered, we seem at least slightly less inclined to look for simple answers and to embrace trendy idealism than we have been in the past.

We are still doom-haunted, anticipating the end of the world by any of a dozen means. And yet…And yet, one of the most successful films at the box office last year—and *the* most honored at the Academy Awards ceremony—was *The Silence of the Lambs*, based on the novel of the same title, in which the simple virtues of one courageous woman are more than a match for the evil of a serial killer who skins his victims; in fact she might eventually prove to be a match for Hannibal Lecter, as well, a psychiatrist whose evil is portrayed as so profound that he might *be* Death himself. Thomas Harris's novel, more than the film, makes the subtle point that Freudian theory—and the utopian desire to render all human behavior understandable—is a misguided attempt to banish

When I Was Twenty-Four
and Dinosaurs Ruled the Earth

the concept of evil by "proving" that even blood-thirsty acts are the explicable response to universal victimization and are therefore pitiable rather than immoral. The best-selling status of Harris's book seems to testify to the mass audience's desire, perhaps still subconscious, to turn away from a century of the pessimism that comes from believing that evil is inculcated in us by childhood trauma, by events beyond our control. Maybe we are ready to hope, if not fully believe, that we are the Fallen but not irredeemable.

As I write this, Clint Eastwood's *The Unforgiven* is packing theaters and delighting critics. Dark, bleak, unrelenting in its portrayal of the human capacity for evil, the film is nonetheless hopeful; we identify with Eastwood's character, a true sociopath, not because we admire his brutality (which might have been the case in earlier films of his) but because we respond to the fact that even this savage beast was, for a period of ten years, redeemed by a good wife who turned his heart away from darkness at least while she lived at his side. The surface of the movie is pessimistic, but the soul of it is optimistic.

Since *Beastchild*, I have been writing stories that, while often dark, are fundamentally optimistic, even blatantly uplifting. For a long time, this seemed to put me out of step with the grim marching armies of the hip and trendy. But in recent years, I've found a growing audience, which is now sufficiently large to confirm my suspicion that an increasing number of men and women want to put the situational ethics and resultant pessimistic philosophies of this aberrant century behind them; they want to seek a future grounded in the wisdom of previous ages and in the hope that sustained the many generations who came before us and built the foundations of our civilization.

Beastchild is interesting to me—if to no one else!—because I see in it the seeds of the viewpoint that informs my work these many years later. There's a natural progression from this thin and stylistically immature science fiction novel to *Watchers*, which I wrote eighteen years later.

For this reason, I intend to revise *Beastchild* eventually and see what happens to the story when I filter it through the past twenty-odd years of experience. I want to give Hulann, the alien lead of the novel, a chance to live more fully than I could make him live in 1969, and I want his relationship with the boy Leo to put down far deeper roots than I could nurture with my level of craftsmanship and insight when I was twenty-four.

Before embarking on that revision, however, it seemed to me that the original version of the novel deserved to be produced for the record in a more durable form than has previously been available—and for the readers who have heard of it and write so often to say they can't find a copy. The Lancer paperback had such a low press run that I half believed the publisher was not in the business to make money but served as a front for the KGB, or a money-laundering operation for the mafia, or an investment vehicle for masochists who wanted to pour their money down a rathole. Relatively few copies of the book remain. No hardcover has ever been published until this edition that you now hold in your hands. If either the original or revised novel merited the beauty of a Charnel House production (you'll be the judge of that), then it seemed to me that the original, created as a response to the times in which it was written, should have that honor. There will be no limited edition of *Beastchild* when eventually it appears at twice this length and in refined prose.

When I Was Twenty-Four
and Dinosaurs Ruled the Earth

Please remember that I was twenty-four when this was written, a poor and struggling and undeniably confused young writer who had not yet found his way. (I had not yet even eaten Mexican food!) That the book still reads well to me is a small miracle; that I've the intense desire to rework it after the Charnel House publication is, frankly, amazing. But the situation and the characters became a part of me more than two decades ago, and they're still in me, waiting to be reborn. Demanding it.

Herein is the future as seen from 1969. Now we're living in the future of that time, and it's not a fraction as bleak as we believed it would be. That humankind continues to look with dread toward the coming decades indicates a perverse streak in the species. That we made it across these twenty-three years without transforming the planet into a radioactive hell speaks well of us and should fill us with hope. But whether or not we can learn to hope again and shed the negativism of this century, I know that my own books will continue to be optimistic at the center, and that I will go on my way, whistling happily, and let events prove whether, by embracing hope, I've been a fool or a sage.

Dean R. Koontz
Newport Beach, CA
August, 1992

Peter and PTR: Two Deleted Prefaces and an Introduction

by Peter Straub

Introduction

→ THESE TWO SHORT pieces represent my effort to get the ball rolling on the novel called Mr. X, then in a condition best described as hypothetical. I had assembled thirty-four single-spaced pages headed "Notes for New Novel" which sketched in the situation I had in mind and, with occasional second thoughts, self-questionings, floating of various leftfield possibilities and pauses for explanation, developed it scene by scene through what I trusted would be the first third of the manuscript, or roughly two hundred pages. In other words, I made it up as I went along, improvising a sequence of events that incorporated the few fixed narrative points I already knew while discovering some others in the process. The "Notes" were more a general guide than an outline, and I broke off when going on would have risked imposing too much order too early. This was the first paragraph:

We may begin with a series—no more than two or three—of unexplained episodes in which first a boy and then the young man he becomes undergo fearful episodes in which he loses consciousness and witnesses hideous crimes. These episodes begin with a charged physical sensation, then a vision of blue light or blue flames, and lead to scenes of physical violence, murder, stalking through various interiors, screams, etc., and these are paralleled with italicized passages which describe the same incidents with greater clarity and from a first-person point of view.

So deeply embedded in the central situation that its first mention does not appear until page twelve was the reason I wanted to write the book in the first place, the presence of a Doppelganger. Secret sharers, unknown brothers, shadow-selves, with their inevitable suggestion that the truly dangerous adversary has stepped out of the mirror, had always appealed to me. They had a lovely eeriness combined with great psychological suggestiveness. Poe, Stevenson and Dostoyevsky had written Doppelganger stories, and so had Daphne du Maurier, Christopher Priest, Orhan Pamuk and lots of other people. Wilkie Collins, one of my ancestral spirits, had virtually built his career on the conceit, continuing to draw upon it well past the point at which he degenerated into unwitting

Peter and PTR:
Two Deleted Prefaces and an Introduction

self-parody. (Collins' life-long laudanum addiction contributed to the speed and severity of the decline, and even a Collins devotee like me, who has no problems with his habit while it was helping him to write his masterpieces, wishes he had detoxed while he was still ahead. In place of unreadable duds like *The Evil Genius*, we could have had his *Edwin Drood*— though *Edwin Drood* almost is a Wilkie Collins novel.)

Once before, I had set out to base a novel on the Doppelganger theme. *Mystery* began as *Family Romance*, a book about two brothers. Tom (Pasmore), raised in well-upholstered circumstances, and Mat (as in doormat), chained in a shed and cruelly mistreated, a matter which rebounds on the mistreaters when he breaks out and...That was as far as I got with the planning, and when I finally sat down before the ready screen, I did not get even that far. Declining to follow orders, the narrative jumped the tracks and turned straight toward the relationship between well-off Tom and the eccentric old boy, an amateur detective, who lived in the peculiar mansion across the street. I cut what I thought were some of the strongest chapters from the manuscript, but they were already pale and useless: the book had rejected them. Mr. X allowed me a second chance at Doppelgangers and secret brothers, and by this time I had thought about the question at least enough to describe it, on page twelve of the "Notes," as follows:

> These two need one another to be whole. They make each other complete. Ned is Ego, Robert is Id; Ned is doubt, Robert certainty; Ned thought and Robert action. Morality/Immorality, Civilization/Savagery, Civility/Raunch.

In May, 1996, no more than a couple of days after I had come to the end of my first foray into Mr. X, my wife and I went on a short vacation to Rome. Our friends Lila and Daniel Javitch, who had a long association with the American Academy in Rome and were living in the city that year, generously guided, directed, piloted us through churches, art galleries, piazzas, avenues, alley-ways and restaurants, over bridges and under bridges, up and down hills in the lively ongoing combat of Roman traffic, several times zipping through the eyes of needles too microscopic to be registered by the untrained eye. On a sunny afternoon near the middle of our stay, Lila Javitch drove us across Rome and up a hill to the Academy, where she introduced us to a number of people, among them a scholarly-looking gentleman whose great administrative significance to the Academy seemed belied by the wispy hair retreating from his high, convex forehead, the protective opacity of his prominent eyeglasses and, more tellingly, the recessiveness of his manner, that of a being forever in retreat. During our tour of the building, Lila showed us into a large, white-walled studio with long windows looking down across the Tiber onto a spectacular view of Roman rooftops and the dome of St. Peter's. These details, clearly, I filed away.

Downstairs, a billboard advertised a lecture to be given that evening by an American painter, an A-list art figure of the generation between Jasper Johns and Robert Rauschenburg's and that of Julian Schnabel, Eric Fischl and David Salle. Susan and Lila were interested in attending, and Daniel was going to be at the Academy that night anyhow. On the grounds that I had not come to Rome to listen to an American painter occupy an hour with reflections upon his own achievements, I took a cab back to our hotel, where a disagreeable, vastly

Peter and PTR:
Two Deleted Prefaces and an Introduction

mustached barman crooned *"Cin-cin!"* every time he produced another drink. I felt as though overloaded with impressions—something was beginning to come into focus, I was not quite sure what. On her return, Susan, for whom the attitudes and opinions of practicing artists held no surprises, reported a conventional though in no way uninteresting event.

At lunch the next day, Dan Javitch, a Professor of Comparative Literature at New York University, described the lecture in altogether more colorful terms. Instead of the familiar spectacle of a self-assured New York art figure expressing a fairly ordinary viewpoint, Dan had witnessed a surly, bad-tempered attack on the Academy and most of its Fellows. Before an audience largely made up of art historians, specialists in Italian literature and other academics, the speaker had condemned scholarly, research-oriented approaches to and considerations of the visual arts as misguided, uninformed and destructive to their contemporary practitioners. The celebrated painter had used the decorous lecture room as a forum in which to complain, bitterly, that the professional scholars who made their livings writing and talking about art believed the only worthwhile artist was a dead artist, the longer dead the better. It got worse, it got ruder, it got personal. Responding to a question (probably a rather hesitant question) from an elderly, much-respected couple who had devoted their careers to the study of iconography, the painter had offered the blunt remark, "Fuck iconography."

After another four or five days of fountains, piazzas, Caravaggios, Raphaels, mopeds, vistas from rooftops, churches, ossified monks the size of orangutans, Mithraic temples, gnocchi, papal symbols, Barolos, Chiantis, *carciofi*, the little rooms in which great poets had died and the little cemeteries where cats sauntered over their bones, tombs, ruins, museums, monuments, *"Cin-cins!,"* restaurants managed by men whose cousins managed restaurants in Greenwich Village, gelatis, cappuccinos, cell phones, guidebooks, walks across bridges, walks across gardens and walks up the Spanish Steps to our hotel, we came back to New York. It was time to start my book.

Or to delay starting it. I still had not worked out exactly where to jump in, nor whether the first sentence should be something like *I reached into my pocket for a quarter to call home, but all I came up with was a lint-speckled cherry Lifesaver,* or something like *Arthur Goodlad, known as "Slats," scuttled around the side of the hotel and spotted a fat billfold nestled into the sawgrass alongside the path to the towel concession.* An interesting notion had just occurred to me. Some of my favorite novels, like *Lolita* and Iris Murdoch's *The Black Prince,* along with a legacy of stories referring to manuscripts supposedly discovered in old trunks, left behind by their mysteriously vanished authors, or inherited by the author's great-nephew, came equipped with Prefaces explaining the circumstances surrounding their publication. They had not been written by the person whose name appeared on the front cover, he or she was merely its conduit. The device distanced the writer from the book by adding another, intermediary layer of fiction which made the narrative itself less trustworthy. It was acknowledged that someone had *written* this story: suddenly, we were in the realm of fable, and all bets were off.

The notion which had occurred to me, interesting enough to allow the fingers (in this case, to allow one finger, the one I used for typing) to maul the keyboard, sending words on a steady march across the screen, was that I could invoke this ancient

Peter and PTR:
Two Deleted Prefaces and an Introduction

but still resonant device in service of the book's theme by calling upon one of my own two Doppelgangers, the dependable, the in fact tireless Putney Tyson Ridge, Ph.D., Chairman and only member of the Department of Popular Culture, Popham College, located in the leafy little burg of Popham, Ohio. Tim Underhill, my other, far nicer second self, a fellow-novelist who had figured in *Koko* and *The Throat*, wouldn't do at all. Tim hardly did anything but work, the poor guy was practically nailed to his desk for ten to twelve hours a day, and he didn't even like me all that much. Besides that, my story would have reminded Tim Underhill too concretely of his own novel *The Divided Man*. He wouldn't have touched the project.

Putney presented none of these difficulties. Old "Put" was never too busy to give me a hand, whether I wanted the hand or not; his presumption of understanding the fictional process much, much more comprehensively than I somehow depended upon his never having written a word of it; and his personal dissatisfactions with my character, my way of life, my habits and my writing did not diminish his attentions but inspired them. My flaws were what Putney liked about me—they gave him material to work with. Putney was perfect for the job.

I'VE NEVER managed to remember Putney's birthday. If he did not come into the world on the day I made my own entrance on the stage, the two events could not have been separated by more than a few weeks. We met in infancy, I know that much. My family and his lived side by side in modest but comfortable houses, with porches and stone front steps to narrow walkways dividing brief, slightly sloping front lawns, on North 44th Street in Milwaukee. Within two months of our births, Putney claims, his mother lowered him into my cradle, or bassinet, whatever it was, whereupon the infant Putney either patted or belted the infant me, depending on which version of the encounter he finds useful at the time. We rattled the bars of the same cribs, played in the same sandboxes, waded in the same wading pools, pored over the same comic books purchased at the same drug store and attended kindergarten together at Townsend Elementary School, where we experienced an identical outrage at the discovery that kindergarten focused on scissors, glue and construction paper. Thereafter, either coincidentally or by design, whenever my family moved from one neighborhood or suburb to another, his invariably took the house next door.

The simplest explanation of this phenomenon would be that our parents were close friends, but they were not. Our parents very rarely, let me amend that to never, socialized. It seems to me that Putney must have spent a great deal more time at my house than I did at his. Surprisingly, I cannot visualize Putney's mother and father with any degree of clarity. Mr. and Mrs. Ridge, Harper and Hunter, I think, but it might have been the other way around, remain hazy blurs hovering in the distance, benevolently waving cigarettes and drinks, like everybody else in those years. I do remember my father saying that Putney's father, Harper, or possibly Hunter, was so stuffy he could get work as a sofa cushion. Another time, I heard him tell my mother that Harper (or Hunter) Ridge never looked at anything another person owned, a car or a lawn mower or a toaster or even a toothpick, without saying that he owned a better one. Putney acted that way, too.

He and I progressed in lockstep, Putney all the while explaining my errors in the spirit of constructive criticism,

Peter and PTR:
Two Deleted Prefaces and an Introduction

through kindergarten and first grade at Townsend, then grades two through six at Daniel Webster State Graded School, grades seven and eight at Marcy School in the suburb of Brookfield, and high school at Milwaukee Country Day. We enrolled at the University of Wisconsin and were assigned adjacent dorm rooms in Siebecker House, Adams Hall. By the time Destiny momentarily nodded off at the beginning of our Sophomore year, with the result that I rented a room in student lodgings at 512 Henry Street and he wound up across the street in 515, the pattern had long since hardened into the form established in the sandbox, if not the crib. My role was to make mistakes, his to point out and correct them. That I was getting tired of the arrangement and had found newer, less judgmental friends—that I thought my Chet Baker record was just as good as his, my Smith-Corona as serviceable as his Underwood, that I preferred Updike to Salinger, continued to dump catsup on my French fries and did not sneer at all American movies, regardless of merit—merely demonstrated my endearing shortsightedness. My efforts at avoiding Putney succeeded only to the extent that, if two or three days passed without my seeing him, no easy feat because we were always taking the same courses, I could count on his barging into my room late in the afternoon, ready to set me straight. True separation came only when Columbia University, which had accepted me into its Graduate Program in English, wait-listed Putney. Irate, insulted, he discovered that Columbia was decadent and its English Department a hothouse of eccentrics, far inferior to the University of Indiana's, into which he had managed to squeak at the last moment. I ignored Putney's lectures on the superiority of Indiana's good common sense over Columbia's corruption, Bloomington's healthy Midwestern ambiance over toxic Manhattan, and once again proved my need of him by making the wrong decision.

Putney stuck to his last. He earned an MA and a Ph.D at Indiana, taught here and there, ascended to Popham, became a tenured Professor and created his private fiefdom, the Department of Popular Culture. In contrast, I went to seed by dropping out of the academic, or respectable, world, getting up to no good in disreputable foreign climes, throwing away what little money I had, living in dank hovels and, saddest of all, pretending to be a writer. After years of dismal failure, I succeeded in developing my few, decidedly unremarkable talents well enough to produce two modestly satisfactory works of fiction, *Julia* and *If You Could See Me Now*. My career since then has been a case study in the destructive effects of misguided praise and vulgar popularity upon a writer too foolish to accept his limitations. If I overstate Putney's view, it is not by much. He writes me every three or four months and, whether invited or not, annually turns up at my front door for a long visit. Putney wants me to know that one person in the world, Putney, can always be relied upon to deliver the uncomfortable truth.

THE MOTIVES that led me to involve Putney Ridge in my professional life were, I confess, less than respectful. Toward the end of the Eighties, I began to take in the existence of a specific attitude on the part of some committed readers and reviewers of horror writing that made me laugh out loud the first time I saw it in print. After I discovered that a number of otherwise

Peter and PTR:
Two Deleted Prefaces and an Introduction

reasonable people shared this attitude, I wanted to drape a cold washcloth over my forehead and lie down in a darkened room. The attitude, really a system for assigning value, in some cases forthrightly rejected, in others denigrated or lampooned, fiction which failed to arouse in its readers echoes of what they already knew they liked. At its most simple-minded, which is to say amongst its dimmest proponents, this view-point yearned for imitations of flash-and-stab horror movies designed for adolescents. Simplicity; swiftness; emphatic narrative punctuations; merciless concentration on creation of suspense, aided by timely interludes of violence; an uncomplicated narrative line; flat characterization; minimal descriptions or digressions (thought of as "padding"); moral structures unambiguously opposing "good" against "evil," as if any such dichotomy existed in life: a valorization of those aspects of pulp fiction its best writers had overcome five decades earlier. When four or five horror specialists in a row had shaken their empty heads at my inability to understand the simple rules of my trade, when too many cardboard productions had been cited as correctives to pieces of my own, Tom Monteleone gave me a way to respond by asking me to provide jacket copy for the Borderlands Press edition of *The Throat*.

I summoned Putney Tyson Ridge. Good old Put, I knew, would loathe the book. He could be counted on eloquently to express the point of view I found comically wrong-headed, even stupid—that I wasn't stupid enough to get things right. Putney came through splendidly. I asked him to perform the same service for the Borderlands Press edition of my HWA anthology, *Ghosts*, and the Gauntlet Books Fifteenth Anniversary edition of *Shadowland*. My old friend performed his task so well that I invited him to add freewheeling remarks about almost everything I have written to my Internet website. Putney's "Comments," as he calls them, are even funnier than I expected. It is a wonderment that I've been able to keep on fooling so many gullible readers over the years.

TWO OR three months after I finished writing Mr. X and edited about two hundred and fifty pages from the original manuscript, I cut the introductory prefaces. My endlessly-revised argument with Putney seemed only to get in the way of the story.

An Explanatory Note

PROFESSOR PUTNEY Ridge's Preface makes it clear that he did not intend this story to fall into my hands. At the time, I put his reluctance down to an unwillingness to surrender "Ned Dunstan's" manuscript until he had figured out how to make hay from it on his own. I should have known better. Old "Put" (his ancient nickname, pronounced "Putt" as in "putty") turned to me as a last resort after waiting months on my former collaborator. When he had wheedled from our mutual agent the telephone number of the Danish farmhouse where Tim Underhill had holed up for the summer, Put's barrage of calls, faxes and e-mailings failed utterly. (Tim so lost patience that he screened his calls and commanded his server to bounce back unread all email bearing Put's code.) If I had

Peter and PTR:
Two Deleted Prefaces and an Introduction

known the history behind my old friend's grim demeanor as he unlocked the desk's bottom drawer with a tiny key, took out the soft, caramel-colored leather hold-all and thrust it toward me, I might have said, "Isn't this more in Tim Underhill's line? After all, he wrote *The Divided Man*, not me." Putney would have wobbled, but only for a moment. Surely, a writer of Underhill's stature would not have betrayed him.

⟲→

MY WIFE and I were in Rome at the invitation of Dennis and Lily Montresor, who were spending a year there while Dennis, a Professor of Comparative Literature at New York University, did research for some essays and articles at the American Academy. Dennis had so little contact with Ridge that he could not remember his name when he first mentioned that one of this year's Fellows had overheard him saying to Allen Stone, a painter we knew in New York, that Susan and I were having dinner with him that night. We were in a Sicilian restaurant in Trastevere after a day of visiting churches under Lily's expert guidance, and Dennis had been describing various goings-on at the American Academy, among them Stone's deliberate offensiveness to a pair of art historians present at a talk he had given that afternoon.

"He knew what he was doing, there wasn't any doubt about that," Dennis said.

"I can't believe it," Lily said. "He wouldn't have insulted them on purpose."

Dennis smiled at me.

I said, "Allen thinks a day without being nasty is like a day without sunshine."

Lily seemed aggrieved, as if I had wronged a friend. "He's never been anything but charming to me."

"In order to be nasty to you," Dennis said, "first he'd have to sleep with you."

Lily opened her mouth, reconsidered, closed it.

"There they are, Ernest and Karen Gold, right in front of him. They've spent their whole lives writing about iconography. Allen spent ten minutes expounding on the sterility of art history, and when Ernest stood up to offer some mild defense of his life's work, Allen said, 'Fuck iconography.'"

"I don't think I'll sleep with him after all," Lily said.

"Most of the audience escaped out to the wine reception. The Golds disappeared. A few kids were hanging around Allen, and I went up to say hello. When I told him that you were here, he said, 'Have him give me a call, I'll show him parts of Rome Lily doesn't know exist.'"

"I know more sewers than Allen Stone does," she said. "But I don't go to them."

"One of the new Fellows came up. Even though I've been introduced to him three or four times, I can never remember his name, but I think he's an English Professor somewhere in the Midwest. A friend of yours. He said he had to talk to you about an important matter. He was sort of guarded. Didn't want Allen to overhear him."

"You have to remember his name," Lily said. "People like Allen Stone forget names, but you don't. What does he look like?"

Dennis looked upward. "He's about our age—mine and Peter's, Lily, not yours. Five-ten. Gray hair. Thin. Thick glasses that make his eyes look enormous. Big forehead. Always seems to be backing away when he's talking to you."

Peter and PTR:
Two Deleted Prefaces and an Introduction

"I know that man," said Lily. "But I can't remember his name."

"That's the one." Dennis frowned, trying to pin down an impression. "When he found out you were in Rome, I could swear that he looked almost…disappointed, as if your being in Rome took some of the luster off his being here."

It should instantly have told me that this was Putney Tyson Ridge, of all my friends and acquaintances the only one so competitive as to be capable of such a feeling. Two factors kept me from making the connection: we see our oldest friends as composite images formed over time, and Dennis's shy, grey-haired scholar had little in common with my picture of the man; the second, less charitable reason was simply that he had never struck me as being good enough at what he did to get a Fellowship to Rome.

By the time we got back to our hotel, I had forgotten all about the mysterious Professor.

The next morning, our tour of Caravaggios having ended not far from the Aventine and their apartment, Lily suggested that we coax Dennis into joining us for lunch in the old Jewish Quarter. "He'll be all stuffy and important about his work if I call him, but if we turn up he'll drop it like a hot coal," she said, which was exactly what happened. The four of us squeezed into Lily's tiny car, Dennis beside Susan in the back seat and I next to Lily. Muttering and squinting, she managed traffic like a cabdriver, griping about other people's ineptitude as she popped the Fiat into a lower gear and whirled into an alley about an inch wider than the car.

"I nearly forgot again," Dennis said. "Remember the man we were talking about last night? This morning, he came up to me in the Academy library, wanting to know if I'd spoken to Peter. I didn't want to admit I couldn't remember his name, so I said, yes, but I hadn't been able to give you his phone numbers. He wrote them on a card so you could call him at his office from the restaurant or get him at his apartment tonight. Maybe you should call him from the restaurant. He wants to talk to you as soon as possible." Dennis fumbled to get the card out his pocket, no easy trick in the Fiat's back seat. "I hate to admit this, but I forgot his name again the minute he went back to his table. Ah, there."

Dennis's hand appeared beside my face with a white business card pinned between its middle two fingers.

"So what's this old friend's name?" Susan asked.

Looking at the card, I didn't know whether to groan or to laugh. "You're not going to believe this, but it's Put Ridge."

"Put Ridge?" Lily said. "That isn't a name, it's a location on a golf course."

"He's that new Fellow," Dennis said. "What's his whole name again?"

"Putney Tyson Ridge," I said.

"Putney Tyson Ridge is in *Rome?*" Susan said. "He's a Fellow at the *American Academy?* We don't have to see him, do we?"

"I certainly don't want to see *Put Ridge*," Lily said. "But you have to tell me what's so awful about him."

"He writes terrible things about Peter," Susan said. "That's all I'm going to say. He's Peter's friend, not mine."

Lily gave me a look of delighted mock-amazement. "He writes terrible things about you? Poison-pen letters?"

"Disguised as articles and reviews," I said. "I've known the guy since we were two years old."

For a moment I saw a succession of Put Ridges: the four-year-old in a natty white T-shirt, his hair cropped to a dark

Peter and PTR:
Two Deleted Prefaces and an Introduction

stubble, earnestly informing me that my clamp-on roller skates were back numbers and dangerous besides; that flat-topped eighth-grader in an oversized gym uniform pointing out the superiority of his basketball shoes to mine; the high school sophomore in a blue button-down shirt, chinos and new, massively rectangular eyeglasses who said, "I'm sorry, but you can't make an intelligent comment about Oscar Peterson until you've heard the Stratford concert;" later on, he read my first published short story and announced it his duty as my oldest friend to inform me that I needed to reduce, to condense, above all, to acknowledge my limitations and *simplify*.

"You still see this fellow?" Dennis asked.

"This fellow is inescapable," Susan said. "When we went to London five years ago, he was staying in the same hotel. The year after that, we walk into a restaurant in Honfleur, and Putney's already standing up and inviting us to his table. We go to Paris and meet him in the Luxembourg Gardens. He goes to all these conferences on Popular Culture! I don't know why I should be surprised he's here. How dumb can you get? Of course he's here. We are, aren't we?"

"I'll call him from the restaurant and get it over with," I said.

AT SIX that evening, Putney Ridge opened a white door on the third floor of the American Academy, checked to see if I was alone and beckoned me into his office. After I obeyed, he leaned out, looked both ways and only then eased the door shut. We shook hands, as we always did—he'd been shaking my hand since we were freshmen in high school. "I didn't know you were acquainted with the Montresors," he said. "How did you happen to meet them?"

Looking at Put, I could see the man Dennis had described: a thin, prematurely aged man with a bulging forehead and a recessed manner who resembled some delicate undersea creature fluttering toward the safety of a submerged rock. I told him that we had met the Montresors long ago when our children had been in the same elementary school.

"Dennis is a fine scholar, but his methodology is out of date. I hope he understood Allen Stone's talk last night. It was like fresh air in a stuffy room. I have to open Dennis up a bit..." He frowned, considering in what manner he might succeed in elevating Dennis to his own level of contemporaneity.

"It's a problem," I said.

"If I could do it at Popham, I can do it here. Then there's Lily, after all. She knows which way the wind is blowing."

"Does she ever," I said.

"Is that a happy marriage? From what I can detect..." He saw that he was going too far. "But you didn't come here to gossip about the Montresors." He gestured toward a wooden armchair in front of his desk.

The office looked as though he had moved in only a few days before. Copies of magazines for teenage girls formed neat piles on the floor, and two stacks of comic books stood like pillars at the end of the desk. The long bookshelves covering the far wall were nearly empty. An enormous window to my left offered a wide view of the rooftops and domes of the city below. Putney sat behind his desk and smiled. I knew that he had never bothered to take in his view. If anyone had mentioned it to him, he had replied that he had better things to do than stare out of windows.

Peter and PTR:
Two Deleted Prefaces and an Introduction

"Have you ever been approached by some young person who wanted you to evaluate a manuscript?"

"About twice a month," I said. "I turn them down."

He brought his eyes up to mine. "I may not have your sense of entitlement. As an educator, I have a responsibility to the young."

"And one young person recently gave you a manuscript," I said, wondering why on earth he or she had chosen Putney Tyson Ridge.

As it turned out, the manuscript had come indirectly to Putney. One night at a restaurant bar, an Academy Fellow named Simon Jackson had found himself in conversation with an American in his mid-thirties. This was the man who shall be called Ned Dunstan throughout these pages. He was not in Rome on business, but neither was he a conventional tourist. Dunstan had visited the Pantheon, the Forum, and a good number of churches, but he had done these things only because he was in Rome: he had not come to Rome to do them. He was making a temporary stop in the course of a longer, less definite journey which had already taken him to Amsterdam, Paris, Nice, Florence and no doubt other places, too.

Dunstan had placed himself at the far end of the bar, where he could keep an eye on the front door. He asked if anyone at the American Academy might be connected to publishers; he was carrying with him the manuscript of a book on which he had been working during his travels, and he wanted to leave it with some trustworthy person who might see to its publication. Was this a novel? No, Dunstan said, it was a memoir. Writing it had been a sort of exorcism, and now he wanted it out of his hands.

The following morning, Jackson brought Dunstan to the office of a classicist whose wife had written a dozen popular thrillers, but a staff member told him that the couple had been called back to the United States. Then the door across the corridor opened, and out came Putney Tyson Ridge.

"As soon as I heard the story, I invited them in," Ridge said. "I got rid of Jackson as soon as I could. He sat right where you are now—Dunstan. Don't ask me why, but I wasn't going to let him walk out until he had given me his manuscript. I have contacts in publishing. I know the editors of half a dozen journals of Popular Culture. I've been in touch with editors at University presses."

All of whom had excruciatingly deliberated over his collection of articles, sometimes prolonging the agony for years, before rejecting it.

"And I know how to get in touch with a number of writers, you among them, who could assure that we get the kind of publication this material deserves. A University press would be too specialized...the people at Popham are going to be royally peeved when they learn I let this get away from them." The thought of one-upping his own college's press evoked gleeful chuckles.

"What was this character like?"

"Calm on the surface and jumpy underneath. He kept turning to look at the door, as if he were thinking about bolting."

"Or being followed," I said.

"That, too," said Ridge. "Of course, I asked him about himself. Not very forthcoming, our Mr. Dunstan. Everything important was in his manuscript, he said. He had written most of it in the States and then finished it over here. He wanted to leave it in safe hands and travel lighter."

Peter and PTR:
Two Deleted Prefaces and an Introduction

"He gave it to you, you read it, and you liked it," I said. "Now you want me to help you get it published."

"Properly," he said. "I have a dual responsibility—to Dunstan and my own standards."

"Old Put," I said. "You're under quite a strain."

A ripple of feeling distended his bulbous forehead and shrank his mouth into a slit. "It's extraordinary. As a story, mind you. As a story, it's extraordinary."

"It's fiction? I thought..."

"A memoir," Put said. His face returned to its normal dimensions as he set me straight. "Anybody can invent outlandish things, but outlandish things actually happened to Dunstan! The story must be handled with tremendous care."

"Alien abductions?" I asked. "Satanic cults? I know—angels."

He was shaking his head, enjoying my ignorance. "More personal. But extraordinary anyhow."

"Do you believe him?"

"If you ask me, yes, everything he describes is absolutely real. To him."

"In other words," I said, "he's out of his mind."

"Not at all. He isn't safe. If I understand his story, he'll never be safe again."

Putney smiled at me, knowing that I was about to take the hook.

"The memoir explains why he'll never feel safe?"

He nodded, still smiling.

"I'll take a look at it," I said.

"If I entrust you with it, you'll have to do more than that."

I asked him to explain, and his smile vanished into a mesh of furrows. He was really torn. Now, I am surprised he didn't ask me to stand outside so that he could make a last appeal to Tim Underhill. Putney leaned forward and looked down. He tapped his foot. Then he leaned back and looked straight at me with his pale, oddly magnified blue eyes. Having reached the end of the diving board, he had decided to leap into empty space.

"I want Ned Dunstan's manuscript published in a form as close to the original as you can manage. It needs work, I know, but I *don't* want you to turn it into a novel. Is that clear? The one change you'll have to make is to take out the material from another point of view—he used two different voices, and it doesn't work. Once you read it, you'll know right away what you have to do to make it publishable. Give it to your editor and instruct him to talk to me."

"Her," I said. "She's a female-type person."

He waved my correction aside. "As Dunstan's agent, I am to be consulted at every step. Upon acceptance, I will supply a preface describing the manuscript, my encounter with its author, my dealings with you, and so on. For services rendered, I want an honorarium of five thousand dollars plus the fifteen per cent agent's commission. I'll set up an escrow account for Dunstan, and when he gets back in touch, I'll let him know exactly what is going on. The financial side of this business has to be absolutely above board."

"You want to handle the negotiations?"

"You'll get fair compensation. Surely, we both understand that money is not the primary concern."

I laughed at his gall. He was getting fifteen per cent plus five thousand dollars, and I would be paid a "fair compensation" already discounted by the agreement that money was not the point. "Let me make it easy for you," I said. "If I think the book is worth the effort, I'll help you for nothing."

Peter and PTR:
Two Deleted Prefaces and an Introduction

He stared at me, weighing the advantages of my offer against his doubts. "That's very generous." A number of parallel creases divided his forehead. "Your offer is accepted." He stood up and extended his hand over the desk. When I took it, I felt a brief electrical shock like the jab of a pin.

Putney fixed me with his stonewashed-denim eyes and rummaged in his pocket for the key-ring, isolated the smallest of its keys, unlocked the bottom drawer and, pausing for another significance-laden glance, extracted the caramel-colored satchel and thrust it toward me. "Fix what has to be fixed, but don't mess with it."

IN SPITE of my old friend's claims to the contrary, I trust the reader to understand that I did follow Putney's instructions. My work on the manuscript consisted of cosmetic surgery: here the removal of an unsightly bump, there the smoothing of a clumsy seam. I let the two voices stand as written. This is Ned Dunstan's book, as the story is his story, despite my friend's protests. Dunstan himself will not, cannot, offer further explanation. Twice a year, Putney dispatches to a post office box in Geneva checks which return counter-signed by a shadowy functionary granted power of attorney. Someone draws on this money, but I wonder if he is Ned Dunstan; I wonder, too, if the real Ned Dunstan was the young man who gave this story to Putney Tyson Ridge, and if the being who continues to move haunted and in flight through the world is someone else, something else, altogether.

Peter Straub

Preface

BEFORE TURNING with a weary heart to the devices of a professional fiction-maker to whom I am long bound by friendship's complex ties, I wish to give an account of the manner in which the record of "Ned Dunstan's" life passed into my hands.

During my Fellowship at the American Academy in Rome, an unknown young man began to attract the attentions of its resident artists and scholars by staging "accidental" or "random" meetings in the course of which he turned the conversation to myself and my work. After several weeks, my colleagues began to suspect that I was being, as the sinister neologism has it, "stalked." When the celebrated painter Allen Stone, a close friend, suggested this possibility to me, I replied that he was a candidate far more likely than I, since stalkers chose famous persons as their targets! Allen's observation that I was unaware of my own fame was seconded by new friends Dennis and Lily Montresor, who offered me the sanctuary of their Aventine apartment. Although appreciative of the gesture, I declined. The "stalker" did not frighten me: the doe-like shyness of his approach aroused quite another response.

Even before I had the privilege of his acquaintance, I had sensed that Ned Dunstan was to be of great spiritual significance in my life. Irrational as it may seem, this feeling struck me with the force of certainty. No such precognition—I may say, a characteristically "Dunstan" precognition—is explicable in rational terms, but, as his aunt, "Joy Crothers," would have it, *c'est la vie*.

Altogether, I spent no more than an hour with Ned Dunstan. Perhaps it was even less, something like fifty

Peter and PTR:
Two Deleted Prefaces and an Introduction

minutes. But every moment of that brief time inscribed itself indelibly upon my memory. Dunstan was easily the most handsome man I had ever seen in my life. His handsomeness was of the order that suggests nobility, courage, deep reservoirs of feeling—a dark handsomeness, thoughtful, sensuous, refined. Dunstan's was an entirely male beauty, comprised of a large, well-cut mouth, a straight, chiseled nose, black eyes of a dazzling clearness and strong, high cheekbones. He wore a soft leather jacket the color of Callard & Bowser toffee, and he carried a satchel or hold-all of the same leather. He resembled a king in exile. *He* did not care about the way he looked; he was anything but vain, he had a great deal else on his mind. From childhood on he had heard people exclaim over his good looks, but that had meant nothing to him.

In one way or another, everyone in Ned Dunstan's story is affected by his beauty. Certain essential turns of the story scarcely make sense unless his appearance is kept in mind. I expected that the writer to whom finally I turned for professional assistance would find a way to highlight this essential point, but my old friend chose not to do so. (We shall, trust me, return to the subject of my old friend's shortcomings.)

As soon as I understood what Ned Dunstan wished of me, I assured him that I did indeed know several people capable of giving his memoir a final polish and placing it with a reputable publishing house. For a time he ceased to glance at the door, his hands unclenched and his left knee stopped jittering. At these signs of relaxation, I enquired as to the substance of his memoir.

Dunstan dropped his head. I feared that I had pressed too hard. When he looked at me again, it was with a comprehensive indecision. I braced myself. Instead of fleeing, he asked who would read his book. "I'd rather not say at the moment," I told him, "but I can assure you that any of the reputable writers I have in mind would give it the same care I would myself."

He nodded slowly, considering, and then did something completely unexpected. He smiled. It was, I believe, the saddest smile I have ever seen on any human face. With that, he began to tell me his story. Not the whole story, but the heart of the story, the discoveries which had become the center of his life. He spoke with the simple gravity of the truth. At certain points, moisture filled his eyes. Never did he glance at me with the anxious reflex of the performer. As is true of anyone with long experience of students, I have been lied to by virtuosos, and Ned Dunstan was not lying.

I recall the awkward position of his wrist (Dunstan was a southpaw) as he set down the post office boxes and other mail drops to which I should write, the combination of eagerness and fatality in his surrender of the satchel, even the flicker of his eyelashes at the moment it left his hands. I can see his backward glance as he departed; I can summon up the compacted scent of apples, summer rainfall and woodsmoke left momentarily behind.

As soon as he left the building, I went downstairs and copied the manuscript.

My next task was to locate Timothy Underhill, the writer most suitable for presenting this story to the world at large. I knew that he used the same agent as Peter Straub, and within twenty-four hours had obtained the telephone and fax numbers of Mr. Underhill's summer residence in Denmark, as well as his e-mail address. The following weeks were a compound of excitement and frustration. Mr. Underhill, "Tim," as I came to know him, quickly succumbed to the spell of the saga.

Peter and PTR:
Two Deleted Prefaces and an Introduction

Not only entranced by the story, he was fascinated by Ned Dunstan. Twice he called me after penning his day's quota of pages to say, "Tim here. Tell me more about Dunstan." (The friendship which developed between us has been one of the great satisfactions of my life.) It was clear to both of us that no one could have been more suited to the job at hand than he.

Yet Underhill had sequestered himself in Denmark to meet the deadline for a new novel. I betray no confidences when I say that he would have preferred working on the memoir to his novel, so passionate was his interest. He told me that if he thought he could go without sleep for six months he would do both projects or perish in the attempt. I assured him of my willingness to wait until his obligations had been met. Considerate to the last, Tim would not hear of imposing an eighteen-month delay upon Dunstan. At this point, after a month of discussion, we realized that the best person, in fact the ideal person for the job would not be able to take it on. For a time we considered which other writers might have been capable of the task.

I wasted another month despairingly making lists of writers without attempting to get in touch with any of those who came to mind. None would do: I despaired.

IT WAS at this fragile point that my old friend Peter arrived in Rome, somehow heard enough to sniff an opportunity and thrust himself into the affair. Eager to press his claim, he insisted on seeing me. That evening, I surrendered Ned Dunstan's memoir. I needed a writer; here was my old friend, who promised to do no more than a mild rewrite; I succumbed to his entreaties. What was the result? Peter took two years to reconstruct the memoir, in the process fulfilling my deepest fears by turning it into another of his "novels." For reasons known only to himself, Straub further complicated matters by introducing a second narrative voice, an affectation nowhere to be found in the original manuscript.

It is therefore with considerable regret that I introduce the following tale. However, I am pleased to conclude these remarks with the observation that Ned Dunstan can in no way be injured by my friend's extravagance. Wherever that endearing, entirely remarkable man may be, he has achieved a level of security he once would have thought unattainable. I wish him well and hope that this particular betrayal causes him less pain than those even an over-zealous author cannot entirely obscure.

I append to the above this blunt admonition to the general reader. The suggestion offered within Mr. Straub's final sentence so surpasses irresponsibility as to be obscene.

Putney Tyson Ridge, Ph.D.
Department of Popular Culture
Popham College, Popham, Ohio

An Abandoned Fragment Starting With "It was an amazing thing..."

by Ray Bradbury

Publisher's Note: This fragment discovered by biographer Donn Albright in Ray Bradbury's archive was originally written in the late 1940s. George Clayton Johnson has said that Bradbury wrote the last three pages of his classic story "All of Us Are Dying" for him and this fragment reinforces that fact.

→ IT WAS AN amazing thing. He turned the corner wearing a black suit, his hair was blonde, his flesh sallow, his face round. There was a sound of running behind him. He himself was running. As soon as he rounded the corner he stopped. He had exactly twenty seconds. He performed the miracle. He touched one button in his suit, a dial, and the suit changed color from black to brown to light tan. He touched another at the base of his neck, and the fine wires of his hair turned from blonde to blue-black. This done, and 12 seconds left to him, he swept his hands over his face which was round but now, the plastic wax in the cheeks moulded to his sculptoring hands, drew itself out thin. Looking down at himself as if in a mirror, he drew a breath, and walked quietly around the corner, almost colliding with the Civil Police.

"Did you see a man in a dark suit!" they cried.

He pointed around the corner, nodding.

Then they were gone, yelling, rushing.

He walked to a cafe, sat down, and ordered a drink.

"The Hunt"

by Kelley Armstrong

Publisher's Note: This story is set in the fictional world of the Cainsville series.

→ WILLIAM ENVIED HUNTERS whose wives allowed them to decorate the family home with their trophies. He sometimes even envied hunters who didn't have wives to complain, like Teddy, who'd just sent him a photograph of his latest trophy, hanging in his living room.

"Did you get the pictures?" Teddy asked when William called.

"They're right here on my screen."

"Nice, huh?"

"Not bad. A little sloppy with the cutting."

Teddy only laughed. "Yes, I'm not at your level yet. But I'm working on it. So, have you given any more thought to that hunting trip?"

"Some."

"I've done my research. It's kosher. Zero risk. Zero responsibility. We pay our money, show up and hunt. A real English hunt. Horses, hounds, the whole works. Like nothing we've ever done before."

That was the kicker, the reason William was even considering it. Novelty. There'd been a time when he'd counted the days between his hunting trips. Not anymore. He was bored.

"Okay," he said.

Teddy paused so long William prodded, "You there?"

"Sure, I just…You said okay?"

"Yeah. Go ahead. Set it up."

Teddy babbled away after that, making plans. William half listened as he admired Teddy's trophy—a necklace hanging from a picture frame—before flipping back to the ones he liked best, those of the woman herself, lying dead on her apartment floor.

↻→

WILLIAM STOOD in the middle of the forest clearing and stamped his feet.

"Little chilly, huh?" Teddy said, blowing into his hands.

William shrugged.

Teddy glanced over. "You aren't worried, are you? It's risk-free, like I said. We're just along for the ride."

That wasn't the problem. The forest…it just wasn't what he'd expected.

When Teddy first suggested this excursion, William's pulse had quickened. Like most of his kind, he was an urban hunter. Born and raised in the city. Stalked his prey through back alleys. Took them down in abandoned buildings. There

The Hunt

was, however, an allure to the forest. The domain of hunters like Dayton Rogers and Ivan Milat and the Larsens. Raw and feral, primitive and wild.

Except…this was a little more wild than William liked. Around them, gnarled trees shot up and slammed together overhead, blocking the moon and stars. The wind didn't bluster and blow like city wind. Here it whispered and moaned and shrieked. And it smelled like death. Not good death—bright coppery blood and fear. This was dank, dark death. Rot and decay.

He glanced at Teddy. "Are you sure—?"

The bay of a hound cut him off. Hooves pounded along the hard path.

THE HOUNDS appeared first. Six beagles, noses to the ground, long ears dragging. Four horses followed. Ordinary looking horses with ordinary looking riders—guys between thirty and fifty, wearing hunting jackets and jeans and boots.

Just regular guys. Except they weren't regular at all. William could tell by the way their eyes took in everything and gave away nothing. Hunters, like them.

"Sorry we're late," said the bearded man in front. "Had some trouble with the fox."

A fifth horse stepped into the clearing. The rider led a sixth. A bound woman lay draped over the saddle. When he yanked the rope, she tumbled to the ground. A leather mask obscured her face, but William could see her eyes, rolling in terror.

"Looks good," Teddy said. "Young. Strong. Healthy. Scared."

The men chuckled, and the leader motioned for William to mount.

"Where's mine?" Teddy asked.

"Coming."

WILLIAM SWUNG onto his horse, remembering how from summers at his grandmother's farm. As his boots found the stirrups, he caught a flicker, like fire, to the left, and he looked over, startled, but it was only a lantern held by a rider.

"Release the fox," the leader said.

The man holding her rope yanked again and, with a snap, her bound hands and feet came free. She pushed to all fours and started to run, still hunched over, so blinded by the mask that she headed for Teddy, who laughed and backed up.

As she ran, her skin seemed to blacken, as if swallowed by the shadows. William gave his head a shake and blinked. When he opened his eyes, the girl was gone. In her place was a massive black dog, running straight for Teddy.

As the beast sprang, Teddy wheeled and ran. The hounds ran too—not beagles now, but huge black dogs with blazing red eyes, tearing after Teddy so fast their paws never seemed to touch the ground.

The leader shouted, "Ride!" and William turned to see five figures in black cloaks, hoods pulled up. Beneath them, their steeds had become great ebony horses with manes and hooves of flame.

The Wild Hunt.

William heard his grandmother's voice from all those years ago, when she'd seen what he'd done to the barn cats.

The Hunt

"The riders will come for you, boy. Mark my words. The Wild Hunt will come."

William's horse plunged after its brethren. He tried to stop it. Tried to scramble off. But he was trapped, watching his friend run headlong through the forest as the hounds pursued, the riders pursued, he pursued.

As they rode, more hunters joined, coming from all sides, silent wraiths atop fiery steeds. Ahead the hounds bellowed and roared, jaws snapping so loud William could hear them.

Teddy ran, but he did not run far. The beasts took him down. William tried to look away, but he couldn't move his head, couldn't shut his eyes. He was forced to watch as the hounds tore his friend to pieces.

When he couldn't turn his horse around, he tried to dismount, but the stirrups snapped like traps, iron teeth chomping into his feet. As he screamed, the reins leaped up, like snakes, wrapping around his hands, tightening until the leather was embedded in his flesh.

The leader's empty cowl turned toward him. "Ride!"

As the group shot forward, William's steed joined them, with a blaze of fire that seared him to the bone and bound him to his mount, and he understood what his grandmother meant. The riders had come for him and now he would hunt forever.

Winter Takes All

by Michael Koryta

THERE ARE GIFTS and there are curses and the perception is that these things are held far from each other, polar opposites, balancing forces.

The year the gift came to Arlen Wagner, the year the curse came, the year good and evil merged and blurred and the world tilted away from his understanding in such a fashion that it would never regain balance again, is remembered in those mountains as the year of the fever and the war. At least, that is, by those who remember it at all. Few do. It's folklore now, an old tale of the old towns, and anyone who connects the name Wagner to the year of the fever remembers Isaac Wagner, not Arlen. Isaac is the father, the lunatic. Arlen is the boy, the son, the one who did right.

Perception, you see. Perception.

The fever came through that summer, the summer the bloodshed in Europe increased and the calls for American aid rose with the toll. Boys from the mining towns left for war, and such thoughts were supposed to occupy the townspeople, but then the illness came, and the sorrows of a world across an ocean seemed ever more distant. Isaac Wagner, the town undertaker, the coffin-maker, was a busy man. In July, 19 died. In the first week of August alone, 22 more joined them. In the second week of August, only five passed, the worst of the fever burning itself out, but among those final victims was Isaac's own wife. It was this, the locals said, that broke the man.

His son, Arlen, believed them.

Summer faded alongside the sickness and the autumn leaves fell and then the year edged toward winter, Christmas carols sung again in the town but with a solemnity this season, the plague of the summer far from forgotten.

It would be a hard winter, the townspeople said, but it could not be as hard as the summer. Summer had taken so many.

For Arlen Wagner, summer had taken one slice of his youth. Winter would take all that remained.

The first signs of concern had come in those blistering weeks when the gravediggers were busy and Arlen's mother took ill and died swiftly. Isaac was spending more time in his shop, particularly at night, when visitors were unlikely. The shop was located beneath the room where Arlen slept, and the sounds drifted up, barely muffled by the thin layer of wood that separated them. He'd long known the sounds of the tools on the wood—his father's paying job, other than a bit of small-time farming, was as a furniture maker—and sometimes Arlen could also hear Isaac humming to himself or occasionally speaking bits of German, his mother tongue. The conversations, however, were a new twist.

They began not long after Arlen's mother died, and they occurred only when Isaac was outfitting a casket. On those long and lovely weeks when no one passed in the town and some level of peace was restored, his father's workshop was silent. Then death would strike, the townspeople would call upon Isaac Wagner, and he would sequester himself and begin to work—and speak.

Arlen told himself that it was a grieving process, his father struggling with the loss and attempting to find a way to cope just as Arlen was himself.

He ignored the conversations.

For as long as he could.

Those floors, though, were so thin. His father's voice, so deep, so strong. The words carried, and Arlen could not help but hear. It was not many weeks before he began to pay attention, and the phrase he heard uttered again and again raised a prickle across his spine.

Tell me, Isaac Wagner would say. *Tell me.*

The more Arlen listened, the more evident it became that his father was trying to speak to the dead. Not only that—he believed he was. The words that left his mouth were parts of an exchange.

There had been several of the conversations before Arlen chanced a trip down to the shop to see for himself. What awaited him was chilling: Isaac spoke with his hands on the corpses. Stood above them and placed his palms flat on their chests or on either side of their heads. When he'd talked himself out, he removed his hands and returned to work and fell silent. Always he was silent unless he had his hands pressed against their dead flesh.

He was a different man outside of the shop, as well—both with Arlen and the townspeople. Moody and unpredictable, given to perplexing statements and a constant tendency to dismiss the worries of the living.

It was a few months before Arlen could admit that his father was losing his mind.

Rumors began to swirl through the town after a teary-eyed man came to the shop with a child's toy in his hand, prepared to ask that it be buried with his daughter, and found Isaac in his now-customary pose, standing above the body with his hands on the dead girl's head like a preacher offering a blessing. The sight rankled the grieving father, and while no more than a heated exchange of words took place, with Isaac taking no steps to pacify the man, simply saying that he'd talk aloud in his shop if he were so inclined, to whomever he liked, it added coal to the fires of suspicion already smoldering throughout the town.

What did you do with a father who was insane? The question haunted Arlen through his days and kept him awake through his nights. It was just the two of them now; there was no other family in the town. Isaac had led the way to this place, and Arlen's mother had been unable to conceive after giving birth to her first and only child. No confidant existed. He listened to his father speak to the dead and thought of what might happen if he sought help, if he told anyone in town the truth, and he decided that it would be better to keep silent. There was no harm being done. It was strange, certainly, unsettling and troubling, but it wasn't harmful. He promised himself that if it ever became so, something would have to be done.

It was a day on the fringe of Christmas when Joy Main died. Three nights of frost had been followed by a final gasp of warmth that faded behind a cold wind and no one in the town had passed in three weeks. Isaac was making furniture instead of coffins, and Arlen had been allowed to slip into something close to a peaceful state. At night his sleep was uninterrupted by voices from below, and the dark rings around his father's

Winter Takes All

eyes had lessened, his strange remarks becoming fewer. Then they brought Joy Main's body to the shop.

The Mains were the power family in town. Edwin's father had been a surveyor—and a damn shrewd man. He asked for, and received, acreage instead of wages, and he had a fine eye for land, acquiring large parcels along the river and through the gorges that bordered it. It was coal and timber country, beautiful land that was soon to become rich land, and by the time Edwin was grown the mining boom was underway and the property he inherited made him a wealthy man. He stayed in Fayette County and filled his father's void. He was large and pompous and charming when he had cause to be. At other times he was harsh and cruel, but the townspeople seemed to believe you could expect that from your leaders.

Joy Hargrove was the most beautiful girl in the county, bright and clever, a gifted piano player and blessed with a haunting, gorgeous voice that turned heads at Sunday services. The marriage was of the arranged sort—Joy's father was vying for purchase of a promising mine. The courtship was strongly encouraged despite the fact that Edwin was past forty and their daughter just seventeen, and it was only a matter of weeks before Joy Hargrove became Joy Main.

They were married for seven years before her death, and during that time she bore three children and grew increasingly quiet, seeming content to offer formalities and then retreat within herself. She was well known in Fayette County but yet not really known at all.

On that December evening when they brought her to the Wagner house just as the burst of warmth from earlier in the day was disappearing with darkness, Joy Main was a week past her twenty-fifth birthday and dead of a fractured skull.

Edwin came with her, tears in his eyes and the sheriff at his side. He explained that Joy had come out to the stable to see him and a horse had bucked and thrown a sudden high kick, a rear hoof catching his bride square in the head.

He'd shot the horse, Edwin explained in a choked voice, and then sent for the sheriff. Maybe it wasn't the right thing to do, shooting that horse, but he couldn't help it. There needed to be blood for blood.

Arlen had heard it all from inside the house, the men standing on the porch with the body at their feet, wrapped in blankets. When Edwin told the story, Isaac Wagner said, "You had the mind to shoot the horse while your wife lay dying?"

The sheriff stepped in then, told Isaac that Edwin was a grieving man, damn it, and there'd be no such questions, who cared a whit about the horse at a time such as this? Isaac had said nothing else but Edwin Main watched him with dark eyes and Arlen, standing at the window, felt the coldness pass through the glass just like the wind that had returned out of the northern hills.

Isaac gathered the body in his arms and prepared to carry Joy Main back to his shop. Edwin spoke up again and told him to make it the finest coffin he'd ever constructed; anything less would be a sin, and how much the box might cost mattered not, he'd pay any price.

Isaac told him that every coffin he made was a fine one.

It wasn't long after they'd left that Arlen heard the dreaded phrase from his father's shop: *Tell me.*

This time he crept to the door. Usually he tried to clear himself away from the sound, but there'd been such tension in the air tonight, with his father asking that question about the horse and Edwin Main staring him down.

Winter Takes All

Not her, Arlen thought, *of all the ones in town for you to speak with, not his wife. We'll be run out of this place if anyone knows, chased into the darkness and the snow.*

The talking persisted, though, and it horrified. Isaac Wagner was pretending to hear an explanation of murder.

"He laid hands on the servant? That girl's no more than fifteen, is she? He intended to violate her? Did she see what happened after? What did he strike you with? Had he beaten you before? Did the children see? Did anyone see?"

Arlen stood at the door and heard it all and felt a trembling deep in his chest that intensified when Isaac said, *"I'll see that it's dealt with. I'll see that he has a reckoning. I promise you that; I swear it to you."*

Arlen opened the door and went into the room then and shouted at him to stop and what he saw was more terrible than he'd imagined. Isaac had lifted the dead woman and placed her hands on his own shoulders so that he could easily look at her face. There was still blood in her hair and her eyelids sagged halfway down but the hint of blue irises remained and seemed to stare over Isaac's shoulder and into Arlen's own eyes.

"She's telling me what happened," Isaac said. "Don't be afraid, son. She's telling me the truth."

"She's not," Arlen screamed, "she can't speak, can't tell you a thing, she's dead! She's gone!"

"No," Isaac said, "the body is gone. She is not."

Arlen stood in the door and shook his head, tears brimming in his eyes. Isaac lowered the body slowly and very gently, then turned to face his son.

"I have to touch them to hear," he said. "There are those who don't, those who can conjure without needing a touch, but I'm not one of them. Maybe in time. It took me many a year to reach them at all. I suspect you'll find better luck. What's in me is in you, Arlen, but stronger. It's stronger and I'm certain of that."

"Stop," Arlen said. "Stop, stop, stop."

"You don't believe," Isaac said. "Those who don't believe can't hear."

Arlen told him he was mad. Told him that they had to find an escape from this before it claimed them both, that they would leave town that winter and find a new place, a happier place, one where the memories would not cut at Isaac's brain in such a way that these mad thoughts came to exist.

Isaac listened patiently, and shook his head.

"My burden is here, son. We all need to understand our tasks. There's a war on, we've spoken of it often, the burdens those men in the field bear for the rest of us. Well, I've a burden to bear for those here. The dead will speak and I will hear them and when they ask something of me, I will provide what I can. I'm prepared to do it. And you will need to be as well. You've got a touch of the gift yourself. I'm sure of it. I see it in you."

"No more," Arlen said, backing away through the door. "Don't say any more."

"Look past your fear," Isaac said. "It's about doing what's right. This woman was murdered, beaten with an ax handle and killed, Arlen! That demands justice. I'll see that it's delivered. I've promised her that. And if there's anything I hold sacred it's a promise to the dead."

Arlen turned and ran.

He spent close to two hours in the wooded hills, stumbling through the underbrush with hot tears in his eyes and terror in his heart. He wondered if his father was still down

Winter Takes All

there with Joy Main or if he'd gone off in search of the promised reckoning. The longer Arlen walked, the more certain he became that he could not allow such a thing to take place.

You've got a touch of the gift yourself, boy. I'm sure of it. I've seen it in you.

It was that statement more than any of the others that drove him out of the woods and back into town, where candles glittered and Christmas wreaths hung from the doors. His father was insane—the dead could not speak to the living; they were gone and nothing lingered in their stead—but Arlen was not insane. He was *not* and he wouldn't ever be.

Let Isaac Wagner bear his own shame, then, and not put the stain on his son as well. If Isaac would show the world that he was mad, his son would show himself to be of the soundest mind, no matter the price. Your actions in the face of conflict defined you, and the time for such action had come.

The sheriff was home, and he stared with astonished eyes while Arlen told his tale. When it was through he gathered himself and thanked Arlen for coming down and told him to go on home and wait.

"I'll come for him shortly," he said. "And you did the right thing, son. Know that. You did the right thing."

Arlen went home. He waited. Isaac was back in his shop, silent. Arlen did not enter, and his father did not exit, and the minutes passed with slow, scalding agony.

Thirty minutes had gone by before the sheriff came, and then he wasn't alone. Edwin Main was with him, wearing a long duster to fight the chill night wind. When Arlen saw them approaching he felt sick. Why had the sheriff told him anything? This was a matter for the law, not for the grieving man.

They came through the door without knocking and saw Arlen standing there and asked where his father was. He pointed an unsteady hand at the closed door of the shop.

They went in for him. Arlen stayed outside, hearing the exchange, Edwin Main shouting and swearing and Isaac speaking in deep, measured tones. When they emerged again, Isaac was handcuffed.

Isaac looked over and locked eyes with Arlen and his face was so gentle, so kind.

He said, "You're going to need to believe. And something you need to know, son? Love lingers."

They shoved him out the front door then and off the porch and down into the dark dusty street. Arlen trailed behind. Edwin Main was still shouting and offering threats. They'd gone a few hundred feet before Isaac spoke to him.

"You killed her," he said, "and it will be proved in time. We'll talk to your house girl and to your children and they'll tell me what Joy already did."

Edwin Main went for him then and sheriff stepped between them. Edwin was a big man but Isaac was bigger, and he stood calm and looked at the screaming widower and didn't seem troubled by him.

"You struck her with the axe handle," he said. "She'd run out of the house to get away from you and you chased her into the yard and killed her there. Then you dragged her into the stable so there'd be blood in it, and you shot the horse because you believed it would add credence to your tale. That's what happened. That's the truth of it."

Edwin Main shook free of the sheriff's grasp. The sheriff stumbled and fell to his hands and knees in the road as Edwin reached under his duster and drew a pistol. Arlen cried out and ran for them, and Edwin Main cocked the pistol and pointed it at Isaac's head from no more than two feet away.

Isaac Wagner smiled. Edwin Main fired. Then Arlen was on his knees in the road and his father's blood ran into the dust and the wind blew down on them with the promise of coming snow and Arlen's heart ached from the weight of the curse his family had been given.

THEY MOURNED for Joy Main that week in the town, and for Edwin and his loss. They mourned for the Main family as a Christmas snow fell and a war surged across the Atlantic. Arlen Wagner wasn't there to see the mourning, but he was on his way to see the war.

He was gone by the second day after his father's death. He enlisted in a recruitment office far from his hometown, where his name would not be known. Lied about his age and joined the United States Marines Corps. The Marines needed good men, sound of mind and body, and Arlen Wagner was sound of mind and body. He would cross the ocean, and there he would fight evil.

It was June, a season apart from those terrible days, a season of new terrible days in a new land, when Arlen found himself in a place called the Belleau Wood, beside a river called the Marne, and his comrades fell around him as the machine guns thundered.

That was the bloodiest battle the Marines had ever encountered, a savage showdown requiring repeated assaults before the parcel of forest and boulders finally fell under American control, and the bodies were piled high by the end.

The sight of corpses was not the new experience for Arlen. No, in the moonlight over the Marne River on a June night in 1918, Arlen saw something far different from a corpse—he saw the dead among the living.

They'd made an assault on the Wood that day, marching through a waist-high wheat field directly into machine gun fire. For the rest of his life, the sight of tall, windswept wheat would put a shiver through Arlen. Most of the men in the first waves had been slaughtered outright, but Arlen and other survivors had been driven south, into the trees and a tangle of barbwire. The machine guns pounded on, relentless, and those who didn't fall beneath them grappled hand-to-hand with German soldiers who shouted oaths at them in a foreign tongue while bayonets clashed and knives plunged.

By evening the Marines had sustained the highest casualties in their history, but they also had a hold, however tenuous, in Belleau Wood. Arlen was on his belly beside a boulder as midnight came on, and with it a German counterattack. As the enemy approached he'd felt near certain that this skirmish would be his last; he couldn't continue to survive battles like these, not when so many had fallen all around him throughout the day. That rain of bullets couldn't keep missing him forever.

This was his belief, at least, until the Germans appeared as more than shadows, and what he saw then kept him from so much as lifting his rifle.

They were skeleton soldiers.

He could see skulls shining in the pale moonlight where faces belonged, hands of white bone clutching rifle stocks.

He was staring, entranced, when the American gunners opened up. Opened up, and mowed them down, sliced the vicious Hun bastards to pieces. All around him men lifted

Winter Takes All

their rifles and fired and Arlen just lay there without so much as a finger on the trigger, scarcely able to draw a breath.

A trick of the light, he told himself as dawn rose heavy with mist and the smell of cooling and drying blood, the moans of the wounded as steady now as the gunfire had been earlier. What he'd seen was the product of moonlight partnered with the trauma from a day of unspeakable bloodshed. Surely, that was enough to wreak havoc on his mind. On anyone's mind.

There were some memories in his head then, of course, some thoughts of his father, but he kept them at bay, convincing himself that this was nothing but the most horrifying of hallucinations.

The curse had tracked him here, but he would not crumble beneath it. He would *not*.

It was not yet dawn when the dead began to whisper. Softly. So softly. He was down in a trench and pressed against his leg was a good boy from Kentucky, a tall blond kid who had once had a high, chirping laugh that sounded like a strange bird and could lift a smile to even the most fatigued soldier. Now he had a gaping hole torn through his throat and jaw, and the last sounds he'd made bore no resemblance to the laugh and lifted no smiles. His had been an anguished passing.

Now, his body cooling against Arlen's leg, he began to whisper.

Arlen rolled away as if he'd leaned against glowing coals, then asked his fellow soldiers, his fellow *living* soldiers, what they heard.

Nothing, he was told. The enemy was out there, but they would wait until dawn to strike. For now, his comrades explained, the woods were silent, and the Americans were safe.

The dead disagreed. The dead warned of an approaching battalion, moving through the night woods like phantoms, unseen but soon to be deadly. And Arlen Wagner, his flesh cold as it had been on the winter night when he'd refused a curse, decided to accept a gift. He reached for a dead man's hand, the blood cool now but still damp, and squeezed it tight.

Tell me, he whispered. *Tell me.*

The Curious Odyssey of James Deacon (AKA James Dean)

by David Morrell

L ONGTIME FANS OF horror remember an inven-
tive small press back in the 1980s and early '90s:
Dark Harvest. Based in Illinois, created by Paul Mikol and
Mark Stadalsky, the company published contemporary clas-
sics, such as Dan Simmons's *Carrion Comfort*. It also created
a series, *Night Visions*, in which a trio of authors each contributed 30,000 words of short stories related to horror and dark
fantasy, with encouragement to be as creative as they wanted.

From 1984 to 1991, these are the authors who appeared,
three at a time, in *Night Visions* volumes: Steve Rasnic Tem,
Tanith Lee, Ramsey Campbell, Lisa Tuttle, Clive Barker,
Dean Koontz, Edward Bryant, Robert R. McCammon,

Stephen King, George R.R. Martin, F. Paul Wilson, Sheri S. Tepper, Ray Garton, Richard Laymon, Chet Williamson, Gary Brandner, John Farris, Stephen Gallagher, Joe R. Lansdale, Thomas Tessier, James Kisner, and Rick Hautala.

Wow. Believe me, Dark Harvest didn't pay much. What attracted these authors was the chance to write whatever they wanted and to be part of what felt like a common spirit. *Night Visions* provided an exciting showcase for new approaches in what turned out to be the tail end of a Golden Age of horror. (Years later, Subterranean Press resurrected the series.)

I feel honored to have been part of it, teamed with Joseph Payne Brennan and Karl Edward Wagner in the second volume, edited by the sorely missed Charles L. Grant. My segment of stories was unified by characters who defined themselves by their professions—a newspaper delivery boy, a football star, and a movie icon—with horrific results.

The third character is the one who's relevant here. I'm obsessed by James Dean. He was only in his early twenties when he rose from small parts in movies and television dramas and headlined three much admired movies, *East of Eden*, *Rebel Without a Cause*, and *Giant*. Shortly after finishing the bulk of his work in *Giant*, he drove his Porsche Spyder toward northern California, planning to participate in a race there. A vehicle emerged from a side road, and Dean crashed into it, dying at the age of twenty-four on September 30, 1955.

Only one of his films, *East of Eden* was released before his death. For it and *Giant*, he received posthumous Academy Award nominations. It's poignant that he never knew how big a star he was. Some of his fans developed such a cult mentality about him that they went into denial, convincing themselves that he hadn't really died but rather that he had

The Curious Odyssey of James Decon (AKA James Dean)

gone into hiding because the accident had disfigured him. He remains a symbol of promise unfulfilled. What fabulous acting heights might he have scaled if he had lived?

If he had lived. That was the subject my wife, Donna, and I discussed on a spring evening in 1984, shortly after I'd been invited to contribute to *Night Visions 2*. We were making dinner and drinking wine. What if Dean somehow came back in the person of a young actor whose age is the same as Dean's was just before Dean starred in his first major film? What if that actor uses a scene from that film as his screen test and is chosen to be the next James Dean? A moment after I suggested a story element, Donna suggested one. We drank more wine. Soon Donna was scribbling notes as thoughts occurred to us.

The need to finish dinner and feed our children interrupted us. The next morning, our creative conversation was only a memory. But when I walked into the kitchen to make coffee, I saw Donna's notes on a counter. Pages of them. In college, she was a legendary rapid note taker, seldom missing a word from a professor's lecture. As I reread our story session, more ideas suddenly came to me, including the title, "Dead Image." I couldn't wait to start writing.

I called the Dean character James Deacon. He never appears in the story, but his short career and too-early death are explained in detail. He is a shadow in every scene, sinking into and controlling the destiny of his alter ego, the young actor I call Wes Crane. The crux of the narrative is as follows: if Wes Crane is a parallel to James Deacon, then will he die at the same point in his career that Deacon did? Or if Crane survives, what great things might he accomplish that Deacon never had a chance to achieve? Or is there a third possibility, horrifying and heartbreaking?

Night Visions 2 was published in 1985. Eventually, I included "Dead Image" and its companion stories in my 1999 collection, *Black Evening*. 1985. 1999. When I revisited the story so many years after writing it, I felt even more obsessed with what happened to Dean and the way I translated that haunting early loss into fiction. I resolved that I wasn't finished with Dean/Deacon and that I would look for the chance to use him on a much bigger scale in a novel.

In 2004, I found that opportunity. November 7. That was the date on the Sunday edition of my local newspaper, the *Santa Fe New Mexican*. I don't usually read the travel section, but as I hurried past it, this is what caught my eye.

LIGHT UP YOUR LIFE
TINY MARFA, TEXAS, BOASTS WEIRD NATURAL PHENOMENA

If something's weird, I definitely want to read about it. Marfa is a town in west Texas, about 250 miles from El Paso. Since the 1880s, when the first Anglo settlers moved in, people have been seeing lights there. These mysterious phenomena hover on the dark horizon, drifting, bobbing, floating. They merge and change colors. They get bright, then turn pale, then become bright again.

Equally weird, not everyone sees them. One night, you might gaze in awe at them while your companions wonder what you're looking at. But another night, your companions might see the alluring lights while all you see is a dark expanse of rangeland. The lights have chased cars. They once guided a lost hiker to safety during an uncommon Texas snowstorm. In the 1970s, the people in Marfa had

The Curious Odyssey of James Decon (AKA James Dean)

what they called a Ghost Light Hunt. They set up triangulation stations, pinpointed the location of the lights, and went after them in vehicles and on horseback, even with an airplane. But despite the determined efforts of hundreds of people, the lights had no trouble eluding them.

Although scientists have come from all over the world to study them, no one has any firm explanation, but these are some theories. Quartz crystals in the soil absorb heat and expand during the day; at night, the lowering temperature makes them contract and give off static electricity. Or maybe radioactive gas gives off a glow. Or maybe the lights are ball lightning. Or maybe they're the headlights of cars driving north from Mexico. Or maybe a temperature inversion in the atmosphere causes far-away lights from vehicles or trains to refract through the air and be distorted in a mirage. Take your pick. Few people who have seen the lights are satisfied by any of these suggestions.

Marfa has another claim to fame. A number of movies were filmed there. *No Country for Old Men* is a recent example. Imagine how interest swelled in me when I learned that the first movie to be made there, back in 1955, was *Giant*. The combination of the Marfa lights and James Dean seized my imagination. I learned that he was mesmerized by them. Many nights, he went to view them and tried to drag his co-stars Elizabeth Taylor and Rock Hudson with him, along with the director. But *they* didn't see the lights and hadn't the faintest idea what he was trying to show them.

As I mentioned earlier, a few days after Dean finished the bulk of his work on *Giant*, he was killed in a car crash as he drove toward a race in northern California. I couldn't resist superimposing all this on the shadowy James Deacon character in "Dead Image." What if I brought Deacon back? I thought. In a novel about the lights he was fascinated with. That would give me the chance I wanted to explore Dean/ Deacon on a larger scale, communicating the sadness of his poignant history. He would still be in the shadows as he was in "Dead Image," never on stage, and yet somehow the reader would feel his hovering presence. I called the novel *The Shimmer*, and just as James Dean became James Deacon, so *Giant* became a movie called *Birthright*, and the town of Marfa—supposedly named after a character in Dostoyevsky's *Crime and Punishment*—became Rostov, which I named after a character in Tolstoy's *War and Peace*.

What follows is a short chapter that I cut from *The Shimmer* in which a television reporter interviews an elderly resident of Rostov about James Deacon and the filming of his last movie in the mid-1950s. If it stimulates your interest, you can then read "Dead Image," which is also reprinted here. Perhaps you'll also enjoy the complete strange odyssey of James Deacon as I present it in my novel, *The Shimmer*.

Where Darkness Is the Only Light

By David Morrell

"**I** HAD A TERRIBLE crush on James Deacon," the seventy-year-old woman said.

Her name was Abigail Grant, and she stood before the decaying façade of the once-magnificent ranch house that had been built for Deacon's last movie, *Birthright*. Three stories high, it had a covered porch that stretched along its wide front. Several chimneys projected from its roofline. A square tower rose on the right corner, ending in a cupola that made the house look like a castle.

At least, that was the way it had appeared in the film, but more than half a century of Texas sun and thunderstorms had ravaged it. Boards had fallen. Part of the porch had collapsed. The ornate front door looked ready to fall off. The gaps revealed that the ranch house was only an illusion. Instead of the high-ceilinged, spacious rooms that were shown throughout the movie, the only things behind the front of the house were rangeland, sky, and the distant Davis Mountains.

Seeing's believing, Brent Loft thought, *but what we see isn't always what's real.*

Brent was the co-anchor of El Paso's First-on-the-Scene TV news team. After twenty tourists had been shot to death the previous night outside this small town in west Texas, he'd rushed here to cover the massacre from as many angles as possible. The killer had been with a busload of tourists who felt drawn to view the mysterious lights that appeared outside town almost every night. After shooting repeatedly at the lights, shouting "Go back to hell where you came from," he'd turned his assault rifle against the crowd.

The lights, Brent thought. *I need to learn about the lights.*

"Of course, I never thought of him as James Deacon," Abigail said. "To me, he was always Jimmy. Still is."

Brent had her positioned so the camera showed both of them in front of the crumbling movie set, emphasizing the ranch house's brooding atmosphere.

"Of course, I was only a teenager back then," Abigail continued. "After Jimmy died in the car crash, I felt that life would never be the same again."

"And he went to the viewing area every night to see the lights?" Brent asked.

"Every night. When he started looking old all of a sudden, I heard rumors that he was drinking or using drugs instead of watching the lights as he claimed. Not that I had any idea of the kind of drugs the movie crew was talking about. This is a sleepy little town." The aging woman looked troubled,

Where Darkness Is the Only Light

seeming to think about the twenty people who'd been shot to death. "Until recently."

"Deacon started looking old?" Brent frowned.

"Drawn and wrinkled. His cheeks started to shrivel."

Brent found himself in the uncharacteristic position of being almost speechless. "Shrivel?"

"Sure. Jimmy was twenty-three at the time. His character was supposed to age until he was in his sixties. For much of the filming, the makeup department did a good job of getting him to look older, but toward the end, Jimmy didn't need the makeup."

"I don't understand."

"He started to look as old as the sixty-year-old character he was playing. I know for a fact, though, that Jimmy didn't look old because he was drinking or using drugs. A lot of nights, I snuck from home after my parents and my brother went to sleep. I rode my bicycle to the viewing area and watched from the darkness on the other side of the road. Jimmy was there every night, leaning against the barbed-wire fence, staring at the horizon."

"What do you suppose made him look forty years older, Mrs. Grant?"

"Ever see anybody who spent a lot of time in the sun? I mean, a *lot* of time. Years and years? Without any kind of protection like a hat or sunscreen? They look like a chunk of old leather. Except that Jimmy also looked sunburned."

"Sunburned? But this was at night."

"I'm just telling you what I was reminded of."

"You're suggesting that Deacon's skin shriveled from heat that the lights gave off?" Brent tried to keep skepticism from his voice.

"Or radiation."

"Radiation?" Again, Brent was caught by surprise.

"That was the theory of my boyfriend at the time. The first atomic bomb was exploded a couple of hundred miles northwest of here."

"Yes. In New Mexico. At what used to be called the Alamogordo Bombing Range," Brent said. "But that was back in 1945. Ten years before *Birthright* was filmed here. I don't see the connection."

"We found out later how closely the government kept the bomb a secret until they were ready to use it. Given how many weird things have happened in connection with the lights, my boyfriend had a theory that the lights might have something to do with *another* secret government experiment. I told him his theory was crazy because other people besides Jimmy would have looked burned, also. My boyfriend's answer was, nobody but Jimmy ever stared at the lights for so long."

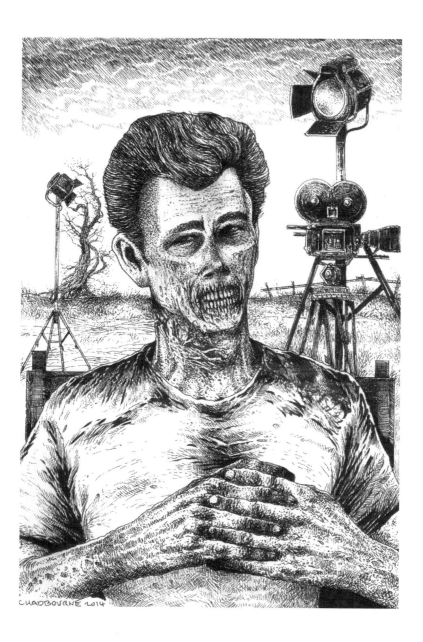

CHADBOURNE 2014

Dead Image

by David Morrell

"**Y**OU KNOW WHO he looks like, don't you?"

Watching the scene, I just shrugged.

"Really, the resemblance is amazing," Jill said.

"Mmmm."

We were in the studio's screening room, watching yesterday's dailies. The director—and I use the term loosely—had been having troubles with the leading actor, if acting's what you could say that good-looking bozo does. Hell, he used to be a male model. He doesn't act. He poses. It wasn't enough that he wanted eight million bucks and changed my scene so the dialogue sounded as if a moron had written it. No, he had to keep dashing to his trailer, snorting more coke (for "creative inspiration," he said), then—sniffling after every sentence—wouldn't understand his motivation for leaving his girlfriend after she became a famous singer, and believe me, nothing's more unforgiving than an audience when it gets confused. The word-of-mouth would kill us.

"Come on, you big dumb sonofabitch," I muttered. "You make me want to blow my nose just listening to you."

The director had wasted three days doing retakes, and the dailies from yesterday were worse than the ones from the two days before. Sliding down in my seat, I groaned. The director's idea of fixing the scene was to have a team of editors work all night patching in reaction shots from the girl and the guys in the country-western band she sang with. Every time Mr. Wonderful sniffled...cut, we saw somebody staring at him as if he was Jesus.

"Jesus," I moaned to Jill. "Those cuts distract from the speech. It's supposed to be one continuous shot."

"Of course, this is rough, you understand," the director told everyone from where he sat in the back row of seats. Near the door. To make a quick getaway, if he had any sense. "We haven't worked on the dubbing yet. That sniffling won't be on the release print."

"I hope to God not," I muttered.

"Really. Just like him," Jill said next to me.

"Huh? Who?" I turned to her. "What are you talking about?"

"The guitar player. The kid behind the girl. Haven't you been listening?" She kept her voice low enough that no one else could have heard her.

That's why I blinked when the studio VP asked from somewhere in the dark to my left, "Who's the kid behind the girl?"

Jill whispered, "Watch the way he holds that beer can."

"There. The one with the beer can," the VP said.

Except for the lummox sniffling on the screen, the room was silent.

The VP spoke louder. "I said who's the—"

"I don't know." Behind us, the director cleared his throat.

Dead Image

"He must have told you his name."

"I never met him."

"How the hell, if you..."

"All the concert scenes were shot by the second-unit director."

"What about these reaction shots?"

"Same thing. The kid had only a few lines. He did his bit and went home. Hey, I had my hands full making Mr. Nose Candy feel like the genius he thinks he is."

"There's the kid again," Jill said.

I was beginning to see what she meant now. The kid looked a lot like—

"James Deacon," the VP said. "Yeah, that's who he reminds me of."

Mr. Muscle Bound had managed to struggle through the speech. I'd recognized only half of it—partly because the lines he'd added made no sense, mostly because he mumbled. At the end, we had a closeup of his girlfriend, the singer, crying. She'd been so heartless clawing her way to the top that she'd lost the one thing that mattered—the man who'd loved her. In theory, the audience was supposed to feel so sorry for her that they were crying along with her. If you ask me, they'd be in tears all right, from rolling around in the aisles with laughter. On the screen, Mr. Beefcake turned and trudged from the rehearsal hall, as if his underwear was too tight. He had his eyes narrowed manfully, ready to pick up his Oscar.

The screen went dark. The director cleared his throat again. He sounded nervous. "Well?"

The room was silent.

The director sounded more nervous. "Uh...So what do you think?"

The lights came on, but they weren't the reason I suddenly had a headache.

Everybody turned toward the VP, waiting for the word of God.

"What I think," the VP said. He nodded wisely. "Is we need a rewrite."

↩→

"THIS FUCKING town." I gobbled Di-Gel as Jill drove us home. The Santa Monica freeway was jammed as usual. We had the top down on the Porsche so we got a really good dose of car exhaust.

"They won't blame the star. After all, he charged eight million bucks, and next time he'll charge more if the studio pisses him off." I winced from heartburn. "They'd never think to blame the director. He's a God-damned artist as he keeps telling everybody. So who does that leave? The underpaid schmuck who wrote what everybody changed."

"Take it easy. You'll raise your blood pressure." Jill turned off the freeway.

"Raise my blood pressure? Raise my—it's already raised! Any higher, I'll have a stroke!"

"I don't know what you're so surprised about. This happens on every picture. We've been out here fifteen years. You ought to be used to how they treat writers."

"Whipping boys. That's the only reason they keep us around. Every director, producer, and actor in town is a better writer. Just ask them, they'll tell you. The only problem is they can't read, let alone write, and they just don't seem to have the time to sit down and put all their wonderful thoughts on paper."

Dead Image

"But that's how the system works, hon. There's no way to win, so either you love this business or you leave it."

I scowled. "About the only way to make a decent picture is to direct as well as write it. Hell, I'd star in it too if I wasn't losing my hair from pulling it out."

"And twenty million bucks," Jill said.

"Yeah, that would help too—so I wouldn't have to grovel in front of those studio heads. But hell, if I had twenty million bucks to finance a picture, what would I need to be a writer for?"

"You know you'd keep writing, even if you had a hundred million."

"You're right. I must be nuts."

"WES CRANE," Jill said.

I sat at the word processor, grumbling as I did the rewrite. The studio VP had decided that Mr. Biceps wasn't going to leave his girlfriend. Instead his girlfriend was going to realize how much she'd been ignoring him and give up her career for love. "There's an audience out there dying for a movie against women's lib," he said. It was all I could do not to throw up.

"Wes who?" I kept typing on the keyboard.

"Crane. The kid in the dailies."

I turned to where she stood at the open door to my study. I must have blinked stupidly because she got that patient look on her face.

"The one who looks like James Deacon. I got curious. So for the hell of it, I phoned the casting office at the studio."

"All right, so you found out his name. So what's the point?"

"Just a hunch."

"I still don't get it."

"Your script about mercenary soldiers."

I shrugged. "It still needs a polish. Anyway, it's strictly on spec. When the studio decides we've ruined this picture sufficiently, I have to do that Napoleon mini-series for ABC."

"You wrote that script on spec because you believed in the story, right? It's something you really wanted to do."

"The subject's important. Soldiers of fortune employed by the CIA. Unofficially, America's involved in a lot of foreign wars."

"Then fuck the mini-series. I think the kid would be wonderful as the young mercenary who gets so disgusted that he finally shoots the dictator who hired him."

I stared. "You know, that's not a bad idea."

"When we were driving home, didn't you tell me the only way to film something decent was to direct the thing yourself?"

"And star in it." I raised my eyebrows. "Yeah, that's me. But I was just making a joke."

"Well, lover, I know you couldn't direct any worse than that asshole who ruined your stuff this morning. I've got the hots for you, but you're not good looking enough for even a character part. That kid is, though. And the man who discovers him…"

"…can write his own ticket. If he puts the package together properly."

"You've had fifteen years of learning the politics."

"But if I back out on ABC…"

"Half the writers in town wanted that assignment. They'll sign someone else in an hour."

"But they offered a lot of dough."

Dead Image

"You just made four-hundred-thousand on a story the studio ruined. Take a flyer, why don't you? This one's for your self-respect."

"I think I love you," I said.

"When you're sure, come down to the bedroom."

She turned and left. I watched the doorway for a while, then swung my chair to face the picture window and thought about the mercenaries. We live on a bluff in Pacific Palisades. You can see the ocean forever. But what I saw in my head was the kid in the dailies. How he held that beer can.

Just like James Deacon.

DEACON. IF you're a film buff, you know who I'm talking about. The farm boy from Oklahoma. Back in the middle fifties. At the start a juvenile delinquent, almost went to reform school for stealing cars. But a teacher managed to get him interested in high-school plays. Deacon never graduated. Instead he borrowed a hundred bucks and hitchhiked to New York where he camped on Lee Strasberg's doorstep til Strasberg agreed to give him a chance in the Actor's Studio. A lot of brilliant actors came out of that school. Brando, Newman, Clift, Gazzara, McQueen. But some say Deacon was the best of the lot. A bit part on Broadway. A talent scout in the audience. A screen test. The rest as they say is history. The part of the younger brother in *The Prodigal Son*. The juvenile delinquent in *Revolt on Thirty-Second Street*. Then the wildcat oil driller in *Birthright* where he upstaged half a dozen major stars. There was something about him. Intensity, sure. You could sense the pressure building in him, swelling inside his skin, wanting out. And authenticity. God knows, you could tell how much he believed the parts he was playing. He actually was those characters.

But mostly the camera simply loved him. That's the way they explain a star out here. Some good looking guys come across as plain on the screen. And some plain ones look gorgeous. It's a question of taking a three-dimensional face and making it one-dimensional for the screen. What's distinctive in real life gets muted, and vice versa. There's no way to figure if the camera will like you. It either does or doesn't. And it sure liked Deacon.

What's fascinating is that he also looked as gorgeous in real life. A walking movie. Or so they say. I never met him, of course. He's before my time. But the word in the industry was that he couldn't do anything wrong. That's even before his three movies were released. A guaranteed superstar.

And then?

Cars. If you think of his life as a tragedy, cars were the flaw. He loved to race them. I'm told his body had practically disintegrated when he hit a pickup truck at a hundred miles an hour on his way to drive his modified Corvette at a race track in northern California. Maybe you heard the legend. That he didn't die but was so disfigured that he's in a rest home somewhere to spare his fans the disgust of how he looks. But don't believe it. Oh, he died, all right. Just like a shooting star, he exploded. And the irony is that, since his three pictures hadn't been released by then, he never knew how famous he became.

But what I was thinking, if a star could shine once, maybe it could shine again.

⟲→

Dead Image

"I'M LOOKING for Wes. Is he around?"

I'd phoned the Screen Actor's Guild to get his address. For the sake of privacy, sometimes all the Guild gives out is the name and phone number of an actor's agent, and what I had in mind was so tentative that I didn't want the hassle of dealing with an agent right then.

But I got lucky. The Guild gave me an address.

The place was in a canyon north of the Valley. A dusty winding road led up to an unpainted house with a sundeck supported on stilts and a half-dozen junky cars in front along with a dune buggy and a motorcycle. Seeing those clunkers, I felt self-conscious in the Porsche.

Two guys and a girl were sitting on the steps. The girl had a butch cut. The guys had hair to their shoulders. They wore sandals, shorts, and that's all. The girl's breasts were as brown as nutmeg.

The three of them stared right through me. Their eyes looked big and strange.

I opened my mouth to repeat the question.

But the girl beat me to it. "Wes?" She sounded groggy. "I think...out back."

"Hey, thanks." But I made sure I had the Porsche's keys in my pocket before I plodded through sand past sagebrush around the house.

The back had a sundeck too, and as I turned the corner, I saw him up there, leaning against the rail, squinting toward the foothills.

I tried not to show surprise. In person, Wes looked even more like Deacon. Lean, intense, hypnotic. Around twenty-one, the same age Deacon had been when he made his first movie. Sensitive, brooding, as if he suffered secret tortures.

But tough-looking too, projecting the image of someone who'd been emotionally savaged once and wouldn't allow it to happen again. He wasn't tall, and he sure was thin, but he radiated such energy that he made you think he was big and powerful. Even his clothes reminded me of Deacon. Boots, faded jeans, a denim shirt with the sleeves rolled up and a pack of cigarettes tucked in the fold. And a battered stetson with the rim curved up to meet the sides.

Actors love to pose, of course. I'm convinced that they don't even go to the bathroom without giving an imaginary camera their best profile. And the way this kid leaned against the rail, staring moodily toward the foothills, was certainly photogenic.

But I had the feeling it wasn't a pose. His clothes didn't seem a deliberate imitation of Deacon. He wore them too comfortably. And his brooding silhouette didn't seem calculated, either. I've been in the business long enough to know. He dressed and leaned that way naturally. That's the word they use for a winner in this business. He was a natural.

"Wes Crane?" I asked.

He turned and looked down at me. At last, he grinned. "Why not?" He had a vague country-boy accent. Like Deacon.

"I'm David Sloane."

He nodded.

"Then you recognize the name?"

He shrugged. "Sounds awful familiar."

"I'm a screenwriter. I did *Broken Promises*, the picture you just finished working on."

"I remember the name now. On the script."

"I'd like to talk to you."

"About?"

Dead Image

"Another script." I held it up. "There's a part in it that I think might interest you."

"So you're a producer, too?"

I shook my head no.

"Then why come to me? Even if I like the part, it won't do us any good."

I thought about how to explain. "I'll be honest. It's a big mistake as far as negotiating goes, but I'm tired of bullshit."

"Cheers." He raised a beer can to his lips.

"I saw you in the dailies this morning. I liked what I saw. A lot. What I want you to do is read this script and tell me if you want the part. With your commitment and me as director, I'd like to approach a studio for financing. But that's the package. You don't do it if I don't direct. And I don't do it unless you're the star."

"So what makes you think they'd accept me?"

"My wife's got a hunch."

He laughed. "Hey, I'm out of work. Anybody offers me a job, I take it. Why should I care who directs? Who are you to me?"

My heart sank.

He opened another beer can. "Guess what, though? I don't like bullshit, either." His eyes looked mischievous. "Sure, what have I got to lose? Leave the script."

MY NUMBER was on the front of it. The next afternoon, he called.

"This script of yours? I'll tell you the same thing you said to me about my acting. I liked it. A lot."

"It still needs a polish."

"Only where the guy's best friend gets killed. The hero wouldn't talk so much about what he feels. The fact is, he wouldn't say anything. No tears. No outburst. This is a guy who holds himself in. All you need is a closeup on his eyes. That says it all. He stares down at his buddy. He picks up his M-16. He turns toward the palace. The audience'll start to cheer. They'll know he's set to kick ass."

Most times when an actor offers suggestions, my stomach cramps. They get so involved in their part they forget about the story's logic. They want more lines. They want to emphasize their role till everybody else in the picture looks weak. Now here was an actor who wanted his largest speech cut out. He was thinking story, not ego. And he was right. That speech had always bothered me. I'd written it ten different ways and still hadn't figured out what was wrong.

Till now.

"The speech is out," I said. "It won't take fifteen minutes to redo the scene."

"And then?"

"I'll go to the studio."

"You're really not kidding me? You think there's a chance I can get the part?"

"As much chance as I have to direct it. Remember the arrangement. We're a package. Both of us, or none."

"And you don't want me to sign some kind of promise?"

"It's called a binder. And you're right. You don't have to sign a thing."

"Let me get this straight. If they don't want you to direct but they offer me the part, I'm supposed to turn them down. Because I promised you?"

Dead Image

"Sounds crazy, doesn't it?" The truth was, even if I had his promise in writing, the studio's lawyers could have it nullified if Wes claimed he'd been misled. This town wouldn't function if people kept their word.

"Yeah, crazy," Wes said. "You've got a deal."

↩→

IN THE casting office at the studio, I asked a thirtyish thin-faced woman behind a counter, "Have you got any film on an actor named Crane? Wes Crane?"

She looked at me strangely. Frowning, she opened a filing cabinet and sorted through some folders. She nodded, relieved. "I knew that name was familiar. Sure, we've got a screen test on him."

"What? Who authorized it?"

She studied a page. "Doesn't say."

And I never found out, and that's one of the many things that bother me. "Do you know who's seen the test?"

"Oh, sure, we have to keep a record." She studied another page. "But I'm the only one who looked at it."

"You?"

"He came in one day to fill out some forms. We got to kidding around. It's hard to describe. There's something about him. So I thought I'd take a look at his test."

"And?"

"What can I say? I recommended him for that bit part in *Broken Promises*."

"If I want to see that test, do you have to check with anybody?"

She thought about it. "You're still on the payroll for *Broken Promises*, aren't you?"

"Right."

"And Crane's in the movie. It seems a legitimate request." She checked a schedule. "Use screening room four. In thirty minutes. I'll send down a projectionist with the reel."

↩→

SO I sat in the dark and watched the test and first felt the shiver that I'd soon know well. When the reel was over, I didn't move for quite a while.

The projectionist came out. "Are you all right, Mr. Sloane? I mean, you're not sick or anything?"

"No. Thanks. I'm..."

"What?"

"Just thinking."

I took a deep breath and went back to the casting office. "There's been a mistake. That wasn't Crane's test."

The thin-faced woman shook her head. "There's no mistake."

"But that was a scene from *The Prodigal Son*. James Deacon's movie. There's been a switch."

"No, that was Wes Crane. It's the scene he wanted to do. The set department used something that looked like the hayloft in the original."

"Wes..."

"Crane," she said. "Not Deacon."

We stared.

"And you liked it?" I asked.

"Well, I thought he was ballsy to choose that scene—and pull it off. One wrong move, he'd have looked like an idiot. Yeah, I liked it."

"You want to help the kid along?"

Dead Image

"Depends. Will it get me in trouble?"

"Exactly the opposite. You'll earn brownie points."

"How?"

"Just phone the studio VP. Tell him I was down here asking to watch a screen test. Tell him you didn't let me because I didn't have authorization. But I acted upset, so now you've had second thoughts, and you're calling him to make sure you did the right thing. You don't want to lose your job."

"So what will that accomplish?"

"He'll get curious. He'll ask whose test it was. Just tell him the truth. But use these words. 'The kid who looks like James Deacon.'"

"I still don't see…"

"You will." I grinned.

⟳→

I CALLED my agent and told him to plant an item in *Variety* and *Hollywood Reporter*. "Oscar-winning scribe, David Sloane, currently prepping his first behind-the-lens chore on *Mercenaries*, toplining James Deacon lookalike, Wes Crane."

"What's going on? Is somebody else representing you? I don't know from chicken livers about *Mercenaries*."

"Lou, trust me."

"Who's the studio?"

"All in good time."

"You sonofabitch, if you expect me to work for you when somebody else is getting the commission—"

"Believe me, you'll get your ten percent. But if anybody calls, tell them they have to talk to me. You're not allowed to discuss the project."

"Discuss it? How the hell can I discuss it when I don't know a thing about it?"

"There. You see how easy it'll be?"

Then I drove to a video store and bought a tape of *The Prodigal Son*.

I hadn't seen the movie in years. That evening, Jill and I watched it fifteen times. Or at least a part of it that often. Every time the hayloft scene was over, I rewound the tape to the start of the scene.

"For God's sake, what are you doing? Don't you want to see the whole movie?"

"It's the same." I stared in astonishment.

"What do you mean the same? Have you been drinking?"

"The hayloft scene. It's the same as in Wes Crane's screen test."

"Well, of course. You told me the set department tried to imitate the original scene."

"I don't mean the hayloft." I tingled again. "See, here in *The Prodigal Son*, Deacon does most of the scene sprawled on the floor of the loft. He has the side of his face pressed against those bits of straw. I can almost smell the dust and the chaff. He's talking more to the floor than he is to his father behind him."

"I see it. So what are you getting at?"

"That's identical in Wes Crane's test. One continuous shot with the camera at the floor. Crane has his cheek against the wood. He sounds the same as Deacon. Every movement, every pause, even that choking noise right here as if the character's about to start sobbing—they're identical."

"But what's the mystery about it? Crane must have studied this section before he decided to use it in his test."

Dead Image

I rewound the tape.

"No, not again," Jill said.

⟲→

THE NEXT afternoon, the studio VP phoned. "I'm disappointed in you, David."

"Don't tell me you didn't like the rewrite on *Broken Promises*."

"The rewrite? The...Oh, yes, the rewrite. Great, David, great. They're shooting it now. Of course, you understand I had to make a few extra changes. Don't worry, though. I won't ask to share the writing credit with you." He chuckled.

I chuckled right back. "Well, that's a relief."

"What I'm calling about are the trades today. Since when have you become a director?"

"I was afraid of this. I'm not allowed to talk about it."

"I asked your agent. He says he didn't handle the deal."

"Well, yeah, it's something I set up on my own."

"Where?"

"Walt, really I can't talk about it. Those items in the trades surprised the hell out of me. They might screw up the deal. I haven't finished the negotiations yet."

"With this kid who looks like James Deacon."

"Honestly I've said as much as I can, Walt."

"I'll tell you flat out. I don't think it's right for you to try to sneak him away from us. I'm the one who discovered him, remember. I had a look at his screen test yesterday. He's got the makings of a star."

I knew when he'd screened that test. Right after the woman in the casting department phoned him to ask if I had a right to see the test. One thing you can count on in this

— 139 —

business. Everybody's so paranoid they want to know what everybody else is doing. If they think a trend is developing, they'll stampede to follow it.

"Wait, I'm not exactly trying to sneak him away from you. You don't have him under contract, do you?"

He ignored the question. "And what's this project called *Mercenaries*? What's that all about?"

"It's a script I did on spec. I got the idea when I heard about the ads at the back of *Soldier of Fortune* magazine."

"*Soldier of*…David, I thought we had a good working relationship."

"Sure. That's what I thought too."

"Then why didn't you talk to me about this story? Hey, we're friends, after all. Chances are you wouldn't have had to write it on spec. I could have given you some development money."

And after you'd finished mucking with it, you'd have turned it into a musical, I thought. "Well, I guess I figured it wasn't for you. Since I wanted to direct and use an unknown in the lead."

Another thing you can count on in this business. Tell a producer that a project isn't for him, and he'll feel so left out he'll want to see it. That doesn't mean he'll buy it. But at least he'll have the satisfaction of knowing that he didn't miss out on a chance for a hit.

"Directing, David? You're a writer. What do you know about directing? I'd have to draw the line on that. But using the kid as a lead. I considered that yesterday after I saw his test."

Like hell you did, I thought. The test only made you curious. The items in the trades today are what gave you the idea.

Dead Image

"You see what I mean?" I asked. "I figured you wouldn't like the package. That's why I didn't take it to you."

"Well, the problem's hypothetical. I just sent the head of our legal department out to see him. We're offering the kid a long-term option."

"In other words, you want to fix it so no one else can use him, but you're not committing yourself to star him in a picture, and you're paying him a fraction of what you think he might be worth."

"Hey, ten thousand bucks isn't pickled herring. Not from his point of view. So maybe we'll go to fifteen."

"Against?"

"A hundred-and-fifty-thousand if we use him in a picture."

"His agent won't go for it."

"He doesn't have one."

That explained why the Screen Actor's Guild had given me Wes's home address and phone number instead of an agent's.

"I get it now," I said. "You're doing all this just to spite me."

"There's nothing personal in this, David. It's business. I tell you what. Show me the script. Maybe we can put a deal together."

"But you won't accept me as a director."

"Hey, with budgets as high as they are, the only way I can justify the picture's a hit, he'll screw us next time anyhow. But I won't risk the money I'm saving by using an inexperienced director who'd probably run the budget into the stratosphere. I see this picture coming in at fifteen million tops."

"But you haven't even read the script. It's got several big action scenes. Explosions. Helicopters. Expensive special effects. Twenty-five million minimum."

"That's just my point. You're so close to the concept that you wouldn't want to compromise on the special effects. You're not directing."

"Well, as you said before, it's hypothetical. I've taken the package to somebody else."

"Not if we put him under option. David, don't fight me on this. Remember, we're friends."

PARAMOUNT PHONED an hour later. Trade gossip travels fast. They'd heard I was having troubles with my studio and wondered if we could take a meeting to discuss the project they'd been reading about.

I said I'd get back to them. But now I had what I wanted—I could truthfully say that Paramount had been in touch with me. I could play the studios off against each other.

Walt phoned back that evening. "What did you do with the kid? Hide him in your closet?"

"Couldn't find him, huh?"

"The head of our legal department says the kid lives with a bunch of freaks way the hell out in the middle of nowhere. The freaks don't communicate too well. The kid isn't there, and they don't know where he went."

"I'm meeting him tomorrow."

"Where?"

"Can't say, Walt. Paramount's been in touch."

WES MET me at a taco stand he liked in Burbank. He'd been racing his motorcycle in a meet, and when he pulled up in

Dead Image

his boots and jeans, his T-shirt and leather jacket, I shivered from déjà vu. He looked exactly as Deacon had looked in *Revolt on Thirty-Second Street.*

"Did you win?"

He grinned and raised his thumb. "Yourself?"

"Some interesting developments."

He barely had time to park his bike before two men in suits came over. I wondered if they were cops, but their suits were too expensive. Then I realized. The studio. I'd been followed from my house.

"Mr. Hepner would like you to look at this," the blue suit told Wes. He set a document on the roadside table.

"What is it?"

"An option for your services. Mr. Hepner feels that the figure will interest you."

Wes shoved it over to me. "What's it mean?"

I read it quickly. The studio had raised the fee. They were offering fifty thousand now against a quarter million.

I told him the truth. "In your position, it's a lot of cash. I think that at this point you need an agent."

"You know a good one?"

"My own. But that might be too chummy."

"So what do you think I should do?"

"The truth? How much did you make last year? Fifty grand's a serious offer."

"Is there a catch?"

I nodded. "Chances are you'll be put in *Mercs.*"

"And?"

"I don't direct."

Wes squinted at me. This would be the moment I'd always cherish. "You're willing to let me do it?" he asked.

"I told you I can't hold you to our bargain. In your place, I'd be tempted. It's a good career move."

"Listen to him," the gray suit said.

"But do you *want* to direct?"

I nodded. Until now, all the moves had been predictable. But Wes himself was not. Most unknown actors would grab at the chance for stardom. They wouldn't care what private agreements they ignored. Everything depended on whether Wes had a character similar to Deacon.

"And no hard feelings if I go with the studio?" he asked.

I shrugged. "What we talked about was fantasy. This is real."

He kept squinting at me. All at once, he turned to the suits and slid the option toward them. "Tell Mr. Hepner my friend here has to direct."

"You're making a big mistake," the blue suit said.

"Yeah, well, here today, gone tomorrow. Tell Mr. Hepner I trust my friend to make me look good."

I exhaled slowly. The suits looked grim.

↩→

I'LL SKIP the month of negotiations. There were times when I sensed that Wes and I had both thrown away our careers. The key was that Walt had taken a stand, and pride wouldn't let him budge. But when I offered to direct for union scale (and let the studio have the screenplay for the minimum the Writers' Guild would allow, and Wes agreed to the Actors' Guild minimum), Walt had a deal that he couldn't refuse. Greed budged him in our favor. He bragged about how he'd outmaneuvered us.

Dead Image

We didn't care. I was making a picture I believed in, and Wes was on the verge of being a star.

I did my homework. I brought the picture in for twelve million. These days, that's a bargain. The rule of thumb says that you multiply the picture's cost by three (to account for studio overhead, bank interest, promotion, this and that), and you've got the break-even point.

So we were aiming for thirty-six million in ticket sales. Worldwide, we did a hundred-and-twenty-million. Now a lot of that went to the distributors, the folks that sell you pop-corn. And a lot of that went into some mysterious black hole of theater owners who don't report all the tickets they sold and foreign chains that suddenly go bankrupt. But after the sale to HBO and CBS, after the income from tapes and discs and showings on airlines, the studio had a solid forty million profit in the bank. And that, believe me, qualifies as a hit.

We were golden. The studio wanted another Wes Crane picture yesterday. The reviews were glowing. Both Wes and I were nominated for—but didn't receive—an Oscar. "Next time," I told Wes.

And now that we were hot, we demanded fees that were large enough to compensate for the pennies we'd been paid on the first one.

THEN THE trouble started.

You remember that Deacon never knew he was a star. He died with three pictures in the can and a legacy that he never knew would make him immortal. But what you probably don't know is that Deacon became more difficult as he went from picture to picture. The theory is that he sensed the power he was going to have, and he couldn't handle it. Because he was making up for his troubled youth. He was showing people that he wasn't the fuckup his foster parents and his teachers (with one exception) said he was. But Deacon was so intense—and so insecure—that he started reverting. Secretly he felt that he didn't deserve his predicted success. So he did become a fuckup as predicted.

On his next-to-last picture, he started showing up three hours late for the scenes he was supposed to be in. He played expensive pranks on the set, the worst of which was lacing the crew's lunch with a laxative that shut down production for the rest of the day. His insistence on racing cars forced the studio to pay exorbitant premiums to the insurance company that covered him during shooting. On his last picture, he was drunk more often than not, swilling beer and tequila on the set. Just before he died in the car crash, he looked twenty-two going on sixty. Most of his visuals had been completed, just a few close-ups remaining, but since a good deal of *Birthright* was shot on location in the Texas oilfields, his dialogue needed re-recording to eliminate background noises on the soundtrack. A friend of his who'd learned to imitate Deacon's voice was hired to dub several key speeches. The audience loved the finished print, but they didn't realize how much of the film depended on careful editing, emphasizing other characters in scenes where Deacon looked so wasted that his footage couldn't be used.

So naturally I wondered—if Wes Crane looked like Deacon's style, would he start to behave like Deacon? What would happen when I came to Wes with a second project?

I wasn't the only one offering stories to him. The scripts came pouring in.

Dead Image

I learned this from the trades. I hadn't seen him since Oscar night in March. Whenever I called his place, either I didn't get an answer or a spaced-out woman's voice told me Wes wasn't home. In truth, I'd expected him to have moved from that dingy house near the desert. The gang that lived there reminded me of the Manson clan. But then I remembered that he hadn't come into big money yet. The second project would be the gold mine. And I wondered if he was going to stake the claim only for himself.

His motorcycle was parked outside our house when Jill and I came back from a Writers' Guild screening of a new Clint Eastwood movie. This was at sunset with sailboats silhouetted against a crimson ocean. Wes was sitting on the steps that wound up through a rose garden to our house. He held a beer can. He was wearing jeans and a T-shirt again, and the white of that T-shirt contrasted beautifully with his tan. But his cheeks looked gaunter than when I'd last seen him.

Our exchange had become a ritual.

"Did you win?"

He grinned and raised a thumb. "Yourself?"

I grinned right back. "I've been trying to get in touch with you."

He shrugged. "Well, yeah, I've been racing. I needed some downtime. All that publicity, and...Jill, how are you?"

"Fine, Wes. You?"

"The second go-around's the hardest."

I thought I understood. Trying for another hit. But now I wonder.

"Stay for supper?" Jill asked.

"I'd like to, but..."

"Please, do. It won't be any trouble."

"Are you sure?"

"The chili's been cooking in the crockpot all day. Tortillas and salad."

Wes nodded. "Yeah, my mom used to like making chili. That's before my dad went away and she got to drinking."

Jill's eyebrows narrowed. Wes didn't notice, staring at his beer can.

"Then she didn't do much cooking at all," he said. "When she went to the hospital...This was back in Oklahoma. Well, the cancer ate her up. And the city put me in a foster home. I guess that's when I started running wild." Brooding, he drained his beer can and blinked at us as if remembering we were there. "A home-cooked meal would go good."

"It's coming up," Jill said.

But she still looked bothered, and I almost asked her what was wrong. She went inside.

Wes reached in a paper sack beneath a rose bush. "Anyway, buddy." He handed me a beer can. "You want to make another movie?"

"The trades say you're much in demand." I sat beside him, stared at the ocean, and popped the tab on the beer can.

"Yeah, but aren't we supposed to be a team? You direct and write. I act. Both of us, or none." He nudged my knee. "Isn't that the bargain?"

"It is if you say so. Right now, you've got the clout to do anything you want."

"Well, what I want is a friend. Someone I trust to tell me when I'm fucking up. Those other guys, they'll let you do anything if they think they can make a buck, even if you ruin yourself. I've learned my lesson. Believe me, this time I'm doing things right."

Dead Image

"In that case," I said, vaguely puzzled.

"Let's hear it."

"I've been working on something. We start with several givens. The audience likes you in an action role. But you've got to be rebellious, anti-establishment. And the issue has to be controversial. What about a bodyguard—he's young, he's tough—who's supposed to protect a famous movie actress? Someone who reminds us of Marilyn Monroe. Secretly he's in love with her, but he can't bring himself to tell her. And she dies from an overdose of sleeping pills. The cops say it's suicide. The newspapers go along. But the bodyguard can't believe she killed herself. He discovers evidence that it was murder. He gets pissed at the cover-up. From grief, he investigates further. A hit team nearly kills him. Now he's twice as pissed. And what he learns is that the man who ordered the murder—it's an election year, the actress was writing a tell-it-all about her famous lovers—is the President of the United States."

"I think"—he sipped his beer—"it would play in Oklahoma."

"And Chicago and New York. It's a backlash about big government. With a sympathetic hero."

He chuckled. "When do we start?"

And that's how we made the deal on *Grievance*.

I FELT excited all evening, but later—after we'd had a pleasant supper and Wes had driven off on his motorcycle—Jill stuck a pin in my swollen optimism.

"What he said about Oklahoma, about his father running away, his mother becoming a drunk and dying from cancer, about his going to a foster home…"

"I noticed it bothered you."

"You bet. You're so busy staring at your keyboard you don't keep up on the handouts about your star."

I put a bowl in the dishwasher. "So?"

"Wes comes from Indiana. He's a foundling, raised in an orphanage. The background he gave you isn't his."

"Then whose…"

Jill stared at me.

"My God, not Deacon's."

↻→

SO THERE it was, like a hideous face popping out of a box to leer at me. Wes's physical resemblance to Deacon was accidental, an act of fate that turned out to be a godsend for him. But the rest—the mannerisms, the clothes, the voice—were truly deliberate. I know what you're thinking—I'm contradicting myself. When I first met him, I thought his style was too natural to be a conscious imitation. And when I realized that his screen test was identical in every respect to Deacon's hayloft scene in *The Prodigal Son*, I didn't believe that Wes had callously reproduced the scene. The screen test felt too natural to be an imitation. It was a homage.

But now I knew better. Wes was imitating, all right. But chillingly, what Wes had done went beyond conventional imitation. He'd accomplished the ultimate goal of every method actor. He wasn't playing a part. He wasn't pretending to be Deacon. He actually *was* the role. Wes Crane existed only in name. His background, his thoughts, his very identity, weren't his own anymore. They belonged to a dead man.

Dead Image

"What the hell is this?" I asked. "*The Three Faces of Eve? Sybil?*"

Jill looked at me nervously. "As long as it isn't *Psycho*."

⟳→

WHAT WAS I to do? Tell Wes he needed help? Have a heart-to-heart and try to talk him out of his delusion? All we had was the one conversation to back up our theory, and anyway he wasn't dangerous. The opposite. His manners were impeccable. He always spoke softly, with humor. Besides, actors use all kinds of ways to psych themselves up. By nature, they're eccentric. The best thing to do, I thought, was wait and see. With another picture about to start, there wasn't any sense in making trouble. If his delusion became destructive...

But he certainly wasn't difficult on the set. He showed up a half hour early for his scenes. He knew his lines. He spent several evenings and weekends—no charge—rehearsing with the other actors. Even the studio VP admitted that the dailies looked wonderful.

About the only sign of trouble was his mania for racing cars and motorcycles. The VP had a fit about the insurance premiums.

"Hey, he needs to let off steam," I said. "There's a lot of pressure on him."

And on me, I'll admit. I had a budget of twenty-five million this time, and I wasn't going to ruin things by making my star self-conscious.

Halfway through the shooting schedule, Wes came over. "See, no pranks. I'm being good this time."

"Hey, I appreciate it." What on earth did he mean by "this time?"

You're probably thinking that I could have stopped what happened if I'd cared more about him, than I did for the picture. But I did care—as you'll see. And it didn't matter. What happened was as inevitable as tragedy.

⟲→

GRIEVANCE BECAME a bigger success than *Mercenaries*. A worldwide two-hundred-million gross. *Variety* predicted an even bigger gross for the next one. Sure, the next one—number three. But at the back of my head, a nasty voice was telling me that for Deacon three had been the unlucky number.

I left a conference at the studio, walking toward my new Ferrari in the executive parking lot, when someone shouted by name. Turning, I peered through the Burbank smog at a long-haired bearded man wearing beads, a serape, and sandals, running over to me. I wondered what he wore, if anything, beneath the dangling serape.

I recognized him—Donald Porter, the friend of Deacon who'd played a bit part in *Birthright* and imitated Deacon's voice on some of the soundtrack after Deacon had died. Porter had to be in his forties now, but he dressed as if the sixties had never ended and hippies still existed. He'd starred and directed in a hit youth film twenty years ago—a lot of drugs and rock and sex. For a while, he'd tried to start his own studio in Santa Fe, but the second picture he directed was a flop, and after fading from the business for a while, he'd made a comeback as a character actor. The way he was dressed, I didn't understand how he'd passed the security

Dead Image

guard at the gate. And because we knew each other—I'd once done a rewrite on a television show he was featured in—I had the terrible feeling he was going to ask me for a job.

"I heard you were on the lot. I've been waiting for you," Porter said.

I stared at his skinny bare legs beneath his serape.

"This, man?" He gestured comically at himself. "I'm in the new TV movie they're shooting here. *The Electric Kool-Aid Acid Test.*"

I nodded. "Tom Wolfe's book. Ken Kesey. Don't tell me you're playing—"

"No. Too old for Kesey. I'm Neal Cassidy. After he split from Kerouac, he joined up with Kesey, driving the bus for the Merry Pranksters. You know, it's all a load of crap, man. Cassidy never dressed like this. He dressed like Deacon. Or Deacon dressed like him."

"Well, good. Hey, great. I'm glad things are going well for you." I turned toward my car.

"Just a second, man. That's not what I wanted to talk to you about. Wes Crane. You know?"

"No, I…"

"Deacon, man. Come on. Don't tell me you haven't noticed. Shit, man. I dubbed Deacon's voice. I knew him. I was his *friend*. Nobody else knew him better. Crane sounds more like Deacon than I did."

"So?"

"It isn't possible."

"Because he's better?"

"Cruel, man. Really. Beneath you. I have to tell you something. I don't want you thinking I'm on drugs again. I swear I'm clean. A little grass. That's it." His eyes looked as bright as a nova, "I'm into horoscopes. Astrology. The stars. That's a good things for a movie actor, don't you think? The stars. There's a lot of truth in the stars."

"Whatever turns you on."

"You think so, man? Well, listen to this. I wanted to see for myself, so I found out where he lives, but I didn't go out there. Want to know why?" He didn't let me answer. "I didn't have to. 'Cause I recognized the address. I've been there a hundred times. When Deacon lived there."

I flinched. "You're changing the subject. What's that got to do with horoscopes and astrology?"

"Crane's birth date."

"Well?"

"It's the same as the day Deacon died."

I realized I'd stopped breathing. "So what?"

"More shit, man. Don't pretend it's coincidence. It's in the stars. You know what's coming. Crane's your bread and butter. But the gravy train'll end four months from now."

I didn't ask.

"Crane's birthday's coming up. The anniversary of Deacon's death."

⟳→

AND WHEN I looked into it, there were other parallels. Wes would be twenty-three—Deacon's age when he died. And Wes would be close to the end of his third movie—about the same place in Deacon's third movie when he...

We were doing a script I'd written, *Rampage*, about a young man from a tough neighborhood who comes back to

Dead Image

teach there. A local street gang harasses him and his wife until the only way he can survive is by reverting to the violent life (he once led his own gang) that he ran away from.

It was Wes's idea to have the character renew his fascination with motorcycles. I have to admit that the notion had commercial value, given Wes's well-known passion for motorcycle racing. But I also felt apprehensive, especially when he insisted on doing his own stunts.

I couldn't talk him out of it. As if his model behavior on the first two pictures had been too great a strain on him, he snapped to the opposite extreme—showing up late, drinking on the set, playing expensive pranks. One joke involving fire crackers started a blaze in the costume trailer.

It all had the makings of a death wish. His absolute identification with Deacon was leading him to the ultimate parallel.

And just like Deacon in his final picture, Wes began to look wasted. Hollow-cheeked, squinty, stooped from lack of food and sleep. His dailies were shameful.

"How the hell are we supposed to ask an audience to pay to see this shit?" the studio VP asked.

"I'll have to shoot around him. Cut to reaction shots from the characters he's talking to." My heart lurched.

"That sounds familiar," Jill said beside me.

I knew what she meant. I'd become the director I'd criticized on *Broken Promises*.

"Well, can't you control him?" the VP asked.

"It's hard. He's not quite himself these days."

"Dammit, if you can't maybe another director can. This garbage is costing us forty million bucks."

The threat made me seethe. I almost told him to take his forty million bucks and...

Abruptly I understood the leverage he'd given me. I straightened. "Relax. Just let me have a week. If he hasn't improved by then, I'll back out gladly."

"Witnesses heard you say it. One week, pal, or else."

IN THE morning, I waited for Wes in his trailer when as usual he showed up late for his first shot.

At the open trailer door, he had trouble focusing on me. "If it isn't teach." He shook his head. "No, wrong. It's me who's supposed to play the teach in—what's the name of this garbage we're making?"

"Wes, I want to talk to you."

"Hey, funny thing. The same goes for me with you. Just give me a chance to grab a beer, okay?" Fumbling, he shut the trailer door behind him and lurched through shadows toward the miniature fridge.

"Try to keep your head clear. This is important," I said.

"Right. Sure." He popped the tab on a beer can and left the fridge door open while he drank. He wiped his mouth. "But first I want a favor."

"That depends."

"I don't have to ask, you know. I can just go ahead and do it. I'm trying to be polite."

"What is it?"

"Monday's my birthday. I want the day off. There's a motorcycle race near Sonora. I want to make a long weekend out of it." He drank more beer.

"We had an agreement once."

He scowled. Beer dribbled down his chin.

Dead Image

"I write and direct. You star. Both of us, or none."

"Yeah. So? I've kept the bargain."

"The studio's given me a week. To shape you up. If not, I'm off the project."

He sneered. "I'll tell them I don't work if you don't."

"Not that simple, Wes. At the moment, they're not that eager to do what you want. You're losing your clout. Remember why you liked us as a team?"

He wavered blearily.

"Because you wanted a friend. To keep you from making what you called the same mistakes again. To keep you from fucking up. Well, Wes, that's what you're doing. Fucking up."

He finished his beer and crumbled the can. He curled his lips, angry. "Because I want a day off on my birthday?"

"No, because you're getting your roles confused. You're not James Deacon. But you've convinced yourself that you are, and Monday you'll die in a crash."

He blinked. Then he sneered. "So what are you, a fortune teller now?"

"A half-baked psychiatrist. Unconsciously you want to complete the legend. The way you've been acting, the parallel's too exact."

"I told you the first time we met—I don't like bullshit!"

"Then prove it. Monday, you don't go near a motorcycle, a car, hell even a go-cart. You come to the studio sober. You do your work as well as you know how. I drive you over to my place. We have a private party. You and me and Jill. She promises to make your favorite meal: T-bones, baked beans, steamed corn. Homemade birthday cake. Chocolate. Again, your favorite. The works. You stay the night. In the morning, we put James Deacon behind us and..."

"Yeah? What?"

"You achieve the career Deacon never had."

His eyes looked uncertain.

"Or you go to the race and destroy yourself and break the promise you made. You and me together. A team. Don't back out of our bargain."

He shuddered as if he was going to crack.

IN A movie, that would have been the climax—how he didn't race on his birthday, how we had the private party and how he hardly said a word and went to sleep in our guest room.

And survived.

BUT THIS is what happened. On the Tuesday after his birthday, he couldn't remember his lines. He couldn't play to the camera. He couldn't control his voice. Wednesday was worse.

But I'll say this. On his birthday, the anniversary of Deacon's death, when Wes showed up sober and treated our bargain with honor, he did the most brilliant acting of his career. A zenith of tradecraft. I often watch the video of those scenes with profound respect.

And the dailies were so truly brilliant that the studio VP let me finish the picture.

But the VP never knew how I faked the rest of it. Overnight, Wes had totally lost his technique. I had enough in the can to deliver a print—with a lot of fancy editing and some uncredited but very expensive help from Donald Porter. He dubbed most of Wes's final dialogue.

"I told you. Horoscopes. Astrology," Donald said.

I didn't believe him until I took four scenes to an audio expert I know. He specializes in putting voices through a computer and making visual graphs of them.

He spread the charts in front of me. "Somebody played a joke on you. Or else you're playing one on me."

I felt so unsteady that I had to press my hands on his desk when I asked him, "How?"

"Using this first film, Deacon's scene from *The Prodigal Son* as the standard, this second film is close. But this third one doesn't have any resemblance."

"So where's the joke?"

"In the fourth. It matches perfectly. Who's kidding who?"

Deacon had been the voice on the first. Donald Porter had been the voice on the second. Close to Deacon's, dubbing for Wes in *Rampage*. Wes himself had been the voice on the third—the dialogue in *Rampage* that I couldn't use because Wes's technique had gone to hell.

And the fourth clip? The voice that was identical to Deacon's, authenticated, verifiable. Wes again. His screen test. The imitated scene from *The Prodigal Son*.

⟲→

WES DROPPED out of sight. For sure, his technique had collapsed so badly he would never again be a shining star. I kept phoning him, but I never got an answer. So, for what turned out to be the second-last time, I drove out to his dingy place near the desert. The Manson lookalikes were gone. Only one motorcycle stood outside. I climbed the steps to the sun porch, knocked, received no answer, and opened the door.

The blinds were closed. The place was in shadow. I went down a hall and heard strained breathing. Turned to the right. And entered a room.

The breathing was louder, more strident and forced.

"Wes?"

"Don't turn on the light."

"I've been worried about you, friend."

"Don't..."

But I did turn on the light. And what I saw made me swallow vomit.

He was slumped in a chair. Seeping into it would be more accurate. Rotting. Decomposing. His cheeks had holes that showed his teeth. A pool that stank of decaying vegetables spread on the floor around him.

"I should have gone racing on my birthday, huh?" His voice whistled through the gaping flesh in his throat.

"Oh, shit, friend." I started to cry. "Jesus Christ, I should have let you."

"Do me a favor, huh? Turn off the light now. Let me finish this in peace."

I had so much to say to him. But I couldn't. My heart broke. I turned off the light.

"And buddy," he said, "I think we'd better forget about our bargain. We won't be working together anymore."

"What can I do to help? There must be something I can—"

"Yeah, let me end this the way I need to."

"Listen, I—"

"Leave," Wes said. "It hurts me too much to have you here, to listen to the pity in your voice."

Dead Image

"But I care about you. I'm your friend. I—"

"That's why I know you'll do what I ask"—the hole in his throat made another whistling sound—"and leave."

I stood in the darkness, listening to other sounds he made: liquid rotting sounds. "A doctor. There must be something a doctor can—"

"Been there. Done that. What's wrong with me no doctor's going to cure. Now if you don't mind..."

"What?"

"You weren't invited. Get out."

I waited another long moment. "...Sure."

"...love you."

Dazed, I stumbled outside. Down the steps. Across the sand. Blinded by the sun, unable to clear my nostrils of the stench in that room, I threw up beside the car.

THE NEXT day, I drove out again. The last time. Jill went with me. He'd moved. I never learned where.

AND THIS is how it ended, the final dregs of his career. His talent was gone, but how his determination lingered.

Movies. Immortality.

See, special effects are expensive. Studios will grasp at any means to cut the cost.

He'd told me, "Forget about our bargain." I later discovered what he meant—he worked without me in one final feature. He wasn't listed in the credits, though. *Zombies from Hell.*

Remember how awful Bela Lugosi looked in his last exploitation movie before they buried him in his Dracula cape?

Bela looked great compared to Wes. I saw the Zombie movie in an eight-plex out in the Valley. It did great business. Jill and I almost didn't get a seat.

Jill wept as I did.

This fucking town. Nobody cares how it's done, as long as it packs them in.

The audience cheered when Wes stalked toward the leading lady.

And his jaw fell off.

CHADBOURNE 2014

Spares: The Lost First Chapter

by Michael Marshall Smith

Spares was my second novel. It's not surprising therefore that it fell foul of dreaded "Second Novel Syndrome"—which dictates that, after enjoying a pretty easy, beginners' luck style of ride completing a first book, you may then struggle badly with self-doubt, lack of direction and pure laziness when trying to write the next (I've subsequently discovered you may have to endure Fourth Novel Syndrome, too, and Eighth and Eleventh, but that's another story).

Spares started quickly, with the chapter that's reproduced here. I then lost all momentum and wound up spending weeks and weeks reworking this opening section to the point where I became trapped within its bubble, unable to move forward. In the end I threw the chapter away (carefully), and started again.

Once the novel was securely underway I experimented with re-instating the opening, but ultimately decided that—decent though I think it remains—it added too much weight at the start of what was already going to be a complicated story. I never truly throw away anything I've written, however, and so here it is.

Chapter 1

I WAITED A COUPLE of minutes after the train had stopped, listening for sounds from the outside. There were none, so I nodded at David. He woke Suej up, and I stood, initiating a complex series of cracking sounds from joints which had remained in more or less the same position for seven hours. I stepped over two of the sleeping bodies and put my hand against the carriage's sliding door. It was cold, colder even than the air in the carriage, which had been minimally warmed through the night by the presence of eight bodies. Well, seven and a half, I guess.

Suej woke slowly, blinking and struggling her way out of sleep. In the night her eyes had twitched and rolled beneath her lids, and though I could not guess at what she dreamed, I knew it would have featured the color blue. I'd asked, and they always did.

David nudged Ragald with his foot, and he woke with a start.

I stood rubbing my hands up and down my arms and sides, casting an eye over the clothing everyone was wearing. It wasn't going to be enough. It was just after dawn on December the

Spares: The Missing First Chapter

18th, the temperature was around freezing and it wasn't going to get better any time soon. I registered that as yet another problem and dismissed the thought. There were about forty worse problems ahead of it in line, and I didn't expect many of them to get solved either. Maybe none of them would.

As the spares came fitfully to life I rested my forehead against the sliding panel. The metal was ragged with rust, but after three hours of slowly increasing light I'd ceased to find the patterns attractive. I felt bone-tired, and most of my muscles ached. I'd stayed awake all the time we were on the train, figuring that someone ought to, but I probably should have slept. There were going to be a lot of someone-ought-to's coming up, and only one candidate for each. The hours had given me space to think, to start reorientating, but they'd also given plenty of time for the adrenaline rush to die to nothing, leaving me hollow and bewildered.

Most of all they'd given me time to stare wide-eyed at myself, wondering what the fuck I thought I had done.

'John, where are we?'

David was standing to one side of me by then, and I raised my head off the door.

'I don't know.'

David glanced away at Jenny and Suej, who were rubbing life into the limbs of other spares. They looked shocked and displaced, shivering constantly as though their bodies simply could not understand the temperature, and were chilled anew every moment. The bad news was that it wasn't even especially cold. Virginia in Winter doesn't fuck around, especially not in the North and on higher ground. It was going to get worse, and soon.

'Can I look?'

I hesitated. My instincts said to wait until all the spares were as ready as they were going to be. Two of them were still staring around in complete bemusement, and Nanune was hunched up against the other side of the carriage, eyes huge, cheeks streaked with tears. Then I nodded. It wasn't going to make any difference. If there was anyone outside we were never going to be in a state to defend ourselves. Whatever we did, the inevitable was rushing towards us like a truck a mile wide and a hundred miles long. Our future wasn't going to be something we could amble into, taking time to look at the flowers. It was going to be right there in our face, apt to smash the flowers into the ground.

'Be careful,' I said.

David smiled without humor, and started to slide the heavy panel. I suppose it was an unnecessary piece of advice, especially to him. He, more than any, possessed enough fury to weld a cold caution onto everything he did.

I picked my way across to the other side and knelt down next to Nanune. 'Come on, little one,' I said. 'What's so bad?'

She burst into tears again, hiding her head under her good arm. I put my own awkwardly around her and tried to warm her up. I noticed Jenny looking at us and smiled flatly. I'd tried to patch things up with her, let her know she wasn't to blame, but she still looked miserable. I wanted to make her feel better, but it was going to have to wait. Jenny was seventeen, and she could pass for normal, on the outside at least. Nanune was thirty, and she couldn't. Not in a million years. She simply didn't understand what was going on.

Suej finished getting Mr. Two to his feet and came over to where I was sitting. She sat the other side of Nanune and slipped her arm round her back, then put her head in close

Spares: The Missing First Chapter

to Nanune's face, making quiet sounds. There were no words, but there was reassurance. Even I could feel it. It was tunnel talk, I guess. Suej knew what to say, and I didn't.

As gently as I could, I moved out of the way.

David had the door open a couple of feet and was standing with his head poking out. Above his shoulders I could see a rectangle of pale grey sky, textured like frosted glass. David pulled his head back in, his features already shiny and reddening with the chill outside.

'It's cold,' he shrugged, stepping back out of the way. I stood in front of the gap for a moment, orientating myself to what was probably going to be outside before committing myself to being revealed.

Then I stuck my head out. What I saw was predominantly white, from the snow-covered ground in front to the hill rising sharply about a hundred yards away. The ground was criss-crossed by innumerable railway tracks, some decaying brown, a few of the others shiny grey. Most were covered in snow, making the yard look like a snake convention hiding under a sheet.

A few carriages lay dotted around the tracks, but all were covered in white and looked like they had been there for a while. Up against the foot of the hill, or mountain, was a small building, one story high. There was no light in either of its small windows, and no curl of smoke from the flue which stuck up from the flat roof. The scene appeared deserted, and had a dream-like tranquility. Had circumstances been different it might even have been nice to sit and look at it a while. It would have made a good postcard, had the intended recipient been interested in industrial archeology.

I leant out further, and checked both left and right. The tracks we'd come on spooled into the distance on the left until they met the fence. To the right there was a slightly higher concentration of carriages. They looked like abandoned toys, spread haphazardly over the matrix of rails, and the interchange seemed deserted, unused and dead. It wasn't, though. The fact that we were here proved that. It was simply arranged to a different kind of order, one created by internal structure alone. The machines which ran CybTrak weren't interested in creating pleasing tableaux. They just ran the trains on time.

'More snow,' said Jenny, from behind. It wasn't a complaint, just an excuse to name it again.

'Is it safe?' David asked, and I glanced at him before answering. He hated the fact that he couldn't tell.

'Well, what do you think?'

He hesitated. 'There's no-one around.'

'I know. Thing is, there never *is* anyone at these interchanges. It's just droids.'

'Like Ratchit?'

'Is Ratchit here?' Nanune asked. She was standing now, and looked better. I winked at Suej, who smiled. I always winked at her—it was a signal that she understood and used herself. For some reason it felt different to the way it always had, but I was careful to hide this. They needed some constants in their lives, even if we were out of the goldfish bowl.

'No,' I said. Nanune looked disappointed. Ratchit had been the support droid at the Farm. 'These are kind of like that, but not as friendly.'

Ratchit had been less than four feet tall and spent most of his working hours sweeping up, repainting the corridors and, for some reason I never established, making endless jugs of coffee. He hadn't been equipped with a laser cannon and the

Spares: The Missing First Chapter

desire to use it as often as possible, and thus was a bad marker for the next set of droids we were likely to meet.

'What are we going to do?' Suej asked.

'We're moving on,' I said. 'Stay here a moment.'

After another quick look around, I slipped through the opening and stepped down to the ground. The snow crunched under my boots with a squeak, sending a shiver up my back, a delicious, wonderful shiver. I took another step away from the train, ostensibly to get a better angle to check if anyone or anything was around, and as I did so I felt a surge of vertigo.

For a moment I was completely alone, for the first time in nearly five years. By myself, without responsibility.

I was back in the real world, and it felt fine. I wanted to keep on walking, find a town and a bar and a line of drinks, wanted to cut yesterday and the day before it off from my life, without looking back. It wasn't a matter of wanting to pick up where I'd left off: it was like I'd never been away. I wanted there to be people around, real people. For just a second I wanted to walk away from all of this, to stride the fuck away and do my own thing, however damaging that might be. I felt like I was standing upright for the first time in forever, as if the recent past was an addled dream and I was free to plummet straight back to my life.

The feeling faded quickly, but it didn't disappear. It made me turn more slowly to face the others than I should have done, but it also made me more ready to deal with them, the situation, and everything else.

Behind the train another steep hillside rose sharply, heavily covered with pines. I could see the perimeter fence right behind the carriage, so it seemed unlikely there was anything behind there to worry about.

I nodded to David and he jumped out of the carriage. Wincing, I held out my hand, and the others followed more cautiously. I have a paranoia about pressure-triggered security mechanisms that goes beyond rationality. A yard that saw trains regularly thudding cross it was unlikely to be wired to blow up in response to a footfall, but it was not a chance worth taking.

David came to stand with me. He stood with his hands thrust deep in his pockets, glancing up and down the track and intermittently kicking one of the rails. His eyes were burning with some unidentifiable emotion.

'Is it always going to be this cold?'

'Yeah. Until we get inside somewhere, this is the way it works.'

'Where are we going to go?'

'New Richmond.'

Within a couple of minutes they were all standing in a huddle by the side of the train, and I let out a heavy breath. David looked at me.

'This going be a problem, isn't it?'

'Yeah,' I said, not bothering to correct his English. It was. When we'd burst out of the Farm, running as fast as we could, I'd only expected to see David, Suej and Jenny behind me. They were the ones I'd banked on trying to take, during the split second in which I'd made the decision. But Ragald had followed, and Nanune tagged along as best she could, and suddenly there were six of us. Then, just as we got to the perimeter and were frantically kicking down the gate, I'd heard a thunderous bellow from behind, and turned to see Mr. Two lurching out of the facility, one of the other spares in his arms.

Spares: The Missing First Chapter

David had run back to help and had kept on going, despite my furious shouts at him to leave them. None of the spares were going to leave anyone behind unless they had to. I understood the impulse but it was going to fuck us up, as David was starting to realize.

He and one of the two girls who were currently corralling people at the carriage could pass for normal. Probably. In a kind light, in the right circumstances, and if I was there to mediate. Suej would have problems, Ragald and Nanune more difficulty still. They were more badly damaged, and neither could speak properly. Mr. Two would stick out like a sore thumb, and the spare he was still carrying was a total disaster. It had no arms or legs, couldn't talk, and I couldn't even remember his name. There was no point in keeping him, really. His life was going nowhere out here, and he would actually have been better off back at the Farm with the other tunnel people, mutely waiting for the inevitable. Now he was here, though, I knew the others wouldn't let me simply abandon him, however much sense it made. Even if I'd been able to convince the key three, Mr. Two would simply not have let it happen. He claimed the spare was his friend, and as Mr. Two stood well over six feet four and couldn't be reasoned with, I guessed the body was with us for the time being.

And in fact, some dark, honest part of me welcomed the fact they were there. Four of us probably wouldn't have stood a realistic chance. With eight it was simply impossible, and so I wouldn't be to blame when we died.

FIVE MINUTES later we were cautiously approaching the low building on the other side of the compound, shrouded in the last few moments of peace that the morning would bring. The yard was silent apart from the sound of our boots in the snow and the desultory cawing of a bird in some distant tree, and the spares had been firmly instructed not to make a sound. I didn't know where the hell we were going, but I didn't want a fanfare.

As we drew closer I could see that the walls of the hut were ragged and unkempt, patches of fallen paint revealing pebbles set in concrete. On the other hand, the windows were intact. Given that no human would ever go inside, it seemed odd they should be there at all, but I'd long ago learnt that machines chose to live in an odd amalgam of our two worlds, and were as much concerned with the rightness of things as anyone else. Buildings have windows. That's the way it is. Just beyond and to the right stood the main gate, and as we approached I made sure that we were never in clear view of it.

In the time it had taken us to walk to the end of the train, I'd turned occasionally, staring at the mountains and gazing the length of the yard. I was making sure there was nothing to be immediately concerned about, but I was also trying to get a fix on where we were. It felt like the Appalachians, but that was no help. We could be anywhere from Blacksburg to the North Mountains above the Shenandoah valley, or anywhere in between. For all I knew we could be in West Virginia. Pinpointing myself on the globe with the aid of nothing but peaks, pines and snow has never been my strong point. I'm a city boy. I need street names, markers. I like to know where the hell I am.

Though we'd been on the train for seven hours, I didn't think we'd have travelled very far. CybTrak trains aren't

Spares: The Missing First Chapter

allowed to go fast, because the regulators are human. The speed limit was their way both of limiting the goods the service could realistically carry, and letting the network know it remained under a carbon-based thumb. CybTrak had accepted the restriction stoically, and concentrated on obstructing the human network in any way it could, with a bloody-mindedness I frankly admired.

At the end of the carriages I glanced behind the train at the fence. It was twelve feet high and wired. I walked a few yards along the tracks and looked towards the low gate through which the trains entered and left the compound. Shut tight, and made of metal: nothing short of the correct key code would open them. Waiting for another train to trigger the gate, and trying to climb out along the carriages, wasn't an option. For a start, less than half the spares were capable of understanding such an undertaking, never mind achieving it. We also simply didn't have the time to wait. We were trespassing, and every second brought the arrival of security droids inexorably closer, droids which recognized no extenuating circumstances, no excuses, and had no sense of humor whatsoever.

So instead I walked back to the spares, who were standing or sitting in a fairly orderly group at the end of the train. Only David and Jenny seemed to have any idea of the danger we were in; David darting looks round and up and down the compound, Jenny glancing in my direction, fiddling with the buttons on the coat she was wearing. My coat, as it happened, one of three currently being worn by the bodies, the rest of whom seemed still to be in a state of shock. They were cold, hungry, and had no understanding of where they were or why. They needed to be inside, and they needed talking to.

For a moment I pointlessly wished Ratchit had made it out with us. He could have started the process of reorientation while I was trying to figure our way out. Hell, he could probably have figured it out *for* me, comforted the spares, and juggled five oranges the while. But even if he hadn't been blown to pieces the evening before, it would have been impossible. At the moment, all we had on our side was that no-one could find out where we were without actually seeing us. Ratchit could have been traced by radio.

Irritably I motioned to the spares to stand up, angry at myself rather than them. I seemed to be walking in treacle, thinking against the wind. I was just a robot myself these days, and it had been too long since I had been anything else. I was barely more used to the outside world than they were, and we were a long way from the things and places I had once understood. Maybe, further down the line, I'd be able to get in touch with someone who could help. Who that might be, I wasn't sure. I just felt I might have to throw out a line to the past, and hope something passed back up the wire to the present. At the moment the battery was empty, and each time I tried to turn the key I got nothing but a rasping click.

David took the lead when I pointed them in the direction of the main gate. Ragald and Jenny supported Nanune between them, with Suej making some use of Jenny's other shoulder to steady herself. Mr. Two lurched straight-backed behind them, the sack in his arms. He hadn't spoken since awakening, and I found it impossible to guess what his mood might be. The spare he was carrying had no moods, of course, but merely took up space. I walked to one side, keeping an eye both on the group and the areas through which we were

Spares: The Missing First Chapter

passing. The spares moved slowly, picking their way over submerged rails as if they were a yard high, and I felt a shout
begin to build behind my temples.

What a crew, I thought, brutally.

And what a fucking captain.

When we reached the hut I sent the others down along
one wall, showing them how to keep low and beneath the
windows. Then I ducked, and slipped round the other wall.
It was to our advantage that CybTrak trains did travel so
slowly. It made them an ill-favored means of transport among
runaways and criminals in flight, and so the yard wasn't
criss-crossed with interrupt beams or wired to monitor pressure on the ground, as the human network was. All we had
to worry about was the droids, little comfort though that
was. We couldn't get to the gate, which we probably wouldn't
be able to get past, without walking in front of the hut, and
so the first thing I had to do was establish if any droids were
inside. They had to be here somewhere, but though I kept
peering closely under carriages and down alleys, they were
still nowhere to be seen.

If you break into the human world, someone with a gun
and a rudimentary education will be jumping on your face
before you've drawn breath. Humans are like that. Excitable.
Machines prefer to approach sideways, and I suspect they see
time differently to us too. Their reactions are so quick, their
ability to act so instantaneous, that they don't value imme-
diacy so highly.

I remember hearing a story once about a man who scored
a magic harp from somewhere. Whenever this man wanted
to interact with a woman and needed a little space, he'd play
a chord on the harp and everyone but him and the girl would

be frozen in slow time, leaving him free to get to work. It's just my impression, and I've never discussed it with a machine, but I suspect they come equipped with such a harp as standard. The knowledge that they must be around somewhere, possibly already aware of us and simply watching with a detached curiosity, was beginning to get me on edge.

I scrabbled along the wall until I was under one of the small windows, took a breath, and straightened up for a moment before immediately crouching again.

In the second during which I could see the inside of the building, I glimpsed nothing out of the ordinary, and little of anything. No table or chairs—but that was to be expected. Though the machines kept up appearances on the outside, when they weren't on show they didn't waste time on things they didn't use. Similarly, the bank of electroware on the far wall had no monitors or dials, no banks of flashing lights. The information they manipulated was not for human consumption, and the computer which ran them simply watched its own thoughts from the inside.

I was about to have another look when suddenly I stopped. For the smallest fraction of time, I had a terrible feeling of stillness, as if someone nearby had played a harp and one second of my life had quickly expanded to fill eternity; as if I'd fallen in a road and turned in time to see the truck wheel which was to roll over my head.

I spun to look behind me, but there was nothing there.

All I could see was a carriage, partially covered in snow, its sides etched and painted with rust. There was something strange about my vision, and after a moment I recognized it. When I swung my head the procession of objects and space in front of me seemed quantized, broken up into still images. It

Spares: The Missing First Chapter

was exactly what happens when an injection of Rapt starts to kick in, and I realized I was almost certainly having a flashback.

I let out a heavy, shaky breath, and realized that my hand was inside my jacket, feeling for a weight which wasn't there. Maybe this should have reassured me, told me something about reflexes which were still miraculously intact. It didn't. It made me feel very bad indeed. For a while the yard ceased to exist around me, and I slid unthinkingly down the wall, heart beating hard and sweat appearing from nowhere on my chilled forehead and neck. The trees on the mountain appeared to shift as one and the sky seemed to blacken, hot at the edges with liquid orange flames. I heard sounds, distant cries and a siren, and it took me a long moment to realize they were coming from inside my head.

'John? What's happening?'

Closing my eyes, I swallowed deeply. The sounds faded, and then when I thought they were gone, I heard something that sounded like a scream, far away, out of reach, hidden behind shadows.

'Nothing,' I said, speaking as quietly as Suej had. My voice sounded hoarse and foreign to me. 'Stay there.'

I coughed quietly to clear my throat, and swallowed. Then I turned back to the wall and rose more slowly to take another look inside the hut. This longer look merely confirmed what I had taken in last time: there was nothing to be directly concerned about, and nothing of any use. I registered this with half of my mind, the rest elsewhere: not thinking anything specific, but simply otherwise occupied, as if watching a complex game, or listening to someone else's conversation. My hands were shaking, not sufficiently to alarm the spares, but enough to scare the shit out of me.

I now had to rely upon a rumor I'd heard a long time ago, and stake our lives on it. When I'd done that, and if it succeeded, *then* it would be time for a drink.

I shuffled round the corner to where the others were waiting. They blinked at me like a huddled family of owls.

'Time to go,' I said. 'Now listen. We're going to head round the corner, and walk quickly towards the main gate. When we get there, I'm going to try something. I want you all to keep watching the yard. Okay?'

Suej got the others to their feet, Jenny offering vague help, and I beckoned them towards me. David nodded curtly, giving me a moment to wish he hadn't seen quite so many action movies. I'd let them all watch television. I didn't have much else to offer. It wasn't much of a role model, I know, but have you seen real life these days? The problem is, in movies you always know if you're going to be able to dodge the bullets, because you've negotiated your fee and seen the script. In real life you get both top and bottom billing, get to be both hero and cannon fodder: you'll never know which until the moment comes, and perhaps not even then.

In front of the cabin was a wide flat area, presumably where goods pickups were made. It stretched to the fence, which ran right up against a nearly sheer face of rock and then turned to lead across to the other side. In the middle was the main gate, which looked suitably imposing. We walked across towards it rapidly, the skin on the back of my neck tightening.

Where were they? Where the hell were the droids? Why didn't they come and put an end to this charade?

'John, can't climb that.'

'I know, Jenny. I hope we're not going to have to.' I said. Because if we did, then we were dead.

Spares: The Missing First Chapter

I motioned the spares to stand in a loose semi-circle facing outwards, and told them to watch. I knew the task was a bit of a long-shot. All of this, from the snow to the sky, was so new to them that it was unfair to expect them to pick out anything unusual. It was all new, and everything was unusual.

A fine flurry of snow had begun to fall, with a persistence that suggested it might be settling in for a while, and this alone was going to distract most of them. Mr. Two couldn't or wouldn't get the message, and walked round in a tight circle, babbling quietly at the sack in his arms in his deep, strange voice. I decided to let him get on with it, and walked towards the gate.

'Hello,' said a female voice.

Everyone turned to stare at the gate.

'It's fine,' I said to the spares, holding out my hands in a placatory way, and backing towards the gate. 'Just keep watching.'

'What are you doing in here? You shouldn't be here.' The gate's voice was reproachful but hardly threatening, and I sent a prayer of thanks down the years to an old colleague who'd told me this trick.

'It's okay,' I said. 'We're tourists.'

'Oh, that's nice,' the gate said. 'Are you having a good time?'

'Great,' I said, carefully. 'We're really enjoying ourselves, aren't we?' I turned to nod manically at the spares, who, after a while, muttered 'yes' in bizarre unison. 'How about you, Miss?'

'Oh, I'm fine. A little cold.'

'It *is* cold, isn't it?'

'Yes. Well, nice talking to you. Enjoy the rest of your trip.'

That seemed to be it, which rather took me by surprise. David suddenly appeared at my shoulder.

'What's going on?' he said.

I turned so we wouldn't be overheard. 'The main gates were built when the compounds were used by the human network, and they made the machines keep them when they took over. The specification was for a gate intelligence which was 'a little mistrustful'. It was supposed to be ironic. But there was a typo in the order and by the time it was discovered 80 million dollars had already been spent, so they couldn't go back. They had to pretend it was deliberate.'

'So?'

'So each main gate ended up being a Little Miss Trustful instead.'

'And what's wrong with that?'

David and I whirled back to face the gate, whose tone had changed for the worse.

'Wrong with what?' I said.

'Being trustful. Is that so bad?'

'No,' I said, packing my voice with sincerity. 'It's lovely.'

'Everyone's so horrible these days, you know, and I just think it's better to be nice to people, you know?' The gate's voice was rising in pitch. 'Everyone has their good side, if you look hard enough for it.'

'Oh, I know,' I soothed. 'You're *so* right.'

'The droids all hate me.'

'I'm sure they don't.'

I looked quickly behind, and saw the spares were beginning to mill around. The snow was falling harder, with flakes half an inch across spiraling down to frost everything that was not already covered. That included the spares, who with few exceptions were staring at the snow with incomprehension. When you looked across the yard it was now difficult to

Spares: The Missing First Chapter

see the other side, as if the area we were in was being made smaller and pulled closer by the moment. Nanune had started crying again, Ragald was looking at the sky and blinking rapidly, and the circles Mr. Two was describing were getting tighter and faster. The snow had broken their concentration, and they were also being affected by the tone of the gate's voice, which was sounding more and more upset. It was also getting louder, which was making *me* unhappy.

'They do *so*', the gate insisted, sounding on the verge of virtual tears. 'They think I'm dumb.'

'Hey, what do they know? They just go round shooting people the whole time.'

'That's *right*. That's all they do.' The gate was now shrill in its indignation. 'What kind of an attitude is that? It's just so *hostile*.'

'Speaking of the droids,' I said, but then there was a wail from behind. Suej and Jenny called my name simultaneously, and I turned impatiently to see that Mr. Two had fallen on his back, the sack still in his arms.

'Oh, get up,' I snapped.

Mr. Two let out another shout, a short bark, and tried to regain his feet. He thrashed about with his legs, at least, but only succeeded in propelling himself round in a circle in the snow.

I turned to the gate. 'Excuse me a moment.'

'Of course,' it said.

I strode over to the spare and throttled back on the verge of yelling at him. Instead I knelt and grabbed his shoulders to stop him spinning. He barked again and stared at me, apparently not recognizing what he saw, and tried to jerk himself upright. The sack slipped from his arms and fell open. The body's head popped out, gazing straight ahead with a meaningless smile on its face.

'Nap,' it said.

'Mr. Two,' I hissed, urgently, 'What the fuck is the problem here?' The sound of my voice cut through some haze or mist in his mind, and he snapped his head to look at me with an expression I'd never seen before. He made three more sounds, shorter than his previous barks, and then shouted a word I recognized.

'There!'

'What?' I asked, trying to get my hands behind to lever him to his feet. 'What?'

He abruptly thrust out one of his hands, and after a moment's consideration, pointed with one of his fingers. The eyes of the spare in the sack rolled with surprising fluency to follow the direction of his finger, and I did my best to follow suit, though Mr. Two's arm was waving wildly around. He seemed to be pointing across the yard in the general direction we'd come from, though at what I couldn't tell. All I could see were the increasingly indistinct shapes of carriages bulking in the snow.

'Moven! Moven!'

'Suej,' I called, desperately, 'What's he saying? We've got to go.'

She ran over and crouched by Mr. Two. David was pacing up and down by the fence, looking across at us with undisguised distaste. Jenny was standing by herself, still fiddling with her buttons, looking lost and alone.

'Whatwhat?' Suej asked. 'Whatwhat see?'

'Moven!' Mr. Two shouted.

'Moven what?'

Exasperated, I let my head drop, and again caught sight of the half body's eyes. A snowflake fell on one and melted

Spares: The Missing First Chapter

slowly as the spare sluggishly blinked, and then he opened his mouth grotesquely wide and clamped it shut again. Something in the movement, in the mindlessness of it, made me shudder in a way I hadn't done since first I'd seen the Farm. Maybe it was because we were outside now, and such things weren't normal any more. Maybe because I was different. Maybe it was just an unpleasant thing to see. I jerked my eyes upwards again and gazed unseeing into the snow, hoping this part would be over soon, that it would *all* be over soon.

'Mr. Two, *whatwhat* moven?' Suej had grabbed the spare by the lapels of the overalls he wore, and was staring directly into his face, trying by force of will to pull sense out of his brain through his eyes. 'Is white fallen? Is...'

'Oh shit,' I said. Finally I'd seen what was moving.

Suej turned, saw the expression on my face, and looked over her shoulder.

Out in the yard, at the edge of what could still be seen through the falling snow, a carriage was now moving.

Not a whole train, but a single carriage, and not in a single direction. With a liquid, unhurried smoothless, the carriage was dismantling itself. What had looked like a sliding door tilted away to connect with two long, jointed sections that had appeared to be runners. The roof divided into four sections like an assembly film run backwards, and peeled back to meet solidly in another shape altogether.

'What's that?' David shouted, stopping dead at the fence. 'What the *hell* is that?'

He walked slowly towards us, eyes wide and mouth hanging open, for once looking as young as he was.

From out of the blur the sounds continued, firm clanks and thuds as the droids reassembled themselves with perfect economy of movement. How clever to disguise themselves as a carriage, to knit their bodies together and let snow fall on them. Very clever. Far too smart for me. For my conscious brain, anyway—some other part had felt something, but I'd let my brain override. Once upon a time the two parts worked together, but that was too long ago, and too far away.

I grabbed Mr. Two's arm, pushed Suej away, and hauled him up. With the other hand I snatched the sack and threw it to David, who caught it clumsily. The chuckle which came from the spare inside seemed somehow entirely consistent with the situation.

I shoved Mr. Two in the direction of the main gate and he lurched towards it, probably more in the hope of retrieving his friend than because he understood what was going on. Though who knows? He was the only one who'd watched well enough to spot when something moved.

I ran to Nanune, who was wrapped in a fetal position, and lifted her in my arms, shouting at Ragald to follow. Jenny screamed suddenly and shrilly, a noise which cut the air for a moment but fell deadened against the falling snow.

I staggered toward the gate, Nanune twisting in my arms, trying not to fall as I glanced across the yard. The carriage was no longer. In its place two large shapes were becoming clearer as they began to move in our direction. No hurry, no waste of effort. Just inexorable and unkind.

Turning back, I saw David with his foot poised to kick the gate and shouted at him to stop.

'Get Ragald,' I said. 'Get him quickly,' and he ran back towards the remaining spare, who was standing alone in the loading area, looking around with baffled terror.

Spares: The Missing First Chapter

When I got to the gate I let Nanune slide out of my arms. Suej grabbed her and held her upright.

'Miss,' I said to the gate, quietly and firmly, trying to keep my voice level. 'We have to go now. Our tour party is waiting outside for us.'

'They'll be here soon, I'm sure. They won't leave you behind, not if they're professionals.'

'You don't understand. We have to go meet them.'

'Oh no, that can't be right,' the robot voice said, primly. 'Pickups are *always* made in the yard. You don't need to go outside. Wait here. You'll see.'

'Oh Jesus,' I muttered, and turned to see if David had Ragald. David was still stumbling towards the other spare, who was staring at him, either not understanding or not processing David's shouts.

Then, terribly, he began to run away.

I bolted after him. Ragald was hooting unintelligibly, his face a churning mixture of excitement and fear, and he was hopping backwards in the snow in the direction of the hut. Maybe he was heading toward it, maybe not. I suspect he was simply running away from everything he could see.

Suej shouted my name. The droids were closer now, bright points of lights in their panels visible for the first time. They made no sound but for the heavy crunch of metal on snow, nor would they. They wouldn't warn or negotiate. They hadn't been constructed to see the need.

I turned to face Ragald again, who was still staggering towards the building. I had a brief, irrelevant glimpse of what it might mean to him, why he might think being inside somewhere would solve all his problems, and then I tripped over a rail or tool hidden in the snow and fell flat on my face.

The momentum was enough to skid me a couple of painful yards across the yard. Before I'd even stopped sliding I planted my hands down hard and started to push myself up again, head raised. I didn't make it to my feet immediately, and the next second was printed on my mind with the still clarity of a photograph.

From behind and to my left a bolt of energy shot across the yard, an absolutely straight burst of rich orange light which lit the falling snow from within.

The bolt hit Ragald in the back of the neck and destroyed everything above his waist. I saw two useless spurts of arterial blood, taken by surprise by the lack of an upper body, and then I shut my eyes.

Moving without thinking I rolled instead of getting up, turning over and over, trying to get away from the line I'd been on, feeling as if I was sliding through a red slick of blood. When I was a couple of yards from the fence I struggled to my feet, slipping on the ice compacted underneath the snow, my hands beginning to lose feeling. Only then, as I started to run toward them, did I notice the rest of the spares were standing absolutely still, staring at what remained of Ragald.

The droids had made a detour towards his corpse and were standing over it, looking like two enormous praying mantises fashioned out of rusty metal.

When I was within ten feet of the gate I started shouting. 'Let us out. Please, Miss, *let us out.*'

'Wait here, silly. It's safer.'

'The *fuck* it is,' I said, reaching out to shake the gate, but stopping myself just in time. 'Miss. Listen to me. Please. Our tour operators are bad. Very bad. Not professional. They've abandoned us.'

Spares: The Missing First Chapter

The droids had concluded whatever purpose they had with Ragald's body, and were turning in our direction with slow and considered intent.

'I'm sorry to hear that.'

'Yes. It's a huge downer for all of us. Look, will you just let us out, so we can look for them? We're cold, it's snowing—'

Another spear of orange light slashed through the curtain of snow, and miraculously missed both Jenny and the gate, neatly bisecting the space between two of its uprights. 'Plus, the droids *are shooting at us.*'

'So I see. Hmm. Well. Will you come back later and sign a form, when you've found your operators? I do think we should make a formal complaint.'

'I'll sign anything you like.' I could feel the ground shaking now, as the droids made their ponderous way towards us. 'But we *really* have to go, Miss. We won't get a refund if we die.'

There was a hesitant pause, and then the gate began slowly to swing open, pushing against accumulated snow on the other side.

The heavy footsteps behind immediately started speeding up. The snow must have been confusing their infra-red: I can't imagine why else they'd bother to close in, unless it was just for sport.

I yelled at the spares to run through the gate. Suej pushed Nanune, and I shoved Mr. Two, who was now carrying the sack with the other spare again. Jenny and David remained motionless, staring down the yard, their faces set.

'Fetch Ragald,' David said.

'No,' I said, grabbing Jenny's arm. 'Ragald's dead.'

'There's some left,' David shouted hoarsely.

'Not enough,' I said, directing my eyes at Jenny, trying to breathe understanding into her. 'Not nearly enough.'

She looked down the end once more, and then allowed herself to be dragged through the gate by the others. David hesitated. He started to follow but then fell, at the same time, it seemed, as another bolt of the sun crashed into the snow at his feet.

He looked up at me, face white except where the cold had turned it red, and I smelt burning.

The droids were now running at us, and another bolt missed my head by about a foot.

'Cut,' David said, quietly. 'Operation. Leg cut.'

I leaned over, grabbed his arm and pulled him out of the yard like a sack of wood. The gate was already closing again, and clipped his feet as they came through. But the charge was off, and he came out safely. I kept tugging at him as the gate swung inward, and we were ten feet away when they finally resealed.

The two security droids stopped simultaneously, an inch short of the fence, a different piece of armament poised and locked on every one of us. They towered several feet over the top of the gate, with nothing resembling a face. We stared back at them, knowing we wouldn't have time to move, and waited in the quiet, snow still drifting down around us like paper rain.

Their world was inside the gates. We were no longer inside, and so no longer existed.

Without turning round, for they had no front or back, the droids moved back from the gate like a pair of skeletal houses.

As the spares watched them disappear into the gloom, I dropped to David's side and looked at his leg.

Spares: The Missing First Chapter

'Just skin,' he said brightly, 'Just a graft'. When I checked, I saw he was right. He grinned up at me like a child, and flexed his leg. It was evidently painful, but not disastrous. I held a handful of snow against the burn for a moment, and after initially wincing, the skin round David's eyes relaxed a little.

As one, the other spares walked over and stood in a circle round us. Mr. Two helped me to get David to his feet, still holding his friend in the sack under his other arm, like a small and shapeless dog. Jenny put her arm round David's back, and I watched as they took a few steps towards the fence. The other spares followed, leaving me a couple of yards behind.

They formed into a line six feet from the gate, and were quiet for a moment. I watched in silence. I had seen them do this before, on the farm, but out here it was somehow weirder. They looked no more natural than the droids had, and I felt very different from them.

'Goodbye, Ragald,' Suej said, and they all suddenly thrust out their arms towards the gate, as if pushing something away, some force they could not control but only resist with all they had. Their eyes were wide and cold, and when they dropped their arms David held his up a moment longer, and flipped the compound the one obscene gesture I'd taught him.

Fair enough, I thought.

The Straw Men: Excerpt from Ch. 29, First Draft

by Michael Marshall Smith

The first draft of *The Straw Men* was quite different to the novel that was eventually published. Different people died, different people survived, familial relationships were altered, and it was even written under a (slightly) different name ("Michael Marshall"). The underlying story motor was a good deal more fantastical, too, though that only emerged in the late stages, and in a low-key way. I was trying to form a bridge between the three quite otherworldly books I'd written before and one set in a more realistic modern-day landscape. My editor judged that I had not succeeded, and she was almost certainly right. After a long period of wailing and gnashing of teeth I re-wrote the second half of the novel pretty much from scratch, and while I sometimes mourn the odder book it might have been, I'm confident that it's much better as it is now.

This excerpt comes a chapter just before the climax of the first draft, and gives some indication (for those who know the book) of just how different parts of it were.

Chapter 29 [Excerpt]

ONCE THERE HAD been two baby girls, just as there had been two little boys. The two sets of twins were born only a year apart, the boys a little older, but they arrived to parents of very different types. The girls were born in Switzerland, to a family which had then come to America when they were three years old. They came because it was known that one day, they would be needed there. As had been predicted, many years previously, the two lines had thrown up extremes at the same time. Their opposites had already been born.

When the girls reached the age of fifteen their parents explained a little of how the world was. They explained that there existed a spectrum of people. That some were of different colours, and some believed different things, but that there was a more important difference underlying these superficial qualities. In the very distant past, something had happened to the people on earth. A change had come upon them, something so deep and intrinsic that for a long time nobody had even questioned it. This change had been so intangible, and varied so widely in extent, that at first it had merely been observed that some people behaved one way, while others were different. That some had become social, while others still

The Straw Men:
Excerpt from Ch. 29, First Draft

howled in the night, prowling outside the gates. It was further
explained that while for thousands of years this situation had
been allowed to progress under the auspices of evolution and
natural selection, science would soon approach a point where
we could intervene in it, for good or ill—and interfere in it
without understanding what we were doing. It would depend
on who did the intervening. Who owned the knowledge.

Because it was in their nature, the girls' parents did not
seek to make a value judgement. They did not insist that one
extreme of this condition was good, the other evil, and they
made it clear that the spectrum of change operated equally
across all races and both sexes. Some people were one way,
some the other. Most lay somewhere in between. One group
was more 'human' in the sense of the species' genetic purity;
the other in the quality of its humanity. In an ideal world,
that would be all that needed to be said. The girls were old
enough to have encountered facial blemishes and bad boy-
friends and nagging anxieties that came and went. They
already understood that this is not an ideal world.

Twins are common amongst people at extreme ends of the
spectrum. They are the natural reproductive means of our species, and only rare for a time because of the conflicting material
hidden within the average human's genetic material—these
small biochemicals that no-one truly understands, even though
we have named and numbered them now and are preparing to
make decisions on an individual's viability on their basis. Twins,
like couples, are a natural feature of our kind, an automatic
group of two, a mutual defence system against the world and
its predators. A litter. Countless millions of people have been
born alone because their twin failed in the womb, the casualty
of two genetic systems failing to work utterly in harmony. Now,

because of in-vitro techniques, they are growing in frequency once more, and that is largely a good thing—another example of how the 'disease' works: slowly, culturally, and in its own time. While the boys had been non-identical, the girls exactly resembled each other. It would be easy to claim that this was a manifestation of the underlying differences between the two pairs, that the boys' fundamental make-up promoted difference, that the girls' tended towards consensus—but in fact it was merely a matter of reproductive chance. Many viral twins are non-identical too. It just happened that Nina and Naomi looked exactly the same.

The girls' parents were murdered, but by then their daughters were out in the world and trying to change it. Neither understood this was what they were doing. They had been told only a very little, and had simply found themselves drawn to certain fields. Nina joined the FBI, and progressed with a speed which earned her the enmity of many of her colleagues. Law enforcement is an area of great conflict, as many of its protagonists are finely balanced on the spectrum: dedicated to maintaining the fabric of a complex society, but fundamentally predestined to hunt. Nina learned to track serial killers, some of whom are the most acutely non-viral men and women in the world, those for whom the culture her disease had helped engender simply didn't exist. Not all of them—many are merely the manifestation of conflicting societal pressures, abuse, and physical damage: but there are those who find themselves drawn to certain ways of behaviour, who murder and maim and kill: who make no distinction between humans and other forms of prey. Such is the way we all used to be.

Naomi meanwhile became an academic, studying the way in which a gracile ape had switched tracks, becoming

The Straw Men:
Excerpt from Ch. 29, First Draft

first a scavenger, then a hunter, and then—quite suddenly—
a farmer.

During all of this time the two women kept closely in
touch, while keeping the other's existence a secret from the
world at large. They had been told from an early age that
they were special. They knew that they must never be in danger together. That they must survive.

Then Nina was killed.

Working now without John Zandt, she had been tracking
a man who appeared to have murdered three black prosti-
tutes. She was drawn to a decayed motor court at night by a
trail of evidence that in retrospect could be seen to be too
self-evident. It was a set-up. There was no such killer. The
FBI is not without Straw Men influence, of course. There
is no institution or town where they do not exist, whether
they know it or not.

There is a loose group of humans across the world who
know the situation, who oppose those amongst the non-virals
who have learnt what underlies our differences. But the viral
conclave acts in an entirely different fashion, never overtly
interfering in the overall march of history. That is not the
viral way, which is predicated upon a long and slow progress
of overall change, on a process of assimilation. Chance is the
medium of evolution, and necessity its engine.

Naomi was contacted, and told she must take Nina's
place. It was not explained why. She was not told that they
had come to believe that a man Nina had worked with might
have been one of a pair of boys who had vanished many years
before. Neither was she told that the killer they had been
chasing was now believed to be a man who had come relatively recently to the Straw Men, awakened after almost being

one of their victims in a small town called Palmerston in 1991, and now a senior figure amongst them. She was merely told where to find John Zandt, and that she must help him to find the Upright Man—using Zandt as bait if necessary.

The Straw Men were gathering.

Where the Upright Man was, they would be.

NINA SPOKE quickly and concisely, as if she'd had a great deal of time to consider what she told us. I suppose she must have done, especially after the death of her sister. I wondered whether she'd stayed on in Hunter's Rock after all, or if instead she'd perhaps gone somewhere to force a little more information out of someone, to get a bigger hint of what she'd become involved in. She kept her head down as she spoke, and didn't make eye contact, but none of us interrupted.

'So how come you didn't tell us any of this in Hunter's Rock?' Bobby asked, when she ground to a halt.

'I didn't know that Ward was what he is,' she said. 'And at that time my job was to help find the Upright Man. Nothing else.'

I held up a hand at Bobby, to hush him.

'And what Mary said back there was true?'

She nodded. 'As far as I know. There was some detail I hadn't heard. But otherwise it fits. It explains what happened, and Don and Philippa were definitely known to the conclave. They gave a great deal of money to the cause. Never mind anything else. I don't know how you've come to think of your foster parents, but they dedicated their lives to you. You should have been very different.'

The Straw Men:
Excerpt from Ch. 29, First Draft

I put my hand out, and took one of hers. She looked at me. Her eyes were of the darkest brown, her face a combination of lines and planes that could not have been better arranged. I knew then that I would always need to see it.

'I want to believe what you're saying,' I said. 'And my father did leave me a message. But he didn't hint at any of this, and there were many far more direct ways he could have used. Like the phone, for instance. Email. A singing telegram.'

'He was not supposed to tell you. But he evidently decided he didn't want to leave you in total ignorance. He set a trail, and left it to chance. That is our way.'

'Okay,' I said, and was quiet a moment. I was picturing my parents in their last days, knowing that something or someone was coming for them. Trying to work out the best thing to do. Knowing they were not allowed to say anything to me, and that doing so might undo something to which they had secretly dedicated their lives. But then leaving something, a small sign, to the son they had loved in spite of where he had come from, in spite of the man who had been his father, and in spite of my lack of contact. 'But in the video it's a girl they abandoned.'

'How do you know?'

'Well,' I said. 'My mother called her my 'sister'. I regarded that as a significant pointer.'

'That's all?'

'She was dressed in yellow, I was in blue.' Suddenly it didn't seem like a whole lot. Pink, for example, might have been a clearer statement.

Zandt spoke. 'Where was she left?'

'I don't know.' I shrugged. 'A city somewhere.'

He waited a long time before continuing. 'Could it have been San Francisco?'

I stared at him. 'Yes. It could. Why?'

'I was adopted,' he said. 'The police found me wandering the streets, a small child, and were unable to trace where I'd come from. I didn't know anything about it until I was sixteen. After my folks had told me, they gave me a bag I'd had when I was found. Kind of small and green. There was nothing in it. Except this.'

He pulled out his keys and held them out to me. 'I drilled a hole in it, used it as a key ring. The people I grew up with were okay. I wasn't going to go looking for whoever dumped me. But I've carried it on me ever since.' He breathed out heavily.

I looked at the key fob. It was about an inch high, and made of oddly-shaped metal. Kind of a blob, with a smaller blob on the top. It looked as if it had been part of something bigger, something which at some point in the distant past someone had hack-sawed in half.

I reached into my jacket and pulled out a small piece of metal which had been handed to me by the woman who now lived at our old house in Hunter's Rock. Now that I'd seen the other half, it was obvious what it was, even before I fitted them together. So obvious I couldn't believe I hadn't identified my half before.

It was a small metal replica, about two inches high, of the Willendorf Venus. A Neolithic fertility symbol, showing a stylised woman, found many years ago in Europe.

'Christ,' I said. 'You guys aren't kidding about leaving things to chance.'

'Chance has nothing to do with it,' Nina said. Or Naomi, I guess. 'You two were always going to meet. Events would

The Straw Men:
Excerpt from Ch. 29, First Draft

have conspired towards drawing you back together. The only question was what would happen then, which is why they wanted someone like me present.'

I handed Zandt his keys back. It felt bizarre. I found I was caught between wanting to stare at him, and the desire to run away.

'But who is the Upright Man?' Bobby asked. 'What's his name?'

Nina shook her head. 'He doesn't have one. The true Straw Men don't believe in names. They say we should live in groups small enough that we can recognise each other by sight.'

I nodded. 'If you don't know me, you don't belong. The cry of street gangs and corner boys everywhere.'

'The Straw Men are strong in the inner cities,' she said. 'The more crowded people are, the more they fight. But actually, it's the same in the comfortable middle classes. The average adult Christmas card list runs to—what? A maximum of sixty people? It's a tribe. Sixty names on a list. The people you *know*.'

She turned to Zandt. Or my brother, I suppose. 'This is why I couldn't explain why Nina stopped her affair with you. It *wasn't me*. And she didn't say why. Maybe she found out what you were and didn't tell me. She could be like that, at times.'

'She could,' Zandt said. 'She truly could.'

There was quiet for a moment, and then Bobby looked meaningfully at the car, and then back at me.

'Yes,' I said. 'Time to get on.'

'We shouldn't go up there,' Naomi said. 'Really. I don't know what they're doing up at this place, but it's going to be bad and none of us should be there. Not me and especially neither of you. We should just turn around and find some-where else to be.'

'No deal,' I said, 'I owe these people a visit.'

'Ward, please. That's not how we do things.'

'Maybe.' I said. 'But you know what?'

Zandt finished for me. 'It's the way *we* do things.'

Introduction to *Ash Wednesday*: The Missing Chapter

by Chet Williamson

When my first two novels, *Soulstorm* and *Ash Wednesday*, were sold to Tor Books in 1985, I determined that I would be as cooperative an author as possible. So when the editor wanted to cut the last fifteen pages of *Ash Wednesday*, I moaned, but agreed, not really knowing that there was any alternative (like digging in my heels and screaming no). The editor felt it would be most effective to end with the birth scream of a new world, while I had preferred to view some of the labor pains and hint at the possibilities of that world. Though I offered several alternate endings, my attempts were unsuccessful, and the book was published without the intended ending.

When readers commented on the book, many felt that the ending was extremely abrupt. I let several people read the original, and the responses were so positive that I tried to have it restored to the paperback, but to no avail.

A warning—please don't read it unless you have first read the book, because it isn't simply an excised *chapter*, it's the bloody *ending*, and you won't have any idea of what's going on, so that it won't be at all meaningful when you find out that all the characters get run over by a beer truck (whoops). So run right out to your local Waldenbooks or Acme Markets or Slim's Sleazy Books or wherever lurid paperbacks are sold in your town, and buy a copy. Then, if you like the ending below, cut it out (buying a second issue of *Detours*, of course), and glue it into the back of the paperback so that it won't fit on the shelf with your other books. If you *don't* like the original ending, keep your issue intact, your paperback unglued, and tell me what a moron I am at the next convention, buying me a drink first to ease the criticism...

What follows are the closing pages to my novel, *Ash Wednesday*, that did not appear in the final, edited book. Bill Munster has been kind enough to offer to print the original ending here to satisfy the curiosity of those who have asked about it. I might add that the following will make no sense whatsoever unless you have first read the book, published by Tor in both hardcover and paperback editions (not-so-subtle plug).

Ash Wednesday:
The Missing Chapter

by Chet Williamson

I T SPREAD OVER the world like ink on tissue, slowly, inexorably, from the center outward until no whiteness remains, its focal point was Merridale, and it began at dawn. Lansford was the first city of any size that it reached, Gettysburg the first site of utter horror. Few tourists were up at that hour, so the battlefield roads were nearly empty. But the early risers—truck drivers, people on their way to six A.M. shifts, anyone awake and about at the time who used the smooth two-lanes that passed the Wheatfield, Devil's Den, the site of Pickett's Charge—all were plunged into a scene worthy of the imagination of a Dante, a de Sade, a Hitler. Thousands of men stood, fell, lay dead in time, as the ball had struck them, as the shell had burst, as the bayonet tore away their lives. They littered the roadways, still warring to occupy the same space in the crisp March air, but warring without motion. Cars and trucks bounced off roads into low ditches and against stone walls. There were new deaths from injuries and heart attacks. When the rest of the town woke and realized, there were several suicides. By the time the first ambulances went out for the injured, the Wheatfield was an unbroken plain of blue.

TWA Flight 405 was the first plane to experience contact with the phenomenon. In the corridor a charred and dismembered corpse seemed to swoop down its length, its left arm and what remained of its right thrown up in the air as if in surprise. Half the head was missing, and a witness recalled later that it looked like a lump of grayish ice cream from which a serving had been scooped.

A man in first class turned away from his window as the ruined body of an old woman shot past, only to catch a glimpse in the seat beside him of a young child whose head was nearly severed from his lacerated body.

A college student went into hysterics as the crushed upper torso of a young woman streamed through his seat back, then rushed through his own body.

In the cockpit, the pilot saw a coalescence of body scraps whirl by as if in the teeth of a storm.

From the time Flight 405 reached the accident site to the moment it left was less than two seconds.

⟲→

THE WIRE services had the story by the time the phenomenon reached New York City, so there were those who were at least partially prepared, although most New Yorkers awoke

Ash Wednesday: The Missing Chapter

completely innocent of the knowledge that the nightmare had come from the two-storied buildings of Merridale to breach their steel and concrete towers. There was panic. There were deaths that led to greater panic. Morning rush hour subway tunnels exploded with screams, crosstown busses turned into cages of frightened children. Taxis, cars all stopped as people ran futilely, quickly discovering that there was nowhere left to hide in this ultimate gridlock.

In Washington, D.C. Clyde Thornton's immediate supervisor had just finished his third cup of coffee and a memorial address to be read before Congress, when a naked, old man in chinwhiskers whom he had never seen before sat in thin air on the other side of his office. The living man sat frozen for a moment, then muttered, "Oh God…oh my God," and grabbed for his telephone. Every number he tried was busy.

At a breakfast in the White House Rose Room, the president and ten congressional leaders all rattled their cups or dropped their silverware when faced with the presence of three undressed men in various reclining postures. Only later, after the officials had run out only to be confronted by similar wraiths, were the three identified as Grover Cleveland, Franklin Pierce, and Warren Harding.

Once over their initial shock, the information transmitting facilities of New York and Washington began to move, so that news of the phenomenon's spread proved speedier than the phenomenon itself, an early warning system of expanding revenants. Though, as in a nuclear attack, there was no way to pull back the array of bombs and the growing stain of fallout, there was at least a herald of things to come. Though the rest of the world would wait with fear, they at least knew that they were waiting. The great majority would not be caught by surprise.

In new, shiny, underground rooms relatively free of the apparitions, it was determined that the phenomenon was spreading at the rate of 1670 kilometers per hour, and showed no signs of stopping or slowing. Calls were made to the Soviet bloc in an effort to prevent any retaliatory strikes against what might be interpreted as a hostile attack. The calls were successfully concluded, thanks in no small part to Soviet officials in Washington who were convinced that the phenomenon resulted from a technology far in advance of any known scientific community, a view which was seconded by their superiors.

Further calls were made to Europe, India, South America, Africa, the Middle East. Explanations were given, preparations were made.

IN MERRIDALE, Joan Craven was vacuuming the living room when the news hit the *Today* show. The Hoover was too loud for her to hear the voices, but she saw the words, "Merridale Disaster Spreading," in fat, block letters on the screen behind the announcer, a thick-set, robust man who looked suddenly pale and sickly. She turned off the cleaner, dashed across the room to the TV, and turned up the volume. After listening for a few seconds, she called to her husband. "Bob? *Bob!*"

He came running shirtless into the room, "What's wrong?" he asked startled. "Are you okay?"

She gestured toward the screen. They both watched, listened.

"My God," Craven finally whispered. "Oh my dear God."

Joan looked at him. His skin was chalky and he was shaking, but his face was filled with excitement, his eyes

Ash Wednesday: The Missing Chapter

with joy. He grasped her shoulders in his big hands. "It's Ash Wednesday. Today is Ash Wednesday." Turning back to the screen, he laughed. "I was right. Even though I didn't believe it myself, I was *right*. There *was* a reason. To get them ready. All the rest of them..."

"You *were* right," Joan agreed, hugging him.

"We'll have to pray now. Pray for all of them." He shook his head, "Imagine what it must be like. In the cities. Other places." The thought of Auschwitz came to his mind. Hiroshima. Even San Francisco. There would be places on earth, he thought with sadness, that would be unbearable, uninhabitable. But that was the price you paid for realization, for truth.

Craven took his wife's hands. "God help them," he prayed. "God help them to bear it. And God help them to *see*."

↩→

The world saw. It saw far more than it could have wished.

Cuba's ghosts, bloodied in revolution and war.

Settlers, massacred and scalped; Indians, tortured in revenge.

Fleshy, blue remnants deep in Chilean dungeons.

Sacrifices with rended chests on the altars of Tlaloc.

The scattered dead on America's highways.

And it was not yet noon.

↩→

THE NURSES and doctors at Lansford General were used to death, so it took them a far shorter time to adjust to what had occurred early that morning than it had the general public.

The patients, unfortunately, were not quite as resilient. Cries of "Nurse! Nurse!" had cut through the halls and rooms for hours, while nurses and orderlies and even surgeons scurried down halls and into rooms, moving beds and shoving the curtained barriers framed by metal poles into place to hide as best they could the forms of the dead from the living.

By 10:00 A.M., when Alice Meadows entered the hospital, the worst of the initial panic was over. US 15 has been heavy with traffic, as people sought to flee, then changed their minds as the radio informed them that there was nowhere to flee to. It had taken her ninety minutes to make what was usually a twenty minute drive. Once in Lansford, the streets were nearly blocked with cars, husbands returning home from work to their families, people trying to reach their friends across town, and everywhere the dogs barked and howled, lending higher, more strident tones to the hundreds of car horns. Finally, Alice had pulled into a small lot a half mile from the hospital and walked the rest of the way.

The hospital seemed far more quiet than she had imagined, although the mingled mass of blue, floating corpses that was revealed when the elevator doors opened persuaded her to take the stairs to the fifth floor. *Dead from trauma*, she thought. Accident, murder. Unnatural death.

The stairway and the fifth floor hall were relatively free of ghosts. When she thought about it, it seemed logical: where do people die in hospitals? In their rooms, or on the operating tables, and even then the heart attack victims, the cancer patients, the more or less natural deaths would be at home, in their offices, the places they haunted in life; and she marveled once again at the *selectivity* of whatever was behind all this. You could no longer sweep the bodies away, bury them

Ash Wednesday: The Missing Chapter

in trenches, or burn them on piles to hide them from the sight of the living. *No. We're stuck with our dead now.*

Jim was smiling when she entered his room. His bed was pushed against the wall in a space that had yesterday held a chair and a small metal dresser. A barrier hid the greater part of the room from her view. She kissed him, then cocked her head toward the curtains. "Bad?"

He nodded. "Not so good to wake up to. There are only three or four, though. This is a newer wing."

"Ring for the nurse?"

"Not right away. I figured they'd have enough troubles. Besides, I was used to them, being from Merridale." He smiled. "I just closed my eyes, told myself the boogeymen all over me and *in* me couldn't do a blessed thing, and decided to go back to sleep."

"Did you?"

"I'm not *that* jaded. Of course not." They laughed together. Then he sobered and pointed to the TV mounted high on the wall. The picture was on, but the sound was off. "It's spreading fast, they say. Soon it'll be everywhere."

She nodded. "I wonder if that's good or bad."

"Bad at first, I guess. The panic, people bashing their cars into telephone poles, maybe killing themselves. But all in all I'm grateful for it. In the long run it could be for the best."

"How is it today?" she asked, taking his hand.

He looked down at his sheeted stomach. "Not bad. Hurts, but they keep me doped. Last night the doctor said maybe another week."

"And then?"

"Then Pittsburgh. If they get all the wrecks off the road by then."

"They will. We're a very adaptable race."

"I hope we're impressionable too. Are you still leaving today?"

She shook her head. "I'd never get back to New York. The trains, the highways, the tunnels, it'd be hell. I'll wait a bit."

"How long?"

"A few days. A week." Alice shrugged. "There'll still be shows, movies. People will still want to laugh, and listen to music. Love songs."

"Stay in the house..."

"We'll see."

"...as long as you like."

"Thank you." She nodded acceptance, although she already had her things packed and in the trunk of the car. She would find a motel when she left the hospital, and wait for things to cool down. The house on Sundale Road was no longer hers. The decision to end their relationship had truly been a joint one. He no longer needed what she had given him, and her need for what he had provided was gone as well. The phone call she'd received Monday evening had helped her make her decision.

"I won't...can't visit you anymore," she said.

"I'll miss you."

"And I'll miss you," she half-lied, "but only for a while."

"Thank you for what you did."

Alice kissed him on the lips, wanting to end it, wanting to leave before Beth arrived. She had not told him she was coming. She still cared enough about him to not want to see the expectation in his eyes. "Goodbye."

When she was at the door he said, "I'll write," and she responded, "Me too," and left knowing that neither of them ever would.

Ash Wednesday: The Missing Chapter

On her way out of the building, she passed Beth, recognizing her from a picture Jim had on the piano. Alice did not introduce herself, but only watched as Beth moved through the lobby with a firm yet graceful stride, eyes set only on the path ahead, the dead past forgotten.

When she finally vanished around a corner, Alice stepped outside into the blaring and barking, and began to resume her life.

↩→

OLD EUROPE, filled with ghosts, was touched during Merridale's early afternoon, at the same time the phenomenon claimed northern Africa, the Hawaiian Islands, and northern Russia via the North Pole. As the circle widened, the rest of the world wasted in horror. Beirut, rebuilt, trembled. Japan's shrines were filled. India recalled its long history, its innumerable plagues and famines, and looked to its ancient gods. China, under its layer of official stoicism toward spiritual affairs, was chilly with fear.

At the moment the sun set in Merridale, the circle closed, populating the world twice over. No country, no continent, no race was spared the sight of its dead. Animals howled and whined and whimpered; adults and older children wept while the young looked on without understanding, often crying only in sympathy for their unhappy parents. For a time the entire planet was mad with grief and fright.

Except for Merridale. And the people who lived, and had lived, there.

↩→

"CHEWING GUM is a poor excuse for a cigarette," Eddie Karl said gruffly from his bed in Lansford General.

He twisted his head uncomfortably and looked up, but was unable to see any more of the TV screen than a thin slash of blue-white light. "Don't know why they hadda move us," he complained to his roommate. "Can't even see the damn TV. That color's somethin', I ain't got color at home." He listened to the newscaster for a while, looking out the window over the tops of the nearby buildings to where an early evening moon shone. He was on the seventh floor, too high to see any of the blue forms below.

"The whole world," he said after a while, "The whole fuckin' world. Startin' here and goin' out and around, like somebody wrappin' the world up or puttin' a glove on it or somethin'. Y'know…" He leaned back and turned his head toward his roommate. Their beds were head to head in a line from the door to the far wall. The rest of the room was hidden. "…if I wasn't a religious man I think I'd become one after this. Now I don't go to church, but nobody said that don't make you religious. But if I was a goddam atheist or an agnostic, I'd change my mind fiddle-fuckin' fast. You just tell me how *else* you can explain this? And on Ash Wednesday too? There's some connection there, betcherass. Don'tcha think?"

Eddie was answered by only a low grunt.

"Sorry. I keep forgettin' that dumb jaw of yours." He listened to a bit more of the news.

"Panic," he said at length. "Don't know why everybody's so shitless scared. Didn't back home and I don't know now. I tell ya, I never done nothin' to no one that I'd be afraid to see 'em dead, y'know? Guess maybe a lot of people are scared to see people they done wrong to or somethin'. Well, if that makes

Ash Wednesday: The Missing Chapter

'em stop doin' wrong to other folks, then I say whoopee and welcome. Now you take your countries—they ain't gonna be so hot to blow each other up, because who the hell wants to live in a place where folks you blew up are all lookin' at you? Huh?"

There was another grunt that Eddie took as agreement.

"Damn right. Now that ain't to say people aren't still gonna *kill* each other. They still will. People did that in Merridale f'crissakes. But I bet they won't do it as often, and like with these countries, not as many at a time. Yessir."

Eddie paused, removed his gum, and dropped it into his water glass. "Hey, we old guys go on and you can't tell me to shut up, so if I'm borin' you, just blink your eyes or somethin'…no, hell, that's no good—I gotta break my neck just to *see* your eyes. Well, I'll shut up for a minute."

Actually, it was a few seconds short of a minute.

"I just thought of somethin'. You ever see that thing on old tombstones, that *Momento mori*? That's Latin. You know what it means?"

The roommate gave a negative grunt.

"It means something like, 'Remember you gotta die.' And that's what this whole thing is like, like one great big reminder that we're all gonna go sooner or later, so we better be damn good to each other while we're here."

Eddie Karl thought about that for a while, then laughed. "Hell, we always knew *that*! That's nothin' new, is it?

"We always knew that anyway…

"You don't got any smokes, do you? Aw hell, I asked you that already…"

↺➜

DAYS, WEEKS passed, and the dogs stopped barking. The tears dried, and those who had fled came home. They returned to Merridale, to thousands of towns and cities over the world, eventually finding their own dead more comforting than those they had not known.

Governments did not topple, kingdoms did not fall. No angels appeared with flaming swords, as the thousands of new prophets predicted. No antichrist arose from the waiting mass of humanity. Siva, Brahma, and Vishnu, though looked for, did not appear. Mohammed remained silent, as did all the gods and avatars, as silent as the hazy dead who shared the earth with awestruck, expectant mankind.

Between the living and the dead lay an uneasy truce that grew easier with the passing of time, a pale blue light that had to darken before it could begin to illuminate.

There was no epiphany, no apocalypse.

But in Africa, a young mother, about to strike her son for accidentally breaking a jar, looked into the peaceful face of her ancient grandmother and stayed her hand, admonishing the boy with a word, impressing it with an embrace.

In the Sinai, an Israeli colonel, craggy and stiff with war, looked over a plain hard-won years before, lost, and won again, and found that there were things more important than land.

And in a tenement in Brooklyn, a machine operator on his way home passed the now familiar forms on the street finally without fear, and for the first time in his life stopped on the corner and spent a dollar for a flower to give the woman with whom he lived.

For the worker, the colonel, the mother, for all who now understood, the blue light blazed with the brilliance of suns.

"Lost Chapter From the First Draft of *Lost Souls*"

by Poppy Z. Brite

A "lost chapter" from the first draft of Lost Souls. In this draft, Christian's bar somehow remained open after he left New Orleans, and now he's back in town working there. I don't remember who "Nick" was; he seems to be the new owner. Later, instead of finding Ann in St. Louis Cemetery, Ghost tracks her down at Christian's place and pulls a John Wayne ("I'm not leaving without her!"). This might have been slightly less ludicrous had I not had him pratfall into the room. Obviously things changed a lot in subsequent drafts—for the better, I hope.

IN CERTAIN BARS there is no time, or time is brought to a stop, or perhaps it only becomes a sepia loop, tail caught in its mouth, circling endlessly but never changing.

Faces are replaced by other faces, the clock ticks off the minutes and the hours until closing time, the levels of clear and amber and green fluids in the bottles sink steadily, implacably lower. But the conversations are the same, the gestures, the kisses and fights, the sharp distilled smell of drunkenness in the air. So it had become with Christian's. When Christian owned the bar, every night had been one ashen moment that stretched out forever. Under Nick's hand it had become filled with a succession of loud bright moments, each one the same as the last, every night.

As Christian served two of his regular customers, he half-heard a dialogue whose lines had been spoken time after time, a hundred nights over:

"Loan me a couple bucks, Mr. Segal. Just till Friday. I got me a date with a lady who likes to go dancin."

"You got you a date with a bottle of cheap whiskey, you mean. Time is money, my boy, time is money, and I got no time to sit here talkin to you." Mr. Segal tossed back his shot of Old Bushmills, but remained perching on the barstool. Apparently his time was not too precious to keep him from having another drink, for he tipped a finger at Christian. Christian served him the whiskey.

How easy it had been to sink back into this life. His boots knew the floor of this bar, had worn tracks in its old glossy boards. His hands knew these shelves, knew which bottle was vodka, which were whiskey or gin or vermouth. He even knew where the Chartreuse was; for the past several nights Nothing and the others had been in, demanding it. Once Nick stopped flitting about, explaining how to make a perfect Bloody Mary or a passable Hurricane—Nick didn't take much stock in sweet drinks—Christian was able to

Lost Chapter From the First Draft of *Lost Souls*

stand behind the bar as he had always done. His hands were a little busier than before, the automatic voice within him called upon more often to answer a question, reply to a tale of woe, smile at an ancient and weary joke.

When his customers left him alone he stood watching the door, waiting for Molochai, Twig, and Zillah to come in, as he had done these past fifteen years. But before, their coming had been only a remote possibility, a cold flicker of hope to pass the nights. Now he knew they would come. Sometime tonight they would stagger through that door, laughing and shoving each other, acting drunker than they were. Nothing would be in tow, or perhaps slung over someone's shoulder. Someday, Christian felt sure, Nothing would be able to match any one of them drink for drink. That was a status symbol to them. Already he could finish off most of a flask of Taaka; already he could put away four or five shots of Chartreuse in rapid succession. But he was a child. For now, Nothing might curl up on the bathroom floor, shame making his dark eyes even darker ... but he would catch up. Give him fifty years, Christian thought. Give him seventy-five. Nothing might outdrink them all. Molochai and Twig would howl with fury, but Zillah would be proud.

Yes, Christian could expect them back tonight. He thought that they would stay with him now, or at least allow him to follow wherever they roamed. If he kept them drunk and happy, Christian would never have to be alone again.

He had been watching the door, but his mind had gone elsewhere. Now a flicker of red caught his eye. A girl with bright hair stood poised between the bar and the street, ready to enter, equally ready to flee. Christian had seen such girls before, with the same anxious searching look. She was looking for someone she wanted badly, perhaps someone who had forsaken her. And if she could not find that person, she was looking for someone who would buy her a drink and give her a place to sleep tonight. A girl alone, Christian thought, a girl alone and afraid. Then he recognized her: this was another of Zillah's castoffs. The girl was Ann.

She saw him a moment later, before he could look away—and would he have looked away? He didn't know. Certainly Zillah did not want her. Still, he had promised himself that, if she came to New Orleans, he would take her in. He would make no attempt to save her life, but he would keep her child and care for it. And she was alone, and afraid.

She came to the bar and nudged herself a place next to Mr. Segal. "I knew I'd find one of you," she told Christian. "I've been looking so long."

BY THE third day in New Orleans, Christian's room had already become a wreck of crumpled brown bags, plastic cups sticky with pink residue, empty bottles that had held cheap wine and every kind of liquor. Nothing lay among the debris. It occurred to him that he might be sprawled on the very spot where he had first drawn breath. He struggled upright, still sore from a wrestling match he had just lost to Molochai and Twig. They were hiding behind the bed pulling the covers off the two figures who slept there. Christian, flat on his back, his face serene. And the hateful shape of Ann, curled on her side with her knees drawn up to her chest and her hands splayed over her face, her gray sweatshirt rumpled, her shoes still on her feet. Christian had put her to bed late last night.

Lost Chapter From the First Draft of *Lost Souls*

She was already asleep when Nothing and the others straggled in. For once. Christian brooked no opposition; he had regarded Zillah with his cold eyes. "She's tired," Christian had said. "She needs a place to sleep."

"Of course you can take in all the strays you like," said Zillah, drawing away with delicate distaste. "It's nothing to me." He had pulled Nothing down on the floor and half-tenderly, half-painfully begun to maul him. After a moment, Christian had turned out the light. Ann slept. And slept.

Still she slept, even with Molochai and Twig dragging the blankets off her. Nothing glared at them. He felt his hair; they had nearly yanked it out of his head. "Some fair fight," he muttered in the direction of the bed. "Assholes. Bet you outweigh me by fifty pounds each." But he was too drunk on vodka to know whether his words were intelligible. His tongue felt like a sodden sponge in his mouth. Only now was he really beginning to understand the habits of his new family. He had thought they slept all day and partied all night: wrong. They partied all the damn time, and only slept when they were too drunk or too exhausted to stay upright.

Light measured footsteps were coming up the stairs. Ancient wood creaked softly; the footsteps crossed the landing. Then a rusty key grated in the lock and Zillah stepped through the door, kicking trash out of his way. Molochai and Twig tumbled out from behind the bed and catapulted across the room toward him, shouting, "Did you get it, did you get the stuff, did you?"

"Of course I got it." Zillah pulled a plastic Baggie full of pot from his pocket and dangled it above Molochai and Twig's heads. He glanced around the room, taking in the situation. "Who," he asked, "has been abusing my dear child?"

"Not us."

"We never touched him."

"He just drank too much."

Zillah quirked an eyebrow. "Nothing?" he said.

Nothing tried to make himself look limp, bruised, broken. He twisted his head to gaze at Zillah. "Get 'em, Joe," he whispered, making each word hang upon the last ounce of his strength. "Get the rotten bastards and make 'em pay for what they did to me."

"Liar!"

"We'll get you back, you little shit —"

Zillah turned upon Molochai and Twig. He was grinning, and Zillah grinning could be a scary sight to see. His teeth seemed to grow sharper and more numerous. His eyes glowed with that mad green fire. "You're the dirty rats who shot my kid brother," he hissed.

"No, Zillah —"

"We'll be good —"

"We'll never ever hurt him again." Saying this, Twig shot Nothing a look of pure murder.

"You'rrrre the dirrrty ratssssss," Zillah whispered again. He moved toward Molochai and Twig, his hands hooked into claws, the pink tip of his tongue quivering between his teeth. Molochai tried to push Twig in front of him. Twig cursed and backed away. Zillah stalked them, licking his lips and giggling.

Nothing raised himself on his elbows to stare. Zillah was playing. Fucking around. Nothing was almost sure he wouldn't really hurt them. Still, Nothing watched with uneasy fascination as Zillah's long nails clawed the air in front of Molochai's face. Molochai whimpered. When a

Lost Chapter From the First Draft of *Lost Souls*

sudden knock at the door caught Zillah's attention, Molochai bolted back behind the bed.

"Who the fuck is that?" Oh, Zillah was in a mood today. Even his anger was exquisite. As he whirled to glare at the door, his hair whipped his face: streaks of purple, green, gold. The sight of Zillah's furious face made Nothing want to pull him down, right here on the faded carpet, even though he knew how hard Zillah could bite at such times. Nothing coveted those red crescents on his throat and shoulders; he always pulled the neck of his T-shirt loose to show them off.

The knock came again, and Zillah bared his teeth at the door. "Who could it be? No one knows we live here. No one followed me." He shoved the bag of pot at Twig, who tucked it under a corner of the carpet. But it wasn't the police, Nothing thought; the knock was too soft, too tentative. "Maybe it's one of Christian's friends," he said in a small voice.

"Christian doesn't have any friends," Zillah hissed, and in one fluid motion grabbed the knob and yanked the door open. The person on the landing had been getting ready to knock again, harder this time. He couldn't stop the motion of his arm: its momentum carried him part of the way into the room, and he stumbled over the laces of his sneakers and fell at Zillah's feet. There he lay in a heap, looking up at Zillah, breathing a little heavily, his eyes wide, pale, scared.

"You again," said Zillah.

"Ghost?" said Nothing. "How did you ever find us?"

"I came for Ann," Ghost told them. His voice was unsteady but stubborn. "I'm not leaving without her."

⟲→

"ALL RIGHT," said Zillah.

"All right?" Ghost stared into those green eyes for a second, then looked away. He had expected anything but this. To plead with them, with Nothing. To pray. To do battle for Ann using the ornate jeweled crucifix Arkady had given him with a doubtful shrug. Each of these possibilities seemed stupider than the last; still, he had expected anything but agreement.

[AT THIS point there are two pages missing from my manuscript, during which it would seem that Zillah toys with the ever-sensitive Ghost and eventually gives him some sort of mind zap. What Ghost was doing smoking a joint with these characters I don't know.]

PRETTY GHOST, if Nothing didn't love you so. The thought lit up the inside of Ghost's skull with luminescent green fire. He stood up too fast and the smoke rushed to his head, making him stagger. He put his hands over his eyes. The others stared at him, grins starting to spread across their faces.

"What if she won't go?" said Nothing, and Molochai, Twig, and Zillah turned their attention to him instead.

The joint burned Nothing's fingers, and he realized he had been holding it for too long. He passed the ragged end to Molochai, stood up, went to Ghost and steadied him. Ghost's eyelids were fluttering, and when Nothing put a hand on the back of Ghost's neck, the skin there felt dry and hot. Nothing didn't want the others to turn their attention back to Ghost,

Lost Chapter From the First Draft of *Lost Souls*

to ask smirkingly what the matter was, so he kept talking. "I mean, she might not want to go. She has this thing for Zillah. We can't just knock her over the head."

"I will," said Twig. "I hate the way she whines." He flung himself into Zillah's lap and started licking Zillah's face. "Ohhh, my true luuuuv, nobody ever porked me as good as you!"

Nothing closed his eyes, made his face stay solemn. He didn't want to laugh at Ann, not right here in front of Ghost, no matter how much he hated her. When he'd seen her tucked into Christian's bed last night, he had felt a rush of possessive fury unlike anything he had known in his fifteen years. It iced his stomach, turned his spine into a vibrating wire. Only the thought that Ghost loved this girl kept him from savaging her then and there: tearing the red hair out of her head, shaking her till her bones came loose, ripping her throat open. He could happily lick her blood off his hands. Zillah would let him. Zillah would help him; the others would too. Even Christian would probably not object; with his strange cold brand of morality, he would not allow them to turn Ann onto the street, but he might let them tear her throat out if they so wished.

It wasn't just the little show that Zillah had put on with Ann outside the Sacred Yew. That had just been fucking. Zillah could have fucked Ann ten times over and Nothing didn't think he would have cared. He himself had enjoyed far wilder scenes. But somehow Ann had fallen in love with Zillah and followed him here to claim him, as if Nothing were some small black-draped shadow, beneath consideration. And that, Nothing thought, was just too damn bad. Zillah was his. By the bonds of blood and spit and sperm Zillah was his, the only one who ever had been. There was no bond between Ann and Zillah — none except the one that grew inside her, the one that would kill her someday soon.

She would die anyway. And Nothing knew he could lick her blood off his hands. He could do it happily. He let go of Ghost and took a step toward the bed where she and Christian still slept.

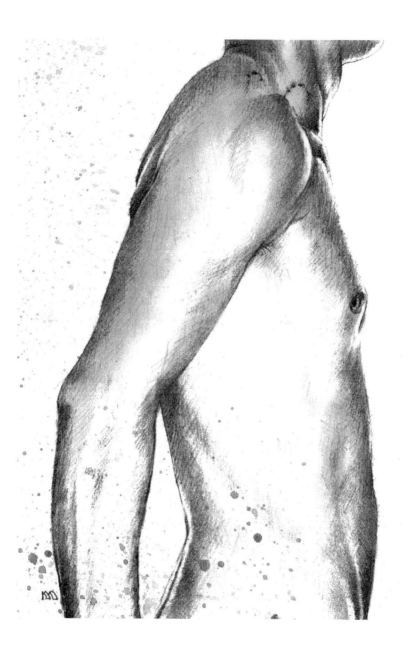

An Introduction to *The Ghost Ship:* An Unfinished Novel

by Stewart O'Nan

I started The Ghost Ship with the idea of writing a big, fun horror novelabout a small town and its huge world-famous amusement park, along the lines of *It*, with a past and a present connected by an indelible local tragedy perpetrated by an Evil Beyond Time, a big, baggy architectonic monster involving dozens of POV characters, the ragtag core of whom we root for to solve the mystery of what happened in the past and, through resourcefulness, teamwork and self-sacrifice, defeat the Evil and learn what's truly important about Life and Love and Time and Faith. Basic stuff.

I studied up on the old trolley parks and their evolution into today'ssprawling theme parks, and even did legwork for my setting, spending a week at Cedar Point, interviewing employees, taking pictures, strolling the empty park after closing. I started a draft, excited about building that world, and wrote a hundred pages, getting some of my major characters in place. The opening had some momentum and some sprawl, and I discovered a ton of opportunities, both in the plotting and the telling, but somehow, as I cast forward, I discovered too much of my storyline, nailed it all down too early, and lost interest.

Instead of a gripping, moment-to-moment inquiry into these people, the writing turned into a paint-by-numbers exercise. The set-up seemed corny, the characters' situations boilerplate, hokey. I stopped, thinking I'd key on just one character and write a small-town novel about this kid who works at an amusement park. Then it was a novel about a small town and a big park. And then a novel about a small town where a girl goes missing. And then a small town that an old woman drives through on her way to a lake cottage she has to sell because her husband died.

That woman turned out to be Emily Maxwell, and that book became *Wish You Were Here*. Later I wrote a sequel called *Emily, Alone*, about her quiet days at home alone with her dog. So it didn't all go to waste—or it led somewhere, finally.

The Ghost Ship:
An Unfinished Novel

by Stewart O'Nan

The Fireman's Carnival

IT HAPPENED EVERY year near the end of school, like a gateway to summer. For weeks on the bus ride home, Katie and her friends saw the silk-screened posters stapled to telephone poles and taped to the window of the dry cleaners. They made plans to go the first night—Friday—badgering their parents, writing it down on the calendar in case anyone might forget, and then one day in the middle of the week the trucks came with their folded-up rides and the trailers that converted into corn dog and cotton candy stands and set up in the grassy lot across from the post office where the Rotary sold Christmas trees in the winter.

Katie was going to go with Mia and Angie and Amy, but Friday after school Amy (it was *so* typical of her) decided she wanted to go with Caitlin Bellingham instead, meaning they were short one person for rides like the Round-Up and had to take turns, one of them standing outside the sectioned metal fence with the parents and little kids, watching the other two fly sideways, laughing and out of breath, getting off wobbly, almost sick from it. You got a discount if you bought the tickets in strips of ten. They went on the Zipper and the Gravitron and the Spider and the big wavy slide at the far end of the lot and the Ferris Wheel where you could see the ore boats way out on the lake from the very top, and still at the end of the night they had two tickets each.

The only ride they hadn't gone on was the Jolly Roger. It was a haunted house, pirate-style. There were mostly older kids in line, but the guy who ran it had a broken arm and was too busy seating people to pay attention to them. Above the name a giant crab with a skull for a head waved its pincers feebly, its eyes two red light bulbs that flashed off and on. Big speakers pumped out the sound of gale winds whistling and waves detonating on rocks—almost as loud as the big diesel generators at the edge of the lot that powered everything, their duct-taped cables snaking underfoot, tripping the unwary. The cars rumbled as they rolled over the steel platform and then banged through a pair of swinging doors. Even with the lights on, it seemed dark. From inside came the shrill, recorded screams of a woman being tortured, echoed cornily by some teenaged guys. On the way out, the cars had to pass through what looked like a solid curtain of water.

"I don't want to get wet," Mia said.

"You won't," Katie said, and showed her the people getting off were dry. "Don't be a chicken. It'll be fun."

"We could go on the Gravitron again."

The Ghost Ship: An Unfinished Novel

"I'm not going on the Gravitron again," Angie said. "And anyway, it's three tickets."

"There's only two people to a car," Mia said.

"Here," Katie said, "you can sit with Angie. I'll go by myself. I'm not afraid."

They didn't give her a chance to say no, slipping into line in front of two guys from seventh grade.

"This is stupid," Mia said.

"You're stupid," Katie said. "It's just a dumb ride."

It was brighter up on the platform, and loud, the steel wheels squeaking. She could see the curtain of water was just a thin mist that turned off when a car came out. The guy with the broken arm stopped a car for Angie and Mia, then locked the safety bar with a pin and pulled a tall lever that stuck out of the floor. The car lurched forward and Mia looked back at her, worried, making Katie laugh.

"Just a single?" the man asked, then locked her in. "Hang on to the bar, else she'll throw you around."

He pulled the lever and the car jerked. It slid along its track drunkenly, gathering speed, and she had to fight the instinct to raise her hands when it bumped the doors open.

Inside it was so dark only the air on her face proved that she was moving. The smell was like their garage, a mix of dust and burnt motor oil, fresh paint and ozone. The wind and waves swirled around her, deafening. Ahead, Mia screamed, and a second later a giant gray seagull with a bloody beak swooped straight for Katie's face, screeching. Gripped in one claw was an eyeball trailing a tangled spaghetti of severed nerves. At the last minute it pulled up, buzzing her.

"That's nothing," Katie called, holding on to the bar.

Far down the hallway a tiny orange glow burned like a nightlight. She could just make out the silhouette of their heads, and then in a blinding white flash saw both of them shy away from something to their right that gave off a burst of mad scientist laughter.

"Katie, I hate you," Mia shouted.

"Yeah, *Katie*, I hate you," one of the seventh graders behind her mimicked.

She stayed quiet, hoping they'd leave her alone.

The laughter was coming from a skeletal prisoner in chains who tried to leap through the bars at her. Its wispy beard was smeared red, and on the floor of the ship's brig were some rubber rats with bloody bites taken out of their backs. As she passed, the lights died again.

"*Kay*-tee," the boys called. "*Kayyyyy*-tee."

"Shut up," she fired into the dark.

"What are you going to do, sic your pizzaface brother on us?"

"If I have to."

"Ewww, we're so scared."

"Yeah—please, Kevin, don't squirt us with your zit-juice."

"Shut up," she said, just as the car banged into another set of doors.

The new room was a huge rotating barrel painted day-glo green, the sides designed to look like the mossy stones of an old fort. It surrounded her, turning. The way the barrel spun made it feel like the car was tipping as it went through, teetering on a narrow bridge, and she leaned against the motion as if to stay upright. There was another set of doors at the end still swinging from Angie and Mia's car. At least she'd get away from the jerks for a while.

The Ghost Ship: An Unfinished Novel

The car banged through into total darkness, or it only seemed that way, after so much light. Ahead loomed a blue glow like a TV in someone's window, and the high cries of seagulls over a calm surf, quieter than the storm raging on the other side of the barrel. Through the screaks of the gulls, a woman was singing sweetly, but far off, as if calling across the water. The car swerved, swinging around a corner, and there, sitting on a fake rock not five feet from her, was a mermaid in a bikini top. She had long blond hair braided with seaweed and a scaly silver tail and a face as pretty as her voice, but when the light changed from blue to red, you could see the skull beneath her skin. Her teeth were fangs. She raised her bony claws to squeeze Katie's neck, and just then the singing stopped, the lights went out and the car ground to a halt.

For a second she thought it was part of the ride. Then she heard Mia through the wall ahead of her, shouting for someone to turn on the lights. The power was out. It was so quiet she could hear voices instead of the generators.

"Get me out of here!" Mia screamed.

"It's okay," Katie called, and twisted sideways on the seat to slide out from under the lap bar. She stumbled stepping down from the car and threw a hand up to brace herself, brushing against the mermaid, which made her flinch and yelp. It swung and came back again, bumping her, its stiff hands in her hair, and she scrabbled blindly along the wall— anything to get away.

She should have stayed in the car, because she now had no idea where she was. The darkness was like the time they went to Perry's Cave and the guide had them blow out their candles one by one. When the last one was out, she tried to touch her nose with her finger and got her eye, then held her hand an inch away from her face. She imagined being lost and trying to find her way out. The guide said they'd found skeletons.

"*Kay*-tee," one of the boys taunted, close by, and with a teeth-clenching rush of hatred she wished them dead—pictured herself stalking them catlike in the dark, slinking up behind their car and reaching around to slit their throats, cutting the first one with a wet gurgle, the second realizing what was happening but unable to free himself in time. She would saw their heads off and throw them overboard for the others to find, a warning. The bodies they could eat.

With a whir the lights flickered on, the siren's voice warbling horribly from the ceiling. Katie found herself crouching behind the boys' car, just starting to move. They hadn't seen her, and before they had a chance to, she rose up until she was at the right height, gathered her breath and screamed as loud as she could.

The Ghost Ship: An Unfinished Novel

Welcome to Edgewater Park

1/ Longtime Resident Missing

A LBERT MANNING HAD lived in the little yellow bungalow on Erie Street for years, though nowhere near as long as his closest neighbors supposed. He was a mystery to them—light-skinned but still noticeably black among the lilywhite new arrivals with their fancy SUVs and minivans, the last survivor of a west side that no longer existed, the great mills and machine shops closed down, the rib shacks and cinderblock corner bars condemned and then replaced by bistros and coffee shops, the whole neighborhood gentrified and unrecognizable.

To the Greives and the Wolfsons and the other young families on the block, he seemed a relic from a different Lakewood, a reminder of another century. They knew little about him, only that he seemed pleasant enough, a fastidious homeowner, waving as he mowed the lawn or raked the leaves, and that he kept his vintage Chevy pick-up in show condition, driving it in the town's Fourth of July parade, bunting hung from the windows, his big tortoiseshell cat Tuffy riding beside him. He carved a pumpkin at Halloween and handed out Tootsie Rolls, he even strung light-up icicles from his gutters for Christmas, but he was a fit and solitary old man and bound to be the target of rumors.

The worst—and dullest, started by the pack of teenagers who hung around the Dairy Barn on Superior—was that he lured white children into his basement, raped and tortured them to death with his woodworking equipment, then chopped them into bone meal fertilizer for his rose beds. And Albert Manning did have a noisy lathe and a beautiful garden, proof enough for the young and gullible, especially at night, when the only light came from the ground-level casement windows and people passing on the sidewalk could hear the wobbly spinning of the shuttle and the high-pitched bite of an awl chipping into heartwood.

Another, less imaginative rumor was that Albert Manning had killed his wife. This, though any responsible adult would have scoffed at it, was true.

Another was that he was an escaped mental patient. This was also true.

But for all the usual suspicions held about Albert Manning, no one speculated, even jokingly, that Albert Manning was not his real name, that he was not from Lakewood, or that the smudged green tattoo of an anchor on his bicep was not, as he sometimes let slip, from a stint in the Navy. And no one would. The man who lived in the yellow bungalow on Erie Street had worked hard to become Albert Manning, and over the years he'd become good at it. If asked, he would have said the initial transformation was the hard part; the rest, like his work around the house, was just upkeep.

The man who'd become Albert Manning had learned that nothing is more comforting to other people than neatness and regularity, and he applied that lesson to everything he did. Saturdays, his neighbors could rely on him to finish his yardwork in time for the Indians' one-oh-five game, which they would then hear blaring from his windows, since, they'd been told (and it was at least partly true), Albert was hard of hearing.

The Ghost Ship: An Unfinished Novel

Albert had never been a great baseball fan, and for years had used the time in front of the tube to ruminate on other business, much of it painful and long past, slowly sipping at his beer while play gave way to commercials, but, as with the roses and the lathe and life on Erie Street, he discovered that somewhere along the line he'd developed a true affection for the game, and for the Indians, a local joke for most of his life. He began to wear an Indians cap whenever he watched them, keeping it on top of the TV, even in the off-season.

Today they were playing the Tigers, an easy win (knock wood), and Albert hurried to put his sandwich together before the first pitch, jamming the zip-locked swiss cheese back in the deli drawer and swinging the fridge door shut behind him. Forget the pickles, he'd get some between innings. He scooted into the room in his socks and grabbed his hat, set the plate and his beer on the TV table and fell back into his recliner.

Tuffy waited at his feet for him to drop a chip or toss him a shred of turkey breast. "No begging," he said, and took a meaty first bite.

The sound was up so loud that he didn't realize someone was at the door until Tuffy suddenly scooted off, spooked.

The bell rang.

Dammit. Couldn't they hear he was in the middle of something?

He swallowed and hollered for whoever it was to hang on—and wouldn't you know, Coco Crisp singled.

The bell rang again.

"Just hold on there," Albert called, already moving toward the front of the house. He looked back to check on his sandwich. He wouldn't put it past Tuff to jump up on the arm and nibble a little.

The front door was open for the breeze. Behind the screen stood Katie Greive in her Girl Scout uniform, her forest-green sash crowded with badges. She was a frequent visitor, at least to the porch. When it came to fundraising, like most of the kids on the block, she was a grim overachiever, a champion hawker of chocolate bars and raffle tickets. Under one arm she held a cardboard box and a clipboard.

"Cookie time again?" he asked cheerfully. "I swear I've still got some in the freezer."

While there was no one on the sidewalk, he was aware of the other houses, their windows like eyes. He unlocked the screen and stepped out on the porch with her to look at the order form. It was a necessary expense, a show of neighborly goodwill. Besides, he had a weakness for the chocolate and peanut butter Tagalongs, and he always bought a few Thin Mints to put away.

"Can I use your bathroom?" the girl asked.

He was going to suggest she just go back next door, but she was hopping from foot to foot.

"Down the hall and to your right," he said, committing himself to standing there until she came out again.

He made his picks and waited, wondering what was happening with the Indians. He couldn't quite make out the announcers over the combined roar of lawnmowers. It was supposed to rain tomorrow, so everyone was out. He added up the total. He didn't have enough cash on him; he'd have to pay by check, another couple minutes wasted.

He listened for the jingle of Tuffy's bell that meant he'd jumped up on the recliner. If she took much longer he'd have to go in and rescue his sandwich, and the devil take the gossips.

"Katie?" he called through the screen. "Katie honey?"

The Ghost Ship: An Unfinished Novel

Inside, something heavy crashed in the kitchen—maybe the pickle jar. It had to be big for him to hear it, and reluctantly he whipped open the screen door, calling the girl's name as he walked down the hall.

She'd dropped her box outside the bathroom door. It was empty, which he thought was odd. On the bottom, a dark stain soaked the paper like old motor oil.

Another crash, and then a steady thumping, like someone driving tent pegs with a sledge. For an instant he flashed back thirty years—to the beating of fists on locked doors, the flapping rush of flames—and slowed, afraid now, treading like a burglar in his own home.

"Katie, are you all right?"

Thunk...thunk...Creeping closer, he could hear a juicy squishing with each blow.

"Katie?"

Thunk.

Though his instinct was to run, he kept taking steps. At the end of the hall he waited a last second before turning the corner.

She was on the kitchen floor, kneeling with her back to him—tending to Tuffy, it looked like. He was worried that she might be hurt. Shards of the pickle jar and a broken plate littered the tile like chips of ice, along with the pickles, the juice and the guts of his sandwich. She raised her joined hands straight up, high above her head, held them there ceremonially, and, unbelieving, he saw that she held a thick silver cleaver.

She brought it down hard on Tuffy—splayed, one leg bent the wrong way, yet still feebly clawing as if to escape. The blade sunk into his back with a thump. It sliced clean through, the tip sticking in the linoleum, and the girl had to wiggle it loose.

So they'd finally come back. It was why they'd let him escape the last time. He could run, except he couldn't; he was stuck there, watching, as if he couldn't believe it was happening again.

The girl turned her head as if she knew he was there, but instead of Katie's face, it was Evvie that last night, pasty in her makeup, green sequined eyelids, the fake blood pooled purple under her eyes. The curls of her long blond wig spilled over her bare shoulders. She filled the costume the way he remembered, the clamshells deepening her green-tinted cleavage, the silver scales accentuating her tiny waist. He was surprised that despite everything he still wanted her—that he still missed her, still wanted to say he was sorry. He wanted to say it wasn't him.

"Hey, Jimmy," she said brightly, flirting with him, and without looking, brought the cleaver down again with a mushy crunch.

It's not real, he thought.

"Like you are," Evvie scoffed, standing and walking toward him, holding the cleaver straight up like a wet paint brush.

It had been thirty years yet she wasn't a day older. He almost felt relief, knowing that he wasn't crazy like they said. Here was proof—as if he could show someone and make them understand.

He knew why she was here. He'd seen the article in the Sunday paper. He knew it was bad luck, but there was the famous picture of the woman running with her hair on fire, and by the time he looked away, it was too late, the knowledge was inside him like a virus.

"You can't make me," he said reasonably, as if they were negotiating.

The Ghost Ship: An Unfinished Novel

"Come on, Jimmy," she said, "we both know that's not true."

He backed into the living room where the Indians were playing. Groping behind him, he found the beer bottle, almost tipping it over before his fingers wrapped around its slippery neck. He gripped it like a tennis racket.

"Mr. Manning," Katie Greive asked, reaching for his arm, "are you okay?"

He looked past her into the kitchen and saw the chopped-up mess that had been Tuffy, the puddle and the trail of bloody footprints. When he looked back, she was Evvie again, grinning and sexy. The danger was giving in to his hate. If he did this in anger, they'd have him, and his whole life would be for nothing.

"I'm fine, darling," he said, and swung for her temple.

He expected her to duck and then lunge at him, burying the cleaver deep in his neck, but he connected solidly, knocking her backward, the bottle breaking in a shower of brown bits, beer splashing, and he fell on top of her, pinning her to the floor with his knees, stabbing the broken shoulder into her face with steady efficiency as she clawed blindly for his eyes. It wasn't until she was no longer struggling that he realized the bottle had disintegrated and he was punching her.

He stopped. The TV was still going. He was holding Evvie by the throat, her mermaid curls twined around his arm, except she'd turned back into Katie Greive, and the hair was actually her sash. The bottle had worked well. Her nose was flattened to one side and her upper lip was gone, showing a crooked row of baby teeth. The carpet was dark under her head.

It was a trap. He'd forgotten how much power they had.

From the kitchen came the clink of broken glass. He grasped the cleaver and wheeled, ready to defend himself.

It was Tuffy, dragging himself across the floor with his front paws. His eyes were drugged, glazed and unseeing as a crackhead's. When he opened his mouth, the man who'd become Albert Manning expected Evvie's voice, but all that came out was a strangled cough, followed by a vomited gush of blood. And still he kept coming, appealing to his master as if he could make him better.

The man held him.

"It's okay, Tuff," he said, "you're all right," and with one hand smoothed the cat's sopping fur to calm him, then raised the other, locked his wrist and drove the cleaver true.

He stood, and out of habit started to clean up, until he realized his socks were leaving tracks. The game seemed louder now, distracting. He tugged his cap down snugly so he could think, leaving a bloody thumbprint on the gray under-side of the bill. He winged it into a corner, stepped over the girl and sat down on the edge of the recliner to pull off his socks. He could clean all he wanted. Ultimately they'd miss Katie and they'd come for him.

The box was still in the hall, and he recalled the dark stain in the bottom.

He needed to leave—every minute meant another mile away from here—but he needed to know. He found his ratty lawnmowing sneakers by the backdoor and tugged them on. The cleaver was too big to conceal, so he chose his sharpest carving knife, holding it hard against his leg.

Outside, it was the kind of day the weather forecasters took credit for, the sun bright on the freshly cut grass, birds chirping, butterflies wobbling over the garden. He detoured around the Greives' big cedar playset and crept up the stairs of their deck. The sliding doors were open, and faintly he

The Ghost Ship: An Unfinished Novel

could hear the ballgame. Don Greive was a fan; it was the one topic they discussed at any length, taking five from their hedgetrimming.

He knocked on the frame. "Hello? Anybody home?" He stood three-quarters to the door, ready if anyone tried to jump him from behind.

He called again and waited, then slid the screen aside and stepped in, leaving it open in case he needed a quick way out.

"Don?" he called, noting the black handles sticking from the knifeblock as he made his way through the kitchen. Besides Don and Margaret, there was Kevin, their teenaged son. If all three of them rushed him at once, he'd have no chance.

In the back hall, a copy of Bon Appetit lay on the floor. The magazine was facedown and open, butterflied as if to cover something. Albert nudged it with the toe of his sneaker. There was nothing but carpet underneath. He kicked it out of the way and inched along the wall toward the front of the house. As he stopped, crouching, bracing himself to spin into the living room, a smell of spoiled meat reached him, heavy and sickening.

It might be a trick.

He couldn't take the chance. He broke into the room with the knife out in front of him, scanning for movement like a hunter.

The Greives were sitting on the couch, or were propped there, the three of them bathed in blood and leaning against each other, Don in the middle. From the stench and the mess, he could assume they were dead, yet he waited, vigilant. It was only when he noticed the letters cut into their foreheads that his arm dropped of its own accord.

Very neatly, she had carved: JAMES EDWARD REESE.

He wondered how deep she'd gone, but really, there was no choice. He hesitated, then remembered what they'd done to Tuffy—what they'd made him do to Katie and Evvie and the others. He had trained himself for this day, hoping, as he grew older, that it would never come. Now that it was here, he knew there could be no anger, no fear, only a cold necessity.

He tested the blade on Kevin, tipping his head back and sawing through his pimples. The skin bled, still fresh. He cut a neat rectangle, but it wouldn't come, and he had to pry it up like a stubborn piece of lasagna. Don's was harder. The EDWARD broke into two sections and he had to scrape the last part of it off, the blade squeaking against bone. By the time he finished with Margaret, he was sweating. He laid the wet lengths of skin on a cushion and took it into the kitchen and ran water while the disposal gargled. He listened to it spin emptily to be absolutely sure, rinsing his hands and the knife until they were clean. Then the man who'd been Albert Manning went home and packed for a journey that could have only one end.

2/ A Problem of Numbers

IT HELPED, Lynn McCourt liked to think, that she liked the survivors. They were regular people, a full half of them women, and after so many seasons interviewing quarterbacks and power forwards who considered her at best a novelty act (she knew perfectly well that most jocks thought a woman reporter a joke), she felt at home in their normal-sized living rooms and kitchens, a bit of a celebrity herself, the newspaper

The Ghost Ship: An Unfinished Novel

reporter come to listen to them remember the most terrifying night of their lives.

She started everyone with the same question: Where were you when you first noticed the fire? Usually that was all it took. The rest came naturally, people being better storytellers than they gave themselves credit for. She made sure her tape recorder was rolling and sat back, trying not to interrupt. They told her who they'd been sitting with—or standing in line with, since most of the people she'd talked to never got inside that night. The few she could find that had actually been in the cars told her about squeezing free of the lapbars (they were teenagers then, it was easy) and groping through the darkened maze, tripping over the double steel rails of the track, stumbling smack into the chickenwire that fronted the gruesome day-glo tableaux they'd come to laugh at.

The ones who made it out unscathed spoke of miracles: a pair of hands pushing them the right way, a flashlight giving them something to run for. Some swore they still had nightmares.

The more unfortunate told her about their burns and the long months in the hospital, enduring first the primitive skin grafts and then, later, the stares of their classmates. Strangely, they seemed more comfortable with their memories, as if, after having been forced to physically confront their pain, all they'd had to come to terms with was their own bad luck. Of all the survivors, they seemed the most even-tempered and generous. They wanted readers to know how brave the firemen and paramedics that saved them had been, and how hard the doctors and nurses had worked, and of course their parents, their families.

She understood that some people didn't want to remember. A dozen times she spent months tracking down leads from old high school yearbooks and hospital records, only to have a voice bluntly tell her no and hang up. Some called her a vulture, and she accepted that, having already accused herself of it. Someone was going to tell the story, she reasoned; at least she'd try to do it with some compassion.

The ones she couldn't fathom were the ones who wanted to talk to her even though they hadn't been there. Like fans, they kept scrapbooks stuffed with disintegrating clippings—some of which were rare, and therefore useful. What worried Lynn McCourt was that they seemed more excited about the idea of the book than the survivors themselves. When she explained this to her editor in New York, Brendan just laughed.

"That's good," he said. "If it was just the survivors that were interested, I'd be seriously worried. You don't have to be a fisherman to like The Perfect Storm, right?"

"You got me there," she said, cursing the day she let her agent convince her that was the best way to pitch the project. All she wanted was a contract, but Betsy thought they could get six figures, which meant Lynn could take an extended leave from the paper. No illiterate bling-bling-dripping bonus babies for eighteen months. She'd thought it was a good deal until she realized Brendan expected a paint-by-numbers bestseller, an instant mix of oddball setting, sympathetic victims, grisly climax and forensic aftermath. What she had, after nearly a year of research, was a puzzle missing its key pieces.

The problem was one of numbers. There were 24 cars total. Since the ride was essentially a creepy tunnel of love, each car held only two passengers. The way the intricate Swiss mechanism that ran everything was designed, the cars passed through the ride in teams of two—one ahead, one behind, perfect for double-dating. The lead car knocked open a pair of doors, passed whatever attractions were in the room, then

The Ghost Ship: An Unfinished Novel

whipped into a turn, throwing the riders against each other, and banged through another set of doors. When one team exited a room, a new team entered. There were nine rooms in all, as well as two long hallways. The entire ride lasted six minutes. Outside, operators sat a new set of riders and sent them in just as the following team of cars emerged, so that at any one time there were 22 cars inside the Ghost Ship, and 44 people, when it was running to capacity, which it had been that night, being a new ride and popular with the high school set.

25 people had died. From the police records and death certificates, she could place 22 of those in cars 5 through 16 (teams 5-6, 7-8, etc.), which had been in the center of the barn, worming their way through the four-chambered heart of the ride and cut off from the exits by the two long hallways. The other three were park employees who'd tried to rescue the dead, using access doors known only to them. All three were found in room five, where team 11-12 ended up.

Lynn McCourt had always been good at math, but it had still taken her a while early in her research to realize the lifelong habit of subtraction had fooled her. Cars 5 through 16 weren't eleven cars, as she'd first figured, but twelve.

Here was Lynn McCourt's problem: at the heart of the Ghost Ship she had 24 seats but only 22 bodies. The two that were missing were the true survivors, and without them, she had nothing.

↰→

SHE DIDN'T expect Joe Barry to solve all her problems, but from what his daughter had told her over the phone, he might be able to help her with some live details of the fire.

It was why she'd driven all the way out to the far suburbs, braving the crazy freeways and stripmall sprawl and then the suffocating, fluorescent-lit sadness of the Meadowview nursing home. He was one of the city firemen who helped contain the blaze, a lieutenant then, hawk-eyed and slim in his dress uniform. Now he was bleary and white-haired, hunched, his wrists bandaged—the thin skin torn, he said, from an orderly lifting him the wrong way. He had difficulty breathing, rasping despite a plastic oxygen line that clipped under his nose and emitted a faint hissing like a gas leak that she knew would bother her when she finally transcribed the tape.

"So," he asked, "how much are you getting paid for this book?"

"Not enough," she joked, and started him with the usual.

He had to sit and consider it, squinting. "I remember driving up, we had to be a mile off. You could see how black the smoke was. The guys thought it was the oil tanks down by the harbor. It wasn't till the causeway we saw it was the park, and I thought: oh boy."

"Why did you think that?" she prompted.

He thought, gazing into the glass of the table between them as if he could read the answer there. He shrugged. "Sometimes you just know it's going to be bad. You work enough fires, you get a sense."

He stopped again, having answered her, clammed up as if he were on the witness stand.

"What was the scene like when you pulled up?"

"We were the first company on-scene. It wasn't five minutes from the station, and the place was just going up. There were people everywhere."

The Ghost Ship: An Unfinished Novel

Actually, according to department records, and verified by testimony given at the state fire marshal's inquest, Engine Company 6 was the third unit to respond, but she didn't contradict him. It had been thirty years, and there was bound to be some scatter. Besides, she wasn't after who got there first or what procedure they followed. She needed the reader to be there with Joe Berry's crew, to see what they saw, feel what they felt. When they moved in to fight the fire, she slowed him down, pulling the details she wanted from him one by one, taking notes in case the tape somehow failed.

What did the smoke smell like?

Smoke.

Can you describe it for me? Did it have a particular odor or taste to it?

It smelled like burning tarpaper, from the shingles. The heat was making them float around in the sky like birds.

What made the fire burn so quickly?

There was a pretty good breeze off the lake—that was its oxygen supply. Add to that the overall area of the building, and how old it was. The place was a pile of kindling just waiting for a match.

So you agree that it was arson.

That's what they say. I got no reason to doubt them.

What would he compare the heat to?

Like sticking your face in a broiler. But that was normal, any good-sized fire. If you didn't go home with pink cheeks, you weren't earning your paycheck.

He coughed and waited for the next question. She needed to be more patient, but she had three more people to see today, and a stultifyingly dry medical text on burns with a glossy insert of pictures she dreaded waiting for her at home.

"Okay," she said, "after the fire was out, what did you do?"

"Mopping up took a couple of hours. We went around putting water on anything that looked like trouble. It was a hell of a mess in there."

"So you were inside the ride."

"Oh yeah. Never seen anything like it." He shook his head, remembering the destruction.

She'd interviewed a policeman who'd teared up at this part, thumbing at the corners of his eyes. She was hoping Joe Barry could help her with the bodies, and knew not to press.

"In my line of work," he said, "you don't see that. You get one, maybe two people, three at the most, and that's a bad fire. I remember walking right by it at first. I thought it was something they put together to scare the people—like a skeleton popping out of something, except it was real, it was some poor girl, and what she was popping out of was a bunch of these other kids, all of 'em in a pile by the door there."

She took out the diagram and had him point to where he meant. He chose the wrong door—the one at the north end of the east hallway, by the exit of room five. It was a common mistake, and she asked if he didn't mean the door at the south end of the west hallway. The kids had stacked up there, trying to get out the way they came in. The doors only opened inward, and the pressure of them pushing kept them shut.

"No, it was this one," he said, stabbing at it, sure.

"That door was open though." She made her hands a gate and spread them. "It opened out like this."

"Smoke's fast. People panic. All it takes is for one person to fall down."

"So you think they trampled each other in the dark."

The Ghost Ship: An Unfinished Novel

"I might have done the same thing if I was in there. You never know what you might do in a given situation."

He was wrong about the door, she was pretty sure—but not positive, because now a sliver of doubt had crept in. He'd been there, she hadn't, and she didn't want to argue with him. She circled a question mark in the margin of her notes and moved on.

An hour later, after she'd packed up and thanked Mr. Barry for his time and set off for her next appointment, the idea of a second pile still bothered her. He had to be wrong, yet there was nothing in her research to positively eliminate the possibility, and that uncertainty naturally called up the larger problem of the two missing witnesses, and the viability of the project as a whole, and her own future, and though she fought for perspective, getting back on the highway and heading for the city again, she thought Joe Barry's moveable pile was typical of her experience so far on the Ghost Ship. It was just one more question she didn't have the answer to.

3/ The House of Horrors

TEN MINUTES before closing, the announcement came over the P.A., a hearty whitebread DJ from the fifties thanking everyone for visiting Edgewater, asking them to please drive home safely. The recording repeated every two minutes as the diehards squeezed in one last ride, one more funnel cake, and then the swoony doo-wop of "Goodnight, Sweetheart" kicked in, playing over and over as the colored lights of the rides flicked off one by one and the concession stands rolled down their steel shutters and security with their orange-coned flashlights slowly herded the patrons from the picnic groves at the back of the park, around the lagoon and along the midway toward the front gates.

It was Owen's favorite time of night, a reprieve from the constant thrum of the compressor that powered the House. Usually he worked alone, but this week he was breaking in Matt to sub for him (and to take over permanently in case he won the job he was shooting for). They dawdled as they swept the platform, watching the crowd saunter past. Even after pulling a double shift, Owen couldn't deny the old-timey gaslights and burbling fountains made the place romantic, a quiet end to a long day. Everywhere in the flood of people, couples nuzzled and held hands. Near the entrance the superstitious stopped by the giant clockface made entirely of flowers. It was good luck, supposedly, if you kissed right at midnight, though it hadn't worked for him and Lorraine.

"Whoa," Matt said, leaning in, "check out Shakira there."

Owen didn't see who he meant.

"Two o'clock. With her ugly stepsisters."

He glanced up again from the line of dust and plastic wristbands and crushed frozen lemonade cups, found the skinny dyed blonde with the navel ring and said, "Nice."

"Not her," Matt said, tipping his head and pointing with his elbow. "*Her.*"

The girl was tall and blonde and tan—long-legged and wide-eyed as a model. She wore jean shorts with a thick black belt and a clinging silver halter top that divulged a dark curve of cleavage. His first thought was that she would make Lorraine laugh.

"Yikes," he said.

"Yikes good or yikes bad?"

"Just yikes."

The Ghost Ship: An Unfinished Novel

"Sometimes you need a little yikes," Matt said. He'd unexpectedly become the ladies' man of the pair when he hooked up with Irina, one of the Byelorussian girls who came for the summer. Matt had been her escort during orientation, helping her with the basic English she'd need to sell buffalo chicken strips and Cokes. She was tiny but plump, with pretty blue eyes and crooked teeth. Her hair was shorter than Matt's, and she was so fair her eyebrows were nearly invisible. She worked in the Doubloon Saloon and lived in a dorm on the inlet behind the family campgrounds. Matt complained about her curfew but said he'd gotten used to her always smelling like french fries. She was his first real girlfriend, the way Lorraine had been Owen's last year, and Owen had to be happy for him. He was sorry too. He thought Matt would be able to brag more if he and Lorraine were still together.

The line of security filed by, spread wide, flashlights swinging like a search party. "Goodnight, Sweetheart" finished, and for a second there was just the wobbly blipping of the needle tracing the groove before the song started again. Owen shouldered the lead car like a blocking sled and drove with his legs to get it rolling. Matt followed with the other one, bulling it through the giant, leering skull painted on the swinging doors.

They went out and grabbed their brooms and came back in again. Owen found the switch, turned off the strobes and blacklights and turned on the overheads. The floor, the walls, the ceiling—everything not designed to leap out at the riders was painted black to absorb the light, making the weak fluorescent wash seem purplish and jittery, as if the bulbs were dying. The floor was terminally dusty, showing the footprints of their sneakers.

It was always a surprise to see how much crap people had dropped—or thrown, since a lot of stuff (hats, stuffed animals, once a bra) ended up gracing the displays. Sometimes there was money, and not just change that spilled onto the seats but bills lying on the floor—scattered singles like leaves, wads folded into quarters. The gold chains and engraved ankle bracelets and sunglasses Owen took to the lost and found, but the money he kept. It was nasty work scraping up gum and swabbing down vomit, and he figured he'd earned it. This week he was splitting the loot with Matt, which was cool, since Matt was a bud. When—if!—he moved over to the Ghost Ship, he'd be teamed with someone—Justin Lauer, Kim Janczuk and Teddy Brox were his main competition—and then it would be finders keepers.

They grabbed a garbage bag and the mop bucket from the closet and did their usual walkaround, following the track through the maze of hallways, picking up the big stuff, stooping to glop tar remover on the knots and caterpillars of gum. The solvent smelled like kerosene mixed with airplane glue and made Owen pleasantly dizzy as he scrubbed up a piece with a rag.

"People are fucking pigs," Matt said, over by the electric chair.

"What is it?" Owen asked, and saw him wiping at a stringy green loogie on the condemned man's boot.

"Why do people do shit like this?"

"Hey, you can always go back to the Turtle."

"At least the little kids don't hawk on everything," Matt said.

"Yeah, they just wipe their boogers on them."

Cleanup went faster with Matt—too fast for Owen, who liked to unwind by himself inside the ride. They were nearly to the tied-up bride about to be run through the buzzsaw

The Ghost Ship: An Unfinished Novel

when Matt's walkie-talkie squawked. Like every night, it was Irina, and Owen remembered what it had been like last summer, rushing to finish up so he could be with Lorraine, racing his bike through the darkened midway, flashing his badge at the startled security guards. He remembered how cold the sand on the beach was, even through a blanket, and how bright the stars were when he opened his eyes after kissing for so long. It hadn't lasted. It wasn't meant to, Lorraine said, like it was something natural and passing, a summer shower. All he could say was that it didn't feel that way to him. Now Lorraine was going out with Keith Perrin from the Ripcord, though the rumor was they'd broken up.

"Go ahead," he told Matt. "I got this."

"We're going to the Crap Shack later, if you want to come."

"Nah, I've got that final on Friday. Gotta study if I want to be the alpha geek."

"Okay," Matt said, but unconvinced. He bopped Owen's fist with his and turned the corner and his sneakers scuffed away up the crazily tilted, day-glo mineshaft. His footsteps backtracked—once, twice—the broom handle rattled inside the closet, and the swinging doors thunked shut.

Really, it was what Owen wanted, to be alone, nowhere. His father was working graveyard so there was no one waiting for him. The house would be dark except for the light in the kitchen. There'd be a note on the table warning him not to stay up too late, signed "Love, Da," something he'd started a couple of months after Owen's mom died and that Owen would never get used to. It was better here.

As if to reward him, there was a dollar on the floor by old Mrs. Bates knitting with her back turned in her rocker, but that was all; the rest was gum and cigarette butts and a couple of empty nips of Jack Daniel's. Kneeling, he could feel the tuolene in the tar remover vaporizing brain cells. Some nights he didn't mind, but he really did have to study later, and tried to breathe through his mouth. That was one habit the job had cured him of—gum. He couldn't see a person standing in line blowing bubbles without thinking about how he'd be on his knees later, cleaning up their congealed spit. Each white or red or aqua blob was like a little ball of disease, and he was glad for the tuolene. With each wad he clawed up he made a face, doubling the rag so he wouldn't get any on his hands. He was nearly to the end, on the far side of the straightaway through the hinged tombstones that clacked against the cars, when he discovered something much worse.

Resting across the nose of the mummified pirate who guarded his cobwebbed treasure chest was a limp ribbed con-dom. It lay wrinkled and translucent, straddling the leathery bridge like a drippy breathe-right strip.

It wasn't the first he'd seen discarded this deep inside the ride. The House of Horrors was one of the few places in the park that couples could be completely alone. It didn't matter that the barn was damp and smelled of mold or that other people might see, with all the strobe lights. This summer he'd swept up dozens of the torn foil packets. No, what shocked Owen was the sheer kooky accuracy of the shot, since the car came swinging hard out of the corner here and with a blast of macabre laughter the pirate popped up, a shaky marionette waving its cutlass. Whoever threw the rubber had shucked it at precisely the right time and tossed it so it stuck, on contact, to a moving target—lucky, Owen would have said, if he wasn't the one who had to clean it up.

He thought he could just brush it off, but it had dried like glue to the dummy's face.

The Ghost Ship: An Unfinished Novel

He swiped at it again. The pirate just lolled on its wires, grinning behind its eyepatch.

He wasn't going to touch the thing. He had rubber gloves but they were buried somewhere in the bottom of the closet. He used the broom like a spear, jabbing at the condom with the bristled end. It was heavy and awkward, and the pirate wouldn't stay still. He looked around for a better tool. If he were outside, he thought, he'd find a stick—and then laughed, because the answer was right in front of him.

"Give me a hand here, Long John," he said, and took the pirate's bony arm with the cutlass and chopped at the condom.

It dropped, followed by the tip of the pirate's papier-mâché nose, rattling across the track like a fallen acorn.

"No way," he said, and closed his eyes as if to make it disappear.

He looked at the blade. It was made of wood and not at all sharp. He must have knocked it loose with the broom. "Stupid."

The dummy was just old, shellacked papier-mâché gone dingy and brittle with age. He'd have to glue the piece back on and let it set overnight. The thing's face was so creased and gnarled that no one would ever know except him—because, honestly, no one gave a shit about anything around here—and while he was bummed and angry at his own care-lessness, there was nothing else he could do.

In the closet he found the crazy glue and dug up the pair of rubber gloves he was supposed to wear when using the remover. They smelled far too condom-like, and pinched the hair on his arms.

After he'd bagged the rubber and tossed all the nasty rags, he sat tailorseat beside the treasure chest, cradling the pirate's head in his lap to keep it still. The nose was surprisingly light, dry as the comb of an old wasp's nest. It had snapped off, leaving a jagged hole in the pirate's face through which Owen could see a glint of white he assumed was the styrofoam form they'd molded the papier-mâché around. He tipped the head to see better, leaning to one side so the weak light could reach past him, and squeezed the tube, guiding the plastic tip along the ragged edge of the hole, leaving an even bead of glue as overpowering as the tuolene. He pressed the crusty nose on and sat there holding it tight. The glue was only supposed to take a minute, but he waited, making sure.

Outside, the belltower atop the Moorish administration building chimed midnight, and as he did every night, he saw himself by the garden clock, bending to Lorraine's face—soft and vulnerable without her glasses—closing his eyes and opening to her, wishing this kiss would keep them together forever. He closed his eyes now to relive it, knowing that, as Matt accused, he was only torturing himself.

Her mouth was warm and still sweet from the Dippin' Dots he'd bought her, and their kiss outlasted the bell ringing nine, ten, eleven, twelve, and the superstition was true, because when he pulled back she was smiling at him with what he knew was love. Only in the daydream she wasn't Lorraine anymore. It must have been the fumes from the glue, because now when he pulled back and opened his eyes, the girl he was kissing was a beautiful blond mermaid who drew him to her again, hungrily, a hint of teeth in her kiss, her breasts pushing against him, insistent, and then just as suddenly he realized that she'd become the pirate, its mildewed breath a foul dust in his mouth, and he reared back, letting go of the nose.

The pirate leered up at him glassily, just a puppet. Outside, the bells were finishing, each clear tone fading away, floating

The Ghost Ship: An Unfinished Novel

off across the lake, and bizarrely, as if the thought was not his own, Owen imagined how lonely it would be under all that water, how cold, forever.

He shook off the vision and the shiver that passed through him and stood. The pirate rose on its wires, held in place by its counterweight. He stepped back to check the face and thought he'd done an alright job. The seam was just another deep crease in the mummy's wrinkled skin. To the unfamiliar eye, it would look like it always looked. In the dark, no one would be able to tell the difference.

4/ *The* Shauna Cheeks

THE PHONE caught her in the middle of heating up some leftover pizza for Mina and Kel while she watched the news on the little kitchen TV. She thought she'd gotten rid of the woman from the Beacon, but here she was again, introducing herself like Shauna should recognize her name, asking once more if this was the Shauna Cheeks who attended Admiral Perry Middle School from 1973 to 1976. It almost made her wish she hadn't changed her name back.

"That would be me," she said, glancing at the doorway to make sure the kids weren't listening, "but I'd really rather not talk about the fire, if you don't mind."

"No," the woman said, "that's not why I'm calling. I just spoke to an old friend of yours, and he said he'd like for you to get in touch with him."

"Is that right?" Shauna said.

"I told him I couldn't give out your number—"

"Good."

"—but that I'd pass his number along to you, then you could decide if you wanted to get in touch with him."

"Thank you," Shauna said, "but if it's all right I'd prefer it if you didn't."

"His name is Tony Booker."

She was surprised at how strange she felt hearing his name spoken out loud after so many years—like an old lover, someone she'd tried to forget. She wondered how much he'd told this Lynn person. Nothing, if she knew him at all. The woman was just fishing. "Sorry, not interested."

"He said to tell you he's coming to the dedication."

"Is that right?" Now she wanted the number, to tell him to stay away. Or was it a lie designed to make her talk? Because it didn't make sense. Tony would be the last person to come back.

"He wanted to know if you were going."

"If you don't mind, I'd appreciate it if you didn't call me again. Please."

"You don't want his number?"

"No, I don't. Thank you though."

"No," the woman said, "thank you. I'm sorry if I bothered you."

"That's all right," Shauna said, but once she'd hung up she paced the kitchen, the anchorman's patter floating around her like another language, some nonsense song.

Tony Booker had had this effect on her since she was a teenager, except the reasons were simpler then. She was supposed to be a good girl, and a brain, almost a gender of its own in those days. The only class they had in common was homeroom, and he was rarely there. He was already too tall for their one-piece study chairs and had to fold himself over

The Ghost Ship: An Unfinished Novel

the arm to write anything. By himself he was quiet, answering Mrs. Pollard with a polite murmur, but out front at lunch with his crew he was the one who goofed the most, doing impressions, mocking Mr. Fisher's daily pronouncements over the P.A. with precision. On gamedays he wore his jersey like the rest of the team, high-fiving each other in the halls, while she moved invisible through the school, quietly nailing every homework, every test, every extra credit question.

The crush she had on him made no sense. Her parents would have said he wasn't serious, that he was just another trifling boy running the streets with his no-account friends. They never had the chance to deliver that lecture (she'd heard it more than a few times concerning Marvin, and ignored it, to her everlasting regret), because outside of her diary she never mentioned her feelings. It was only after the fire that they discovered how much they had in common besides their secret, but by then they were entirely different people, and she was too confused to hold on to him.

The last she knew, he was squatting in a trailer on government land outside of Phoenix, raising bonsai trees for the golf resorts, hiking the foothills and staying stoned for days on what he called his vision quest. He said he needed to listen to the land if it was going to teach him true peace. He needed to be one with the world instead of one alone. That had been five years ago. He'd called a few months after the 25th anniversary and asked if she'd seen the special on PBS. She purposely hadn't. It was after midnight and he was wasted, far gone, a blurry voice from the desert.

"Y'ever wonder?" he asked, and then there was silence, as if he'd lost the thought. "I mean, seriously, Shauna, think about it…why us?"

It was a question she'd lived with a long time, so long that she'd learned to put it aside. "There is no why."

"There *is*," he insisted. "We were *chosen*. I can't prove it yet, but I know there's a connection."

"It doesn't change anything."

"It changes *everything*. It means it wasn't our fault."

"It wasn't," she said. "We were just babies."

"That's exactly it," he said, as if it sealed his case. "We were babies."

"Tony, are you alone there?"

"Always."

The divorce was still a year away, but she could have said the same thing, and yet she wanted to get off, stayed silent while he rambled on, becoming hopelessly tangled in his own cosmic thoughts, then said it was late there and that she had to get up early for work. He let her go, haltingly, apologizing for forgetting the time difference, assuring her he was fine, just fucked up. He didn't expect to see his best friends burn up on TV, that was all. "It's just, you know, I'm feeling a little ambushed here," he said, and after she finally maneuvered him into saying goodbye, that was exactly how she felt.

"Let me guess," Marvin said when she finally came back to bed. He held a hand to his forehead like a mindreader. "Big Chief Smokes-a-lot."

She worried about him the rest of the night, yet never called to see if he was okay, as if it would have been fine with her if he ended his misery and left her to hers.

Five years. Now he was coming back, and wanted her to know that. She wasn't sure she wanted to know why. She supposed it didn't matter. Ultimately he'd find her. He always did.

The Ghost Ship: An Unfinished Novel

5/ Walter Lawson, Beloved Husband and Father

HE DITCHED the Apache the first night, reluctantly trading it for a Ford F-150 with Pennsylvania plates in the dim lot of a suburban multiplex. On instinct he headed south, away from the lake and the busy interstates and across monotonous farmland, tooling through sleepy crossroads towns where the stoplights went blinking yellow after a certain hour. He drove with the radio tuned to the news, expecting to hear his name, weighing the risk of taking a motel versus sleeping in the truck. Several times he found himself turning to try out a thought on Tuffy, but the only thing occupying the seat was his duffel, stuffed with everything he'd need.

He stopped after midnight, killing his lights and bumping down an access road on the edge of some state forest. He slept with the cleaver within easy reach under the bench seat, and wished that he had a gun. The next morning he did the drive-thru at a McDonald's and bought a Plain-Dealer from a machine. There, beside the formal family portrait of the Greives, was a picture of him as a much younger Albert Manning, smiling as he received an award for starting a community garden in University Circle. They'd darkened the contrast to make him look blacker, and he thought he could use that. When he was finished with the article, he traded his reading glasses for his shades and tried out a frown in the rearview mirror. All he needed was his Indians cap to top off the look—crusty old cuss. He'd have to stop at a Wal-Mart and pick up a replacement.

He'd need a new name again too. The obituaries were full of possibilities, and as he chewed through his greasy sausage biscuit, he tried on the lives of the dead like so many discontinued suits at a thrift store.

Vaguely he thought of running, heading south, paying cash for gas and eating bad truckstop speed, but he knew what would happen if he didn't stop them. The fact that they'd used Katie to get to him convinced him it would be worse than the last time, and he cursed the idiots who ran the park for not knowing their own history. To him, a certifiably crazy person, it couldn't have been more obvious.

Half the names in the paper were either Polish- or Italian-sounding, useless to him. He settled on an ex-Marine who'd been a deacon in his church and a counselor at a group home, as if the dead man's history might steady him. He'd had luck with veterans before.

The first thing he needed was ID—easy enough, but he didn't want to go back into the city. He decided it could wait. The truck was stolen; if the cops stopped him he was finished anyway. Once he was in Sandusky he'd find a place to stay and start working on becoming Walter Lawson.

He thought he'd feel better moving, but the drive gave him too much time to think, and every town he slowed for made him paranoid. At each stoplight he watched the people on the streets—all white—as if they might turn as one and mob the truck, drag him screaming from the cab and finish him right there, kicking and stomping till they were satisfied. He kept the doors locked and his foot on the clutch, ready to peel out, and then the light changed and he went on, glad to be in the country again, pushing the limit.

The Ford was comfortable but just as bad on gas as the Apache. Even with the air conditioning off, he didn't have enough to make it all the way. He thought he should stop while he still had a choice. Once he got up around the interstate he'd be dealing with massive travel plazas with dozens

The Ghost Ship: An Unfinished Novel

of pumps and people everywhere. The thing spread like an infection. All it took was one person. He'd step inside the convenience mart to pay and they'd be on him.

He scouted the outskirts of Clarksfield for a station, finally settling on a Kwik-Fill with two empty islands and a doorless pillbox the cashier sat in, watching him like he might drive off. Cars bombed along the highway, and he used the bulk of the truck to shield himself. He slid the twenty into the pull-out tray and stood back as if the cashier could grab his wrist and yank him through. Once he got his change, he locked the doors and got back on the road and didn't stop until he reached Fairview.

Unlike Lakewood, the old neighborhood hadn't changed for the better. There was trash matted in the gutters and the rowhouses on Columbus Street were boarded up, yet he couldn't resist taking a peek at their old place.

Soot darkened the vanilla-colored brick of the Chandler Arms, and the evergreen hedge that bordered the doors was gone, otherwise it was much as he remembered it, still handsome and imposing, despite the sketchy-looking youngblood hanging out on the steps, eyeballing the passing traffic, from time to time loping over to see what people needed. He found their window on the third floor and the whole apartment flowed back into him—the rose wallpaper and the view of the lake, the way the morning sun lit up the narrow kitchen. It was their first place—their only place—and he could see Evvie reading over a script in her robe, drinking orange juice and eating dry toast to keep her figure. She wanted to be an actress, just as he hoped to work as a mechanic for NASA outside of town, but that was in some distant, perfect future. That summer all they could get were jobs at Edgewater, and they'd taken them, glad to have rent money and each other.

Down the block, a police cruiser crossed the intersection, scaring off the punk on the steps, and Arthur thought he was being stupid. He could do this later. He waited another minute before pulling out, checking his mirrors obsessively.

Some things about Fairview hadn't changed. The group of heavyset ladies at the bus stop on the corner of Huron could have been waiting there since 1975, headed off to their jobs cleaning the mansions of Sandusky's gold coast. He and Evvie used to take the 87 to work, and he was tempted to stop and offer to chauffeur them, and felt badly that he couldn't. Driving the route was different—quiet, that much faster—but when he turned onto the causeway and the cloudless wall of sky filled the windshield like a painting, the feeling was the same.

The lake was a dark line on the horizon and all around him now, the roadway suspended above the blue, pitching water. In an emergency pull-off, several men in ballcaps were sitting on the hood of a rusted Buick, fishing. Traffic was thick but fast, and most of the plates were from out-of-state. They were all headed for the same destination, making it feel like a race. Ahead, shimmering in the heat, Edgewater rose like a mythical city, the humped lifthills of roller coasters crowned with space-age towers capped with flags, and all the excitement he'd felt as a child rose and collided with all he'd suffered as an adult, reminding him not to trust anyone or anything here.

The road opened into a toll plaza, but instead of slowing, the other cars sped up, jockeying for position. He stayed to the left, trailing a minivan in which the children were watching cartoons. The lines were surprisingly long, giving him time to note the automated lanes for employees all the way to the right—they probably used some kind of bar-coded sticker or EZ-Pass. He wondered where the employee lot was

The Ghost Ship: An Unfinished Novel

now. Attached to each fanciful, candy-colored tollbooth was a camera, and he wished he'd stopped to grab a hat. When he'd worked here, parking was free and the lot was five times smaller, but he didn't tell the attendant that, just handed him a twenty and waited for his change, hoping his shades would protect him.

He couldn't believe how the place had grown. He didn't recognize any of the rides that jutted into the sky—steel corkscrews and loop-the-loops, all new. Inside, he had to drive another half-mile to find a spot, then walked back across the shadowless asphalt toward the front gates, where he tried to lose himself among the clamoring families and grab-assing packs of teens. The little kids worried him the most, with their sudden tottering rushes. He thought one would latch on to his leg and then they'd all attack, the crowd raging after his blood—unlikely, but he was vulnerable out of the truck, constantly on guard, and had to fight the urge to retreat. The sheer size of the place gave him some cover, but he felt conspicuously single, and old, and he thought it was a mistake coming during the day. After dark, he could buy a ticket and walk around all he wanted.

He found a kiosk labeled Guest Services, and while the attendant was busy with a couple of mothers, he helped himself to a map of the park and a glossy brochure. The girl's uniform was a cobalt polo shirt with EDGEWATER embroidered over her heart, and khaki pants; through the gates he saw a security guy in the same shirt in canary yellow, khakis and black tennis shoes. He could come close enough to duplicating those. The only tough thing was the plastic nametag, and he figured he could lift one. There had to be a locker room somewhere, and a laundry, maybe at one of the hotels.

The guard's walkie-talkie would be tuned to a common channel, simple to pick up.

So there were ways in, and ways to become invisible, at least for a short time. That was all he needed. The map and the brochure would give him enough information to begin. He knew it would be harder than he thought, but right now he didn't see how exactly. He had the feeling something was wrong, as if this was all a trap. And it was, he'd known that from the moment Katie Greive turned to him with the cleaver, but there was something else too. The whole thing felt set-up, as if they were using him. Why else would they come for him after all these years? They could get anyone to do it, they'd proven that.

He squinted at the sun-blanched park with its gardens and arcades, soaking in the blend of the new and the familiar, fending off nostalgia and loss—as always—by paying attention to the work at hand. He stayed in the shade a minute, watching the security guard wave a black device like a Dustbuster over some teenagers, then turned and headed back to the Ford.

6/ Public Relations

HE WAS just gulping down some Advil with his third coffee of the morning when line five lit up. Christ in a sidecar, what now?

Lines one through four were internal, connecting Warren Atwood with the rest of Edgewater, a world he considered his, having worked there his entire life. Nothing on lines one through four could surprise him. Line five was the outside line, bearer of demands and threats and impossible requests,

The Ghost Ship: An Unfinished Novel

especially now, a week away from the reopening. He thought of not picking up, but in the end, as always, his curiosity as much as his sense of professionalism got the better of him, and then he wished he'd let the machine answer.

It was Lynn McCourt with more questions about the fire, exactly what he didn't need. The great and powerful Adam Fitch had reamed him out last week for granting her access to the park archives, then given him strict orders not to talk to her, as if they could afford to piss off the Beacon. News flash: like every other burg in the Midwest, Sandusky was a one-paper town now. Unless the park wanted to pay for direct mail, they had to play nice. It was a mistake Ben Fitch—the real Fitch, with whom Warren Atwood had spent many a boozy night and many a contentious board meeting—would have never made.

"Lynn, Lynn, Lynn," Warren Atwood said, "to what do I owe the pleasure?"

"Just a minor detail I'm trying to nail down. I was going over the old plan maps the other day, and I think I figured something out. I just wanted to run it by the expert."

"Shoot."

"The location of the first Ghost Ship, that was where the Satellite was in the '50s."

"And the Scrambler. The barn overlapped both lots."

"Before that, there was another dark ride there."

"The Laff in the Dark." It was all in the archives; he wasn't giving anything away.

"Before that?"

He blew out a puff of air. "Couldn't tell you. The Laff in the Dark goes way back—well before my time, believe it or not."

"It looked from some of the earlier maps like there might have been a pond there."

"Very possible. With the water table we've got, all you have to do is dig a hole and you've got a pond."

"Have you ever heard of Caroline Sharp?"

"Nope," he said, honestly.

"She drowned in a pond at Edgewater back in 1905."

"Is that right? I'm surprised I've never heard of her."

"What I'm interested in is which pond she drowned in."

He could see where she was going with this thread—the site's unlucky history. It was too easy, he thought, a cheap hook. In the late '60s one of the carpenters framing the original Ghost Ship had died in spectacularly gruesome fashion, and after the fire the papers recalled that accident as if the two were mysteriously related. He was disappointed but not surprised Lynn had decided to pursue the theory.

"You tried the morgue already?"

"The one piece I could find just says 'an ornamental pond.'"

"There were more than a few of them back then," he commiserated.

"And from what I can tell only the bigger ones were named."

"It couldn't have been one of the beaches."

"No, that would be too easy."

"Nothing in Dietrick?" he asked, referring to the reverent official history sold in the gift shops.

"Nothing useful, and the tax maps before that only show buildings."

He knew the archives held hundreds of recently discovered glass-plate negatives from the era. She'd have to get lucky, and there was no way she'd find a name, but by comparing them she might be able to confirm that there'd been a pond there. It wasn't out of loyalty to Adam Fitch that he didn't offer Lynn McCourt this information, or craven

The Ghost Ship: An Unfinished Novel

self-preservation either, but something simpler and more powerful: Warren Atwood loved Edgewater Park and would do whatever he needed to protect it.

"I don't know what to tell you," he said. "At this point you know the territory better than I do."

"Thank you, but I doubt that."

Line two flashed—Barbara in marketing, probably wanting to go over this weekend's promotion. Last month he'd failed to catch a typo (not his) in the ad copy, and hundreds of families had shown up expecting to ride all day for ten dollars. It was a simple mistake, but one he'd never made before, and though he denied it, at 65, deep-down Warren Atwood worried that it might be the first sign of slippage.

"Anything else I can help you with?"

"No, that's it for today."

"Hey Lynn, do me a favor, huh?"

"What is it?"

"When you publish this thing, do it off-season, okay? Makes a great Christmas gift and all that."

"No promises," she said, thanked him again and let him go.

Line two was still blinking, but he was in no mood. He took his coffee to his window overlooking the midway and stood there sipping, watching the crowd and thinking about Caroline Sharp and how the park had been a hundred years ago—women in bustled skirts with frilly parasols, those chaste bathing suits. The people below him would probably seem as quaint and outdated in fifty years, the way the groovy hairstyles of the '70s already seemed ridiculous.

Styles changed, people didn't—that was why Lynn McCourt's history of the fire scared the shit out of Warren Atwood. People came to Edgewater to be thrilled and frightened within an inch of their lives. That inch was critical, whether it was the metal pipe of a lapbar or the woven nylon of a shoulder harness or the chrome tongue of a seatbelt. Caroline Sharp and the carpenter who got splashed all over the Ghost Ship (Minton? Fenton? Ben Fitch had dictated the press release to him) and the kids who got fried alive were a reminder that the park wasn't special at all but operated by the same rules as the rest of the world.

It was a proposition he knew to be untrue, despite those few exceptions. There *was* something magical here; he felt it the first time he crossed the causeway and passed through the ornate terra cotta gates emblazoned with gold stars and sickle moons, vaguely oriental, as if he were entering another kingdom. He didn't know how much of it was the land—the marshy point jutting swordlike into the belly of the lake, facing sunset—and how much was the park's history, but, like summer or youth, there was something eternal and otherworldly about the place.

In this, and maybe only this, Warren Atwood was absolutely right. Whatever power inhabited Edgewater had been there long before he arrived and would be there long after he was gone.

Behind him, the phone trilled. Line one—Fitch. He juked around his desk chair, almost spilling his coffee, and caught it before the second ring.

7/ Calling Buddy Lee

IT WAS that boring time around four in the morning and K.J. was coming back from running doorchecks on the lakeside when he turned a corner too fast and had to brake and then swerve hard to miss hitting another Cushman sitting in front of the new ride.

The Ghost Ship: An Unfinished Novel

"The hell you doin," he said from reflex. "Try and kill me like that."

There was no one there to answer him. The cart's lights were on, aimed at the chainlink fence. The gate hung open, the lock popped. The engine was running as if whoever was driving had just stepped inside to investigate.

The lights were weak, even joined by his. They barely reached the open porch of the loading platform, showing a maze of ropes surrounding a gallows. Skulls grinned in the dimness. Past that it was black.

"Naw, naw," K.J. said, cancelling the whole idea with a shaky wave of his hand, "I don't think so."

He called in on his walkie-talkie.

"What you want?" Cherise asked.

"Where Reg at?"

"How'm I sposed to know?"

"I got a cart here by the Ghost Ship."

"What you mean a cart?"

"I got *someone's* cart here. I need to find out whose it is."

"It's not mine," Reg cut in. "I'm just getting the Raptor."

"Who else is on?"

"You're it," Cherise said. "Darryl's sick."

"So it's no one's cart," K.J. asked.

"You want me to call Buddy Lee?"

"*Hell* no," Reg said. Buddy Lee was the city cop on grave-yard assigned to the park. His real name was Leroy Detwiler, but his forehead was round and hairless like the doll on the jeans commercials, and he was just as useless. He had his own office in the administration building that he hated leaving, and he couldn't be bothered to learn anyone's name. Everyone was "cuz" or "chief."

"What you want me to do?" Cherise asked.

"Nothin," K.J. said. "I'll check it out."

"You wait, I can back you up," Reg said.

"Nah, I'm cool."

"Cause I can be over there in like three minutes."

"That's all right."

He left the Cushmans on and took out his flashlight. As he crossed in front of the gate, his shadow loomed, huge. The lock wasn't just open but broken, the long silver prongs of the shackle bent against themselves as if by a giant's hand. He had to force himself to go in, holding the flashlight out in front of him like a gun. The gallows in the middle rose like an empty altar. He couldn't take his eyes off the loading platform, a black gap under the palm-frond roof, and had to blindly highstep over the ropes until he found a handicapped lane that ran along one wall. As he advanced, he kept glancing back to be sure of his escape route. It was dark back here, and his single beam threw a wavering circle across the face of the ride, picking out doubloons and skulls and bloody cutlasses, the black background and one knobbed crossbone of the Jolly Roger. He was almost to the ramp when he looked up and saw something large and ungainly dangling from the yardarm that jutted from the front, something that didn't belong at all. He stopped and trained his light on it, and had to step back, ready to run.

It was a charred body with a sign hung around its neck, the skin melted in dirty lumps, the limbs warped and bubbled black—or not a body, just a dummy, a department store mannekin. $HAME! the sign said.

"Shame on your own damn self," K.J. shouted. "Think you can scare me with that."

The Ghost Ship: An Unfinished Novel

He kept his light on it as he fumbled for his walkie-talkie.

"Hey, Reg?" he said.

"What you got?"

"Why don't you come on over here."

8/ Kill Switch

HE WAS squeezing in some last-minute cramming at the kitchen table when he heard the stuttering squeal of the Taurus turning in the driveway and then a minute later his father clumping up the back stairs and the crunch of the key in the lock.

His father had on his olive janitor's uniform, his hospital badge clipped to his pocket. Owen gave him a flip of a wave and concentrated on the diagram of the control panel. He was trying to memorize the position and shape of the red kill switch in case they made him find it in the dark. Last summer the big blackout had trapped dozens of riders in the House of Horrors, and when the power came back on, the cars nearly ran some of them down.

"You're up early," his father said, peering at the mess of papers spread around him.

"I've got that test." Owen had told him about it just yesterday, but it didn't seem to register. That happened when you drank yourself to sleep every morning. "For the new ride?"

"I know what test, and I don't care for that tone, so try another."

His father popped a beer and sat down across from Owen so he had to work to ignore him. His father watched him, letting out a satisfied gasp after each long draw until he was done with the can, and then he didn't go and get another, just sat there staring at Owen.

"I wish you studied that hard for school," he said.

It was a sore point, and when Owen looked up, his father reached across and chucked his shoulder. "I'm kidding! Jesus, aren't *we* touchy."

He got up and cracked another Bud and searched the cupboards for something to eat. "You get breakfast yet?"

"Yes," Owen said.

"What'd you have?"

"Cereal."

His father used this as an excuse to quit looking and sat down again, slurping and gasping, leaning back in his chair and staring into space between tugs as if distracted by some longplaying internal conversation.

"Yepper depper do," he finally said.

Three years ago Owen's mother had died of ovarian cancer in the same hospital where Owen's father punched in every day, and by now Owen was used to his random comments. "It's all shit anyway," his father would philosophize after seven or eight beers. "Fuck it in a bucket," he'd joke, "know what I'm sayin'?" and Owen could only agree. The other thing he said that Owen hated was "You and me, kiddo," but that came later, mumbled blearily as Owen was unlacing his boots and getting him to bed, often just tossing their old Browns blanket over him on the couch and clicking the TV off. Those intimate moments also served as occasions for his father to reminisce about Owen's mother's legs and brains, her laugh and her standing rib roast and her courage in the face of a wasting death, and to tell Owen how much she had loved him—as much, his father said, as he loved him. Today, thanks to the test, he was spared that litany.

The Ghost Ship: An Unfinished Novel

He wasn't finished studying, but he wasn't getting any-thing done here, and he pocketed his pen and fitted his handouts into the glossy Edgewater folder they gave him. He grabbed his I.D. and his keys and a bottle of water. He was hoping to make a clean getaway, but his father trailed him to the door, can in hand.

"So how much extra do you get if you ace this test?"

"Nothing," Owen said. He'd told him this already, but was prepared to take shit for it again.

"You like working there," his father said, as if the idea had just occurred to him.

"Yeah, sometimes."

"Sometimes is enough. A lot of people don't even have that."

"I know."

"All right," his father said, "go get 'em, Tiger," and clapped him on the shoulder like a coach. His touch made Owen cringe inwardly, and after he closed the door he still felt it on him, pushing him down the stairs and away from the duplex and their crappy neighborhood like a phantom hand.

↺→

THE GATES wouldn't open for another two hours, but already long lines of cars inched through the booths at the end of the causeway. Inside, the park was quiet, the rides still. Without the clank and clatter of the coasters and the PA's relentless cavalcade of hits, there were only the haphazard sounds of work. The Byelorussian girls wiped down their counters, fir-ing bottles of Windex like gunslingers. Vendors' trucks parked incongruously on both sides of the midway, unloading soda cannisters and boxes of frozen fries.

To Owen, this time of the morning felt like the final minutes backstage before a play, the crew calmly setting all the props in place. It filled him with the same sense of ownership as the slow moments after closing. He'd planned to hole up in the House and review the safety procedures, knowing they'd make up the bulk of the test, but as he passed the back fence of the Blue Streak he saw Lorraine doing her daily walkaround.

She was walking the ties in her Nikes, following the track up the last gentle hump of the old coaster before the station, her eyes on the rails, looking for problems. She had on her skinny glasses that made her look brainy; when the gates opened, she'd trade them for contacts and then complain after closing that her eyes hurt. At school she ran every morning for crew and the tendons behind her knees were taut as bowstrings, her arms tan and lightly muscled. She stopped and knelt down to check something in the brake pit, pulled a rag out of her back pocket and wiped at it. Her face was composed and serious, intent on the problem—a face he knew from when they played Ms. PacMan at the Crap Shack. Her ponytail, blonder than her severely pulled-back hair, waggled over the strap of her Edgewater visor. If this was last year he would have stopped to admire her and waited until she saw him, making a joke of her beauty and its effect on him; instead, he turned as if slapped and made for the corner of the Dodgems, hoping she wouldn't see him. He'd have to detour around the Calypso and the Wildcat and come back the long way by the marina, but it was worth it.

Fuck that, another voice said, and as if this opposite thought had seized control of his body, he stopped, spun on his heel as if challenged and stalked directly for her. A whole different set of facts surfaced—unpleasant but indisputably true. She was pretty and smart and strong, but so what? So

The Ghost Ship: An Unfinished Novel

were a million other girls in the world—ten million, a hundred million. He'd treated her better than anyone he'd ever known in his whole life, and she'd dumped him so she could go off to college and screw whoever she wanted, so fuck running away and fuck shutting up. He'd climb that fence and tell her to her face what a slut she was, and if she tried to run from him she wouldn't get far. He might not be the best-looking guy in the world or the smartest, but he could sure as hell outrun the bitch. He'd take that rag and stuff it down her throat, then drag her under the platform and kneel on her shoulders so he could work on her face—

The fence stopped him. His clenched hands gripped the chainlink like a prisoner's. He looked at them as if they belonged to someone else, and his anger vanished, drained away to nothing. It was like being shaken awake. He wasn't exactly sure what had just happened. Lorraine was looking down at him from the track, a hand on her glasses as if she couldn't believe what she was seeing.

"What the hell are you doing?"

"Nothing," he said.

"You call that nothing?"

"What?"

"Hel-*lo*? Shaking the fence like you're insane? If you want to talk to me, Owen, just talk to me."

Blair Lockwood from the Old Time Photo Gallery walked by and gave them an appraising look. They both waited until she was gone, as if they were playing by some unspoken rules.

"I'm sorry," he said, but couldn't find a way to explain himself. "Forget it."

"Matt said you'd been acting weird. I thought he was kidding."

"I've been studying all week for this stupid test."

"Kim's taking it too, and she's not freaking on me."

"I guess I'm just stressed out."

"It couldn't be that you're still mad at me." She rested both elbows on the rail, tilting her head in her hands—greasy from the track—and he was defenseless.

"Did Matt tell you that?"

"You don't hang out anymore."

"I don't feel like it."

"Too many bad memories," she guessed.

"Too many good ones, actually."

"Awww, poor Owey," she said, sticking her bottom lip out, like she hadn't sentenced him to the longest winter of his life, the longest spring. "You should come out tonight."

"Why?"

"You never know. You might get lucky."

"Is that right?"

"You won't know unless you come out, will you?"

It was a game, he thought, not serious, but just talking with her made him want last summer back, the long cool nights they parked by the water, the ghostly green light of the dashboard and the kiss of her Mustang's leather seats on his skin, the eternal puzzle of the emergency brake. The reality of her—of them—overwhelmed him. She was his first, and he'd loved her blindly, completely, thinking she felt the same way. He would always feel foolish for that, and for losing her. Now here she was again.

"I thought you were going out with Keith Perrin."

"Why do I have to be going with anyone? We went to the movies a few times, that doesn't mean we're getting married. I'm not Amish, okay? I'm nineteen."

The Ghost Ship: An Unfinished Novel

"Hey, I know that," he said, holding up his hands to show he was blameless, but secretly he was pleased the rumors were true: for whatever reason, she and Keith had broken it off.

She was grinning at him enigmatically, challenging him to say something else.

"I gotta go," he said, tipping his head back at the rest of the park.

"Maybe I'll see you tonight."

"Maybe."

"Hey," she said as he was walking away, and he turned and walked backwards. "Good luck on your test."

"Thanks," he said, "I'm gonna need it."

He would. When he got back to the House he was too scattered to study. He hovered over the dull handouts, replaying their conversation and the way she looked at him, daydreaming about tonight. He'd have to clean out his car, stick in a new box of tissues. He wished he'd worn that yellow Aeropostale shirt she always tried to steal. He wondered if he'd have time to go home and change. She might notice, but that could be good too.

He'd barely gotten through the placement of the fire extinguishers when Matt came banging in, hungover and sipping a giant Icee. "Man, you shoulda come," he said. They'd played quarters with these sailors from Nigeria who gave them all rides in a Zodiac. It was his first time setting up by himself, and every few minutes Owen had to stop and show him what to do. Owen didn't tell him about Lorraine, not wanting to jinx anything.

He was afraid of being late and headed over to the administration building a little early. They were all waiting in the upstairs hall—Kim Janczuk and Teddy Brox and

Justin Lauer, Benny Pena and Cara Rosenstein, the pair of quiet first-year girls no one knew and the two Byelorussian guys no one could understand. They were all paging through their handouts except Justin, who was nodding along with his headphones. Owen claimed a spot against the wall and opened his folder, hoping to consolidate his grasp of the reset command. He was still confused about how to use it for more than just a single car, but didn't dare ask anyone.

He hated tests. He'd always been bad at them, even when he knew the material, and as he stood there he could feel his throat closing and had to swallow. A queasy shiver vibrated inside him, and he remembered freezing on the word "postcard" during a classwide spelling bee, stagefright combined with the panic of sudden blankness and then everyone laughing at him.

Mr. March was right on time, carrying a thin manila folder and a box of number 2 pencils. He unlocked the door and they poured into the stuffy room behind him, assuming their usual seats. He asked Justin to take his headphones off and then everyone to please stow their belongings under their chairs. "You have fifty minutes," he said, handing the tests out. "I seriously doubt any of you will need all of it, so please use the extra time to check your answers."

Owen sat in the back corner, and was the last to get one. It was a single sheet, multiple choice, twenty questions on each side. He took his time, making sure to completely blacken the oval for the computer. The first few seemed too easy—the start-up sequence, the location of the emergency exits—and he recalled most of the first aid techniques from the handout, but by the back of the page they were beyond memory and into competing hypothetical situations:

The Ghost Ship: An Unfinished Novel

28. Standard evacuation procedure should be implemented in all but which of the following:
   A. Electrical storm
   B. Hailstorm
   C. Tornado
   D. Terror threat
   E. None of the above

He skipped to the next one, and the next, and the one after that, but the answers were just as baffling.

Teddy Brox got up, handed in his test and left, and Owen backtracked. Evacuating people into a hailstorm or tornado couldn't be right, but you'd have to after a bomb threat. The contradiction gave his brain a twinge like a mini-stroke. Maybe there was a special evacuation plan for terrorism they'd gone over in class that he somehow missed. After studying so hard, he felt helpless guessing, as if he were giving up, but the clock was running. E—all but none. The next question was even worse. He filled in the oval answer key with steadily increasing anger, grinding the dark lead into the page. Fuck it in a bucket, right?

In front of him, Cara Rosenstein stood and looped her purse over her shoulder. Benny Pena pushed his chair back with a scrape. And there was March, leaning back against the desk all cool and calm, letting the rest of them sweat. Where was he the last time Owen had to tell a line of people who'd been standing for an hour in a hundred-degree heat that they had to shut down the ride? Probably sitting in some air-conditioned office drinking a Coolata and playing free cell, the fuckhead. Owen would show him what he thought of his test, and with a swift and vicious efficiency he filled in the rest of the answers at random, grabbed his shit, slapped his paper on the desk and bulled through the door.

It wasn't until he was in the stairwell that he could breathe again. "Asshole!" he spat, so loud that it echoed, accusing him.

"No shit," Justin Lauer said, coming down. "Fucking trick questions. What'd you put for the heart attack one?"

He couldn't remember the question, let alone his answer, and he didn't care. He wanted to push Justin Lauer over the railing for caring and watch him fall, flailing, all four stories.

"It's bullshit, man," Justin said. "They want someone to run that thing, they can write that shit down on a piece of paper and tape it to the console like every other fucking ride in this place."

He was just as pissed off as Owen, and instead of punching his thumbs into Justin's windpipe, Owen found himself agreeing with him (because he was right: that was all they needed, a card with the emergency procedures), and once they made it downstairs and outside and Justin skulked off to the Demon Drop, he'd completely recovered.

Walking back along the midway in the bright, mocking sunshine, he thought it was like a panic attack, the way the feeling had come over him, incapacitating. Part of it was how stressed out he was about the test. He'd stayed up late and gotten up early to study, and then he'd tanked it. Two months he'd been busting his ass, and for what? The needling fact returned like a headache, and he thought maybe it wasn't so strange that he went off—either time. No, in both cases—because deep down he was afraid Lorraine was playing him again and he wasn't strong enough to resist her—he had good reason to be angry, if only with himself.

The Ghost Ship: An Unfinished Novel

9/ For Your Security

THEY HAD him from the minute he ducked through the sliding doors—this huge black dude in a sky-blue Hawaiian shirt and sandals, probably a ballplayer once, maybe down for Charles Barkley's Pro-Am at Camelback. The other passengers had to catch themselves, doing cartoon doubletakes to prove they'd actually seen a person that big. He smiled down at them like someone famous, forgiving their stares. Even lugging two massive duffel bags, he moved with an easy grace, as if he might break into a run. Shaved head, muscled neck, gold-rimmed glasses that looked dainty hooked over his ears. The floor agent monitoring that end of the United line ducked his chin and whispered into his lapel, and his supervisor on the far side turned and found the guy immediately. The supervisor was not a basketball fan but had grown up in L.A., and his first thought was inescapable: Kareem.

His second was that they needed to be careful here; they might be dealing with a celebrity, and possibly a Muslim one.

That impression only lasted until the guy passed by the empty set of ropes welcoming First Class passengers and installed himself at the end of the switchbacked line for everyone else. It simplified things. Now they could pull him out at the counter. There was no way he could complain, a single guy traveling alone.

Standing there with his bags at his feet, Tony Booker was aware of the men checking him out. He was used to this kind of scrutiny, not just in airports but in supermarkets and shopping malls, at gas stations and video stores, even in the luxury hotels that were his loyal clientele. It was a lesson he'd learned young: he was just too big and too black to blend in with

America—with the rest of the world, really. He'd tried to remedy the situation in the '80s, moving to Ghana briefly to teach English, but people there didn't like Americans, and he never got used to the cramped formality of the culture or the dulling daily loneliness of exile. If the ranch was solitary, it was also his, though lately he'd come to see it, in its own way, as a trap. He'd wasted too many years digging a hiding place for himself. Whatever might happen at Edgewater, he didn't expect to get them back, but at least he'd be done running.

As the line shuffled along, a gate agent came around the outside of the ropes and checked people's tickets. There was a flight to Dallas in half an hour, and the agent was bumping people up to get them on. When she came to Tony, she gave him a professional smile and asked him where he was headed today.

"Cleveland," he answered.

She scribbled something on his ticket in blue pen. "You're all set."

"Thank you," he said, though he knew exactly what it meant.

When he finally made it to the counter, the woman who printed out his boarding pass looped the luggage stickers through the handles of his bags and asked him to take them over to the screeners at the big machine. He didn't have to come back; they could process them there.

On his way over, he nodded to the floor agent.

The screeners wore rubber gloves like EMTs. "You don't have to wait," the one promised, loading the first bag onto the conveyor.

The other screener behind the machine held up a hand and the belt stopped. The screener leaned in, squinting to read the image, then gestured the other guy over. They both looked at the image as if it couldn't be right.

The Ghost Ship: An Unfinished Novel

The first guy glanced at Tony, as if to make sure he hadn't taken off.

Tony gave him a salute of a wave to show it was no problem.

The man came over. "I'm sorry, sir, but I'm going to have to ask you to wait right here." He stood beside him like a guard.

The floor agents converged on the machine like a zone press. They didn't ask him if they could open the bag, they just set it on a table, unzipped it and dug in.

The screener suddenly stopped, up to his elbows in Tony's drawers, and told the floor agents to step back. He couldn't pull whatever he was after out, but didn't want to lose his grip on it, and had one hold the bag down for him. The two of them wrestled the duffel as if they were fighting over it, the screener tugging with both arms, dislodging balled socks and one high-top Nike and a CD case, until finally the gate agent pawed aside a stack of once-neatly folded shirts and the screener extracted a mass of bubble wrap the size of a bowling ball. The bubble wrap was wound tight with strapping tape which the screener carefully sliced open with a boxcutter. Inside the translucent cocoon was a cloudy plastic bag. Inside the bag, staring blindly out at them from within, was a woman's head.

They all paused, as if no one knew what to do.

The gate agent stepped away from Tony and muttered something into his lapel, and in less than ten seconds a state trooper was there to take his place. He asked to see Tony's I.D.

"Is this your personal property, Mr. Booker?"

"Yes, sir."

"Is there any reason for us to believe it may be dangerous?"

"No, sir," he said, and when the trooper kept trying to read his eyes, raised both hands to show he was being straight with him.

The trooper nodded to the screener, who undid the twist tie, leaning back as if the head might explode. When it didn't, he gently parted the mouth of the bag with his gloved hands and peered in. The woman was some kind of weird puppet, her skin ice-white, with bluish lips and vampire fangs. She had tiny lightbulbs for eyes.

"What the hell *is* this?" he asked.

"It's a gift," Tony Booker said. "For a friend."

The stones and branches and bags of dried herbs in the other duffel took even longer. In the end, the only thing they confiscated was the butane torch, and he could replace that for five bucks at any 7-Eleven.

10/ The Breakdown Lane

TWICE A day Shauna Cheeks passed the causeway where it intersected Shoreline Drive. It was the quickest route to work, and while she hadn't been back to Edgewater since the night of the fire, she saw no reason to detour around it either. That was in the past, along with Marvin and all the needless sorrow the two of them had put each other through. She had her hands full trying to raise Mina and Kel right without calling up a lot of old stuff.

Today she happened to be stopped at the light on her way home and was sitting there with the radio on, mulling over what she had planned for dinner, when the engine started missing. The car sputtered and shook as if it wasn't getting enough gas. She slipped it into park and pumped the accelerator, gently revving. She was second in line, and when the light dropped to green, she shifted into drive and the car surged forward, bucked, jerking, then flooded and died.

The Ghost Ship: An Unfinished Novel

The radio stayed on, then stopped when she turned off the ignition.

The semi behind her blared its air horn.

"Come on, baby," she pleaded, twisting the key hard, as if the car might respond to force.

Nothing, not even a click.

She was still in drive.

She cursed herself and rammed the gearshift into park and tried again. The starter ground on, coughing, but refused to turn over.

"No, no, no, no," she said.

She turned off the radio and gave it another shot—not close.

The honking was constant now, outraged. In answer, she put her hazards on and stuck her arm out the window to wave people by. The truck was right on her bumper and couldn't get around. The others had to wait for the left lane to clear out, and then they glared and gestured as they shot past, mouths twisted, showing teeth like pit bulls. Not all of them could make it. The light changed, and another wave of traffic swallowed them.

"Good car," she cooed, petting the dash. "You can do it."

But it couldn't.

Her nose was halfway into the intersection. As she tried to start the car again, there was a knock on her window. The fist belonged to an arm with a green tattoo of intertwined hearts skewered by an arrow. It was a beefy white guy in a t-shirt and biker vest—the driver of the truck.

"Need a push?" he asked, and gestured to the wide open causeway beside her.

"I think it's flooded."

"Put her in neutral and we'll get you out of the way for now."

She didn't protest, just cut the wheel as he shoved against the trunk. The car slowly rolled into the gritty breakdown lane of the causeway, the blue water pitching beneath them. He came around to her window, red-faced and gasping a little.

"Thank you," she told him, as a minivan whistled by, dangerously close.

"You got triple-A? I can call you in if you want."

"I've got a phone, thanks."

"All right," he said, as if the problem was solved, and left. A minute later, the light changed and the truck rumbled across her rearview mirror.

She waited for the engine to drain, looking out over the lake and the twin curving bridges of the causeway, the hump where the freighters went under. Every minute or so, another few cars shot by, rocking hers. The park was a mile off, an island on the horizon, featureless from this distance, yet it unsettled her to know it was there, waiting for her. Marvin never understood why she wouldn't let Mina or Kel go there for the annual school picnic. He thought it was a weakness in her, and unfair, her inability to overcome her own fear depriving them of a normal childhood. She could hear how she'd sound if she told him the truth—that she was protecting the children from something evil, some *thing* that knew her in a way, if he was lucky, he never would. No one ever would except Tony, but she couldn't tell Marvin that, so she let him believe she was weak. It was easier, or so she'd thought. When they fought, that last bad year together, he accused her of not telling him anything. She said she wasn't keeping any secrets. That's not what I mean, he said, angry that she didn't understand. I don't know what you're feeling. It's like you've got this mask on all the time and you're afraid to take it off, and

The Ghost Ship: An Unfinished Novel

I don't know why because you won't tell me. Are you happy, are you sad? I have no idea what you are anymore.

I'm just me, she said, knowing it wasn't a good enough answer.

I can't do this, Sha, he said. She could see he was hurt, and while she wanted to help him, she knew it was best to let him go. Those first nights alone, she'd had to stop herself from calling him, or calling Tony, asking if he had room for one more in his fortress of solitude. But the next morning there were Mina and Kel to feed and get off to school, and work, and dinner to think about, the force of dumb routine buoying her, keeping her evenly drifting forward, and she surrendered to the tide of days—exactly what Marvin couldn't bear.

Now, gazing across the water, she thought she'd been wrong, that she should have confessed everything, but just the thought of telling Marvin dredged up a single, bitter laugh. She shook her head at the dashboard and the keys dangling from the ignition. It made sense that she'd break down here. She was tempted to see it as more than a coincidence but squashed that possibility before it could take hold.

Another pack of cars rocketed past, headed for Edgewater. She thought she'd waited long enough, and tried the engine.

It fired up immediately, running quiet and steady as if nothing was wrong.

The road in front of her beckoned, empty. It was one way the whole way; there was nowhere to turn around, just a mile-long gauntlet of lightpoles crowned with nesting seagulls. It was where the local teenagers staged their races until one of them flipped his little fast and furious Honda over the rail and disappeared, still belted in.

Here was a chance to prove that the past was truly behind her. She could drive out and back in less than five minutes and still be home in time to make dinner. Except now she questioned the timing of everything. It seemed too convenient, with Tony coming and the woman from the Beacon calling. Her Uncle Charles was famous in the family for being court-martialed for refusing to board an Army transport that later crashed in a blizzard in Nova Scotia. When the presiding officer asked him why he didn't get on the plane, he said, "I didn't feel right about it." Shauna had felt the same way about The Ghost Ship, but she was fifteen and in love; she would have done anything to be with Woody Campbell then.

Now, at forty-five, she didn't have that excuse, and before the light could change, she swung the car into a U-turn. The causeway wasn't wide enough, and as she backed up, broadside across the dotted line, the engine knocked and strangled and died.

11/ The Vertical File

LYNN MCCOURT loved to go fishing in the morgue. It was more than research to her. As a girl, her most prized possession had been her library card, and that was still true. Even now, the quiet shelter of a library felt like a second home, though she did miss the musty old card catalogs with their hand-typed citations, the tops worn soft from decades of seeking fingers. Computers weren't the same. For the photographers at the Beacon, the digital revolution was a godsend, but every time she searched for something on-line, she found herself lost in a directionless maze, the screen smothered in pop-ups urging her to take a vacation.

The Ghost Ship: An Unfinished Novel

She liked microfilm. Like most papers, the Beacon had committed its entire run before 1990 to hundreds of reels stored in pleasingly identical, neatly indexed boxes and available to any reporter willing to deal with Philip Edson.

Edson ran the morgue with a near fetishistic attention to detail. He was somewhere in his mid-forties, though it was hard to tell because he was vastly fat and already bald. He drove a perfectly preserved Lincoln said to have been his dead mother's and wore a black formal suit like a mortician. He was rumored to be a poet, scratching away in his basement cubicle, though no one had ever seen a thing he'd written, and when he spoke he seemed genuinely unaware that what little he deigned to say was invariably condescending. The first time he heard Lynn was doing a book on the Ghost Ship, he frowned thoughtfully and said, "I suppose it was inevitable."

Lynn didn't mind Philip Edson for the simple reason that he knew everything, as if he'd not only catalogued but consumed every bit of information under his command. He was the one who remembered Caroline Sharp and then helped locate the sole article about her.

Today, when Lynn came down and presented him with her I.D., Philip Edson pointed at her like a mindreader. "Leon Golub, 1955."

"1955," she said, signing in.

"July 4th—July 5th actually, since it was after midnight."

She looked up and he was grinning broadly, seeing he'd hooked her. "Okay," she said.

"Killed his wife and three children in their sleep. Used a claw hammer."

"Park employee?"

"Not quite. There were fireworks that night. Mr. Golub helped set them off. Ah, but the best part—" He opened a manila folder to show her several photocopied articles. "After he killed his family, he killed himself—with the hammer."

"Nice."

"How, is the question I asked myself. Read on."

The story said the man's body was found in the kitchen. Apparently he used the hammer to smash a number of glasses, the shards of which he ate before caving in his own skull.

"It seems Mr. Golub was very determined," Edson said.

"Or very murdered."

"Ah, but notice—" He pinned a sentence with a fat finger. "He didn't kill the dogs."

She checked the second article. "He only hit himself once."

"—then bled to death."

It was interesting, but she didn't see any useful connection. Over the years, millions of people passed through the park. One nutcase going postal off the property proved nothing.

"Thanks," she said, closing the folder.

"I thought you'd appreciate that. Now, what other old business can I interest you in today?"

She wanted to look at 1947, the year the Laff in the Dark shut down. She was hoping for a farewell feature on it that might hit the high points, then maybe an off-season piece on the demolition for continuity. Edson gave her the boxes for May through July and August thru October. It was a gesture of trust—usually he made people return a reel before checking out a second.

She installed herself at the reader in the corner by the map cabinet, threaded the film between the glass plates and around the take-up reel and with a whirring shuttle forwarded

The Ghost Ship: An Unfinished Novel

through the morning-fresh news of 1947. Truman was president and there were ads for wingtips and fedoras in the margins. In Boston there was a bad hotel fire, jumpers crumpled like dirty laundry on the sidewalk. The Indians were in first place. After the first few days she was quick to leapfrog the sports and comics and classifieds, pages flashing past at the touch of a thumb. She slowed only to scroll through the front page and then the local news and living section, sweeping from top to bottom, alert and unblinking, trying not to miss anything. Headlines slipped by like streets glimpsed from a speeding train. It was tiring, and every so often she had to stop and close her eyes. A small bright bulb shone toylike beneath the glass. Somewhere inside the machine a fan purred, dispersing an electrical smell of heated dust. The ergonomic office chair made her conscious of her posture; she pulled it closer and sat up straight, but in fifteen minutes she was hunched and leaning into the screen again, lost in that forgotten world of cookie-cutter suburbs and H-bomb tests.

Edson left for lunch in the middle of June and returned noisily in July with a fistful of mail. It was his job to handle outside requests, and as Lynn slogged through August he went about it with an efficiency that bordered on disdain, striding to the correct file cabinet to select a reel, then striding to a reader to print out the desired articles, then striding to his mailing area to fold them into an envelope along with an invoice and drop the whole package in his out basket—all without a word—and soon he was back in his cubicle again, tapping at his computer as if he'd lapped her.

The feature she was hoping for was in the roto section the Sunday before Labor Day, a big puff piece complete with pictures she immediately coveted. She'd assumed from its name that the Laff in the Dark was a lighthearted ride, and maybe it was inside, but in stark black-and-white the cut-out of the giant, leering clown that served as its facade seemed menacing, as did the shabby Depression-era line of patrons entering the stretched, yawning maw of his mouth. Unlike the Ghost Ship with its kitschy Gilligan's Island decor, it looked like a ride that *should* burn to the ground. She hit the print button and ran out a copy, adjusted the contrast and did another.

The piece itself was unenlightening, a pastiche of sentimental recollections. The writer had interviewed several married couples who remembered their courting days, and the park superintendent, who lamented the end of a tradition and plugged the technical improvements of the new Old Mill ride, opening next spring. If anything more interesting than some heavy petting had happened in the Laff in the Dark, the article didn't mention it. She dutifully printed it out, added it to her folder and sped on.

She was cruising for anything about the demolition when Helen Fielder came rushing in, trailing a nervous intern. She rapped on the counter for Edson, then spotted Lynn and abandoned the intern to him.

"I swear, it is *kismet*," she said, and glanced up to acknowledge this divine intervention. "You are exactly the person I need to be talking to. Who else have you talked to?"

"About what?"

"Tell me you haven't talked to anyone. Please tell me that."

"Helen, you're going to have to tell me what the hell you're talking about, because I have no idea."

"James Earl Reese."

"James *Edward* Reese?"

The Ghost Ship: An Unfinished Novel

"Earl, Edward—I need everything you've got on him."

"Why?" Lynn asked, feeling suddenly protective.

"It just came over the wire. They think he's the Cleveland Cookie Killer."

"What?"

Helen said something about a matching fingerprint, a secret identity, and while it registered, in the minute it took Lynn to process the idea—impossible, seeing he'd been missing for twenty-eight years—she thought it was wrong that her first concern wasn't for the slaughtered family or the public at large, but for her own unformed, unwritten book.

You Must Be This Tall to Ride

1/ A Gift

WARREN ATWOOD HAD stopped answering line five. He'd been in the business long enough to know there was no damage control on a hit like this. He could stonewall all he wanted; there wasn't enough lead time before the dedication for it to blow over. Some days you just had to take your lumps.

He checked with Adam Fitch's secretary. He was on his way to L.A. for a meeting. In the good old days that would have bought Atwood a couple of hours. Now he had to gather himself and call the familiar number to show he was on top of things, all the while hoping he wasn't the first.

"I heard," Adam Fitch said through a wall of jetwash. "Talk about timing."

"I've got everything buttoned down for now, but they're going to expect some kind of release. I figure we want to go with something low-key, reassure people—"

"Warren, listen, I don't want to tell you how to do your job, but it seems to me we're talking about front page news here, is that right?"

"Yes, sir, at least locally. The Beacon's got us scheduled for page—"

"Screw the Beacon," Fitch said. "And while we're at it, screw the Blade and screw the Plain-Dealer too, okay? Now, I'm just a dumb businessman, but I'd say we're talking *national* news here, feature stuff."

The Ghost Ship: An Unfinished Novel

"That depends on what else is happening." Like, say, your plane crashes.

"You're not listening to me, Warren. I'm saying we *are* going to make the national news. Psycho killer comes back after thirty years to finish the job he started. It's like something out of Scooby Doo. Business is about recognizing opportunities. We just got handed a gift. Let's recognize it for what it is and make sure we take advantage. Are you reading me, Warren?"

"Yes, sir."

"Play up security for all it's worth. Find a way to bring in terrorism, I don't know how. It doesn't matter. We want to focus on the product and the event. We do that and everything else will follow, okay? Ghost Ship Ghost Ship Ghost Ship. Opening opening opening. They want it, they got it. Ram it down their throats. And Warren?"

"Yes, sir?"

"Remember that it's a game, okay? Have some fun with it."

2/ Lake Views

HIS NEIGHBORS at the Sunset Cottages started cocktail hour early, circling their lawn chairs and coolers and hauling up dripping cans of beer well before the firehouse down the road blew its siren for quitting time. The two families seemed to know each other, or maybe they were related, the kids cousins, clamoring for sodas and chips after swimming all afternoon. They scooped up dip from Tupperware containers while their fathers grilled chicken and burgers, the smoke drifting through his open window, making his stomach clench. He'd been trying to sleep so he'd be fresh tonight but their laughter made it impossible, and he lay in bed, sweating, the fan he'd bought at Wal-Mart on low, blowing over him. Under his pillow, in a makeshift tape-and-cardboard sheath, rested his carving knife.

He'd gone to Wal-Mart last night, hoping to pick up something more lethal, but as he stood in the camping and fishing aisle, scouting the counter at the back of sporting goods, he realized there were cameras dedicated to recording his face if he so much as applied to buy a gun. Another commanded the display of grooved and gleaming hunting knives, some of the blades a good foot long. He fiddled with a Coleman stove, wishing he had any kind of skill with a bow and arrow. It was a risk being here; whatever he was going to get, he had to get it now.

He thought of Katie Greive. Of all the assassins to send after him, she was the weakest, probably just a warning. From now on they would be stronger, and there would be more of them. He needed to prepare himself to fight on the run, stick and move like the young Ali, except he felt like the old George Foreman, impossibly heavy, definitely outgunned. Here, now, if they came for him, what would he do?

On the shelf beside him were reels of nylon line tough enough to pull muskies up from hundreds of feet deep, and practically invisible. It could be used to garrotte someone quietly from behind, or as tripwire—ankle or neck-high. He could picture it working its magic in the dark, and added a box to his plastic handbasket.

Propane was attractive as a bomb, except he didn't think he could rig a reliable detonator. The barbed lures were sharp but expensive, and the filleting knives were kept inside a locked plexiglas cabinet. He moved to the next aisle but it was all harmless tents and sleeping bags.

The Ghost Ship: An Unfinished Novel

The next section was automotive, stocked with tire irons and flares and aerosol cans of Gumout that could be made into flamethrowers. After that was hardware, with its cold chisels and nailguns and Raid and paint thinner. Casually he returned to the front of the store and exchanged his basket for a cart.

Now, waiting for darkness to fall, listening to the buzz of his neighbors talking, he fantasized about gunning the truck through the lit-up midway, scattering people, open cans of paint thinner splashing in back. The cab had a sliding window behind the driver. He could pop a flare and drop it in the wet bed—that easy, as if no one would stop him.

A thunk on the side of the cottage knocked him out of his reverie. Instantly he was up and pressed against the wall by the window, the knife in one hand. He could hear someone nearing, footsteps bending the dry grass. They were headed steadily, stealthily for him, then when they got close, they suddenly stopped. He could hear the person breathing. He braced himself to see Evvie again, then twisted and peeked through the screen. Directly below him stood a blond-haired boy from next door, seven or eight at the most. The boy was looking up at him, wide-eyed, reminding him that all he had on was his boxers.

"Can I help you?"

"We're sorry," the boy said innocently. He knelt so his head disappeared, and Albert Manning shifted so he could punch the knife through the screen if he had to. He envisioned the other kids spread in a perimeter around the cabin, the truck's wires cut.

The boy came up with a frisbee. "It was Jessie."

"No problem," Albert Manning said, giving him a neighborly wave with his empty hand, and watched him scamper off.

There was no safe place for the knife in the shower, so he slipped it under the pillow again. The water resounded hollowly in the flimsy tin stall. He'd had to pass on the cheaper, more remote Catawba Campgrounds farther up the peninsula because it had communal bathrooms. Here the cabins were closer together, but he could hole up inside all day if wanted. They were also situated on a wooded bluff high above the lake, and though he knew intellectually that whatever was coming for him wasn't going to crawl onto the dock and drag itself slithering up the long, stepped set of whitewashed stairs that climbed the hillside, it was better than being right on the water.

This time of day hot water was scarce, plus he didn't like the idea of being trapped inside the noisy stall, unable to tell if someone was out there. He rinsed quickly and whipped the curtain aside, dried himself with his one towel and put on clean jeans and a billowy mustard-colored shirt he'd picked up at Wal-Mart. The khakis and polo shirt were for later, when he knew what he was doing; for now he was a tourist, someone's laidback grandfather. Sneakers and a new Indians hat topped off the costume, and for a final bit of camouflage, his reading glasses. He'd had them since the '80s and the frames were too big. He appraised himself seriously in the mirror. The hat was obviously new, too boxy. Even smiling—especially then—he looked like a man trying to disguise himself.

Outside, the last light of day was fading, the flood of warm gold giving way to cool gray tinged with pink as the sun flared a final time before dropping over the horizon. The cicadas were loud now. The neighbors put on sweatshirts and fired up their citronella candles. Dusk was supposed to be the hardest time to see. He would be outside for twenty seconds at most, crossing from the door to the truck. Still, he waited

The Ghost Ship: An Unfinished Novel

for dark, lying on the made bed with the lights off, looking up at a flattened coffee can used to patch the roof. When he could no longer see it, he swung his legs over the side and sat on the edge a minute, then rocked to his feet.

He tried to be quiet locking the cottage and slipping into the truck, but once the engine roared to life there was no hiding it. He turned on his parking lights and crept respectfully over the narrow gravel road, obeying the owner's handpainted 5 mile-per-hour signs. After he turned onto the highway, he kept checking his mirrors, as if someone might be following him. It was the country; for miles there was nothing but utter blackness. He still had to catch Route 2 and cross the bay bridge, then navigate his way through the city. Weekdays Edgewater was only open till eleven, and it was already ten to nine. He should have left earlier.

He'd just passed the last exit before the bridge and was starting up the long slope of the approach when he heard his name on the radio—not Albert Manning, but his real name.

He turned it up, as if he might have imagined it.

"Reese is wanted by authorities in connection with the June 23rd murders of—"

A horn blared and dopplered past, trailing a pair of taillights. The bridge was fast, and he'd slowed to listen; now he stood on the gas out of frustration. If they knew who he was, they knew where he was going, and here he was, obliging them.

According to the story, the police considered him armed and dangerous, a suggestion that made Albert Manning shake his head. His neighbors back in Lakewood must have helped with the description, because James Edward Reese was also reported to be a Cleveland Indians fan. "Damn," he said, and there went his 12.99, literally, out the window.

3/ Eleven at 11

SHAUNA CAUGHT the fallout on the late news. The silent home movie that had haunted her for so much of her life ran in grainy slow-motion, flames knifing skyward, the burning whirlwind billowing the sails of the Ghost Ship as the anchorwoman coolly recited the official version of events. The kids had long gone to bed. As if to protect them, she lowered the sound and crouched close to the set to get every word, then muted it, keeping her finger on the button through the weather and sports in case they said something else.

It was impossible, and yet, thinking back, she had a queasy feeling that somehow Tony had known. Everything made sense then. *That* was why he was coming. And she'd been so quick to dismiss him, afraid he'd drag her back into the past. She thought he was bothering her with the same old shit, when all along he was trying to warn her.

She turned off the TV and flicked on the light in her little office off the hall, knelt by the file cabinet next to the computer and dug in the back of the bottom drawer. There, rubberbanded together, were her old address books, dating back to the '80s. In the most recent one she had a number for him with an area code she couldn't ever remember calling. She took the book over to the phone and punched in the number, expecting the high, three-toned chime that meant it was disconnected. Instead, it rang.

Immediately she wanted to hang up, as if this was a mistake. What if she was wrong and it was all coincidence?

By the third ring, she was hoping no one would pick up. By the fifth, she was strangely disappointed. The line clicked, as if she were being transferred.

The Ghost Ship: An Unfinished Novel

A woman's schooled and honeyed voice came on, so smooth that at first Shauna thought it was a Southwestern Bell recording. "You have reached the offices of High Desert Concepts. Our hours of operation are 8 a.m. to 6 p.m. Monday thru Friday and 10 a.m. to 6 p.m. Saturdays. Please leave a message at the tone, or, if you require immediate assistance, feel free to page any of our sales associates. Your business is important to us. Thank you."

The beep beeped. She hesitated, debating it. She wasn't sure it was him; it sounded too professional. On the other hand, if it was and he was already gone, she'd sound like a fool.

Well, she was, wasn't she? And a frightened one at that. This was no time to stand on her pride.

"Tony?" she said. "It's Shauna. Call me." And then, after pausing, as if she were giving away a deep secret, she left him her number.

4/ A Private Party

THEY BLEW through clean-up, finishing before Irina called on the walkie-talkie. Owen hadn't mentioned Lorraine all day and let Matt believe he'd convinced him to come out and celebrate nailing his final. Matt seemed more excited than he was.

"You'll see, *mi amigo*," he said. "There's gonna be some *muy serioso* females there."

"We'll see," Owen said, noncommittal, and headed for the lot.

He had to stop home and change, giving him a last chance to bail, but his father's note on the kitchen table and the fresh memory of Lorraine standing long and tan above him on the track kept him moving. He'd done laundry that weekend and his yellow Aeropostale shirt was clean. It was too obvious, he thought, but pulled it over his head anyway.

The Crap Shack was on the far side of town, tucked into a rusty strip of old boatyards and marine salvage places in the shadow of the bay bridge. He drove fast, knowing he'd be late, passing on the right and sneaking through yellow lights. "Let's go," he urged an oversized pick-up hogging the left lane. The guy must have been lost because he slowed and put on his blinker and then didn't turn.

"Come on, jackass."

When he did it again, Owen punched his middle finger at the windshield and flashed his brights.

The truck's taillights flared, making Owen brake.

"Motherfucker!"

The guy took off again, and before he knew what he was doing, Owen gunned around him on the outside, pulled in front of the truck and slammed on his brakes.

The man in the truck *was* lost. He was also medium-drunk. His name was Mike Weideman, and he was looking for a party he'd heard of at another party that was breaking up. He was a burly guy in his thirties, a welder by trade, and played league softball to keep in shape. As the stickers on the back of his cab proclaimed, he rode a Harley and had No Fear, but he wasn't familiar with this part of the city, and kept his doors locked. For protection he had an arm's length of iron pipe under the passenger seat. When the prick cut him off and stopped short, he leaned over and reached under the seat, fumbling until he felt the pleasing cold of steel.

It was a white kid who jumped out of the little shitbox riceburner and walked toward the truck, yelling and pointing at him like a psycho. He wasn't a bulked-up jock or a gym rat ripped on steroids, just some scrawny high school puke in a yellow t-shirt. The kid's hands were empty, so he popped his lock and stepped out and showed him the pipe, thinking that would be enough.

"Come on then, shitass," he said.

The kid didn't stop. Instead of eyeing the pipe and weighing his chances like a normal person, the kid bared his teeth like a dog and charged, linebacker fast. Mike Weideman had downed twelve or thirteen beers over the course of the evening, and his reflexes were like wet pretzels. He realized what was happening a full second too late and swung, but by then the kid was inside his defenses and the pipe thumped harmlessly off his back. As the kid took him to the pavement, he heard the pipe chime against the road.

He'd been in fights before, he'd even lost a couple, including an ugly one in the crowded men's room of Richland Arena that he tried to forget. He knew he had to get off his back or even a wiry little shit like this would work his face like a heavyweight. He clawed for the kid's throat, stretching, and had him for a second, but lost his grip.

The first punch caught him on the top of the jaw, stunning him, the pain in the bony hinge flaring up into his ear. The next mashed his nose, snapping him back to reality. He thrashed his head from side to side to dodge the flurry, trying to use his legs, arching for leverage. The kid pinned his head with both hands and banged it against the road, twisting his neck. As he kicked, he felt fingers digging into his scalp, tearing out hair, yanking his head up as if he was going to pull it off, then slamming it down.

The back of Mike Weideman's skull bounced off the asphalt, sending a shock wave through his body. All thoughts of fighting evaporated, given over to damage control. He was aware of a deep, sustained numbness back there, and understood it was bad—that he was probably already bleeding and in a minute a hot wave of pain would catch up to him.

The kid was above him, his hands tangled in his hair again, his face growing closer as he lifted him, teeth clenched with the effort. The kid grunted and flew away, and a blinding white flash went off, bloomed and then lingered like dying fireworks on his field of vision.

He discovered he couldn't move. Above him hung the sky and its stars, partly eclipsed by a nearby streetlight. The kid's face hove up like a half-moon. Beside it, glinting silver, was the pipe.

Okay, he wanted to say, you win, but all that came out was a gurgle.

The pipe descended so slowly that he thought it was a special effect brought on by his concussion, but no, the kid wasn't swinging at him, he was holding it above his face, showing it to him as if he was supposed to memorize this mistake and learn from it. Mike tried to lift his head but couldn't. He tried to say something, and the kid's hand covered his mouth. The touch was dulled, as if his lips were numb. He could barely feel them being pried apart. It was like being at the dentist, his face made of clay, except he could feel all too well the kid pulling his chin down and then the unforgiving steel inserted between his teeth, the chilly, oily taste of it on his tongue. It slid deeper, jabbing the back of his throat so he gagged, choking for breath, his eyes tearing. The kid was straddling him, and reached down as if to remove the pipe. Instead, he lifted him by the shoulders so that his head sagged back, aligning his throat just so. He held him there with one hand gripping his collar while the other passed over Mike's face and took hold of the end of the pipe jutting from his mouth. The kid jiggled it from side to side, bearing down steadily, forcing it in, all but the last threaded inch that grated against his upper front teeth.

Impossibly, it fit. He could breathe.

And then the kid yanked him up by the shirt so he was almost standing—gasping, the pipe making his throat spasm—and let go.

He landed with his head flung back unnaturally. His own momentum drove the pipe against his teeth, hammering them in one swift stroke up into his gums. The pain was orbiting now, swarming, yet he was still conscious, and as he bled onto the pavement, choking for every breath, he clung to the hope that he might live through this. After the first few kicks, even that didn't matter.

5/ 10-22

HE'D BARELY hung up his windbreaker when another call came in: suspicious activity, on the lakeside behind the waterslide. Probably some married couple from the campground taking a moonlight stroll, Roy Detwiler thought, but called back to confirm and grabbed his jacket.

It had been like this since that fool protester broke in. Instead of the nice quiet nights he was used to, they had him chasing all over creation. Fitch had torn the head of security a new one, so now to cover their asses they buzzed him whenever a seagull crapped on the beach. It wasn't right, a bunch of punk-ass kids who didn't know shit delegating to a decorated officer of the law.

At 56, Roy Detwiler was a great believer in the maxim that shit rolls downhill. He himself had been the beneficiary of that specific gravity his entire life, including this, his final assignment. While internal affairs and the courts had cleared him and his partner of any charges (and in truth they were innocent of more than they were guilty), they were an embarrassment to the force, and when they returned from suspension, Henry quietly drew parking enforcement downtown and Roy this friendless exile—permanently friendless, it seemed, since after three weeks of writing citations and taking shit from pissed-off motorists, Henry went home and fulfilled the promise he made during those last few uncertain minutes the two of them spent alone together in the holding pen right before the verdict.

Henry's verdict was final, and while Roy had never subjected himself to the glossy photos he knew existed in Henry's case file, he'd covered enough swab jobs to color his nightmares. Henry sat on the custard yellow couch in his den across from the big TV and his grandfather's hand-carved mallard decoys above the stone fireplace and leaned back, the muzzle denting the soft flesh beneath his chin, and Roy, who'd come up with the scam, could only watch, over and over. The gunshot woke him up. His wife Delia had grown tired of asking. "You have the dream again?" she'd say from the door, and he'd nod groggily and try to shower away the feeling. It never left him completely, just as the disgrace of standing trial like some common criminal ate at him daily. Occasionally he thought of taking himself out, had weighed it soberly, like an important purchase, and might have if the insurance policy didn't have that one clause. No, his only way out now was making his pension. Two more years and he was free. Like a prisoner, all he wanted was to do his time.

The Ghost Ship: An Unfinished Novel

He took the Cushman, splashing over the hosed-down midway. According to the boss's new orders, the halogen gaslights lining the walkways were blazing, surrounded by clouds of fluttering mayflies. The brightness was distracting, throwing harsh shadows across the blacktop. It made him feel watched, as if he was being followed. He knew as long as he stayed in the open security would have him on their monitors—not exactly reassuring. He guessed, correctly, that right this minute they were probably laughing at him.

He picked the inland route because it was less buggy, cutting through the parking lot of the Breakers, where the night clerk was taking a smoke break beside the front doors. He lazily returned Roy's wave. Over the whole rear face of the hotel only two random squares were lit, the walkways deserted, nothing but the tireless mayflies mobbing the lights. On the far side the mini-golf was dark, and the two-tiered figure eight of the go-cart track, lined with tires. In the water park, the artificial river was still, the blue inner-tubes stacked neatly.

The Cushman whined, climbing the handicapped ramp onto the boardwalk. It was a clear night and the wind was chilly, bringing the dank, muddy smell of the lake. The distant lights of the islands glistened like stars.

The boardwalk was just a prop; a hundred feet past the manicured hotel beach it abruptly ended in a warped set of stairs. He drove the cart as far as he could and swung himself out, then reached back in and removed the key before setting off across the sand. The tide had just gone out, and the shingle grabbed at his old brogans like wet cement. Beyond the reach of the last gaslight, the beach was dark as a mineshaft, only the treetops outlined by the glow of the park. The bull's-eye of his flashlight beam wobbled ahead of him, picking out stones and driftwood and the occasional pale, tail-nibbled fish.

When he was a kid growing up in Huron, he and his friends used to go beachcombing at the foot of the bluffs. They never found anything valuable, it was more of a make-believe adventure, a way of wasting the long summer afternoons. One day they came across a dog that had washed up. It had been in the water a long time, because it was eyeless and earless, its fur gone except for a Brillo-y patch on its chest. The rest was bare skin gone white and rubbery as a pickled egg. When someone jabbed at the belly with a stick, water and a knot of writhing white worms spilled out. Roy remembered the ring of boys standing there speechless, maybe a little afraid but fascinated too, bearing witness to the truth. That was what happened when you died—you turned to mush and the worms ate you.

Henry had been dead for five years now, and Roy couldn't help but wonder what natural processes were going on inside his coffin. They lined them with polyurethane to prevent seepage, if you could trust the brochures. Henry was probably oozing into a stew of himself. Roy wondered how long he would last now if, to get a confession, someone made him get in the box with Henry?

"Not fucking long," he answered himself, sweeping the light back and forth. It glinted off a beer can jutting like a shiny turret from a sand castle, and he ventured over to make sure it was nothing. On his way, he noticed intermittent tracks in the sand—sneakers, except they were huge. He wore 10s, and these were at least 13s. He followed them with his flashlight along the water's edge and then up the beach toward the jetski rental. When the concrete started,

The Ghost Ship: An Unfinished Novel

they disappeared. He checked and saw that his own shoes were leaving prints, so it had probably been a while.

The jetskis were chained together loosely, a sloppy job but good enough. It had been a problem a couple years back, kids who worked at the park taking them out for joyrides after hours. It was dark on the water, and the things didn't have lights. One night one of them had run out of gas a half-mile out. The lake was calm but cold, and while it looks doable, a half-mile is a long-ass swim. The kids were smart enough to stay with the ski until the Coast Guard rescued them; otherwise you were talking fish food. Now even the rowboats had to be dragged up the beach, their oars locked away for insurance purposes. He banged the butt of his flashlight against the metal hull of one and kicked another, as if someone might be hiding under them. He rattled the doors of the boathouse and the storage shed where they kept the life vests—all solid. The single gas pump was turned off. He stood there a second, playing the beam around, then showily checked his watch.

"Gettin' kinda late to be out and about," he said. "Tomorrow'll be here soon enough."

No one argued the point. Probably scared Ma and Pa Winnebago back to Camper Village. Just to be thorough, he walked back down to the sandcastle and smoked a cigarette, using the beer can as an ashtray and looking out at the dark islands. He wondered how long he could swim for, and how far the dog had floated. He'd read in one of Delia's holy roller pamphlets that in Hell there was a crowded river where the damned floundered for eternity, and he could see himself neck-deep in the black water, struggling with the others, trying to grab on to the low ferry as it passed. He could see Henry looking down at him, his round, pudgy face intact, no wet hole where his nose had been, no explosion of teeth. Henry watched him silently, his eyes filled if not with understanding then at least pity, staying on Roy's as the ferry slid by, growing smaller and smaller, leaving him behind.

In his reverie, he'd forgotten the cigarette. It burned his hand and he dropped it, shaking and then sucking his fingers. Goddamn Henry, he didn't *make* him eat his gun.

He could almost believe this when he was pissed off, but he knew it was untrue. He'd convinced Henry to go along with his scheme. It came to the same thing.

He sighed and gazed out at the islands again. He could go whole weeks now without thinking of Henry. Why was he fucking with him tonight? He needed to get back to the office where he could read or watch TV—anything to occupy his mind.

He waved his light around a last time, then keyed his mike. "This is 232 checking on that 10—22, over."

"Yeah?" the heifer who ran the board said, instead of "copy." Goddamn amateurs.

"All clear here," he said. "232 over and out."

6/ The Four Directions

FROM THE rustling, windswept woods, standing still as a treetrunk, Tony Booker watched him go. He waited until the rent-a-cop climbed back in the golfcart and putted away before breaking cover and tending to the pit again.

It was naturally camouflaged, tucked into the shadowy edge of the beach and the scrubby underbrush. The ground was loose and sandy here. All he needed was a shallow bowl,

The Ghost Ship: An Unfinished Novel

but the e-tool he'd picked up at the army surplus was dull, and the walls of the hole kept collapsing. After having the cop suddenly pop up, he felt exposed, and every so often he froze, sweating from the effort, peering back at the lit boardwalk like a graverobber.

When it was deep enough, he mounded the dirt around the edges to serve as a windbreak, then wiped his palms on his jeans. He reached into the backpack at his feet and lifted out the raw sticks of kindling and today's newspaper. Squatting in the pit, he balled up some pages and set the crossed sticks on top of them in a teepee. He had his new butane torch cocked when he remembered the water.

Like the torch, the cup had come from the 7-Eleven. On one side it had a bad likeness of Ewan MacGregor as Obi-Wan Kenobi waving a light saber. Tony hustled down to the water and back, setting the cup to one side so he wouldn't kick it over.

He squatted to shield the light of the torch from the boardwalk and watched as the newsprint bloomed and the kindling darkened and caught. He fed it the sports section page by page, steadily building it up. He'd brought more kindling, just in case, but decided to save it. When the fire was thriving on its own, he felt around in the bottom of the pack and pulled out a bundle wrapped in plastic.

It was the size of a license plate and thick as a box of chocolates, but seemed smaller in Tony's gigantic hands. He scratched at the strapping tape with a nail, then unwound the package in his lap, turning it over and over. It was mostly padding, which he gathered with one hand and shoved back in the pack. In the end, he held a short length of black, lacquered plywood.

Like Lynn McCourt, Tony had done his homework—in his case, homework he'd put off—unsuccessfully—for most of his adult life. Once he'd begun to seriously pursue the issue, it had taken him eight years to track down the source of this nondescript piece of wood, following browned carbons of demolition contracts and barely legible salvage invoices to A-1 Entertainment, Incorporated of Seaside Heights, New Jersey, a mob-connected outfit that ran several summer concessions along the shore, including Ocean Playland Park. There, under thirty seasons worth of latex paint, the original, undamaged cars from the Ghost Ship ferried teenagers through its dark ride, The Frighthouse. This piece had come from one that had been cannibalized for its chassis and left to rot in a storage shed. Posing as an aficionado, Tony had bought the useless shell for five hundred dollars, saying he'd restore it—as if the man counting the stack of brand-new twenties cared.

He U-Hauled it across country in a fishtailing trailer, all the way afraid that something would happen to it, and then when he pulled into the ranch and had to find a place for it, he chose the quonset farthest from the house, and locked it in like a prisoner. He still wasn't used to the sight of car 23 with its molded plastic nose and discolored benchseat. It seemed too small to hold both him and Vi. Once he'd even sat in it, tempting memory, twisting his legs sideways to prove that it could be done, and then felt foolish and disrespectful, as if Vi could see him. From then on he was businesslike, staying just long enough to cut what he needed.

From his pack he took a baggie and sprinkled a handful of dried sage over the flames, then a tangle of spiny creosote and finally some bitter devilroot. He zipped the baggies closed again and waited. The fire crackled, fragrant and mesmerizing. Without ceremony, he reached in and set the piece of car

23 on it. The lacquer sizzled and caught, feeding a guttering green flame.

He stood and took his shirt off. He was a big man, paunchy if not fat, and the firelight deepened the creases under his breasts and belly. A patch of skin over his heart was rucked and puckered like a burn. He squatted again to shield the fire, stoking it with more newspaper so it flared, engulfing the piece, charring its raw edges. He watched it burn awhile, then pulled a quilted asbestos mitt from the pack and fitted it on his right hand.

He took the cup of water in his left hand and reached into the fire with the mitt. He stood and raised the piece to his lips, blowing on the edge so it glowed orange-red, then, facing east, pressed the live ember to his chest.

In the desert he'd learned silence for this very purpose, and he returned there, a hawk soaring through the high white sky.

He poured water over the burn, bent and scooped a handful of dirt and rubbed the mud into his skin, then stood, letting the wind cool him.

There was no sign of the cop and his cart, only the black water, the lapping waves.

He set the piece of wood back on the fire and waited.

7/

IT DIDN'T make sense, but part of him thought she wouldn't be there, or that she would be with Keith Perrin—that it was all a set-up. He was prepared to see them together, turn right around and leave, but when he walked into the Crap

Shack, there she was, in their usual corner booth with Matt and Irina and Cara Rosenstein. It was Owen's first time back since last year, and even with the jukebox thundering some old Cake tune he was aware of the pause in conversations as the regulars watched him make his way to the table.

There was a space by Lorraine, but he squeezed in next to Matt so they were facing each other. She had a half-finished draft, and the whole table was picking over a plate of chili fries, or Matt was.

"What took you so long?" Lorraine asked.

He didn't want to say he'd gone home to change, and just shrugged. "Traffic." He reached for the fries to cover his answer. He was reeling in a long one when Lorraine caught his wrist.

"What did you do to yourself?"

"Nothing," he said, but his knuckles were raw and swollen. He flexed his fingers to show them he was okay. "I must've banged it on something cleaning up."

"So," Lorraine said, "Cara says tomorrow's the big day."

"I don't know," Owen said. "I'm pretty sure I bombed the test."

"Please," Cara said. "It was *so* cinchy."

"For you, maybe."

"Dude, it was multiple guess," she said, and everyone laughed.

It was strange. He'd known Cara since he started working at Edgewater yet he'd never noticed what a bitch she was. Sitting there grinning, he could see himself snatching up her mug and bashing her over the head with it—one solid knockout blow crushing her skull. The idea flashed like a bad memory, just long enough to shock him back to reality.

"I know," he said. "I blanked on it. I studied hard too."

The Ghost Ship: An Unfinished Novel

"He did," Matt said.

"I'm sure you did fine," Lorraine said. "How many are they going to take?"

"Just the top three," Cara said, like she was in charge of the process, and again—from nowhere—Owen had the urge to hurt her. It was like a painful headache, that same ruthless impatience with the rest of the world he felt after the test, and then, when he looked at Lorraine, it vanished and he was fine again.

"Who are the three, you think?" Irina asked.

"Kim's one," Cara said.

"Der," Matt said.

"You," Owen said.

"Thanks. I would have said you, but it sounds like you're not very confident."

"Maybe Justin," he said.

"Justin Lauer?" Lorraine said.

"I don't think so, bro," Matt said. "Justin Lauer couldn't pass a breathalyzer test. Seriously."

"I don't see why he's even in the class," Cara said. "He never says anything."

"Exactly," Owen said, pointing. "Why is he in the class?" It seemed obvious to him, but no one guessed. "He wants the job. He wouldn't bother if he didn't think he had a shot."

"I would be very surprised," Cara said.

The fries were history except for some burnt slivers like cigarette butts, and suddenly he was hungry. By the time he flagged a waitress, they were ready for another pitcher. It had been a while since Owen had gone out drinking, and he tried to pace himself, never forgetting that he had to drive home. The fries took forever to arrive, and Cara couldn't stop talking. He sat beside Matt, trying to include Irina in their conversation, wishing Cara would take off—willing her to. Shut up. Go away. In the middle of his fries, as if she could read his mind, Cara bailed, waving to the other tables as she went, leaving Lorraine alone on her side, and as naturally as he could—knowing the whole place was watching—Owen moved over.

"Hey," she said.

"Hey," he said.

"Nice shirt."

"Thanks."

"I see you're still a slob." She leaned in and dabbed with a napkin at a dark drip on his chest, but it was dry.

"So you and Cara are best friends now."

"She's funny."

"Okay," he said, hedging, because he didn't see it. "Where's Kim?"

"Big date."

"With who?"

It wasn't awkward talking. It could have been last year, except for the invisible forcefield between their bodies. When Lorraine excused herself to go to the ladies' room, Matt gave him a sly nod.

"Don't you have to be back for curfew?" Owen joked.

"Thanks for reminding me."

"We go," Irina said, definite.

"I'm just kidding."

"No," Matt said, "we should."

"Yah, we should," Irina said. "You want to be alone weet you girlfriend, no?"

"She's not my girlfriend."

The Ghost Ship: An Unfinished Novel

"Oh!" Irina said, "it's a lie you say," and they both laughed at him. He dipped his head and smiled.

"Be careful, meng," Matt said.

He promised that he would, but after Lorraine came back and they paid their share of the bill and said their goodbyes, Owen asked if she wanted to go out on the deck and talk. She accepted, and again he felt watched by the entire room as they crossed to the doors.

It was chilly out, windy, and they huddled at the railing. He'd hoped for an ore boat or a partyliner to watch but there was nothing, just the bay bridge looming at their backs. She slid her hand into his to show him how cold her fingers were.

"Maybe this wasn't such a good idea," he said.

"Let's walk," she said, and led him down the stairs and across the soft, trucked-in sand of the volleyball court and through the toppled resin chairs and wire spool tables down to the hard flats by the water. The spotlight on the deck threw his shadow over her, eclipsing her face so he caught only an ear and a honey-colored wave of hair as they walked, until they reached the corner of the salvage yard where the darkness was solid. Last year they seemed to end up here a lot, trashed on sweet margaritas and kissing sloppily. The memory confused him, as if it had never happened.

He thought she would stop, but they kept going.

"What did you mean I might get lucky tonight?" he asked.

"What do you think I meant?"

"I don't know. I was kind of surprised."

"You were surprised? I was surprised you even talked to me. You've been avoiding me ever since I got back."

She said it like he had no reason to, so he answered her with silence. Before he could help it, that strange new part of him was calculating how long it would take for someone to find her.

"I know I hurt you, and I'm sorry, Owen, but…are you going to be like this the rest of your life? I hope not, because you're a good guy. We used to have fun. I liked being able to talk to you. Now it's like you don't care about me."

"I care about you."

"Uh-huh. Then why don't you talk to me? Why does it have to be all or nothing?"

For months he'd been thinking, almost exclusively, about what he'd say to her, but he hadn't anticipated an attack. He knew he needed a strong comeback, but nothing came. His whole life, this was how he lost every argument, freezing up, not fighting and then feeling stupid afterward for letting people walk all over him. He felt a twinge like the beginning of a headache.

"Because it *is* all or nothing," Owen said. "You're either with me or you're not with me, and that's your choice."

If There Were Demons, Then Perhaps There Were Angels: William Peter Blatty's Own Story of *The Exorcist*

By William Peter Blatty

In 1949, while a junior at Georgetown University in Washington, DC, I read in the August 20 edition of the *Washington Post* the following account:

IN WHAT IS perhaps one of the most remarkable experiences of its kind in recent religious history, a 14-year-old Mount Rainier boy has been freed by a Catholic priest of possession by the devil, it was reported yesterday.

Only after 20 to 30 performances of the ancient ritual of exorcism, here and in St Louis, was the devil finally cast out of the boy, it was said.

In all except the last of these, the boy broke into a violent tantrum of screaming, cursing and voicing of Latin phrases—a language he had never studied—whenever the priest reached those climactic points of the 27-page ritual in which he commanded the demon to depart from the boy.

In complete devotion to his task, the priest stayed with the boy over a period of two months, during which he witnessed such manifestations as the bed in which the boy was sleeping suddenly moving across the room.

A Washington Protestant minister has previously reported personally witnessing similar manifestations, including one in which the pallet on which the sleeping boy lay slid slowly across the floor until the boy's head bumped against a bed, awakening him.

In another instance reported by the Protestant minister, a heavy armchair in which the boy was sitting, with his knees drawn under his chin, tilted slowly to one side and fell over, throwing the boy on the floor.

The final rite of exorcism in which the devil was cast from the boy took place in May, it was reported, and since then he had had no manifestations.

The ritual of exorcism in its present form goes back 1,500 years and from there to Jesus Christ.

But before it was undertaken, all medical and psychiatric means of curing the boy—in whose presence such manifestations as fruit jumping up from the refrigerator top in his home and hurling itself against the wall also were reported—were exhausted.

The boy was taken to Georgetown University Hospital here, where his affliction was exhaustively studied, and to St. Louis University. Both are Jesuit institutions.

If There Were Demons Then Perhaps There Were Angels: William Peter Blatty's Own Story of *The Exorcist*

Finally both Catholic hospitals reported they were unable to cure the boy through natural means.

Only then was a supernatural cure sought.

The ritual was undertaken by a Jesuit in his 50s.

The details of the exorcism of the boy were described to the *Washington Post* by a priest here (not the exorcist).

The ritual began in St. Louis, continued here and finally ended in St. Louis.

For two months the Jesuit stayed with the boy, accompanying him back and forth on the train, sleeping in the same house and sometimes in the same room with him. He witnessed many of the same manifestations reported by the Protestant minister this month to a closed meeting of the Society of Parapsychology in a laboratory at Duke University, who came here to study the case, and was quoted as saying it was "the most impressive" poltergeist (noisy ghost) phenomenon that had come to his attention in his years of celebrated investigation in the field.

Even through the ritual of exorcism the boy was by no means cured readily.

The ritual itself takes about three-quarters of an hour to perform. During it, the boy would break into the fury of profanity and screaming and the astounding Latin phrases.

But finally, at the last performance of the ritual, the boy was quiet. And since then, it was said, all manifestations of the affliction such as the strange moving of the bed across the room, and another in which the boy's family said a picture had suddenly jutted out from the wall in his presence—have ceased.

It was early this year that members of the boy's family went to their minister and reported strange goings-on in their Mount Rainier house since January 18.

The minister visited the boy's home and witnessed some of the manifestations.

But though they seemed to be naked eye unexplainable— such as the scratching from the area of the wall in the boy's presence—there was always the suggestion, he said, that in some way the noises may have been made by the boy himself.

Retaining his skepticism in the matter, the minister then had the boy stay a night—February 17—in his own home.

It was there, before his own eyes, he said, that the two manifestations that he felt were beyond all natural explanation took place.

In one of these the boy's pallet moved across the floor while his hands were outside the cover and his body rigid.

In the other the heavy chair, with the boy immobile in it, tilted and fell over to the floor before the minister's amazed eyes, he said. The minister tried to overturn the chair while sitting in it himself and was unable to do so.

The case involved such reactions as neighbors of the boy's family sprinkling holy water around the family's house.

Some of the Mount Rainier neighbors' skepticism was startlingly resolved, it was reported, when they first laughed it off, invited the boy and his mother to spend a night in their own "unhaunted" homes, only to have some of the manifestations—such as the violent, apparently involuntary shakings of the boy's bed—happen before their eyes.

THE ARTICLE impressed me. And how coolly understated that is. I wasn't just impressed; I was excited. For here at last, in this city, in my time, was tangible evidence of transcendence.

If There Were Demons Then Perhaps There Were Angels: William Peter Blatty's Own Story of *The Exorcist*

If there were demons, there were angels and probably a God and a life everlasting. And thus it occurred to me long afterwards, when I'd started my career as a writer, that this case of possession which had joyfully haunted my hopes in the years since 1949 was a worthwhile subject for a novel. In my youth I had thought about entering the priesthood; at Georgetown had considered becoming a Jesuit. The notion of course was unattainable and ludicrous in the extreme, since with respect to the subject of my worthiness, my nearest superiors are asps; and yet a novel of demonic possession, I believed—if only I could make it sufficiently convincing—might be token fulfillment of deflected vocation. Though let me make clear, if I may—lest someone rush to have me canonized—that I would never write a novel that I thought would not engross or excite or entertain, that I thought would have a readership of fifteen people. (It has often worked out that way, yes; but I didn't plan it.) If walking out of church you should pick up a Daniel Lord homiletic treatise from the vestibule pamphlet rack, you will not, I can virtually assure you, see "as told to Bill Blatty" under Father Lord's name. But if one has a choice among viable subjects and one can do good along the way by picking that one…well, that is the little one can say of my motive.

AS THE years went by, I continued my studies in possession, but desultorily and with no specific aim. For example, I made a note about a character on a page of a book called *Satan:*[1] "Detective —'Mental Clearance Sale.'" The words, in quotes, would turn up eventually very deep in the story, as a thought of Kinderman, the homicide detective in the novel; but at the time I made the note, I knew nothing of its context. Finally, however—I think it was in 1963—the notion of possession as the basic subject matter of a novel crystallized and firmed.

But the problem was that no one else liked the idea. Not my agent. Not Doubleday, my publisher at that time. Even my dentist thought the notion was rotten.[2] So I dropped the idea. I was a comedy writer; I had never written anything "straight," except a few forged letters of excuse from my mother when I'd been absent from school the day before. ("Well, it hurt right here, Sister Joseph. Pardon? How could I have cancer for just one day?") I was doubtful I could do it; even more doubtful than Doubleday, perhaps, which would extend us from doubt into negative certitude.

But sometimes something, someone, helps. In December 1967, at a New Year's Eve dinner at the home of novelist Burton Wohl, I met Marc Jaffe, editorial director of Bantam Books. He asked me what I was working on. Finding the shortest line at the unemployment office, I told him; and then spoke of possession. He warmed to the subject matter instantly. I wondered if he was drunk. He suggested publication of the book by Bantam. I was then supporting the entire cast of Birnam Wood and requested an advance large enough to carry me for a year. He said, "Send me an outline."

What could I send him? The small scrap of paper with the cryptic notation about the detective? I had no plot. I had only the subject matter, some hazily formulated characters and a theme.

So I wrote him a long letter. I began by detailing what I knew of the incident of 1949, including some rather bizarre phenomena that had been bruited about on the Georgetown campus at the time: for example, a report that the exorcist

If There Were Demons Then Perhaps There Were Angels: William Peter Blatty's Own Story of *The Exorcist*

and his assistants were forced to wear rubber windjammer suits, for the boy, in his fits, displayed a prodigious ability to urinate endlessly, accurately and over great distances, with the exorcists as his target.[3]

I went on to discuss the position of the Church on the matter:

⟵→

IT CAUTIONS exorcists that many of the paranormal phenomena can be explained in natural terms. The speaking in "unknown tongues" (unless it is part of intelligent dialogue), or possession of hidden knowledge, for example, can be explained in terms of telepathy—the possessed may simply be picking the knowledge out of the brain of the exorcist or someone else in the room. And as for levitation, Hindu mystics reputedly can manage it now and then, and what do we really know about magnetism and gravity: The "natural" explanations are, of course, somewhat mystical themselves. But the occurrence of one or two of these phenomena, exorcists are cautioned, does not justify assuming one is dealing with true possession. What the Church does tell its exorcists is to go with the laws of chance and probability, which tell us that it's far less fanciful to believe that an alien entity or spirit has control of the possessed than to believe that all or most of these paranormal phenomena are likely to occur all at once through purely natural causes. When all of them occur, and psychological causes are eliminated, then try the cure.

⟵→

STILL LOFTILY avoiding such crass considerations as a discussion of plot, I nimbly leaped to the next sure peak—my intended theme:

IS THERE a man alive who at one time or another in his life has not thought, Look, God! I'd *like* to believe in you; and I'd really like to do the right thing. But twenty thousand sects and countless prophets have different ideas about what the right thing is. So if you are out there, why not end all the mystery and hocus-pocus and make an appearance on top of the Empire State Building. *Show me your face.*

We follow through by thinking that God doesn't take this simple recourse, this *reasonable* recourse, and therefore isn't there. He isn't dead and he isn't alive in Argentina. He simply never lived.

But I happen to believe—and this is part of the theme of the novel—that if God *were* to appear in thunder and lightning atop the Empire State Building, it would not affect (for long, at least) the religious beliefs of anyone who witnessed the phenomenon. Those who already believed would find the incident a reinforcement of their faith; those who did not already believe would be impressed for a while, but with the passage of time would convince themselves that what they saw was the result of either autosuggestion, mass hypnosis, or hysteria, or massive charlatanism involving nuclear energy and NASA. On a theological level, I happened to believe that if there is a God who is somehow involved with us and our activities he would *refrain* from appearing on top of the Empire State Building, because he would ultimately only cause trauma for

If There Were Demons Then Perhaps There Were Angels: William Peter Blatty's Own Story of *The Exorcist*

those who *did not have the will* to believe, and thereby increase their guilt. The Red Sea's parting and the raising of Lazarus are not viable entries to religious belief. The trick of faith lies not in magic but in the *will of the individual*.

THE NOVEL would ask, I went on to explain, what effect a confrontation with undisputed paranormal phenomena would have on the book's main characters, the atheist mother of the boy (as I then intended the victim should be; I had named him Jamie), and the priest of weak faith called in for the exorcism, whom I first named Father Thomas.[4] This thematic aspect would prove only a suggestion of what it would become in the book I eventually wrote, expressed by Father Merrin as follows:

I THINK the demon's target is not the possessed; it is us...the observers...every person in this house. And I think—I think the point is to make us despair, to reject our own humanity, Damien: to see ourselves as ultimately bestial; as ultimately vile and putrescent; without dignity, ugly, unworthy. And there lies the heart of it, perhaps: in unworthiness. For I think belief in God is not a matter of reason at all; I think it finally is a matter of love; of accepting the possibility that God could love us...

AND PERHAPS even this would seem merely an insight compared to the stronger, more encompassing theme that would spring from the Jesuit psychiatrist's act of ultimate self-sacrifice and love: the theme I call "the mystery of goodness." For in a mechanistic universe, where the atoms that make up a human being should logically be expected, even in the aggregate, to pursue their selfish ends more blindly than the rivers rush out to the seas, how is it there is love in the sense that a God would love and that a man will give his life for another?[5]

Because it is true and embedded in reality, this theme would appear of itself in the inevitable developments of my plot, that plot which at the time of my letter to Jaffe was a beast as mythical as the unicorn. And so I "vamped," as we mental swindlers often say. And then a murder, predicted long before by my subconscious[6] when I scribbled that note about a "detective," indeed did appear to me. "The killer is the boy;[7] the mother knows this, and against the eventual arrest of her son," I wrote to Jaffe:

THE MOTHER seeks psychiatric help to establish the boy was deranged at the time of the murder. The effort proves unpromising. She then seizes upon the device of calling in the psychologically intimidating forces of the Catholic Church in an effort to prove (although she doesn't believe it for a moment) that her son is "possessed"—that it was not Jamie but an alien entity inhabiting his body who committed the murder. She resorts to the Church and requests an exorcism; and soon it is arranged for a priest to examine the boy. She grasps at the desperate and bizarre hope that if the exorcist concludes that the boy is possessed and is able to restore him to a measure of normalcy, she will have a powerful psychological and emotional argument for securing both the release of the boy and the equally important release (even if the boy is imprisoned) from humiliation and degradation. The exorcist selected for the task is, by the one coincidence permitted us, the priest who has lost his faith.

Ultimately, the boy is exorcized. Although his fate at the hands of the law is not the concern of this novel. Our concern is the exorcist. Has his faith been restored by this incredible encounter? Yes. But not by the exorcism itself, for finally the exorcist is still not sure what really happened. What restores—no; *reaffirms*—his faith is simple human love, which is surely the fact of God made visible.

VIRTUALLY NONE of this plot survived; nor did my notion that "the alien entity possessing the boy should be a woman who claims to have lived in some remote period of history, possibly Judaea in the time of Christ; and who attacks the exorcist psychologically by claiming an acquaintance with Christ, then proceeding to describe him in demythologizing, disillusioning terms."

Jaffe shopped my letter at some hard-cover houses, hoping to bring them in on the deal and thus share in producing the required advance. But a book about possession by a writer of comedy? Whose books, while they didn't sell fewer copies than *The Idylls of the King* in its Tibetan translation, certainly didn't sell any more? No one was interested, a phenomenon to which I'd grown accustomed, but which surely should have given Marc Jaffe second thoughts. But Jaffe held fast, and Bantam, on its own, at last came up with the advance. Only then did I begin to believe that perhaps I could write the book.

After some intervening screenplay assignments, I undertook a period of intensive research early in 1969. From the outset I was biased by training and religion in favor of belief in genuine possession. Furthermore, replace the word "demon" with the words "disembodied malevolent intelligence," and one has a concept not repugnant to reason or in apparent contradiction to the laws of matter, whatever they happen to be this year. Aldous Huxley's *Devils of Loudun* makes a devastating argument to the effect that the seventeenth-century epidemic of demonic possession in a convent of Ursuline nuns in France was a fraudulent, hysterical manifestation; yet even Huxley observes:

I CAN see nothing intrinsically absurd or self-contradictory in the notion that there may be non-human spirits, good, bad and indifferent. Nothing compels us to believe that the only intelligences in the universe are those connected with the bodies of human beings and the lower animals. If the evidence for clairvoyance, telepathy and prevision is accepted (and it is becoming increasingly difficult to reject it), then we must allow that there are mental processes which are largely independent of space, time and matter. And if this is so, there seems to be no reason for denying a priori that there may be non-human intelligences, either completely discarnate or else associated with cosmic energy in some way of which we are still ignorant.[8]

TEILHARD DE Chardin, the Jesuit philosopher-paleontologist, once proposed that what we think of as matter and spirit are but differing aspects of something else, some third and

If There Were Demons Then Perhaps There Were Angels: William Peter Blatty's Own Story of *The Exorcist*

fundamental reality in which matter and spirit commune. And indeed, the views of modern physicists on the ultimate nature of matter seemed to be leaning towards support of Chardin, seemed increasingly to be edging towards something like mysticism, a paradoxical consequence of the steadily deeper probing into the Chinese box of the atom. Consider the neutrino. It can speed through a planetary thickness in a twinkling, yet has no mass and no magnetic or electrical charge. Real, yet lacking fundamental properties of matter, the neutrino is a ghost.[9]

All well and good. Possession is possible, I thought. But where were the documented cases? Where was even one well-documented case? 1949. I thought of that. The story in the *Washington Post* seemed factual; and yet, finally, how could I tell? Only an eyewitness could corroborate it for me. In an earlier try at tracing the exorcist, I had queried the *Washington Post*, but couldn't find the reporter who had written the story, and the names of the exorcist and the fourteen-year-old boy who was the victim had never been known. I'd also queried the Jesuits I'd known while at Georgetown who were still on the campus. None could help.

SO I searched the literature of possession. To begin with, though in time they reached back to ancient Egypt, the published sources, notably those in which the insights of psychiatry were fully reflected, were not only few in number, but also repetitious. And of the cases cited, over 90 percent were conceivably attributable to fraud, delusion, a combination of both, or misinterpretations of the symptoms of psychosis, particularly paranoid schizophrenia, or of certain neuroses, especially hysteria and neurasthenia. 80 percent of the victims were women, moreover, a ratio so disproportionate as to suggest, as opposed to possession, a common disorder once alluded to as *furor uterinus*, an expression that speaks, I would think, for itself. This would surely account for the extraordinary lewdness of speech and behavior that I found to be present, without exception, in every case of so-called demonic possession. And it surely is significant that Tourette's syndrome, a still mysterious neurological disorder only recently isolated and labeled, is primarily characterized by the sudden, apparently unmotivated and unpredictable onset of a usually irresistible compulsion to shriek out a torrent of verbal obscenities not noticeably lacking in nauseating grossness.

A few of my findings were intriguing: the reporting of a common symptomology in cases widely separated with respect to both time and place; and cases where the victims were very young children. Both tend to make hysteria, fraud or delusion more remote as explanations of possession. How would an eight-year-old boy, for example, come to know its classic symptoms? It is possible. But likely?

And consider what happened to four of the exorcists sent to deal with the outbreak at Loudun. Three of them, Tranquille, Lactance and Lucas, successively appeared to be possessed themselves, and while in that state died, perhaps from cardiac exhaustion. The oldest of these men was forty-three. The fourth, Surin, a noted intellectual and mystic, a truly good man, only thirty-three, became totally insane and so remained for twenty-five years. If these exorcists were faking, they carried it far; if temporarily hysterical, they were so in defiance of a psychiatric principle that tells us that hysterics do not blossom overnight; and if hysterical beforehand, though of differing backgrounds,

If There Were Demons Then Perhaps There Were Angels: William Peter Blatty's Own Story of *The Exorcist*

then their hysteria must surely have been the determining criterion employed by the cardinal who picked them for the mission, for how could we otherwise account for the coincidence involved in his selecting four closet hysterics? I do not find these possibilities alluring to reason. And it was certainly known well before the events at Loudun that symptoms suggesting possession could in fact be caused by mental illness: "The too credulous," The Church warned would-be exorcists in the Acts of the Synod of Rheims, "are often deceived, and…lunatics often declare themselves to be possessed and tormented by the devil; and these people nevertheless, are far more in need of a doctor than of an exorcist." That statement was made in 1583.

Moreover, what was I to think of cases of possession in which the subject's personality, voice and mannerisms altered so radically that people around them actually believed they were dealing with someone else? It is useless to resort to "dual personality" as an explanation. The competent psychiatrists[10] who authored *The Three Faces of Eve* make the candid admission that while Eve's disorder disappeared in apparent response to treatment based upon a certain diagnosis of the problem, that diagnosis depended on the interaction within equations of concepts like "mind," "personality" and "hysteria"; but in fact the reality of these labels is still unknown. In physics, when working certain equations, one assumes that light is composed of particles; but in working other equations, the assumption is that light is composed of waves. It probably is neither.[11] But it cannot be both. And that either type of equation "works" does not prove either assumption concerning light; it proves only that the equation works. So in attempting to explain possession, one might as well say "demon" as "dual personality." The concepts are equally occult.

BEFORE EVE Black's case, the great psychiatrist Morton Prince had treated a case of dual personality in which one of the newcomers, hardy "Sally," who knew everything her other personalities were doing whereas they knew nothing of her activities, claimed to be a "spirit"; and refused to be therapeutically murdered, so that Prince at last resorted to "exorcism." By taking her on her own terms he was able to argue her into returning whence she had come. In a like vein, following publication of *The Exorcist* I was to hear from a noted psychologist that he believed that some of his former patients had been "obsessed," the second stage of possession in which the attack is from the exterior. This psychologist, Dr. Alan Cohen, a Ph.D. from Harvard who practices in San Francisco and coauthored *Understanding Drug Use*,[12] told me that in paranoid schizophrenic subjects experiencing auditory hallucinations, the verbal patterns of association of ideas should be identical to the patterns in the content of what is hallucinated, since both patterns have a common source. But in certain of his patients, Cohen told me, these patterns were totally dissimilar, thereby suggesting separate intelligences. Cohen alluded to the two little boys, aged ten and eleven, who killed by crucifixion a three-year-old boy in San Francisco, each explaining independently that "a voice" had told him to do it; he told me further that the former chief psychologist at Mendocino State Mental Hospital in northern California, Dr. Wilson Van Deusen, believed that many patients in the disturbed ward in that institution were possessed;[13] and that he went so far as to practice therapeutic exorcism on occasion.

All interesting, indeed. And yet all these findings taken together did not constitute the slimmest reed of evidence.

If There Were Demons Then Perhaps There Were Angels: William Peter Blatty's Own Story of *The Exorcist*

The case for demonic possession had finally to rest on what was plentifully lacking at Loudun: the reliably witnessed and reported occurrence of so-called paranormal phenomena. Levitating mattresses are very "out front."

Of course I found many such cases reported in the literature. And at times the eyewitness observer—the noted ethnologist Junod, for example—surely had to be counted as reliable. So too must William James, the great psychologist, who investigated the case of a girl in Watseka, Illinois, who underwent a total and abrupt transformation of personality and identity, claiming for months to be someone named Mary Roff, who turned out to be a real person whom she had never met: a sixteen-year-old girl who had died in a state insane asylum years before. James declared the "spiritist explanation" of the case "the most plausible" one available. And Carl Jung, it is perhaps little known, was connected with another case of possession for almost a year.[14] The case involved a fifteen-year-old girl, the daughter of friends. Normally dull-witted, she manifested three distinct personalities, one of them a chatty and eloquent old man who spoke High German, a dialect completely unknown to the girl. She demonstrated telepathic abilities and an astoundingly accelerated intelligence, all of which phenomena were frequently witnessed first-hand by Jung, who found in them no possibility of fraud.

BUT THE case involving James lacked paranormal phenomena, and the case involving Jung, while it apparently did exhibit such phenomena, was, however, totally lacking in the fits of rage, the malevolent activity and the demonic self-identification that characterize so-called demonic possession. And of all the other cases of demonic possession I studied, almost all exhibiting paranormal phenomena had occurred no later than 1900, with some dating back several centuries. I constantly found myself asking: Who were the witnesses? Who had written the report I was reading? Could I trust his veracity and judgment? Did he witness the phenomena himself? If so, how much time intervened between events and the preparation of the report? Or was the record based on hearsay? And if so, how far removed was it from the eyewitness source?

In an ordinary circumstance when there is continuing and universal testimony that such-and-such a thing has occurred, we allow for inaccuracies and falsehood but accept the main core. There are extant a number of differing Deluge stories. There are those who cannot accept the Old Testament account of a massive ark that bore animals two by two in its hold. And who can take literally the Gilgamesh epic? The point is that we do accept the core of these stories: that at some point in history mankind experienced a devastating flood.

Yet I could not apply that kind of thinking to possession. Not that such reasoning is invalid, for in life—and sometimes in science, especially physics—very little is "proved" before we give it assent; instead, what we do is make prudent judgments. But prudent judgments do not satisfy when dealing with the supernatural, for the ultimate issue is too important; the issue is God and our hope of resurrection. Thus, on hearing a second-hand report from Martha and Mary to the effect that the tomb is empty, that "He is risen," I would first stroll over to the tomb and examine it myself; and then, if the women claimed to have personally witnessed the actual resurrection,[15] I would have a little chat with them to try to determine if they had been "stoned" at the time. I would also pull their files from Roman Intelligence to check out their character, their integrity and their record of "prowler" calls to the police. Only then would I begin to formulate a prudent judgment based on what they had said.

And so with possession. I felt that if I couldn't write the novel with conviction I probably wouldn't want to write it at all; for how could it possibly turn out well? A hollow heart cannot excite.

I found a case that was relatively recent: 1928. In Earling, Iowa. There was only one account of the event, a printed pamphlet written by a monk. The pamphlet carried photographs of the principals. Paranormal phenomena were cited. One in particular gave me pause. It was stated that the victim, a forty-year-old woman, who would repeatedly and forcefully fly up from her bed as if hurled like a dart, head first, at a point above the bedroom door, where she would hang suspended by her forehead, as if tightly glued to the spot. An extraordinary image! I instinctively felt that it could not have been invented. Moreover, while phenomena tended to repeat themselves in the cases I had studied, this was one I had never before heard the likes of. And yet my overall reaction to the pamphlet was a shrug. Perhaps some who are familiar with the pamphlet were impressed, by which I do not imply that my threshold of credulity is higher than theirs, as should be evident to anyone who examines my record of box-top mail-ins at the Post Toasties plant, notably the one in response to an offer of a Dick Tracey "two-way radio ring." But the tone of the pamphlet seemed so overly credulous, so replete with pietistic asides and exclamations, that it turned me off. I reacted illogically, I suppose, as the basic phenomena might still have been factual; but the pamphlet made me think of "Crazy Mary," a friend of my mother's who during my boyhood visited seven churches a day and saw Our Lady of Fatima in the alphabet soup. I simply didn't trust it. And the people involved were unfortunately dead. That ended Earling, at least for me.

NEXT I called upon numerous Jesuit friends in the hope that they might lead me to someone now living who had actually performed an exorcism: maybe someone from the foreign missions, for in Asia and Africa possession is common. But I had no luck. I came closest with Father Thomas Bermingham, who had taught me at Brooklyn Prep and was master of studies at St Andrew's-on-Hudson, a Jesuit seminary, at the time I sought him out. He recalled that in his earliest years in the priesthood a Jesuit quartered at the seminary was known to have performed an exorcism. Withdrawn and never known to speak, he haunted the wooded walks alone, a blank, burned-out look in his stare. He was late into his thirties. His hair was shock-white. It had happened in the exorcism, I was told.

The story caused my pilot light to flicker back on; and in the back of a book that I used in my research, I have recently discovered a small notation that it doubtless inspired: "Exorcist white-haired man called out of retirement to do it again. He dies early and assistant takes over." But Father Bermingham couldn't remember the original model's name.

So I tried something utterly illogical: instead of asking more Jesuits who'd been in the neighborhood when the

If There Were Demons Then Perhaps There Were Angels: William Peter Blatty's Own Story of *The Exorcist*

incident had taken place, I called a Jesuit friend of mine in Los Angeles, thousands of miles away from the event. He gave me the exorcist's name and address.

I wrote to him. He answered with the following letter, from which I have deleted certain information for reasons that will be apparent:

☞

YOUR LETTER, addressed to me at the—Retreat House at—, was forwarded to me here, where I have been stationed for the past year. We have a mutual friend in Father—, SJ.

As you stated in your letter, it is very difficult to find any authentic literature on cases of possession; at least, I could not find any when I was involved in such a case. Accordingly, we (a priest with me) kept a minute account each day of the happenings each preceding day and night, one reason being that our diary would be most helpful to anyone placed in a similar position as an exorcist in any future case.

My hesitancy in giving you the details of the case of possession is due to two facts. First,—, who delegated me as the exorcist, instructed me not to publicize the case. I have been faithful to his instructions. Secondly, it would be most embarrassing, and possibly painfully disturbing, to the young man should he be connected in any way with a book detailing events that took place in his life some years ago. Since a case of possession is a very rare occurrence, he would certainly connect his own experience with any such account.

Some Jesuits living with me at—at the time were conversant with some of the events in the case, and, as often happens, as a story passes on, events are not correctly reported.

My own thoughts were that much good might have come if the case had been reported, and people had come to realize that the presence and the activity of the devil are something very real. And possibly never more real than at the present time. But I submitted my judgment to the instructions which I received from—.

I can assure you of one thing: the case in which I was involved was the real thing. I had no doubt about it then and I have no doubts about it now.

Should I be of any assistance to you within the limitations I have set forth in this letter, I would be glad to accommodate you.

I wish you every success in the important apostolate of the pen. You can do so much good with that gift.

↩→

THE LETTER was electrifying, for at last I felt I was in touch with reality, with a good and sensible man. I wrote again and asked permission to see his diary, not for the purpose of reproducing any of its details in the novel I would write, but because I am Thomas and needed to put my own fingers in the wounds. But again the exorcist declined, citing the need to protect the boy; he would only assure me that the case had indeed involved unambiguous paranormal phenomena.

I later would learn that even a priest who had requested the material from the Washington archdiocese was told in 1952 that "His Eminence [the Cardinal] has instructed me to inform you that he does not wish the case of exorcism of the boy in Mount Rainier discussed publicly. The parents of the boy made a very strong request to that effect and we have tried

If There Were Demons Then Perhaps There Were Angels: William Peter Blatty's Own Story of *The Exorcist*

to shield them and the boy from any embarrassing publicity." After *The Exorcist* was published, a number of periodicals and newspapers resurrected the original account of the case given out by the victim's minister; I had changed the boy in my story to a girl, although more to ease the exorcist's anxiety than from fear of doing any real harm to the boy, inasmuch as the specific locations, the characters and the story in my novel were not taken from the actual case, there being, as I have said and now repeat, no murders or deaths of any kind in the latter; and in addition, I utilized no paranormal phenomena peculiar to only *this* case of possession. Nevertheless, all this being said, it is a fact that the diary maintained by the exorcist was submitted, for their guidance, to two other people who were in contact with the boy and were to keep a watchful eye on the course of his recovery, and to the archives of two archdioceses; and that it came somehow to be in the files[16] of a city hospital where the boy for a time was confined and where some of the exorcism was performed. And it is also a fact that I have read it; that I have long known the name of the boy and where he lives; and can attest that the diary kept by the exorcist is in part, and beyond any doubt, the thoroughly meticulous, reliable—even cautiously understated—eyewitness report of paranormal phenomena.

↩→

THE STORY in the *Post* proved accurate, except where it implied that the boy knew Latin. It is true that he was able to parrot long phrases, and even sentences, in Latin just spoken by the exorcist as part of the ritual; and that he always burst into fury at the exorcist's command of *"principio tibi..."* the beginning of the first of the stern adjurations of the Catholic ritual of exorcism. But the parroting is easily attributable to the heightened unconscious intellectual performance—sometimes fifty times normal—that is cited by Jung as a possible concomitant of certain forms of hysteria. And the rages were doubtless cued by the abruptly loud and commanding tone recommended for delivering the adjurations in the Catholic "Instructions to Exorcists." The "unknown language" specification used by the Church as a sign of possession requires that the person allegedly possessed be able to engage in *intelligent dialogue* in that language. I cannot vouch for what may have happened prior to the exorcist's appearance on the scene; but certainly no intelligent dialogue in Latin was ever in evidence thereafter, even though the exorcist frequently demanded it of the alien intelligence controlling the boy's response in Latin to certain questions required by the ritual ("What is your name? When will you depart?") and although the "demon" (whatever ultimate reality may lie behind that name) protested at one point, "I speak the language of the persons," a seemingly childish, if not fraudulent, evasion.[17] But there was nothing evasive about the levitation of a hospital nightstand beside the boy's bed, which was witnessed by a physics professor from Washington University; nor could one so characterize a repeated and striking phenomenon not mentioned in the *Post* account: the various markings—described as "brandings"—that appeared spontaneously and without apparent case on various parts of the victim's skin. Many times they were words clearly etched in fiery red block letters that were usually a little over two inches tall; other times they were symbols; at still others, pictorial representations. One of the words that appeared was

If There Were Demons Then Perhaps There Were Angels: William Peter Blatty's Own Story of *The Exorcist*

SPITE. One symbol was an arrow that pointed directly at the victim's penis. And a very clear picture was that of a hideous satanic visage. But by far the most frequent and alarming of the brandings were lengthy lines that at times broke the skin, as if the boy had been raked with the prongs of an invisible miniature pitchfork. Or, one could say, claws.[18]

During brandings, the boy wore only his undershorts. No bedcovers hid his movements. His hands were at all times in view of the exorcist and his assistants and others in the room. One branding that ran from the boy's inner thigh to the top of his ankle, drawing blood, occurred while the exorcist was seated on the end of the bed, his eyes on the boy, and no more than about a foot away. Other of the brandings were on the boy's back. And one, the word SPITE, did not fade from his skin for over four hours.

☙→

THE PHYSICS professor from Washington, having seen the hospital bedstand levitate rapidly upwards from the floor to the ceiling, later remarked that "there is much we have yet to discover concerning the nature of electromagnetism," an observation impervious to challenge. But when we are confronted with the paranormal, is it valid, in this age of scientific awareness, to resort at the last to 'unknown forces'? We do not know all of the positive efficiencies of natural forces; however, we do know some *negative* limitations. In the words of the Jesuit Joseph Tonquedec, "By combining oxygen and hydrogen you will *never* get chlorine; by sowing wheat you will never get roses…If anyone, sowing wheat, should believe that 'perhaps' he might get roses, he must be in an abnormal state of mind."[19]

I wrote the novel. It was finished by the summer of 1970.[20] As soon as I had made several Xerox copies (for I never made carbons, which must mean I have a death wish), I took one to my neighbor, Shirley MacLaine. I had always felt inadequate and insecure in my handling of female characterizations, a bulletin certain not to stun like oxen any of the women in my life. And so when starting the novel, I had looked about for a model for Chris MacNeil, one who lived in a milieu that I knew very well and who also had a mental set and personality that would make the story work: a flipness of manner (masking vulnerability) and an earthiness of tongue that would help to keep the situation rooted in reality; whose "I'm from Missouri" attitude would serve initially as the reader's point of view. This device would later provide what Anthony Burgess has called the "nice irony" of *The Exorcist*: an atheist heroine who comes to believe that her daughter is possessed, in opposition to a Jesuit hero who does not. Though Shirley leaned more to agnostic at the time, she'd have been perfect as the model for Chris. And now I was bringing her the novel because I hadn't seen her in a very long time and because I'd had a little bit[21] too much wine and hoped to give her a happy surprise with Chris MacNeil. I lasted twenty minutes. I think my line about "saved her career" must have done it, though it could have been my effort to show her some card tricks that I told her I head learned from Roy Rogers's horse. She steered me gently to my car after giving me a bag full of rocky road candy, which has always had an instantly sobering effect upon me, a reflex triggered by my need to be alert to defend the rocky road from aggressors, namely anyone at all who might ask me to share it. The candy was decidedly better than the dog food I'd once spied on a daintily wrapped dish

If There Were Demons Then Perhaps There Were Angels: William Peter Blatty's Own Story of *The Exorcist*

in her refrigerator just before she conned me into taking several bites of it, calling it "White Fang Pâté Parisien"; but I felt a bit glum at her fluffing off the novel as something she would read when she had "a little time." Four days later, though, she called me to tell me she had read it. She seemed touched by the characterization of Chris. There were even lines of dialogue scattered through the novel that she recognized as having said many years ago. How did I come to remember them? She asked me.

She asked me to drop by. I did; and at her home she spoke more about my memory. And then said that she would like to do the book as a film. Of course when I had brought her the book I had imagined that it might be a film; and certainly Shirley would play Chris MacNeil. But I had no idea how such a film could be made; and now Shirley, who had entered into a partnership for the making of feature films with Sir Lew Grade, the English producer, was talking of cancelling the first of the films in which she was set to star and going with *The Exorcist* in November.

IT WAS all too sudden. I had labored nine months, often fourteen hours a day, every day, at a novel that had to be convincing to work. To achieve this texture of reality, I had resorted to techniques such as setting up a situation (Chris' party) where the reader would assume that Chris and Karras would finally meet, that seemed designed in fact just in *order* that they meet, and then after this buildup *not* having them meet; to having Chris called "Mrs. MacNeil" by some characters and "Miss MacNeil" by others; and even to writing in varying styles, each matched to the major character being dealt with.[22] So now I was tired and, as I said, unsure that a script could be done at all, at least by me. There were so many problems involved in adapting the novel to the screen. First, the internalizing by Karras. And how could the paranormal happenings be shown? How could Regan's demonic transformations be managed? How could the complex events of the novel be accomplished in a film less than eight hours long? Finally, how could I write such a script by September in order to shoot it in November?

I thought it was impossible. And immediately agreed to do it.

But the wearier part of me set conditions. First, we had to make a satisfactory deal and, second, I wanted to produce the film. Have you any idea why I insisted on the latter, or what can happen to a screenplay when it leaves the writer's hands? Film is an industry[23] in which writers are either broken or wind up senselessly murdering strangers in the streets. For example: Ivan Tors, the creator of the *Flipper* series, had, in addition to the dolphin, a monkey and a pelican in subordinate roles in his "pilot" (establishing) script. The head of NBC television called Tors to his office and assured him that the project was "fantastic." In fact, it was going on the air that autumn with a guaranteed run of thirty-nine weeks. Tors was elated but—"There's just one little change that I'd like you to make," the head of the network went on to tell him. "Get rid of the dolphin and build up the part of the pelican." And when *The Wizard of Oz* was first screened for studio heads, MGM's Louis B. Mayer recommended that the Kansas sequence, in which "Over the Rainbow" is sung, be cut from the picture because it was "boring," an act which was followed by Paramount's head of production, Marty Rackin. At the cocktail party celebrating the showing of the "rough cut"

If There Were Demons Then Perhaps There Were Angels: William Peter Blatty's Own Story of *The Exorcist*

of *Breakfast at Tiffany's*, Rackin remarked to Blake Edwards, the film's director, "Well, I can tell you one thing, Blake: the song has got to go." The song in question being "Moon River." ("Are you running with me, Jesus?")

Fortunately, none of this advice was followed. But too often the producer or the director or the actor or his wife will commit more obscenities of change upon a script than Launce's dog wrought against the gentlewoman's farthingale in *Two Gentleman of Verona*. Oh, there are times when it can work in reverse: when direction and editing and performance can transform a weak script into something wonderful and essentially other than it was. But more often, and especially in the area of comedy, substantial tampering with the script inevitably leads to its destruction. I once wrote a caper script, for example, in which the first two acts built to an effort by talented rogues to rob "the unrobbable bank of the West," a bank constructed by bank robbers specifically for storing their stolen loot, since in no other bank would it be secure. For two whole acts we are shown the bank's impregnable defenses. We come to like the rogues, and hope they will succeed, since if they don't they will die. For two whole acts we watch them make elaborate preparations, while being kept in the dark about the specifics of their plan. How will they do it, the audience wonders. And that was what the film was supposed to be about. But the director,[24] known in the business as a genius with comedy, suggested "just one little change" in the script: namely, that the leader of the rogues do a "High Hopes" type of song with a bunch of kids complete with choreography. Never mind that it paralyzed the momentum of the plot and utterly destroyed the pace; far worse, it put us on *overtime*. And the film would run long. To solve this problem, the director suggested[25] that we cut out the entire robbery sequence. The robbery! "We just see them coming up on the bank and then dissolve to them loading the gold on the cart," he explained. The advice wasn't followed, thanks to Malcolm Stuart, the producer. But the role that was written to be played by Rex Harrison ended up being played by Zero Mostel, and the role intended for Melina Mercouri was played instead by the ever-iridescent Kim Novak.

I was determined that this wasn't going to happen with the script of *The Exorcist*. Thus my insistence on producing it. But we never came to terms. In spite of Shirley's great enthusiasm, Lew Grade's offer for rights to the film was very low. In my straitened circumstances I probably would have accepted it except that in that case the producer would not be me but Robert Fryer, then most recently the producer of *Myra Breckenridge*. Shirley was upset that I'd rejected this offer and instead took the lead in a rival work, *The Possession of Joel Delaney*. That decision ended, if for no other reason,[26] any chance of her playing Chris MacNeil. Chris still haunts her, however.[27] Since *The Exorcist* was published, she had several times told me of her conviction that the very blurred photo representing Regan MacNeil that appears on the jacket of the book is in fact a photograph of her daughter which I'd "lifted" surreptitiously from her house. "Have you ever seen 'baba au rhum in a blender' written in lipstick on your bathroom mirror?" I asked her the last time she made the accusation. I explained that whenever I burglarize movie stars' homes to steal photographs of their children, I write those words in lipstick on a mirror. "It's my mark," I told Shirley. In reality the jacket art and photo were created by Harper Row. When first I saw the photo, in fact, I thought that it strongly resembled *my* daughter.

If There Were Demons Then Perhaps There Were Angels: William Peter Blatty's Own Story of *The Exorcist*

Around the time the Lew Grade negotiation ended, Bantam put the novel out to bid for publication by a hardcover house. Of the four good firms to whom it was submitted, two became active, if not vigorous, bidders, with Harper & Row at last bravely doubling the previous last bid that had been made by Random House. A third house receiving a submission, Knopf, had Thomas Tryon's *The Other* upcoming on its schedule; and a four person editorial staff at McCall Publishing (now defunct) unanimously rejected the novel altogether, which may prove some consolation to frustrated writers.

I WENT to New York and heard Harper's suggestions for revisions of my first draft. I was asked to drop the prologue, which I considered but didn't do; and to make the ending less obvious, which I did. In my original version of the epilogue, both Chris and the reader realized fully what Karras has done; that he has lured the demon out of Regan's body into his, and after doing so is aware that the demon, when in total control of his body, will murder Regan and anyone else in the household and then leave him, once more in control of his body, to face the horror he has wrought. Karras, apprehending this, makes a superhuman effort to regain full control of his body and battles the demon's will just long enough to hurl himself out the window in a final, saving act of love. But the ending, as I'd written it, flirted with bathos, and perhaps even married it. You may judge for yourself. Here is the relevant section of the original epilogue:

CHRIS WENT upstairs to Regan's bedroom. She looked in from the doorway and saw her standing at the window, staring out. Her hands were clasped lightly behind her back. Chris paused. She felt a twinge of worry. Slowly she moved forward to the window. There she stopped. She examined the child's face. Regan was slightly frowning as at sudden remembrance of forgotten concern. She looked up at her mother. "What happened to the man?"

"The man?"

Regan nodded. "The one who jumped out of the window. Ya know? The man in the funny black dress."

Wide-eyed, Chris sagged to one knee. She took hold of her daughter's hands and held them firmly. "You saw a man jump?"

Regan nodded solemnly. "Is he all right?"

Chris held her breath. "Honey, tell me." She paused, controlling her voice. "Can you remember—can you remember what happened?"

"Well he jumped."

"Honey, why? Do you know?"

Regan frowned.

"Do you remember why he jumped?"

"Well, it's kind of…well, funny." Regan looked off. "I mean, I think I might have dreamed it." Regan shrugged. "Well, it sort of was crazy."

"Just tell me, honey! Tell me whatever you remember!"

"Well, the man…well, he was saying…I mean, talking to some animal or something…"

"An animal?"

"Well something…" Regan bit her lip, her brow furrowed. "He was telling it to go, like—to get out. You know? And then he said…" She paused, as if groping for the memory, "He

If There Were Demons Then Perhaps There Were Angels: William Peter Blatty's Own Story of *The Exorcist*

said—if it came out it could go inside *him*. And then—well, it seemed like it *did* go inside him. This animal or something. It went in him." She looked at her mother. "I think that part I *must've* been dreaming. Don't you think?"

Chris stared numbly. "Honey, tell me what else!"

"Well this man started acting real crazy an' stuff. Like he was fighting with someone."

"Fighting?"

"Uh-huh. But there was nobody there, though. Just him. An' he was saying..." She squinted at the forming recollection. She turned to her mother. "I remember. He was saying that he wouldn't let it hurt you."

"Let it hurt me?"

"Well, hit you, sort of. And me. I mean, all of us. He said he wasn't going to let it hurt us. And that's when he jumped." Regan pointed to the window. "I mean he ripped off the covering, first. *Then* he jumped." Regan frowned. "Mother, why are you crying?"

"Because I'm happy that you're well again, baby. I'm just crying 'cause I'm—happy—you're well."

"Is the man all right, Mom?"

Chris looked down. "Yes, honey. The man is all right. He's resting."

"In the hospital?"

Chris nodded.

"Can we go and see him, Mom?"

Chris lifted her face. The tears ran freely. "Yes, honey," she smiled. She clasped Regan's hands. "Someday..."

AND SO I rewrote it. The basic elements remained the same but I made the exposition more oblique.[28]

While still in New York and in the midst of revising the manuscript, I received a call from a William Tennant, representing Paul Monash, who had just produced *Butch Cassidy and the Sundance Kid*. Would I enter an exclusive negotiation with his client for an option on the book? Tennant asked. I would. For Monash offered to meet my terms. We made a deal whereby Monash would have six months to get a major studio to make the film. If he failed, all rights to the property reverted to me and I would keep the money he had advanced. If he succeeded, I would write the script and produce, with Monash acting as executive producer. And he did succeed. He made a deal with Warner's to make the film.

But soon we had some disagreements. Paul, a bright man and a writer himself, was in favor of changing the locale of the action from Washington, DC, as it was in the novel; didn't like the "colorful" treatment of Kinderman; thought that Chris shouldn't be an actress, said we shouldn't use the prologue of the novel, which introduces Merrin in Iraq;[29] and wanted to eliminate Merrin entirely. None of this pleased me. Then came further disagreements involving the studio. I don't remember what I did then; I must have blacked out. But according to a rumor abroad in some circles, I pilfered some documents (Shirley MacLaine just sat up and paid attention) relating to my deal that showed a lack of…well, shall we just call it due regard for fair business practice?[30] According to the rumor, which of course is preposterous, I picked a day to go to Warner's when I knew that Paul Monash would be at Universal. And it being the lunch hour, and Monash's temporary secretary busy chatting in an office opposite, it is said

If There Were Demons Then Perhaps There Were Angels: William Peter Blatty's Own Story of *The Exorcist*

that I entered the reception area of Monash's office; and that the secretary then returned to ask me who I was; and that I told her, "William Faulkner," requested some coffee, the urn being visible in Monash's office, and then inquired if I might use the phone; and while using the phone—now being seated behind the reception desk and in view of the secretary, who'd gone back across the hall—I rummaged through drawers for a key, found it, went into Paul's office for another cup of coffee, lunged at a file drawer labelled "A to E," unlocked it, found some documents filed under "Exorcist" that I thought of unusual interest, tucked them in a copy of *Fortune* magazine, went out the office and two doors down to the Warner Bros. Xeroxing room, made copies of the documents, tucked them back inside the copy of *Fortune*, returned the originals to the file, locked it, sat down again at the desk, picked up the phone and dialed "time and temperature" while returning the key to where I'd found it; and then disappeared into the Burbank fog with a clutch of documents which seemed to prove conclusively that crimes against the author had indeed been committed and which because they were in my possession, impelled the studio to buy Monash out and make me sole producer of the film.

I BEGAN the script. I compressed the first third of the book into only thirty-three pages. And then I further decided to eliminate the subplot relating to Elvira, the servant Karl's daughter. I hated to do that. The Elvira subplot not only added a dimension to Karl, but was intended to illustrate Merrin's belief that out of evil there finally always comes good; for

Kinderman's relentless investigation of Dennings' murder results in Elvira, a heroin addict, at last being hospitalized and on the road to cure. But there simply wasn't time and the subplot had to go. So too did the novel's subtle hints that the killer and desecrator might be Karras. *Though* I did insinuate it, at first, in the sequence that begins in the Jesuit refectory at Georgetown and ends with Karras and a young Jesuit on a platform at the top of the steps from which Dennings was probably[31] pushed to his death. Karras says he always tries to make it to the platform around that time to watch the sunset. The Georgetown University clock booms the hour: 7:00 p.m. Dennings plunged to his death at 7:05. And Karras, who once blacked out at a time when a desecration was taking place, is surely a candidate for somnambulism produced by an "unconscious rebellion" against the Church; for not only is he filled with compulsions of guilt but he was refused in his request for a transfer to New York so that he might be close to his mother, who since that time has died alone.

Again, though, there wasn't time and most readers of the novel had failed to pick up on the suggestion anyway. And so finally I cut the scenes. Even so, I wound up with a first-draft script that ran to over two hundred pages. If shot, it would result in a four-hour film. But I decided, like Scarlett O'Hara, that I would "worry about that tomorrow."

It was June and by now the novel had been published. I could tell by the mail I was getting. Some of it was nice. Some was not. And some of it, letters from a number of readers seeking help because they thought themselves to be possessed, was very pathetic.[32]

I heard from Jack Douglas, the humorist, who began his letter with the comment, "I sure wish Karras was still

If There Were Demons Then Perhaps There Were Angels: William Peter Blatty's Own Story of *The Exorcist*

alive—I've got a couple of kids I'd like to have him take a look at." Another who wished that Karras had lived was my friend the exorcist. For in a letter which remarked on the authenticity of the book, he decried the impression that Karras had "lost." I was stunned. For he thought it was the *demon* who impelled Karras out through the window to his death. It was a view shared by many other readers, I learned, and accounted in part for my hate mail. With such an interpretation, my novel was received by the reader as a definite "downer" and construed by many to mean that evil finally triumphs. I really don't know what to do about "speed readers."[33] Shooting them certainly comes to mind. Although most of the hate letters that I received—and by far the most virulent—had nothing to do with sloppy reading, but came instead from those who presumed to lecture me obscenely about obscenity. Useless explaining to them that obscenity lies not in words but in every contravention of the Sermon on the Mount; useless citing favorable reviews in a number of religious periodicals, among them the *Civiltà Cattolica*, the Vatican literary journal.[34] One woman to whom I had pointed out the latter, in fact, wrote again to me, screeching, "If the Pope likes your book that *proves* it's rotten." And that helped. Until then the attacks had hurt a bit. But at that point I realized that they had come, in the main, from people who hated themselves.

NOT SO with some others, perhaps mainly those who felt the book's shocking aspects were unnecessary. I did not share their belief. To begin with, the descriptions of demonic behavior are authentic (as are also the descriptions of rites at Black Mass; and everything else in the book that relates to satanism or possession). Furthermore, and purely apart from dramatic considerations—the need for something so unthinkably horrible (the crucifix masturbation scene) that it drives an atheist to a priest—if you're attempting to present possession as possible evidence of an unutterably evil and malevolent intelligence, then you must back it up both in concrete detail and in the viscera. You cannot say, "Regan then did something awful"; for if demons exist, that is not the way to argue it; and not the way to make us abhor what is evil. Oddly—and significantly, I think—the only blast at the novel, in print or in the mail, from any formal religious source, emanated from a Jesuit named Raymond Schroth who assailed me in *Commonweal*, basing his attack not on "obscenity" but on his feeling that *The Exorcist* fostered belief in Satan, thus prompting a return to "the superstitions of the Middle Ages." He suggested I ought to be writing about social action. Perhaps he was right.[35]

I myself, in considering the question of Satan's existence, reflect upon the fact that every primitive culture has had a myth about an evil being or "magician" who comes to earth and spoils the work of the Creator; who introduces hatred, disease and death. Then I think of the soldier who deliberately throws himself atop a freshly hurled enemy grenade in order to shield his comrades from the blast. Not his children; not his sweetheart; not his mother. Fellow soldiers. And I cannot help feeling, when I consider these things, that the world holds far more monstrous evil than can be accounted for solely by man, who is essentially good. I have not reasoned to this. I *feel* it.

↻→

If There Were Demons Then Perhaps There Were Angels: William Peter Blatty's Own Story of *The Exorcist*

BUT IS Satan a single personal intelligence? Or Legion, a horde of evil entities? Or even, as has been conjectured, the stuff of the universe: matter itself, Lucifer working out his salvation through the process of physical evolution that ends in Teilhard de Chardin's "omega point." I surely do not know, nor can I even make a prudent judgment. Whatever my beliefs concerning Satan's existence, however, we have no record of reliable data that would link him to possession. I know that will surprise many readers and reviewers. But historically, the "demons" involved in possession and pseudopossession rarely identify themselves only as Satan. And surely the chief of the fallen angels has far worse things that he could be doing. Even in terms of my novel, I have never known the demon's identity. I strongly doubt that he[36] is Satan; and he is certainly none of the spirits of the dead whose identity he sometimes assumes. If I had to guess, I would say he is Pazuzu, the Assyrian demon of the south-west wind. But I'm really not sure.[37] I know only that he's real and powerful and evil and apparently one of many—and aligned with whatever is opposed to love.

Now I put away the mail. It was time to select the film's director. My contract with Warner's called for a form of mutual approval whereby, before the signing of my contract, we were to shape a list of directors agreeable to both. The list we had agreed upon finally included Arthur Penn, Stanley Kubrick and Mike Nichols.

I had also suggested Billy Friedkin. I had met him years before. I'd been working with Blake Edwards on the script of a Peter Gunn feature called *Gunn*. Billy was up for the job of directing it; in first position in fact. Billy had never directed a full-length feature film. But all he had to do to change that fact was to read the script and then tell us he liked it.

He read the script and met with Blake and me for lunch at the Paramount commissary. Straight-on and very articulate, he was only twenty-six and with his horn-rimmed glasses looked like *Fiddler on the Roof's* Tevye as a boy. But he wasn't about to ask God for any favors and proceeded to tangle with Blake on a sequence in the script that he thought should be cut, a sequence I had written. It was a very small point and he might have let it slide. But he didn't. And blew the assignment of course. But I never forgot him. My previous experience with most directors had been that they would tell you your script was sensational, their only reason for taking low money, because frankly, they would confide, they needed a hit; and then when they'd been hired and were safely under contract, they would give your script to the FBI chief, instructing him, "This should never see the light of day." Friedkin, in that context, was a wonder.

Years later, I saw his *The Night They Raided Minsky's*. I thought it had movement and grace and sensitivity. It wasn't commercially successful but I liked it very much. I had a pet script in my trunk at that time. It was based on the novel I had written before *The Exorcist, Twinkle, Twinkle, "Killer" Kane* (a.k.a. *The Ninth Configuration*), my first exploration of the mystery-of-goodness theme, although, despite the lurid jacket copy on the Curtis paperback edition, it had nothing at all to do with the occult.[38] It was set in a military rehabilitation center and centered on a war of nerves between the psychiatrist in command of the center and a number of inmates led by an astronaut who refuses to go to the moon on the grounds that it might be bad for his skin. Just prior to being committed, he is observed, while dining in the officer's mess, as he picks up a plastic ketchup squeeze bottle, squeezes a thin red line across

If There Were Demons Then Perhaps There Were Angels: William Peter Blatty's Own Story of *The Exorcist*

his throat and then staggers over to a table where the head of the Space Administration is dining, falls across it in front of him and gurgles, "Don't—order—the swordfish." Another of the inmates, to round it out for you, is adapting the plays of Shakespeare for performance by a cast of dogs and "cannot abide a Dalmatian that lisps." ("Shrieking terror!") It was what you might call bizarre material. I had hoped to direct it myself. But after seeing *Minsky's* I thought that the script would be safe with Friedkin. I sent it along to him. He liked it. But we couldn't find a studio that liked it. We'd put it away. Now, with *The Exorcist* film in preparation, his name leaped to mind and I submitted it to Warner's for inclusion in the list. They turned it down. But then one by one the directors on the list were penciled out. Some had commitments that would keep them unavailable for almost a year. Arthur Penn was teaching at Yale. Stanley Kubrick could produce for himself, thank you kindly. And Nichols said he didn't want to hazard a film whose success might depend upon a child's performance.

THEN THERE were none. So I suggested Friedkin again. Again they said no. And they asked if instead I'd be willing to consider another director whom I personally liked and who was talented and sensitive but whose work I nonetheless loathed. He'd been critically acclaimed for a film that consisted in the main of interminable reaction shots in which the characters stared at each other piercingly, thinking presumably staggering thoughts. Let us say that the name of that film was *Hypnosis* and the name of the director, Edmund de Vere. If he were to wind up directing *The Exorcist*, with a script of over two hundred pages, its running time couldn't be under three weeks. However, I agreed—to be fair[39]—to screen a rough cut (generally, the first edited version, but minus music and finished sound, and in some cases optical effects) of de Vere's most recent work, which, I was assured, would "change my mind"; it was "absolute dynamite," "so sensitive," I was told.

I screened it alone at the studio while a studio executive sat awaiting my reaction. And yes, it was sensitive. But so were Leopold and Loeb. And I felt that I was watching another murder, the victim in this case being pace. Entire novenas could be said during pauses in the dialogue.[40] This was all very well at Cannes, I supposed, but would surely be deadly for *The Exorcist*. Thinking the locale of the novel was Boston was but one indication of how readers often flew through the pages of the novel to gulp down further developments of plot. Slow pacing on screen would result in frustration and diminishing tension.

Midway through the screening I thanked the projectionist and left. I returned to the executive's office. On seeing me back an hour early he did a little leap about an inch off his chair, and I imagined his hair standing straight up on end just like Little Orphan Annie about to say, "Yike!" when the news isn't really all that smashing.

He asked that I return to the screening room. The ending, he insisted, "was the picture." And how could I judge after seeing only half of it? There was also the need to forestall "bad word of mouth," which would start with the projectionist's report to his friends that "Blatty walked out on it halfway through, and he isn't even *bright*"; and which is how the public comes not to queue around the block on opening night for a film that hasn't been reviewed yet.

If There Were Demons Then Perhaps There Were Angels: William Peter Blatty's Own Story of *The Exorcist*

The executive had his secretary call the projectionist. She told him I'd had a headache but was feeling much better now and would be back to see the rest of the film. I returned to the screening room. And liked the second half of the film only very little more than I had liked the first. I didn't return to the executive's office. Depressed, I had dinner and then went to a movie. I went for diversion, not to study. But the film was Friedkin's *The French Connection*. And I went quietly berserk. The pace! The excitement! The look of documentary realism! These were what *The Exorcist* desperately needed.

I called the head of the studio. And soon the executives at Warner Bros. were screening *The French Connection*.

Billy Friedkin was hired.

---

1 Frank Sheed (New York: Sheed & Ward, 1952). I cannot recommend this book too highly for those interested in studying certain aspects of possession.

2 He endeavored instead to seduce my interest, the cosmic rays being strong that day, towards fictionally exploiting "the romance of dentistry."

3 This report was false and later proved to have been a distortion of a similar and factual phenomenon whereby the boy could *spit* in such a manner, even with his eyes shut tight, or, as they sometimes were, physically shielded from his targets.

4 Later on I renamed him John Henry Carver. I thought this aspect of the theme would work better if the priest were black and had come to the priesthood to escape from the slums and his boyhood identity; for then his resistance to the notion of possession in the face of levitating beds could be partly ascribed to his rejection of what he thinks are the superstitions related to his Haitian parents. The reason I abandoned this characterization was my fear of falling into the trap of writing Sidney Poitier.

5 It is useless to argue that unlike atoms, men have a higher intelligence, for this merely serves to help us rush all the more quickly.

6 I believe that my subconscious, once it has the necessary raw material (data and research) and sufficient prodding (sweat), does most of my plotting; and that it knew, by the time I had made that notation, almost the entire plot of *The Exorcist*, slipping portions to my conscious mind a little bit at a time. I remember, for example, being so surprised at the moment it occurred to me that Burke Dennings, and not an offstage character as originally planned, would be the demon's murder victim, that from the desk I cried out aloud, "My God, Burke Dennings is going to be murdered!" Yet an early and seemingly accidental detail— Denning's habit of tearing off the edges of pages of books or scripts and then nervously twisting and fiddling with them—would later prove vital to a major piece of plotting. What we often call inspiration, I think, are in fact subconscious disclosures.

7 I wish to make it clear that in the 1949 case no killings or deaths of any kind were involved. Two priests were injured, however, one to the extent that for weeks he could use only one hand for the lifting of the chalice when saying mass.

8 *The Devils of Loudun* (New York: Harper & Row, 1952).

9 Physics now tell us that on the subatomic level matter as we know it does not exist; that on the subatomic level there are no "things," only processes; and that the clockwork universe of the mechanists has been destroyed. We have the additionally mystical notion, which won for its discoverer the Nobel Prize, that a positron "is an electron *moving backwards in time.*"

10 Corbett H. Thigpen and Hervey M. Cleckley (New York: McGraw-Hill, 1957).

11 Or, like the neutrino, evidence that matter is finally sprit?

12 *Understanding Drug Use: An Adult's Guide to Drugs and the Young,* Alan Cohen and Peter Marin (New York: Harper and Row, 1971).

13 As reported in *Newsweek* (11 February, 1974, p.61), other psychiatrists agree: "...there are some psychiatrists who no longer dismiss exorcism as a crude, pre-Freudian method of handling emotional disturbance. Milwaukee psychiatrist Alan Reed Jr says he will not rule out possession as an explanation for some forms of extreme psychic disorder. 'In the whole field of spiritualism, mysticism, religion and the human spirit,' says Reed, 'there are things so minimally understood that almost anything's possible.' 'I believe all that stuff,' admits Dr. Walter Brown, a psychiatrist at Mount Sinai Hospital in New York

If There Were Demons Then Perhaps There Were Angels: William Peter Blatty's Own Story of *The Exorcist*

City. 'In a way, all psychoanalysis and psychotherapy are forms of exorcism, of getting rid of demons.'"

14 Fully described in his "On the Psychology and Pathology of So-Called Occult Phenomena," *Psychiatric Studies*, in the *Collected Works of C Jung*, Bollingen Series XX (Princeton, NJ: Princeton University Press, 1957).

15 Merely a "for instance." According to Gospel accounts, they did not.

16 *Not* via the exorcist, who continued to exhort me never to reveal the boy's identity.

17 Although an identical claim in two earlier cases of possession was further explained by the possessing entities as relating to the absence, in the bodies of their hosts, of the muscular formations in the physical speech apparatus that develop with the use of a language; thus their efforts to speak another language not known to the host would be halting, if not laughable. In the cases cited, however, the languages were French and German; whereas Latin has never posed any such problem for high-school freshmen, with the possible exception of myself.

18 In both the novel and the film the levitation of the bedstand would translate into the levitation of the bed itself. Other phenomena taken from the actual case would be the rappings; lesser manifestations of telekinesis, such as the drawer popping out and objects flying around the room; the "brandings" (the words on the victim's flesh, as just described); the transformation of the voice; new abilities (such as perfect pitch) never before manifested by the subject; paranormal strength; the bellowing; and a few lesser and more ambiguous phenomena, such as the accurate "blindfolded" spitting. The transformation of Regan's face, the furring and lengthening of the tongue, did not come from the actual case, but were taken from countless other cases, and in fact are no less marked than occurs in certain types of hysterical disorders. The icy cold, the shaking of the room and the cracked ceiling did not occur in *any* of the cases I studied. Neither, of course, did the turning of the head, at least to the extent depicted in the film. As this scene was first shot, Regan's head turned 360 degrees! When I pointed out to Billy Friedkin that in such an eventuality the head would likely fall off and that 'supernatural' was not synonymous with 'impossible,' the head turn was modified in the editing room. I still believed it to be excessive and unreal, but audiences loved it. Moreover, there is *some* factual basis for it. In the state of possession, and among hysterics, you will find one medical case after another in which the subject— no acrobat—was nonetheless able to perform such incredible physical

contortions as bending over backwards and touching his heels with his head. What distinguishes possession—and pseudo-possession—from hysteria in this context is that the possessed subject, when performing these actions, seems to be doing so involuntarily, for throughout he shrieks in pain.

19 *Les Maladies nerveuses ou mentales et les manifestations diaboliques*, p.230; see also *Satan* (cited in note 1).

20 Had it not been for a friend, William Bloom, it might not have been finished until the following year; for on an evening in June, when I allowed him to read what I had written thus far—which was up to the point of Merrin's death—my plan was for Karras to continue the exorcism for one or two more months. Bloom said the reader would kill me if I did that; the action was crying out to be at an end. This conversation convinced me to have Karras perform the actual exorcism in less than a minute of time.

21 Staggering quantities.

22 Merrin, complex and poetic and filled with concrete images of nature. Chris, simple, and direct and ordinary as a supermarket shopping cart. Karras, elegiac and haunted by images resonating pain in the minor particular. The styles blended with the appearance of Kinderman.

23 I use the word advisedly and in a sense that could be sobering to some. For a film is made with stockholders' money. Its purpose is profit. When an artist isn't using someone else's money, he is free to create his art for art's sake. But when his creation is financed by a studio, which borrows the money from a bank, the loan must be repaid; otherwise the value of the stock goes down and some pensioner may lose her life's savings. Simple decency therefore dictates that the artist not make a silent film in which the actors all meditate for seventeen hours.

24 Whom I do not name, for he has suffered enough, his crime having served as his punishment as well.

25 On three separate occasions in my presence, which eliminates the possibility that he wasn't really serious.

26 Billy Friedkin preferred Ellen Burstyn for the role of Chris. Ellen got the part and proved to be magnificent.

27 As the novel in a way haunts Sachi, her daughter; for various columnists, hearing that Shirley was the model for Chris, have published irresponsible innuendoes that Sachi was "possessed" at the time, and

If There Were Demons Then Perhaps There Were Angels: William Peter Blatty's Own Story of *The Exorcist*

that the novel is her story, an absurdity cruelly put to use by Sachi's schoolmates. I repeat, there is not a shred of truth in the report.

28 In view of widespread misunderstandings of both the novel and the film, I now wonder if I made the correct decision. And certainly do miss the implication of Chris accepting faith, indicated in her "Someday…"

29 As an archaeologist working on a dig at the ruins of Nineveh, for Merrin was modelled on Pierre Teilhard de Chardin, even his self-confessed frailties, which are taken from letters that Chardin wrote to his friend Madame Zonta; his love of matter; and his view of the relationship existing between matter and spirit, which he thought to be merely differing aspects of some third, more fundamental reality.

30 More commonly known as "screwing the author."

31 The likely assumption at that point in the story.

32 Although one from a woman who complained she had an incubus (demon lover) seemed not only rational but touched with humor. She'd taken her complaint to a psychiatrist who told her "most women would give their right arm" to have her problem.

33 One reviewer thought the action took place in Boston. Another complained that I knew nothing about construction, citing my introduction of a character in the prologue (Merrin) who one "never sees again." And the *Saturday Review* somehow got the notion that Karras was Jewish.

34 Religious press reactions to the film have been widespread and equally favorable. Among them is a review in the *Catholic News*, the official newspaper of the archdiocese of New York, which states that *"The Exorcist* is a deeply spiritual film" and the arch-conservative *Triumph* magazine, which published a rave review.

35 Though not about everything; for in the article in *Commonweal*, he asserted that "Père de Tonquedec, the old Parisian Jesuit, one of the most renowned exorcists of recent times, reportedly told his fellow Jesuits that he had never encountered an authentic case of diabolic possession." But another Jesuit who read Schroth's article wrote to me stating, "In 1961 I stayed for a few days at the Jesuit residence on the Rue de Grenelle in Paris. After dinner I was sitting next to Father de Tonquedec in the recreation room. In the course of the conversation, I asked whether he had ever been involved in a real case of possession. I kept a diary during my trip with no thought that what I recorded would ever be of any significance. I just checked it and I find this entry under date of October 23

1961: 'Father de Tonquedec told me that he certainly had encountered one real case of diabolical possession, and possibly two others.'"

36 Perhaps the one instance of dreaded male chauvinism not bound to irritate women's liberationists.

37 The novel is ultimately what Billy Friedkin calls a "realistic look at inexplicable events." And only in fantasy can the author be omniscient. We can get inside the heads of humans; not of demons.

38 Let book people never cast stones at Hollywood. Compare the quotes that were used on the *first* Curtis edition of *Twinkle, Twinkle, "Killer" Kane*—"Nobody can write funnier lines than Blatty" (Martin Levin, *New York Times*) and "Wild…with the verbal virtuosity of S. J. Perelman" (Richard Armour, *Los Angeles Times*)—with their jacket copy and front matter on the edition published following *The Exorcist*: "The nerve-twitching chiller from the author of *The Exorcist*" and "INVITATION TO EVIL! A grotesque old mansion that once used to belong to a silent horror movie star, and now was home to shrieking terror…"

39 I lie. It was to give the appearance of being fair.

40 Directors who come up from the ranks of cameramen sometimes subordinate other considerations in a scene to what will make the best-composed "picture." De Vere had been an actor (and though never a star, was truly outstanding), and thus no doubt tended to indulge his casts.

The Curator

by Owen King

→ D, FOLLOWING THE COUP d'état, contrived to obtain a job at the National Occult Collection. Prior to the outbreak of hostilities, she had studied library science, and harbored besides an unusual degree of interest in the afterlife, whether there was something. Her brother had died young, fourteen, of a blood-borne disease. (His final words quiet but clear: "Yes, I see you. Your—face." Whose face? He'd been nothing if not secretive, her brother, forever slipping off with his slingshot and returning flushed and vague in response to their mother's inquiries as to where he'd been. In her memory he wore his gray school suit, bowtie and cap, drawn low, so his cool eyes were shaded, the slingshot tucked into his belt at the hip.) So, D's gentleman friend, a lieutenant in the revolutionary brigade, made a call. What he discovered, to her disappointment, was that the National Occult Collection had been destroyed in a fire. The very night of the coup the building's boiler had exploded—or at least, that was the assumption. There had been a fire, anyway. In the city-wide chaos the fire crews had been dispersed to several more important locations and the blaze ate itself alive long before anyone noticed, leaving nothing but a smoldering brick shell. However, her lieutenant explained, eyebrows lifting hopefully, the National Museum of the Worker, next door, yet stood, and whoever had been in charge there had abandoned the post with the rest of the government rats.

D shrugged, said okay, and was summarily awarded the position of new head curator, and the keys to the building.

A GROUP of boys, loitering outside a shop on the opposite of the road, taunted them. "Oh, what a pretty baby!" one boy howled. D was carrying her cat doll. It wore an ivory night-gown. Her brother held her hand. He was twelve and D was six.

D sniffed at tears. She thought her baby was pretty.

The boys made cat sounds, hisses and growly screeches.

"Never mind them," her brother said quietly.

D said it was hard, though. He promised it would get easier—and when they rounded the corner, and the calling soon faded to nothing, he was proved correct. This was an important lesson. Her brother loved her and her brother told the truth.

A BROAD, red brick structure with pea green shutters and a tarnished steel door made of melted hammers, the National

The Curator

Museum of the Worker was second from the corner on a leafy street in the government district. Peen and hammerhead fragments jutted from the door's surface like fingers and faces pushing up from under a sheet.

To the left of the Museum, at the corner, lay the debris of the Occult Collection. Visible in the midst of a lean-to of charred, fallen beams was a tall, blackened rectangle that D immediately recognized from a pre-fire tour she had made of the Collection as a student. It was a closet belonging to a conjurer of the previous century known as "Salvador the Gentle." D clearly recalled the tour guide's description of the conjurer's trick: after selecting a female volunteer, the Gentle would withdraw with his new assistant into the closet; a few minutes would pass, and suddenly the conjurer would burst out again, but with the head of the woman atop his body and vice versa. While the audience roared in horrified delight an orchestra would strike up and the two abominations would perform an elegant waltz, he laying his head wistfully upon his own velvet-caped shoulder. At the conclusion of the song they would reenter the closet and shortly emerge again with their respective heads put right again. There were no photographs of the trick, of course, but according to contemporary reports, rival conjurers disapproved. They remarked, in one way or another, that the Gentle was playing with things he had no business playing with—and indeed, this proved to be the case when a series of his willing female volunteers turned out to be pregnant. "This is not my soul's doing!" the conjurer protested. There must have been someone else in the closet, he claimed. The vengeful husband who shot the Gentle in the crotch and let him bleed to death on the rug of a gentleman's club was not swayed by this excuse. D was intrigued, though. It occurred to her that, perhaps, the face her brother had glimpsed in the moments before his last breath belonged to that other soul.

To the right of the Museum was the embassy of an imperialistic ally of the former government, the diplomats of which had fled during the coup.

Together, D and her lieutenant went around the Museum building's six floors, opening the windows and the shutters to air the museum's capacious halls. Dusty light flooded the exhibitions, which ranged from working factory models to agricultural displays to examples of various kinds of printing presses. In the boiler room D's lieutenant puzzled over the gauges and switches before shrugging and abruptly pulling a red lever. "Let's just hope," he said. D plugged her ears and told him, "If this is farewell, Lieutenant, I hope I'll see you in the afterlife!" A clanking started up, and heat began to express from the radiators. "Yes!" D's lieutenant shot his arms up as if he had scored a goal. He appeared starved inside his scarlet officer's uniform, his body the same weedy university student's body that it had been when the college closed the previous spring and the revolution broke out.

"Wait." Frowning, he dropped his arms. "I'm having dark thoughts. What if heaven is a museum that hasn't been swept in a month?"

"Lieutenant." His name was Robert, but it amused her to address him by his rank. D shook her head in a regretful way. "You know very well that neither of us is going to heaven."

"Oh, right," he said. "Then: maybe this is hell?"

She pulled her dress over her head and threw it. A draft captured the thin flowered fabric, and sent it rattling across the basement, a frightened ghost, until it plastered itself across a crate, exorcised.

The Curator

"Okay, then. Definitely not hell, either," said her lieutenant, stepping toward her.

"Definitely not," she said.

D felt protective of her lieutenant; he was so puppyish, blathering on about boring holes through the economic strata and quenching the people's thirst for knowledge with the run-off; about the committees being formed in every town and village across the countryside on female advancement and resource theory and efficient management; about the brigade's artillery pressing the retreating government forces; about his dull-witted parents who meant well but couldn't conceive of the world beyond the lawn of their quaint little inn and worried only that there would be a shortage of cheese for their guests; about the paintings and the bottles of wine and the blocks of currency that the prosecutors wheeled into the courts day-after-day, and how the ministry men in the docks, like plucked chickens without their wigs and sashes and medals, claimed never to have seen any of it. Color rose up in his cheeks and sweat gathered on his forehead, where the angry scars of his teenage acne glowed purple. In school, she had been the only one who called him Robert; his friends all called him Bobby. Maybe calling him Lieutenant was an effort to get as far away from that boy's name as possible. It didn't seem to make a difference. It was still so easy to picture him on a field with lines and squares painted in the grass, shouting and elbowing in the scrum around a ball. And there was the problem: as lovable as D found her lieutenant, he was a disappointing, often irritating lover.

They did it once in the basement, and a second time upstairs, where the sawmill exhibition had caught her lieutenant's attention. Here, they positioned themselves on the chute that passed underneath the blade. For leverage D hung onto the empty crossbar that would have held the razor-sharp circular saw blade in a working mill, but in the exhibition contained only a large wooden washer. "What a show you're putting on for them! They're all waiting for their turn to grab you with their massive workers' hands, their massive calloused mitts that will scrape you, and—" His lips were in her hair, and D could feel his smile, his satisfaction. Her lieutenant tried too hard; he talked about fucking her in a desert, about pounding her into the sand while coyotes watched and howled; he talked about fucking her on a flat rock in the middle of a river, and people on boats passing by, leering and groping themselves; he talked about fucking her in the street, fucking her before an audience at the opera, fucking her in a zoo cage for the amusement of tourists. None of it excited her. Maybe it would have if she thought it was something he actually fantasized about. D knew he wasn't like that, though, that her lieutenant was too sweet and eager to be a real threat, sexual or otherwise. Her affection for him was grounded in his well-meaning nature, but so was the ambivalence she felt toward him when they were intimate.

"Sick," she said to him, which seemed to make the lieutenant happy. He cackled.

There was a shout, cut off by a gunshot. D and her lieutenant lay on the cutting board under the roof of the model sawmill and listened. A minute or two, and a heavy door banged open at street-level.

The lovers slipped off the slide and went on their knees to the nearest window. They peeked over the sill. From a rear door of the embassy emerged a massive, shirtless man, a man of the revolutionary brigade by the red uniform pants that he wore. Over his shoulder he toted a body-shaped object inside a canvas bag. It was early evening, light enough to discern stains on the canvas of the bag. A thick black beard ran down from under the soldier's eyes to his Adam's apple, beneath which a thin band of pale skin interrupted the river of hair before it spread into a pelt that covered his shoulders, chest, and torso. The soldier crossed the courtyard and dropped the object against the base of the stone retaining wall.

D glanced at her lieutenant: his jaw was shifting around inside his closed mouth.

THE MEN who removed her brother's corpse from their apartment took him out wrapped in the bedding. They wore gloves and handkerchiefs knotted over their mouths to guard against contagion.

D watched from the doorway of the living room as they passed through with their burden. Her nurse, breathing fumes of gin, rested a hand on her shoulder, as if in comfort, but really, to keep from falling over.

Her parents were already gone to choose the coffin.

THE LOVERS dressed in silence. Her lieutenant spent a few minutes irritably scrubbing at a dark spot on the wooden slide, but the mark wouldn't come away. She told him it was fine, and he said, "I know," and announced that he had to be off. There was, he explained—sulkily, sounding a lot more like a Bobby than a lieutenant—a reapportionment committee he needed to attend.

The last sun broke in shards off the tin roofs of the National Bank in the distance and D held a hand over her brow to keep from being blinded as she locked the doors. When the bolt was settled and she turned to leave, the glare momentarily cleared. D stopped. The imperialist ally's flag had been taken down from the pole that extended from the wall of the embassy and a new one—solid black—had been run up. Through the fabric D could just discern the form of the sun, a coal on the verge of collapse. The next morning, the bag that had lain by the courtyard wall was gone.

A group of schoolchildren came to the museum conducted by a pretty young teacher named Miss Clarendon. D followed the instructions written on a note card in the slanting hand of a previous curator to turn on the model waterworks and the children took turns rotating the wheel, sending bits of kindling surfing down the model river. She wheeled around a mobile printing press, brought out paper and pencils, and set them to drawing pictures of the machine. Miss Clarendon circulated among the children, the sheet of auburn hair that fell down her back swaying lightly with her steps, and her arms crossed tightly over her chest. It surprised D, how quiet the children were, the only noise the scrape of pencil leads. "They're so good," she told the teacher. "They're scared," Miss Clarendon replied. "Why?" asked D. Her lieutenant had assured her that the combat was essentially over. The other woman blinked and laughed in a way that D didn't like; it sounded less like a laugh and more like the nervous inhalation a person took to brace for a splinter being pulled. Miss Clarendon had wandered to the window. "I thought that was an embassy there," she said, not turning, leaving D to respond to her shimmering hair.

"They fled," said D. She added, defensively, "They were aligned with the criminals," and immediately regretted it,

The Curator

because what reason did she have to be defensive? D was not a soldier or a revolutionary. She was a curator.

"My fiancée is a—was a stenographer for the government—I mean, the criminals. He went there to record meetings sometimes—about trade agreements and mineral rights—shipping lanes and—and he's been missing and I wondered if during the fighting..." The teacher touched the tips of her fingers to the windowsill, as if she feared it might be hot.

"So you knew it was an embassy," said D.

"Yes," said Miss Clarendon. The women stared at each other then. One of the children sighed, perhaps dissatisfied with his picture.

"It's not an embassy any more," said D. "They do other things there now."

Miss Clarendon gathered the children. Several of them left behind their drawings of the printing press. In their crude renderings the printing press tended to resemble a spider, wide and rigid, body swimming with letters.

↪

"I AM looking for stones like this one," her brother explained, perhaps a year before the sickness took hold, and held up a smooth egg-sized rock for D to see. "Can you find me some?"

There was a park not far from where the boys had yelled at them that time. There was no sign of them now, though. From a little pond D fished four or five stones like the one her brother had shown her, stuck them in her pockets, and rushed home, the damp weights soaking through her dress and knocking against her hips.

Her brother thanked her; she was a fine sister. They were exactly the kind of rocks he needed.

⟲→

HER LIEUTENANT was happy that night. They did it inside the engineer's compartment of the train exhibit. He sat on the stool and she rode him. "Wave to the people, you dirty girl! Wave to all the people watching us pass by!" Over his shoulder, at the engine, a waxwork man was forever bent, shoveling coal into the iron belly. He was stripped to the waist, navy-colored suspenders dangling around his hips. The waxwork man had a dog's grin, wet and wide and stupid; but his shifty eyes—glass—seemed to sneak a peek. She liked that idea and followed it while her lieutenant babbled. She imagined the waxwork man continuing to shovel, not saying anything, but chuckling to himself, calmly enjoying the view, plunging the blade into the coal, lifting, pitching, plunging, lifting, pitching. The waxwork man would take his time, D thought, and he would stink, and there would be nothing said, just the force between them, as they tried to break each other apart. Her lieutenant reached up and pulled the rope for the whistle, and the shriek boomed and echoed off the vaulted ceilings of the Museum. "Oh, no." He groaned. "I think we crashed." She patted his damp red cheek. "Sad." Her lieutenant laid his head against her chest, not realizing that the pat had nearly been a slap—the whistle had ruined her concentration.

As they dressed he related to D how the deposed prime minister had killed himself in his cell, taking the coward's way out. There hadn't been any rope or sharp implements at hand, so it did have to be conceded that the son-of-a-bitch was

The Curator

tougher than one would have expected. Initially, it seemed that the deposed prime minister had tried to knock a piece of stone off the wall, probably so he could cut his wrists. But he'd just managed to crush all the bones in one of his hands. His second attempt had gone better: he successfully drowned himself in the cell's commode. "Certain poetry there, I suppose," said her lieutenant. "The guards should have stopped him, obviously. Rule of law. They must have been deaf."

"Must have been," said D.

In the provinces, meanwhile, their artillery had shattered the main body of the government's forces. It would be done in a couple of weeks, a month at most. Elections could take place before the new year began. Her lieutenant was walking around staring at the ground. "Oh, and I dropped in next door. They are holding some prisoners there—overflow from the jails—but what we saw, the bag? A dog. Belonged to someone at the embassy. Bastard left his dog behind and it went crazy, rabid probably, so they had to put it down. Shit, I can't find my button. Do you see it? It's gold."

THEIR MOTHER asked questions. People had seen D's brother with the butcher, the vividly disreputable one who sat in the chair in his bloody apron with his boots off and his fat, pale feet sticking out onto the walk, laughing at everything that anyone said to him.

This annoyed her brother. "Most people are gullible," he said. "It's a survival instinct. Because they aren't strong like we're strong. The thing she can't see is that for actually wanting to know, she's one of the stupidest ones."

Sometimes, watching her brother, their mother wore the queerest expression, a mix of confusion and irritation, as if she did not quite know who he was, what to call him, how they were related, or how he had ended up sitting on the couch in the living room in his gray school suit and cap even on a Sunday, carefully oiling the strap of his slingshot with a cloth, but the answer was right there, so close, she could almost catch it in her fingers.

"What's that butcher to your brother?" their mother wanted to know. She jerked the hairbrush through a snarl in D's hair.

"I don't know," said D, trying not to flinch, and answering honestly, even as she hoped, that if she were loyal, he would eventually tell her.

THEY DEPARTED the Museum together, splitting up outside: her lieutenant to the left, toward his next committee meeting, and D, to the right, to the tram stop, and the line that would take her home to the apartment she shared with a girl who studied at the Medical College to be a pharmacist and was almost never around. D's path brought her past the wreck of the Occult Collection building. In the lean-to of fallen beams, inside the conjurer's closet, she saw an unidentifiable animal scurry. The stench of smoke had dissipated.

While she waited at the stop, a street performer, a man with a rubbery face and a stovepipe hat, strummed a guitar and made everyone laugh by singing a song about a penguin and waddling. Miss Clarendon, the teacher with the sheet of auburn hair and the missing fiancée, approached. D greeted her. The teacher said hello, but sat down at the end of the far

The Curator

bench, head low over her purse, snapping and unsnapping it, as if she hoped that some lost thing might materialize if she searched enough times. It occurred to D that maybe Miss Clarendon had been following her, though she couldn't say why, except that the teacher had come from the same direction. The tram arrived, dragging a limp corkscrew of steam from its exhaust pipe.

A few nights later D couldn't sleep. She left her apartment and returned to the Museum.

Screams from next door at the former embassy: "Please!" someone begged and there was a crack of gunfire, and no more was heard from that voice. Other voices cried out, but following two more cracks there was silence.

THERE WAS a game her brother invented called, "Stray Cat." In this game, he would wait in a dark place—behind a door, say—and then, when either their mother or father or the nurse passed by, leap out and yowl and paw at their legs. If they hit you to get you off, you won.

FROM THE window across from the sawmill she watched the soldier—the bare-chested one from before—lug out another large bag, and another, and a third bag. This time he wore his shirt. Though it was dark she could tell that the shirt was sticking wetly to his torso. He stopped by the retaining wall, the bags piled at his feet. D thought he was listening, aware of her, but she didn't move. Why don't you move? she asked herself, and stayed right there, continuing to not move. D realized, then, that she wanted to see his face, and the desire was more important to her than any sense of self-preservation; because even though she had seen it before, seen his great beard and caught a flash of his deep-set eyes, D had the sudden implacable feeling that if he were to look up now, raise his face to find her in the window, there would be no face, just a black hole. The idea held her, while at the same time she felt like she was tipping forward, turning fast and tilting forward, like a spun coin.

He went back inside the former embassy without looking up at her window.

D wandered the museum. On the third floor she examined the splayed pelts tacked to the walls of the animal skinners' hut; the fur was as brittle as the teeth of a comb. Close by, the skinners, burly waxwork men draped in furs, ate waxwork meat off the waxwork bone and warmed themselves at a black pit that had never held fire. Seated cross-legged in a nest of hemp strands in a corner of the fourth floor was an old woman waxwork. Her ragged dress was spread around her and she was contentedly winding rope. D bent to study the ancient grooves in the cordeur's fingers, the webs of wrinkles that radiated from her bright eyes. There were no unhappy workers at the Museum.

She found herself at the massive, oaken, glass-topped display case of drill bits. There were keys to all the display cases on the key ring that her lieutenant had given her when she took over as curator. D opened the case of drill bits. She ran her fingers along their threads. The biggest bit was as long as a sword and as thick as a lamppost; FOR BORING MINE SHAFTS, read the label. The smallest was as thin as

The Curator

a toothpick. Its label said, FOR TAKING SAMPLES FROM SMALL METEORITES. D took this tiny bit without thinking, slipped into her pocket, and locked the case again.

On the basement level there was a bunkhouse diorama. She pushed aside the waxwork of the sleeping fruit picker in the bottom bunk and slid under the wool blankets.

In the morning the three bags were gone from the courtyard. Flies circled around a dark splotch that glistened on the spot where the soldier had dumped them.

ON BOTH of his hands there were long, crimson scratches, puffy and infected-looking. "What happened?" D asked.

"It's nothing. I just got a little too close," her brother said, and yawned. He never worried, so D never worried.

Too close to what, though? A little after that was when he came down with the cough that was the first sign of his illness.

NEVER MORE than a dozen visitors passed through the National Museum of the Worker each day. D approached them with a basket to collect donations. Most of the visitors were old, meticulously choosing a penny or two from their wallets and plunking them into the bowl. They swayed in front of the exhibits and blinked, sometimes clearing their throats and nodding to themselves. It was, D thought, like they were running down a list in their heads of what they needed to do, but the list must have been short because the same elderly museumgoers came back day after day. She saw the anxiety in the way one scarecrow of a man stared and nodded and sniffled with a light cold, and at the same time rubbed the lapel of his worn jacket.

The coup itself had been almost entirely bloodless, more a pageant than a fight, the revolutionaries arresting the quivering state officials and tearing down statues in the parks, but now the military convoys rolled past all day. For the sake of her lieutenant D tried to think about the revolution, to feel enthusiastic about it. It was hard, though—not that she cared about the old government. In the orphanage, after her parents died, a big-bellied, rooster-legged, glaring personage with medals on his shoulders and a gold-tipped cane visited them. He had been a vice-mayor. They lined up in the dining hall so he could inspect them. He roughly ran his hand across a few of the children's scalps, as if he could read them, like a phrenologist. With his cane's gold tip the vice-mayor had raised the shirt of a skinny boy to grunt at the sight of his scrawny body. "You might teach them how to smile," the man snapped to the mistress of the orphanage when he reached the end of the row. The vice-mayor had undoubtedly choked to death on a bone, or drowned in some pudding, or otherwise farted his last years ago, but she didn't doubt that there were plenty of others like him in the government who wore medals on their shoulders and treated people like livestock, and if they were having an uncomfortable few months, that was fine with D. But when her lieutenant talked about the Struggle, she couldn't help flashing back to her first meeting with him. Before he had a rank, before he was Robert or Bobby or anyone particular, he had been a skinny boy pulling on his unruly hair with one hand, while he frantically ran the index finger of his other hand along the spines of books on a shelf in the university library, and moved from side to side and peered up and down, as if they were an optical illusion he was trying to solve.

There was a biology textbook that he needed for "a very, very important test," he said.

D found it for him immediately: right there, filed in the correct spot, a finger tip away, but turned wrong, spine inward and pages out. The young man's outrageous shout of relief— "That's it!"—caused D to laugh in surprise and a hundred students had glanced up from their book-strewn tables to shame them down with a thunderous "Shhh!" The book was right there, though. They had wonderful ideas, D supposed, her lieutenant and his comrades, but what if they couldn't see what was right in front of their faces?

"MOTHER ASKED me about the butcher. What should I tell her?"

"Whatever you like."

They arrived at a wide, low building with a blue door. Painted on the door was a silver triangle. There was a sign posted at the foot of the path that led up to the door: National Occult Collection. It was spring and the breeze was scented with the rhododendrons and crocuses that spilled from the window troughs of the embassies and the government buildings that made up the neighborhood. Her brother told her to wait.

D watched him knock on the door. The door opened, and her brother handed the book he had been carrying to an unseen figure within. When he came back, he read D's expression. "We have an arrangement, all right." He sounded amused.

"What sort of an arrangement?"

"He lets me use his alley."

"For what?"

"To practice my slingshot."

"Will you take me there?"

Her brother flexed his hand. The scratches had swollen to up to purple seams. He caught her gaze and jammed the hand into his pocket. "Sure."

The alley was back in their neighborhood, running along-side the butcher shop. Out front, as was often the case, the butcher was perched, barefoot, on a stool with his leg crossed over his knee. "Not a bad day, eh?" he winked at her brother. The butcher's toenails were the color of lemon rinds.

"Oh, I guess it'll do," said her brother and made a large, open-handed gesture, like a conjurer who has made some-thing—a handkerchief, a coin, a lady—vanish into the air.

The butcher went *heh-heh-heh* and D's brother led her into the alley. Damp leaves of newspaper were plastered across the floor of the alley. There was a bucket set by a back door. D peered inside. There was a small pile of gray bones soaking in cloudy water.

"Were they cows or pigs?" D asked.

Her brother broke out coughing. He made a brushing ges-ture. "You've seen. Run home now. I have things to do."

↩→

NEXT DOOR in the ruins Salvador the Gentle's closet stood black inside the grip of the fallen beams. On clear days, in the late evening, the lowering sun cast its shadow out from the wreckage, like a clock hand with the arrow snapped off.

The Curator

D wondered how the randy old sleight-of-hand artist had done it, made the switch, made love to his volunteers.

Set inside a tall glass cabinet was a model foundry. You inserted a coin, pressed a button, and watched as painted figures on rails raked the coin onto a fire, where it melted down; at which point another team of painted figures tipped the molten stream into a mold shaped like a cat, and a last group of mechanical ironworkers doused it with water from tiny buckets. It took about five minutes. The machine ejected the little cast metal cat for a souvenir. D thought the cat resembled a mouse at least much as it did a cat. She used the donations to make herself a pack of cat-mice and set them along the base of her bed in the bunkhouse, where she had begun to sleep most nights. In front of the bunkhouse diorama D had drawn a curtain and pinned up a CLOSED FOR REPAIRS sign.

Some nights there were more screams from the former embassy and sometimes laughter now, too, mighty bellowing laughter, the kind of laughter you heard at weddings during the toasts. Other nights there were dull, distant thumps—cannon fire. There was a homesteading exhibit in the Museum; here visitors could test their mettle by using a wooden mallet to drive a wooden pike into a bed of sand, like a real fence builder. The invisible explosions sounded like a muffled versions of such strikes, but D could only imagine what the blasts were hammering into the ground. They came from the south, close against the hills that ringed the city.

Her lieutenant related that the revolutionary brigades had suffered a series of setbacks in the field. In rural areas many of the uneducated people were inexplicably loyal to the aristocracy. "They've poisoned wells," he said, "killed their animals, pulled apart sections of train track—" The lovers had fucked on the glass surface of the creek bed where nearby smiling waxwork prospectors panned, boot-deep in the fake water, and on the bank, their smiling waxwork women draped laundry on boulders. D had almost enjoyed it for once. Her lieutenant had been unusually subdued, not once telling her what a lovely whore everyone thought she was, or how after the fighting was over he ought to become a teacher, and lecture to great halls on the proper way to fuck her, or any of the other things that D mentally predicted he would say. Now they were lying on their sides atop the glass. She pondered the pebbles beneath the transparent floor, studded with bits of false gold, and twisting past, hung by bits of white wire, tiny brown minnows with dusty black eyes.

THE SAME sickness took her parents soon after. Men removed them in sheets, too, her mother's hair dangling from the end of one bundle, like the rotted silk from the end of a cornstalk. But the sickness had not wanted D. Her time to know—what her brother hunted, what he had come too close to and been wounded by, whose face he glimpsed—did not arrive. So, D waited: waited first in the orphanage halls where the weak girls cried and fought and made treasures of worthless junk just to have something, and waited then at the college, in the highest, deepest stacks of the library, where the oldest books were made from animal skins and even the deans could not translate them; and she waited now, while the stuffed fish hung from wires just on the other side of the glass.

The Curator

"—LIKE MY parents, too stupid to understand that the government leaves them just enough to live, and when the crops are poor, not even that—"

"—hey," said D, "get dressed, I have an idea. Something fun."

She showed her lieutenant how the heads of the waxworks were mounted on posts that protruded from the necks. D then demonstrated how, if you unhitched the clasp, they came right off.

"Why hello there, young fellow," he said to the head of a prospector she had plopped into his hands. "I think you would look very nice on—yes! On her!" Her lieutenant plucked off the head of a burly washerwoman and stuck the prospector's head on the female body. D giggled and clapped her hands. "Let's do them all!" They dashed from exhibit to exhibit, their arms full of waxwork heads, swapping the heads of lumberjacks planing logs at the sawmill with the heads of miners riding in a coal cart; changing out the seamstresses' heads for the shipbuilders' heads; the shipbuilders' heads for the bricklayers', and the bricklayers' for the seamstresses'.

To amuse each other, they conducted conversations with their creations, ventriloquizing for the waxworks:

Her lieutenant spoke with a bricklayer who found himself stuck on a matron's body: "Well, word ye jes look at me wunnerful tits!" "Yes, well, they're very nice, but let's not get distracted. You've got a lot of sewing to do." "I b'lieve I'll sew me a bag fer my tits and take 'em home!" "Listen here, you devil! You'll do no such thing. Those are museum tits and the museum is a national trust. Those are the people's tits." "No, no, no! My tits, is what they is! Mine what to swaddle an ah'dore to me art's cont'en!"

D tried to calm down the seamstress who found herself on a scaffold, tapping pins into a bulwark: "What's this then now, a damn boat? I don't e'en like to cross a bridge, now do I, and I'm s'posed to make a boat?" "I know you're upset, madam, but we've all got a job to do. Everyone works their share now." "My share's all well and good, it is. Trouble is, if'n you put me in charge of boats, people'll be gettin wet or drownt." "I'm sure if you just listen to your supervisor's directions everything will be fine." "My sup'rvisor! Her up there? That's Matilda! Why, she's no better'n me when it come to water! Matilda don' e'en warsh but once a week, now do she?"

They were stupid little plays, but it amused them, and D was reminded again of how much she liked her lieutenant, what a ready person he was when he wasn't talking about politics. Eventually they found themselves having sex for a second time on a pile of musty costumes that must have belonged to discarded waxworks.

D told her lieutenant the story of Salvador the Gentle, how he exchanged bodies with his volunteers inside the closet before they emerged to perform a waltz. Her lieutenant clucked at the second part, the pregnant women and Salvador's insistence that it was not his "soul's doing," that someone else must have done it, and the husband who sat by while the conjurer bled to death. "What about the bastards, the babies?" he asked. "Who knows," said D. She vaguely recalled that around the exhibit area for the conjurer's closet there had been some framed four-sheet tabloids, the headlines howling that the babies were stillborn with the heads of animals, but these were—obviously—just an excuse to print an artist's rendering of a baby with a snarling wolf's head. Her lieutenant asked if the story didn't make her envious. "They found out what it was like to have a cock, the

The Curator

conjurer's lucky ladies." D conceded that she was faintly envious, but maybe he could do something to soothe her. Awhile later, as they were drowsing off, her lieutenant admitted that he was uneasy. "You know I was a boarder as boy? During the school semesters? I shared rooms with four other boys, provincial fellows like myself, hardly able to dress ourselves, let alone keep house. Of course we had a guardian, but still. Anyway, we used to get up to a lot of trouble to impress the city boys. Steal things. Cheat. Start fights. Pick on smaller kids." He ran his hand along D's bare hip. "I used to feel horrible, you know, afterward. 'Why did I do that?' I'd ask myself. I feel like that now." D's lieutenant stayed quiet for a while. Then, he said, simply, "I guess I didn't realize so many people would die."

D wondered what he expected it would be like. Did he believe that the government would just step away, like workers coming off a shift, and let them take over? How often he must have cried, her lieutenant, playing as a child, as a Bobby, shocked by every shove, devastated by every bump. It was a thought she'd had so often before that she could no longer be angry at his naiveté. It just made her afraid for him.

He sat on the edge of the fruit picker's bunk, lacing up his boots. It was morning. "Robert," she said.

"Addressing me by my first name?" He twisted to squint at D. "Have we abandoned all decorum? You know I'm an officer, woman."

D didn't laugh. "It's going bad, isn't it?"

Her lieutenant smiled. There were bags under his eyes, stubble on his cheeks. "It's not going great."

"This isn't like when you were a boy. It's not like yelling at some little girl on her way to school and giving her a fright," D said.

"I told you about that?" he asked.

She went on as if he hadn't spoken. "People are dead, Robert. People with friends. You should go, get out of the city."

"I can't do that." Her lieutenant shook his head. He yawned and stood, pulling himself up with the frame of the top bunk. "You know, it's funny—this will probably surprise you, but I was always the worst sport when I was kid. Hated to lose."

"I want you to go home for awhile," said D.

"And leave you behind?" Her lieutenant bent to kiss her where she lay. His beard scraped her lips. "I'll see you later. Don't let anyone switch your head in the meantime, okay?" He stepped out through the curtain.

"Unless it's with the woman in the bakery! You know the one! You can switch with her!"

She closed her eyes and traced her lips with her fingers and listened to his steps recede.

Much later, as the day was deepening into twilight, there was a new, discordant sound, a crunch and an echoing twang. D went to her lookout. The soldier had already gone back inside the former embassy, but at the place where he deposited the bags there was now just the smashed body of a guitar, its strings spraying off the snapped neck in frozen bolts.

↺→

D NEVER saw her brother weep. Their mother wailed and wailed, sprawling theatrically across the divan in the parlor, as the boy withered in his sickbed.

"Who does that woman think she's fooling, anyway?" he croaked.

"I don't know." D wasn't fooled, either.

The Curator

Another howl of sorrow ricocheted down the hall and into the sickroom. Her brother winced. D held his club of a bandaged hand, the infection inside hot enough to feel through the fabric.

D LEFT the museum to sit on the stoop in the fresh air. The teacher with the long auburn hair was standing in a doorway across the street. D waved to her. Miss Clarendon did not wave back, but walked, shoulders hunched, toward D.

"Hello, Miss Clarendon," she greeted her, "how are you today?"

The woman grabbed D's forearms and squeezed. "You need to help me." The teacher's lips were chapped. "They took my fiancée into that place." One of her false eyelashes was dangling from the corner of her eyelid, like the waxwork in the windmill exhibit who perched from a rope swing in front of the rotor, tightening a bolt. "He's just a stenographer. He just writes down what people say. He doesn't have a horse in the race."

"Please take your hands off me," said D.

"That man you fuck. The one who takes care of you," said Miss Clarendon. Her bitten lips widened in a smile. Tears formed in her eyes, and began to drip down her cheeks. "He's an officer. He could find out where my fiancée is."

D inhaled and exhaled; she held the teacher's gaze.

SHE ONCE asked her brother about the kids that taunted them when they walked together that time. "They didn't bother you?"

"No," he said. "No one bothers me."

"I don't understand how that's possible."

"If anyone bothers me I imagine trapping them at the dead end of an alley and hitting them with rocks from my slingshot."

"Oh," said D.

"Then I imagine myself going closer and smashing apart their faces," he said.

"Is it hard?" asked D.

"No," he said. "You just keep hitting until the skin splits and the bone breaks."

"You're joking."

"Ha-ha," he said, "ha-ha."

☾→

"LET GO of me right now," said D.

Miss Clarendon blinked, dropped her hands. The false eyelash came loose and wafted down.

"Your fiancée went over there. You know? You're certain?"

"Yes." The teacher nodded rapidly.

"Then he's dead," said D.

"Oh." Miss Clarendon sniffed. The tears stopped, but the smile had hardened in place. "Thank you." Her voice was a wheeze. The teacher left, moving at a bend, like a storybook crone.

A convoy carrying wounded soldiers passed in the street while D was sweeping the steps a few days later. One had a blood-soaked bandage wrapped around the center of his face; the bandage was plastered down where his nose should have been, but clearly no longer was; it was as if the man's nose had

The Curator

been scooped out. His muddy eyes sat above the bandage like small animals huddled on top of a wall. Some of the wounded soldiers were lying on the benches. Some had wrapped stumps at the ends of their wrists, at the bottoms of their legs.

At the tram stop, two teenage girls in red berets pinned with the insignia of the revolutionary brigades were whitewashing a mass of graffiti scrawled over the walls. The messages they were obliterating had to do with fighting back, about the lies of the uprising, about secret trials, about the duly elected government, about rapists in red, about the devil's many masks. "There used to be a street singer at this stop," D overheard one girl remark to the other. "He was quite amusing."

Shots from next door at the former embassy awoke D that night. The reports continued, sporadically, for almost an hour. At the window, D observed her neighbor carrying out bags in the dark. She counted a dozen. Once again, he paused at the back steps of the former embassy, seeming to listen. Again, D remained in the window, ordering herself to hide, but not hiding. The moonlight glossed a slickness in the soldier's beard: silvery beads clung to the hairs. He removed a knife from a sheath at his hip and returned to the pile of bags. The soldier squatted, peering around, and then plunged the knife into a bag, working the blade around in a circular motion.

The courtyard was empty come daylight, but there was a pool at the foot of the retaining wall, hundreds of flies diving and darting above it.

Days elapsed without a visitor, not a single old man, not her lieutenant. D sat by the skinners on their log by the fire that didn't burn. She got down on the floor and pressed her forehead against the deeply etched forehead of the beatific cordeur. For an hour she tried to sketch a picture of her

– 409 –

brother, but his features were impossible; in the end, there was just the suit and the hat, empty of a body. She left the Museum, locking the doors behind her.

Her feet took her to the ruins of the Occult Collection. She shifted a few chunks of masonry and unearthed scraps of burnt cloth. On one piece she could make out embroidered stars, on another symbols like pyramids. She found the blackened, jagged mouthpiece of an ivory horn. D imagined savages, a fire, a screaming maiden, a priest blowing a song to their gods. She laughed at herself. There were other fragments in the scree: a cracked gong, a charred pillar with a barely discernible etching of roses and brambles, an iron key melted into a droop and with no lock to open. D climbed over a jumble of brick and found herself at the lean-to of timber that held the conjurer's closet.

The rich, purple velvet fabric that had covered the inner walls of the closet, which she remembered from her visit to the Collection, had burned away. It had been a match for the material of the conjurer's cape, which was also displayed, draped on a hook on the wall nearby, as if Salvador the Gentle had only stepped away for moment and would be right back. It was destroyed now, too, of course. D felt along the walls to either side, felt the back wall, felt the bottom. She wished, half-heartedly, to push through somehow, and find her brother, as he had been, young and beardless, dressed in his gray school uniform and cap. But there was just some dirt on the floor. The closet was a closet, plain and empty. "You there!" someone yelled. Her pulse tripped and her breath caught. D, instinctively, shoved her hands in her pockets as she spun around. There was a sting of pain—the miniature drill pricking her hand—and behind

The Curator

her, a gust of wind licked at her dress, a hot gasp against the exposed skin at her calves, as if a stove grate had been opened at the bottom of the closet's back wall, and a puff of grit tinkled across the floor.

A soldier in tall boots stood at the edge of the ruins. Other soldiers perched on the benches of a convoy in the street. They were searching for the woman who was in charge of the museum. D's mind was still in the closet or else, she realized later, she would have thought that she was in some sort of trouble. Instead, she said, "Oh, that's me," and stepped up over the bricks and picked her way to the foot of the lot.

The soldier in the tall boots gave her a note of requisition signed by the acting chairman of the Committee for the People's Defense, Sector Six: they were to be permitted to remove whatever they saw fit from the Museum, specifically any heavy metals weighing more than five kilos, and she was to assist them.

D guided them around to the applicable exhibits: the giant gears that children liked to run on, the cannon ball pyramid, the sling blades in the farm exhibit, the rifle parts at the gun assembly display, the anchor at the shipbuilders', and so on. The soldiers hauled these items to the wagon; they were to be liquidated for raw materials. "Of course," said D. She thought of the painted men on rails in the little foundry model, melting coins for cats.

"Jus' you 'ere?" asked a soldier with a bulge of tobacco in his cheek and a stained grin. The tobacco-chewing soldier had a strange eye; it wobbled obscenely, like a wad of spit. He and another soldier were carrying an oversized gear the size of a table down the Museum steps. D was standing by at the bottom of the museum's stoop.

"No," said D. "Of course I'm not the only one. There's a large staff. Researchers, curators, restorers. Guards."

"I keep an eye out, too," said a voice. Her neighbor from the former embassy had appeared, striding up the sidewalk. Today, he was wearing a shirt, but it was unbuttoned, hanging loose around his muscled upper body. Sweat shone on his neck, glittered in the hairs of his beard. D had never seen him in broad daylight and was too startled by the sight to be alarmed.

The executioner—for that was what he was—wore a happy, tired face; he could have passed for a waxwork at any number of exhibits inside the museum.

"Ah," said the other soldier, and didn't say another word after that.

Last the soldiers set to the door of peens and hammers. "Sorry," said the sergeant in the tall boots as one of his men banged and wrenched at the hinges. As a courtesy they dragged a good-sized sheet of timber from the ruins and set it across the gap, an improvised barricade.

D and the executioner stood, side-by-side, as the operation was conducted. She wanted to slide away from him, wanted to shrink inside of herself, pop like a soap bubble into nothingness, but she couldn't. Whatever was between them in the dark, whatever made her fearless then, here, in the late day, in the sun, D knew that he was death. The executioner had shoulders like a casket. The stench of him was beyond unseemly; he smelled like meat and blood; he smelled sick, rotten, worse than shit; he smelled like he had been killing people late into the morning.

"Bullets, buckles, knives." Her neighbor meant the metal.

"Of course." D made herself look at him. "Everything for the war effort."

The Curator

"I apologize about the noise," the executioner said. "At night."

She told him it was no bother.

"Of course it isn't," he said, and winked at D. "But I should warn you—between us—" He lowered his chin to his chest in an expression that emphasized how he was taking her into his confidence. His beard crackled as it was pressed. "—they says I should expect an influx. And that means it's liable to be louder, for longer."

D summoned a laugh that came out as a flute-y breath. She worried she might throw up if he didn't move away soon. In her mind, she pictured maggots wriggling out of his beard and plinking to the ground, and his expression not changing.

"I would invite you in," she said, "but there's not so much to see now."

"Very kind. Can't, though." The executioner shook his head. "I'll have to come over eventually, I'm afraid, but not now." He indicated the former embassy. "Duty calls. Pots left simmering, as the saying goes."

There was a clatter of metal and one of the soldiers swore. The executioner said, "Oh," and moved toward the spill. "What's this?"

The rope around a bundle of tools had come loose. D recognized the tools scattered on the sidewalk pavers: they were from the masonry display. There were chisels, trowels, scrapers—and the long-handled tool that the executioner had picked up. It had a cedar handle, like an ax, and on the business end, a two-sided implement of iron, a sharp pick the size of a trestle spike pointing one way and a wide, curving claw pointing the other, like the front teeth of the world's largest, meanest beaver.

"I'm not sure what you call it," said the soldier who had dropped the bag. He was a codger with a drunk's ruby nose half-buried in a florid white mustache. Up until a few months ago D guessed that he had been a street sweeper or a jack-of-all-trades with a rented room above a tavern; now he was a sergeant in the revolutionary brigades. "It's for breaking up the tougher types of ground, I believe."

"A mattock," said D. She had read the exhibit. The waxwork that had wielded it was posed in mid-swing, about to shatter a mound of rocky earth.

"Ah," said the executioner, weighing it in his hands. "I'll take care of these."

D and the codger watched silently as the executioner gathered up the chisels and mallets and trowels and scrapers, too, and carefully retied the rope around the bundle. The codger glanced at D. The little shine that had been in his eyes when he spoke up was gone. Now his gaze was flattened, the gaze of a man in a painting who had been dead so long that no one living had ever known him.

"Wait. How did you know I slept here?" D called after the executioner as he departed, the bundle under one arm, the mattock slung over his shoulder. The question was out of her mouth before she could catch it.

The executioner raised a hand, but did not turn.

A loose phlegmy sound came from the codger. D could see him vibrating, legs and shoulders and florid mustache and ruby nose. "Heaven save me," he said, "heaven save me."

"DON'T WORRY."

This was right before the end. Her brother was shrinking in his sick bed. His boy's school suit and cap were gone, replaced by the nightgown he would die in. "I'll save a place," said her brother.

"Where?"

"To my right."

"When?"

"Eventually."

"How?"

"D—" he began, and swallowed down the rest of her name. His eyes slipped up to the whites. "I see you. I see your—face."

"Whose face?" asked D, but her brother was dead.

↩→

BY THE failing light she picked her way back through the ruins to the burned box of the closet. She felt around in it again: the walls were solid, the floor was gritty. From her pocket she removed the tiny drill bit and dragged it across her palm. D winced, bled. Nothing happened. What if she had only had one chance? She closed her eyes. In the dark of her mind she searched for a face and found no one.

At the edge of the wreckage, she stubbed her toe: a perfect gray egg of stone.

Her lieutenant was waiting for her at the Museum. He had discarded his red uniform and was dressed like the student he used to be: baggy trousers and a ratty sweater. A scab marked the corner of his mouth where he'd been punched. "What happened, Lieutenant?" D asked.

"Long story. But—I'm out. I lost my command," he said.

"Well," she said. "We can still pretend, can't we?"

"Sure." Robert tried to smile then, like it was nothing, like they were flirting in the library again, daring each other for permission. She pulled his face against her shoulder as he started to weep.

The reverberations from the shelling were close that night, the giant hands of giant potters punching down into mounds of wet clay outside the Museum's walls. D thought she might have slept through them. The screaming coming from the embassy was the problem, an unholy chorale of wails falling up and down the scale. She climbed from her bunk and went upstairs to the window. Robert was already there. Below, the executioner moved from the back stairs of the embassy to the area by the wall, a bag over each shoulder. He was naked except for his soldier's boots. There was blood on him, down his back, down his front. The pile of bags was high enough to climb.

"This is… " Robert trailed off.

"A bad dream." D began to tug him away from the window. "Listen, come back to bed. I want to tell you a story about my brother."

Robert shook her off. "I have to go over there."

"No," said D. The idea was so insane, she blurted a laugh.

"I'm sorry," he said. "You can tell me about your brother when I come back." Robert kissed her on the forehead. "You better. I didn't even know you had a brother."

He strode away down the hall, down the flight of steps, and out through the empty doorway.

"Lieutenant?" D waited for his dramatic reemergence, his second thought, his shoes clapping against the steps. "Robert?"

Dust snowed from the ceilings with each blast, but the Museum would never fall unless it took a direct hit. D removed the head of the shovel man from the engine of the train and put him on the body of the fruit picker with whom she shared her bunk. She lay beside him, comforted by his

The Curator

sly grin. "I see your face," D said to the waxwork. "Let me see your face, let me see your face, let me see your face," she prayed again and again, while the building rattled and the dust tinkled, and eventually she did sleep.

⟲→

NIGHT, A dream monster, the scrape of its claws like shovels dragged across cobblestones, the shameful warmth of her urine, the drunk nurse snoring in the rocking chair. She called, "Mommy!" She called, "Daddy!" They weren't even home, she remembered, and D's bladder found more water and let go a second time. Her brother then, slipping so quietly into the room that it was as if he had materialized beside her, placing a cool touch against her cheek: "You're okay. It's not real."

"How do you know?"

"I am real. You are real. Everything else is a dream and dreams are less than nothing."

"How do you know?"

"I know."

"How? How? How?"

"A man told me. Now: sleep."

⟲→

A FOG of smoke tumbled over the wood that half-blocked the door into the Museum, and unraveled across the first floor of the Museum of the Worker in a mustard-colored blanket. D walked through the knee-deep mist to the barrier. She climbed over it, made her way down the steps and into an opaque world. "Robert?" she whispered. "Robert?" D guided herself with a hand pressed against the wall of the Museum building. When it ended, she counted sixty steps—the empty space in front of the Occult Collection—and reached out again, finding her away around the corner to the main thoroughfare where the tram tracks ran. Here the smoke was wispier; D glimpsed shards of reality in the shifting air: the windows of a bakery, smashed out, the shelves empty; out in the middle of the street on the tracks, a dog biting and pulling at a sleeve that belonged to a crumpled body, trying to compel it to rise; a toy boat on the sidewalk, dropped, snapped in two pieces where it had struck the pavers.

"Robert?" she asked the murk.

A gunshot popped, ricocheting off something nearby. She pressed tight to the wall, feeling the report in her palms. A large, bulbous bird, turquoise feathered, hurried by chattering softly, ruffling against D's ankles, and disappearing into the chalk and dust, its claws typing lightly on the stone.

She tried to backtrack, but soon found herself in an alley. She was about to backtrack a second time when she heard a growling somewhere in the smoke that did not belong to an animal. It was a man and he was also giggling and banging a metal object, a pan, maybe. D thought it wisest to keep moving forward.

The alley abruptly opened. The smell of cordite was strong enough to make her gag. D frantically waved her hands in front of her face to make a breathable pocket for herself, but the air was thickening. Somewhere not far behind her the growler with the pan had switched from giggling to sobbing, and he was closer. A few steps ahead she fell forward onto a bumpy incline. D grabbed at a rounded, textured handhold and began to crawl

The Curator

on all fours up a small hill. A person inside the hill inhaled. D stopped. Between thumb and forefinger she rubbed a piece of the hill: canvas—a small tent-like shape—a nose—a face... The hill groaned. D scrambled backwards and the hill shifted, the dozens of bodies rolling and coming loose, and she banged her head on the courtyard pavers, coughing and wheezing and clawing for open air, as the crazy person yelled from inside the vapor that he was he taking a census of everyone who told lies. What was the name of the sneak he heard he wanted to know, and he was clanging his pan as D found her knees again and scrabbled toward the rear wall of the Museum building.

For a long while she worked her away around the opposite side of the building. She smelled fire. There were people running. There were more shots. Her palms were scraped and her knees were scraped and her head hurt where she had hit it. The mad man was still banging his pan, but the sound receded as D got closer to the street. She let her hands draw her around the stoop of the Museum and up the steps to the crosswise board set across the empty doorway. D threw herself over the side and landed on the floor of the Museum.

In the nearest bathroom there was some water pooled in a basin and D splashed it on her stinging eyes. She spat, trying to get the taste out of her mouth. She told her brother she was afraid. She told him she needed him. The dirt-clouded water slopped around in the bottom of the basin.

D went down to the fruit pickers' bunkhouse and got into bed beside Robert. "You're here," she said, but he didn't respond. His eyes were closed. He was frowning. "Are you okay?" His eyelids were red-rimmed at the edges. D realized that his body was cold and hard, a waxwork's body. There was the slightest gap between his lips and—he has no teeth because the executioner has used his tools to chisel them out, D thought, and even as she thought this, she was easing herself from under the wool blanket, never allowing her eyes to drift to the place where the severed head had been mounted on the neck pillar.

On the other side of the curtain the hall was quiet. Slicks of ambient light glistened on the hardwood lane that ran between exhibits for plowing and scything and husbandry. D, as lightly as she could, walked toward the stairs at the far end.

"You know," said the executioner. "People look forward to coming here. Simple people such as myself. A place that celebrates the common person. 'Look,' they says, 'here's what Daddy does. Here's why Daddy's so invaluable to our society.' It's something special for us, they says. They bring their children. If I had children, I'd want to bring them. And then, someone comes along and makes a joke of it." On a stool in the husbandry exhibit he perched with the mattock across his knees. Beside him was the bull whose head her lieutenant had, in the course of their game, switched with the bespectacled head of an exchequer from the sixth floor exhibit on money printing.

In his other hand the executioner held the bundle of chisels and mallets and planers and trowels. He was shirtless. There was gore in his chest pelt and gore in his beard and something gunky and glistening at his scalp, so his hair was partially flattened.

D was stuck to the floor of the hall directly across from him.

"Well?" asked the executioner. "It was you, wasn't it? You've defiled a national treasure. What have you got to say for yourself? Anything?"

She cleared her throat. "We were playing."

He shook his head.

The Curator

D went on. "You saw them take everything out. There's barely anything left. And no one was coming any more anyway."

The executioner rose. His knees cracked. He pointed his mattock at her. "I held off killing you because I thought you were taking care of this place. I made an exception for you."

"Thank you," said D. She touched her chest, as if she could feel the gratitude beating there, like a bat in an attic. "Thank you."

For a few seconds the executioner squinted at her. "You're fucking welcome."

She ran. His boots thudded behind her. Six stairs and at the landing she yanked down a tapestry of men threshing wheat and hurled it down without looking backward. She heard the executioner grunt, heavy flapping as he fought with the fabric. D made the first floor and went rightward for the door, lung hitching, the smoke tearing apart across her body, the whistle of the mattock cutting space somewhere close behind.

A black shadow stood against the slate gray of the smoky hall and in the shadow's hand was a glittering pistol. "Shoot!" screamed D. "Shoot! Shoot!" D dropped.

The teacher moved forward, emptying the pistol, each successive crack shattering against the last. Miss Clarendon continued to press the trigger, more than a dozen times, even though the gun was small and had been empty after four.

D sat up.

The teacher was standing over the body. Somehow the executioner had ended up on his back atop the threshing tapestry. The smoke oozed over him, the wooly tatters seeming to catch and tangle around his shoes, around the long claw of the mattock that he still clutched in a limp hand. One of the shots had taken off most of his jaw, but his tongue was still there, wet and pink in the bloody cave that remained. There was another neat hole in his chest and a third by his bellybutton. His other tools had scattered as he flopped. The chisels, the trowels, the mallets, and the scrapers were strewn all over the glossy surface of the hardwood hall amid the smoke, like the leftover pieces of some child's game.

Breath lifted a long tassel of red spit off of the pink meat of his tongue. The executioner's eyes blinked at D, focusing.

She crouched down beside him, brought out the smooth, egg-shaped stone from her pocket. "Do you see my face?" she asked.

The executioner blinked: yes.

The first blow cratered the executioner's left eye socket; the second made the eye itself disappear; bloody gray matter welled up at the third strike. D slammed the stone, raised it, slammed it, raised it, and by the time she stopped, the teacher had moved well away.

D flung away the stone. It clunked against the floor and slid away, eaten by the smoke. "You saved me." She got to her feet. The teacher had retreated to a bench. Smoke had gathered around her skirts; it looked like she was sitting on a cloud.

"Was that...?" asked Miss Clarendon.

"Yes," said D. "He was from next door."

"Good." But her voice, nears tears, confessed that it wasn't.

"Let me help you," said D. "I know what to do. We need a safe place until the fighting settles down." D accepted the pistol and some bullets from the teacher. She reloaded it, helped Miss Clarendon to her feet and, hooking an arm around the other woman's back, they moved together from the museum.

It was reminiscent of the way that D had, as a ten year-old, led her old nurse away from her brother's corpse in the sick

The Curator

room. They had been the last two, mother and father having gone to see the funeral director to select the coffin. She fixed the nurse a series of drinks and once the old lady passed out, D pulled on mittens and switched her parents' pillowcases with her brother's pillowcases. Although this action had its downside—her father's wealth had turned out to be figmentary, his death unleashing a landslide of debt that crushed the fine contents of their apartment and left D a penniless ward—she had been justified by the way her mother carried on, practically screaming her brother out the door of this life, and sending him to the next world with a headache.

Outside, they pressed their faces into each other's shoulders, and sidled in a huddle toward the wreckage of the Occult Collection building. "Where are we going?" asked Miss Clarendon. "There's a safe spot in there," D said. Their shoes crunched on the crumbled brick and stone. D put a hand out, touched a charred timber, and led them into the lean-to of beams. The rectangle of the conjurer's closet emerged from the smoke. D eased the teacher forward into the closet.

"What's it go to?" asked the teacher. "A basement?"

A shell whistled through the invisible sky and D fired the pistol into the base of Miss Clarendon's skull. The teacher fell forward through the black rear wall of the conjurer's closet. D stepped after her.

THE DEAD woman sprawled a few feet away on the floor of white stone.

Set into the columns of the temple were sconces holding flickering candles. Dozens of penitents sat upon the white stone floor with faces lowered and arms held close. There was a dais at the far end of the room, a plinth, and atop the plinth, a voluminous red bowl that contained a leaping fire. One of the penitents in a rear row wore a familiar gray jacket and a gray cap.

"Brother," D whispered. "Brother."

The figure in the gray jacket pushed to his feet. He turned to D. Beneath the gray cap his face was a cat's face, one side cleaved, at the fissure the shine of bare bone. Her brother raised an arm; his hand was a trembling gray rat.

A hush fell over the assembly. A figure limped from the darkness behind the plinth, made its way past the fire, the light finding a glossy reflection in the purple velvet of his cape, and along the aisle, coming to greet the new arrival, to learn her name.

-- For Big Pete

A Night's Work

by Clive Barker

I RETIRED TO BED a little after one, exhausted. Sleep came readily enough, but it wasn't an easy slumber.

Somewhere in the middle of the night I dreamed a story of great elaboration.

It involved, as far as I remember, a race of miniature men, and a pair of escalators on which I was pursued up and down, up and down, for reasons I have now forgotten, but which seemed, in the grip of this dream, essential to the plot.

I was highly excited by my story; so much so that in the midst of it I thought to myself: *When I've dreamed it all, I'll wake up and write it down. This is a best-seller; I'll make millions!*

The story came to a wonderful conclusion, satisfying every question it posed. I woke up, and hurriedly started to write. Oh, I could scarcely believe it! Every idea—every image—was crystal clear. And yes, it was just as riveting now as it had been when I dreamed it. My body ached by the time I'd finished, but I was ecstatic.

I turned off the lamp and lay back in bed. But as sleep seemed to come over me again I realized, with a kind of leaden disappointment, that I had not truly woken; merely dreamed that I'd done so.

The story was still unrecorded.

I fumbled to recollect what had seemed so pungent moments before, so inevitable, while telling myself, *Wake! Wake, damn it! Quickly now before you lose it!*

It seemed to work. Again, I took the pen in my hand and scribbled out the dream I'd had. But this time I didn't get through half of it before I realized that it was delusory.

I let the dreamed pen drop, and struggled to catch hold of what was left of the story. Miniature men, yes! Escalators, yes! A woman in a gold dress, perhaps? Or was that something I'd read before I went to bed? And the dog with the blue tail; where did he belong? Had he been an intrinsic part of my immaculate plot, or had he strayed in from somewhere else?

Oh Lord, it was getting muddier by the moment.

I woke again. And again I picked up the pen. This time I was deeply suspicious of my state. With reason. After just a few words I knew I was still dreaming. And now my previous story was little more than a few senseless wisps. I would never catch it now, I knew.

I despaired of it. And once I relinquished all hope of having my vision intact, I was at last awake.

It's pathetic, I know, to be setting down *these* words, as though the tale of how a glorious thing was lost can be the equal of the thing itself.

And as I write—now, this very *word*, this very *syll ab le*— the suspicion rises in me that even this faint echo is insubstantial, and must be given up if I am ever to open my eyes.

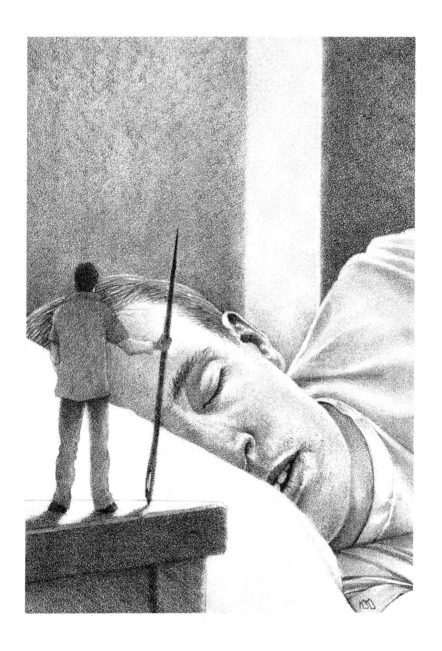

Made in the USA
Middletown, DE
18 October 2024

62863789R00241